"Charles Bukowski would feel disturbingly at home in this darkly hilarious anthology. He would try to bum a smoke but might find he is actually better off financially than many of the wonderfully twisted writers herein!"
--- Sandra Tsing Loh, The Madwoman in the Volvo

"A heartbreakingly contemporary collection of stories. Mundane desperation abetted by high unemployment rates and the realities of our messed up cultural cage. Like Steinbeck's Tortilla Flat for the Internet Age, but instead of scamming bottles of wine, the characters here deign for Nick Cave tickets, sell their belongings on eBay, and sneak into bougie pools high above their class bracket. We need to read this."
--- Maxwell Williams, Technology Editor, Good Magazine

"HA HA!"
--- John Baldessari, Artist

"Tweets are the new short-story today, so this anthology might rank as the new long-form. When you join Holly Myers on the #302 bus going east on Sunset, your imagination drifting past all those changing buildings on the Strip, somehow you can sense a crash waits up ahead."
--- Christopher Knight, Art Critic, Los Angeles Times

"For the startlingly fresh and eclectic anthology Gen F, Shana Nys Dambrot contributes a shining and mysterious work of fiction that blurs the lines between dream, memory, and experience -- evoking the mechanics of the subconscious mind and inviting us to embrace its absurd logic of love, desire, and acceptance. Her work speaks to the place the book occupies, a generational moment of simultaneity, shattering, and surreal transcendence. It's everything!"
--- David LaChapelle, Artist

Praise for GEN F

"There are 33 reasons to read this book but number one is the ir-repressible and unrepentant James Hayward. But none of these Gen F writers hold back. Diplomacy and tact are not for them and if they are not for you, read on!
--- Hunter Drohojowska-Philp, Rebels in Paradise: The L.A. Art Scene and the 1960s

"This collection, Gen F, is a wild zig-zag of a journey into fasci-nating discordant realms. Every time it changes direction, the new view is equally as interesting. Gen F keeps the reader on their toes more than any book I've read in ages."
--- Greg Escalante, Curator and Co-Founder Juxtapoz Art Magazine

"His prose floats like a dragonfly and stings like a beaver. No, not a beaver, a scorpion. It's also funny as hell, and always grounded in his generous spirit. I love Dave Shulman's work."
--- Calef Brown, New York Times Bestselling Author

"Before lamenting the ten-percent retrenchment of your 401(k), consider the plight of this new Lost Generation. These fine stories, dripping with disillusionment and ca m'est égal, prove that even dire circumstances can't crush the artistic spirit."
--- Gary Buslik, Author

"Sarah Hunter's wit and sense of irony has pleased people in both her original plays and poetry. Her energy transmits through the page."
--- Victoria Patterson, Award Winning Author

"The short stories pick us up where Nathaniel West, John Fante and Charles Bukowski dropped us off. Reading Gen F gave me the feeling of being ecstatically high and stone cold sober simultane-ously. Not for the faint of heart. Great work Gordy Grundy!"
--- John Philbin, Actor and Surfer

Praise for GEN F

"Victoria Looseleaf writes with the passion and - occasionally the vitriol of a twenty-something wordsmith, but tempered with the wisdom of a sage who has experienced the broad spectrum of humanity's foibles and triumphs."

--- Benny Rietveld, Bassist, *Santana*

"Dave Shulman is more than an amazing writer, he's a unique, twisted and beautifully hysterical visionary."

--- Jerry Stahl, Novelist and Screenwriter

"This collection reflects the cacaphony of our infobesity era - we know too much, we are too clever and our geniuses are more likely to be our baristas as our stand-out celebrated talents. That they are gathered under one roof if only for this collection is a chance to peer thru the collective keyhole into the pulse of a time that is demolishing its own memory before history can catch up and do the same."

--- Mat Gleason, Coagula Art Journal

"Gen F is a virtual roadmap to the end of the world."

--- Ed Moses, Artist

"The book promises to provide spectacular narratives--that is, unwitting narratives of Guy Debord's spectacle--updated by the contemporary allure of hipness."

--- Frances Colpitt, Art Educator and Art Writer

GEN F

Los Angeles

This is a work of fiction. Names, characters, places, and incidents are the products of the author's imagination or are used fictiously. Any resemblance to actual events, locals or persons, living or dead, is entirely coincidental.

2014 Gordy Grundy Trade Paperback Edition

Copyright © 2014 Gordy Grundy

Published in the United States of America.

ISBN-10: 0692214917
ISBN-13: 978-0692214916

Library of Congress Control Number: 2014908526

Design by Gordy Grundy
Photography by Tyler Hubby

Printed in the United States of America.

www.GordyGrundy.com

GEN F

Gen F is a Collection of Short Stories for Our Times, an Ensemble of Comic Tragedies and Humiliations for Those Displaced by a Reversal of Fortune, the Toxicity of Failure, Psychological Downsizing, Class Disparity, Vanished Industries, Outsourscing, Mortgage Collapse, Bank Bailouts and Stimulus Recovery for the Wealthy.

Edited by Gordy Grundy

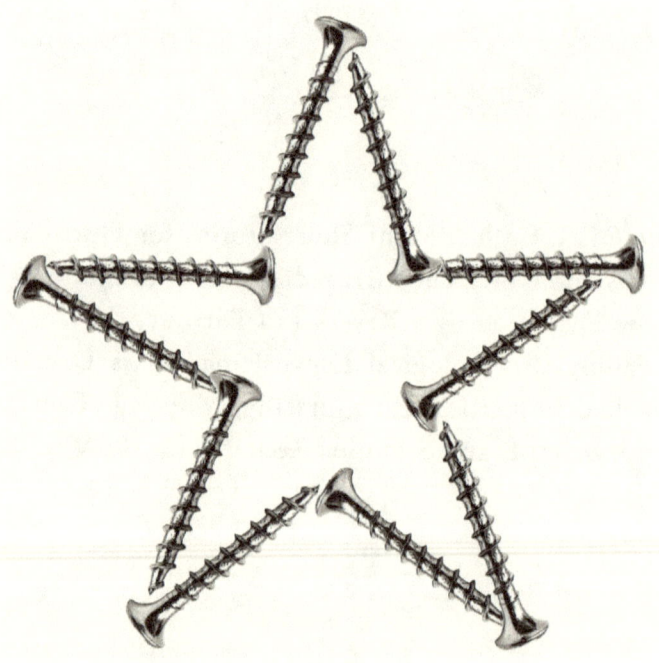

INTRODUCTION

We are becoming one. Regionality is no longer distinctive. We are losing our accents. We talk alike. Local cuisine has lost its flavor. We dress alike. In every city across the nation, we shop in the same stores and eat in the same restaurants. We listen to the same music. East Coast and West Coast no longer have longitude.

The ranks of the unemployed grow faster than the disillusionment of the *under*employed. Once revered talents are now inconsequential and easily outsourced. Many wage earning skill sets are obsolescent. Pride and dignities have soured to shame. Necessary functions - journalism, for example, which is fundamental to the mechanics of a free society - have been monopolized, minimized and redlined.

A scheduled revolution or a runaway train is on the tracks. The puppeteers have never been so agile nor has their job been so easy. Utility is confusing. Clear answers are not forthcoming.

By contrast, the Industrial Revolution was a slow phenomenon. Today, our world is changing fast. Innovation and progress have a quick, hard byte and humanity has taken the back seat. As the landscape blurs in the velocity, fundamental identities are no longer distinctive. We all listen to the same playlist.

Where does one fit into the new Spa-based Economy? Are you getting the massage or are you giving one? Within the warm embrace of our commiseration, there are many stories to be told.

Gen F is a wickedly eclectic collection. The 30 authors come from a wide variety of disciplines, interests and genres. Every age is represented. Many are visual artists. Eight authors are related to journalism. Most are writers that dance around the art world. Easy to say, laughter to tears, Gen F offers something for everyone.

We are all one. We are all Gen F.

Gordy Grundy, Editor

CONTENTS

Transition A.K.A. Night of the Preditor
Luca Celada
17

Letter from New York
Andrew Berardini
37

Disappearing
John Tottenham
41

Loved in Spite of Great Fault
Matty Byloos
49

Faith-n-Fire
Diane Mooney
57

25 Random Things About You
Matias Viegener
67

Panache
Sarah Hunter
75

Transcribed, from Boxes
Josh Herman
81

Zen Psychosis
Shana Nys Dambrot
85

The Twelve-Thousand Dollar Reindeer
Rich Henrich
101

CONTENTS

Freedom
Nicolas (Dimitri) Vorvolakos
113

Old Songs
Betty Ann Brown
115

Dear Mr. Lake or How to Make an Omelet
Christopher Michno
119

Savage Cut
Tulsa Kinney
123

In Addition, It Is the Best, (AKA F for Howl)
Doug Harvey
127

"We're Here to Help."
Kurt Thomas
137

Sliding into Home
Hills Snyder
147

Dog-Man
Paul Chavez
149

The Oudist
Victoria Looseleaf
175

I Don't Ever Want My Kids to Work in the Entertainment Industry
Harry Dunn
179

Post Orgasmic Guilt
Josh Herman
183

CONTENTS

Love?
Mary Woronov
189

The Magruder Film
Martin Mundt
195

Almost a Year
Nicolas (Dimitri) Vorvolakos
209

Stumps
Dave Shulman
211

I'm Working Here
Jill Paris
215

Miguel
Michael Delgado
221

Inertia Variations
John Tottenham
229

I Shit Like a Tough Guy
James Hayward
237

Dark Land of the Sun, Excerpt: The 302 Bus
Holly Myers
249

An Extremely Short Classic Story
Ronee Blakley
273

CONTENTS

The Big Paddle
Gordy Grundy
275

Luck
Buffy Visick
287

Biographies
293

Credits
306

GEN F

Luca Celada

Transition A.K.A. Night of the Preditor

PREDITOR

Seeking a Producer/Editor (Preditor) who embraces the opportunity to create daily stories for multi-platform publication. This preditor must be eager to tell amazing stories which resonate with millennial audiences. An organized self-starter with proven experience as a team player, a strategic thinker with an absolute passion for the promise of journalism in the digital age.

The bus, number 208, lurched to a halt and the loudspeaker scratched to life: "Central and 2nd".

A stampede of exiting passengers was halted by an equal and opposing force of people waiting to board. The momentary impasse was caused by the old woman who was hopelessly trying to maneuver her walker down the steep front steps. She was snarling the foot traffic. She looked helplessly at the driver who shrugged and averted his gaze.

A couple of more enterprising passengers finally took matters into their own hands, uncoupling the woman from her aluminum contraption, loaded with plastic shopping bags, and gingerly handing both to the waiting hands of the ground crew. With the flow restored, Maxi eventually made his way down the steps and into the morning glare. He briefly wondered if that last impatient glance from the driver had been tinged with condescension. Or was it pity?

Maxi found himself standing now in front of a low-slung building on which institutional lettering spelled *Career Transition Center – East Division*. Yeah, well, he couldn't really blame the driver, solidly perched on his union-backed job, for the look of scorn with which he disgorged his cargo in front of the government job office. Several of the disembarked passengers were in fact making their way toward the drab building. To Maxi, the belch of black diesel smoke left behind as the bus departed the curb did not seem like a cheer of encouragement. More like the dismissal of a group of leprosy patients to their bleak fate at the shores of Molokai.

Since his dismissal from the American desk of the Italian network, he had often felt like someone finally smitten by a deadly plague. Reports of the mortal malady had come, faint at first, from the periphery of the land. Then, ever more insistent and close. Scouts had been dispatched and more detailed accounts had been filed from the ravaged provinces; ghostly pictures of foreclosed tract homes and homeless camps had danced on the Network feed and in turn produced more assignments to document the advancing pestilence which presently overtook the news cycle. Sure, he himself had filed stories on the ominous tide; like everybody else, written about the job crisis and blogged on the scourge of unemployment. Then, suddenly, it had been here, inside the city walls like a Red Death from which there was no further escape. He himself was laid off, forcibly made to join the ranks of the sad sacks he had heretofore been accustomed to filming for the b-roll.

The fateful call had come from HR, confirming the swirling gossip.

"It's not a big deal", Lopez had lied, "You'll still work. Just freelance. It's probably better, work at home, flexible hours… See more of the kids…"

Sounded great.

Except for the missing assignments. And it soon became apparent; there had been no freelance gigs forthcoming. None needed in the wondrous new world of digital media where continuous content, like homogenized slurry, was fed into the maw of the ravenous Web. The great needy machine which converted an endless supply of narcissism into oceans of tweets, posts, comments, likes and bile, all equally useful as spacer between banner ads, all free and volunteered by anyone with Wi-Fi and a pulse.

This was not a kind place for Maxi and other mastodons, whose futile resistance simply made them sink faster into the tar-like sludge of

Transition A.K.A. Night of the Preditor

New Media.

Bewildered, they inevitably joined the other superfluous and disoriented wildlife caught staring into oncoming traffic.

At first he felt as if black welts had appeared on his face, which caused people to recoil in horror and pity. He began avoiding employed friends and acquainted himself instead with his couch.

After a couple of months he filed for unemployment. As foreign as this had been, initially it had also been a pretty aseptic affair: A couple of phone calls to sign up with the Employment Bureau and then the online form every two weeks. A formality, really, easily absolved straight from the laptop.

But after the allotted months, the aid had run out and Maxi had been summoned to the Transition Center for Evaluation and Orientation – mandatory, the letter had stated - for those wishing to extend the checks into the supplemental period that had been authorized as part of the Emergency Stimulus.

Out here now, in the morning glare, this condition suddenly acquired a tangible, unavoidable shape, that of the beige building and its metal lettering that assigned him irrevocably to the ranks of the transitional, the infected. To Maxi the sign might as well have read: *Quarantine Center.*

Swallowing his dread he swung the door open and stepped inside.

The lobby of the Center was crowded with fellow applicants raring to transition into new stimulating career adventures. Parallel lines formed in front of the desk where three receptionists checked Social Security cards and handed out registration forms that were to be filled in black ink before proceeding.

Beyond the desk, a large room was furnished with rows of orange plastic chairs. On the far wall, next to the classroom clock hung a corporate inspirational poster, slightly askew. A Monarch butterfly was fluttering into a golden light streaming into the dimly lit room from an open window. An empty chrysalis was left behind on the table in the foreground. Large lettering spelled: *CHANGE!* Below it milled a small crowd, similar to the haphazard collection of citizenry that you get in the average DMV, a random cross section of individuals slightly bewildered by their momentary station as supplicants to a stern and inscrutable government.

He had covered similar assemblies before, as a reporter. Filmed and interviewed them, seeking the right sound byte to edit into a piece about the economic recession. Or was it the mortgage crisis? They had been his subjects, a hapless collective framed for maximum dramatic effect. Back then. Not the fellow applicants they now so incredibly, impossibly purported to be.

Completed forms in hand, Maxi was directed to take a seat and await further instructions by the impassible security guard who sat at her own wooden desk next to the entrance.

"And no talking on the phone" she advised, as amiably as a correctional intake officer could.

CONTINUOUS CONTENT REPORTER

This reporter's smart phone is as important as his or her notebook – it allows him or her to shoot quick, on-scene or look-live video, record interviews, email photos and push updates via twitter and email. Looking for an enthusiastic and tireless Vine and Gif programmer who loves pop culture and geeking out at the best media has to offer. Must have solid grasp of the competitive media and Internet landscape, good CMS skills. Ideal candidate consumes online video — day and night — because it's fun.

"Hello, my name is Gloria," said the short stocky woman with large amber glasses held around her neck by a gold chain. "Welcome to Transition Orientation."

Still settling into the school-style desks the crowd half-heartedly murmured a greeting in return.

"We're here today to help you find a job. The first thing is you'll need to watch the reemployment and eligibility assessment video."

Maxi heard an audible groan coming from his neighbor to the right, a large woman in her sixties who had placed an overstuffed red bag on her desk and had, up till then, been thoroughly absorbed by her little screen (in flagrant violation of the posted no cell-phone policy). Now she was holding it aloft as she waved her hand. "Excuse me?!"

Gloria acknowledged her with an air of resignation.

"What if you've seen the video already? Do we have to watch it again?"

"Every time you come to an assessment you have to watch the

20

video."

"Is it he same one?"

"Yes. Look, I don't make the rules. But those who've already seen the video can take a seat in the back two rows. We'll see if we can't slip you out early. The rest of you sit up front."

Some reshuffling ensued as the group, now much like a high school class, reorganized the seating arrangement as per the teacher's instructions. Maxi's neighbor gathered up the red bag and the smart phone with an air of satisfaction and glanced at Maxi as she wriggled out of the desk, on her way to the frequent-viewer VIP section in the back.

"I've seen it already," she confided to him definitively.

She was replaced by young Latino man in a Dickies shirt holding a squirming toddler in his arms that he sat on the desk.
Gloria finished maneuvering a video projector in front of the portable screen and announced, "OK we're ready to go. The video is about an hour long. Try and pay attention because it covers a lot of useful information."

She asked the citizen closest to the door to dim the lights, and pushed Play.

The emblem of the State Reemployment and Career Stimulus Agency filled the screen as a speaker intoned slightly off-speed. "In February", the female voice recited by way of introduction, *President Obama signed in to law HR 3630, the Middle Class Tax Relief and Job Creation Act of 2012"*

The middle-classers in the room sat at attention, eager to glean useful tips in order to right the reversals, which had temporarily, mistakenly, landed them among the losing classes. Either that or they were simply constrained into unnaturally straight postures by the diminutive desks into which they were shoehorned.

The video now listed innovative employment hunting techniques such as checking the 'jobs offered' listing on the local paper, checking online job sites, or even applying in person at the companies' places of business.

Some seekers appeared to be taking sporadic notes, so as to not forget any possible epiphanies provoked by the audiovisual support module unfolding on the screen.

The monotonous drone was now listing other actions that were required by applicants seeking to further their Emergency Assistance

Eligibility, such as regularly seeking employment and keeping a log of their dealings with potential employers.

"The job must be within your usual occupation and must be based on your past experience, skills and your prior earnings," recited the speaker.

"Like that was a ever going to happen!" Maxi scoffed to himself. He thought of attaching the quote verbatim from the video to any future correspondence with news organizations that had recently retired the job description for *Journalist* and replaced it with *Social Media Specialist*. It allowed them to downsize the pay to intern grade.

Outside the sun beat hard on the squat building, oblivious to the middle class travail unfolding inside. Maxi contemplated the contours of the linoleum tile floor and how it edged the frayed, mauve colored carpet right in the center of the doorway leading to the side room, the one Gloria had disappeared into after starting the video. His eyes now wandered onto his fellow postulants. Latino Dad was struggling to contain his writhing daughter on the desk. He was attempting to hold her attention with a pacifier she had long lost interest in. The commotion drew scornful sideway glances from the tattooed Asian girl in short skirt and Doc Martins, whose gaze was otherwise lost in the middle distance.

Next to her, in a long-sleeve button down and a patterned tie, sat a young man with red hair, mustache and sideburns, who seemed bewildered by the unfamiliar world of career transition, unfolding on the screen. "No doubt recently orphaned by his cubicle," Maxi thought to himself, "That has to be Bob. Definitely looks like a Bob".

In front of Bob was Homeless Lady. Maxi assigned the mental moniker on account of her shapeless black orthopedic trainers, sunburned face and the maroon velour trousers that she was wearing, worn at the knees and not particularly clean.

All the way in the back, against the wall, sat the Twins. Maxi had noticed them earlier, in the reception line, animatedly talking Armenian, in their tracksuits and loafers. Now the brothers seemed transfixed (or was it mystified?) by the many possible paths to a successful career transition enumerated by the benevolent Reemployment Fairy narrating the video. Next to them sat the Red Bag woman who "had already seen the video." She was chewing gum and lifted her stare from the screen of her unauthorized phone just long enough to knowingly wink at Maxi.

Time seemed to be slowing now to a crawl, as the useful video facts being delivered by the monotone drone piled onto each other in a face-meltingly tedious amalgam of info-points.

"The current recession has affected job seekers at all levels," the voice was reciting. *"If you were employed in a professional, managerial or technical field such as information technology accounting or engineering, the Experience Unlimited Program might best serve your needs. Motivated and skilled individuals can network through EU clubs throughout the state…"*

Maxi tried to picture himself in the group photo of able and ambitious job seekers currently depicted on the screen. They wore broad smiles as they sat at their monitors; looks of strong technical aptitude behind safety goggles and lab coats, secure in their productive destinies. Maxi could not see himself rise to anything resembling the determined motivation simulated by the models hired by the producers of the state video. Maybe if his ex-profession had required specialized attire, regulation gloves or steel-tipped boots---it might have stood a chance, against the tweeters and the tumblrs, the hordes that had burst into the citadel of Maxi's former life and ransacked it.

It had barely been a few months, but his life of work and gainful employment seemed like another lifetime already. When he occasionally bumped into former colleagues he now felt embarrassed by their pity and by the chasm he felt between they and him.

He steered clear and avoided contact.

Unfortunately, sometimes, it just happened. Like when he bumped into Zane in the Trader Joe's cheese aisle. Zane with his television hair and his freelance gigs for the bottom feeders at DZ-TV. Right up his alley. Hadn't seen him in ages, nor missed him. He, on the other hand, had heard about Maxi's layoff, just like apparently everyone else. So Maxi had had to accept his cheese-aisle commiseration, and then listen to his generous offer. He was working on a pilot now, some entertainment news magazine for Malaysian TV, "You know: Hollywood…Blah blah…Red carpet, blah… Stars, glamour…" Maxi could just picture the glossy canned graphics and jingles, tight suits and gowns and the Happy News chatter. It was a done deal pilot, Zane was explaining, just a formality, really. He had a cousin at Cal State who was roommates with the daughter of a head honcho at Malay TV. He was going to sign off on 30 shows. How about he, Maxi, come aboard on the ground floor? Come over and produce? Budget was tight for the first year, YouTube channel stuff, so he wouldn't be able to, you know, actually pay or anything, not the first cycle. But you know how it is… Bigger things down the line for sure. In the meantime you can get back in the game".

"Give me a call" said Zane, "Let's talk. Listen, I know times are tough but, hell, what are friends for? One day maybe you can pay me back…whatever."

That's it! No irony, no shame, no nothing! Why sure Zane, you're doing me a solid. How awfully big of you… The snappy retorts finally came to his mind. 'How many shows did you say? 30? Alright, so at zero dollars per hour and zero per story that'll come to let's see…. Tell you what, let me pay you back now, in advance. That way the air is clear and I can do the slave labor with no misunderstandings. Wouldn't want to let you down or anything like that. Let's see I could write you a check… Or you wanna take my car?'

Maxi could see Zane recoil in shame at his witty sarcasm, now as he pushed his cart through the parking lot. But inside the store, instead, he'd feigned appreciation. Zane had been a little more brazen than most, but this is what now passed as normal in the brave new *content market*. That's what it had come to: You are expected gratitude for free work.

"That's what's out there!" Maxi wanted to yell at the screen, at the motivated accountants happily shaking hands with the new employers they had connected with thanks to Experience Unlimited, the Department of Employment's Networking Clubs.

The thud of a pacifier bouncing off a desk on its way to the linoleum tiles brought Maxi out of his reverie. He reached sideways around the mini school desk to retrieve it and hand it back to Señor Dickies who was losing his battle with the squirming girl.

Supplemental wage replacement may be available for workers over 50 who start a new career and earn less money. Please refer to the Department of Labor website…Schedule 'F'..

The Career Fairy was winding down her Magical Misery Tour with a series of sunny pictures of beaming families and eminently employed breadwinners at construction sites wearing brand new tool belts. Smiling nurse practitioners at their newfound workstations and youths in spotless aprons and visors holding unbranded fast-food bags and soda cups from behind a counter in a land of happier meals…

Transition A.K.A. Night of the Preditor

"Thank you for attending this presentation and best wishes for your continued career transition," the voice signed off.

The screen faded to black and the neon above flickered back to bring the room back to its off-white drabness.

Maxi glanced at his watch. It was 12:35.

People stretched and blinked back to the glum reality of their school desk stations.

A new person addressed the group, a heavy-set black man in light blue shirtsleeves and tie, visibly perspiring.

"So, that was the video. What you need to do now is fill out the worksheet and drop it back out at reception. This form right here," the man held up the piece of paper everyone had been given at registration.

"Please use a pencil or black ink. Print clearly. You have plenty of time and you can grab some lunch or stretch. The workshop that is the second part of orientation starts at 1:30. You'll meet Gloria out in the waiting room where you first came in, OK? Any questions?"

The Armenian Twins looked like they may have had a few, but the man didn't really wait for any. "Ok, see you back in an hour".

ROBOT WRITER SOFTWARE ENGINEER
Our patented System applies complex and sophisticated artificial intelligence algorithms that extract the key facts and interesting insights from the data and transforms them into stories that are as good or better than your best analyst, and are produced at a scale and speed only possible with technology. We are seeking a motivated data engineer to support data ingestion, process and analysis. As part of the Platform Team, you will provide the foundation for developing applications and services for auto-generating narratives and news stories from data.

A group of applicants had found the lunch truck strategically stationed in the alley behind the transition center. Having just put in her order for the Special (California burrito, no-cheese, medium diet Mountain Dew) the Red Purse Woman joined Maxi and the others waiting at the pick-up window.

She winked again "I hope they make them good here" and then getting closer, almost whispering, "Usually I go to the center over there in Azusa. There's less waiting and they got free coffee. But this time I was staying at my daughter's house so I thought I'd try over here. It's OK, but the video? Uh-huh. I seen that already."

A couple of people were talking on their phones. Latino Dad was playing with his daughter whom he had hoisted onto the bed of his pickup truck and was now holding as she practiced walking. One of the Twins was intently sucking on a cigarette while his brother appeared to make a point gesturing towards the worksheet he held in one hand. The heat seemed to radiate from the very air, still and bone-dry, and the midday sun drew only the slimmest rims of shade around the edges of the concrete buildings.

Maxi looked at his watch and started towards the career transition door. People were going back inside.

Back in the classroom Gloria was adjusting the projector and reordering her notes. "Hello, and welcome again," she said, looking up to the class.

A few newcomers had joined the group, or so it seemed to Maxi. He hadn't noticed the pimple-faced youth with the precocious comb-over now making his way into the room holding an overstuffed folder under his arm. Another return customer, judging by the way he addressed several Center workers by name.

"Hi, Judy how's things?" To another, "W-What's up Brian?"

Stuttering, he made his way to a desk in the front of the room, spilling papers on the floor as he tried to unload his folder.

Next to Maxi on his right, another new member had squeezed himself into the desk. He was built like a Mack truck; looked to be about 6'3", shaved head and a t-shirt bearing the logo of a malt liquor brand that featured the likeness of an angry Grizzly bear.

"The next unit of the orientation," Gloria now announced, "consists of the Career Transition Workshop. We are going to touch upon some key aspects of professional redeployment, as well as some fundamental strategies for maximizing desirable job placement outcomes. The workshop is just one of the resources we like for you to take advantage of, here at the Center. We also offer job search assistance, interview counseling, computer resources, fax machines and bus route schedules. The Center's aim is to help you successfully complete your career transition and we are continually placing applicants into new employment. Last week we had a rep come here from the new Ross Dress for Less store, just opened up at

Transition A.K.A. Night of the Preditor

Westfalls Mall. That location will accommodate forty-*two* new retail positions. Straight up!" On that triumphant note Gloria paused for effect, as if to let the fact sink in.

The general reaction was muted although some people dutifully nodded in celebratory acknowledgement of the Dress for Less landmark, notably the newcomer up front who even ventured the beginning of a clap, quickly aborted as soon as he realized that no one would follow. In the excitement his folder once again fell to the floor spilling papers on the linoleum.

Gloria glanced at him with the indulgent tolerance of a mother for her slightly special child. Maxi was now sure Folder-Boy was definitely a frequent customer at the Center.

In the meantime, she seemed satisfied with her intro and she pulled up the first PowerPoint slide on the screen. On it were listed a half dozen bullet points. "Nowadays its hard," she started with a practiced tone, "It seems everyone is losing their job," she added with the level objectivity of a climate scientist assessing the melt-rate of a glacier. "Having said that, you are not just your job, you are more than that," she now conceded, with a hint of protective, maternal, encouragement. "So," she paused as if gathering her thoughts and to double-check the power-prompts. "Everyone here needs to find a job. The days are gone where you needed to be ashamed of being out of work. Everybody's out of work nowadays."

The mantra-like repetition of this truth was apparently calculated to put the audience at ease, although its only tangible effect was to induce sideways glances among fellow non-workers, apparently trying get some sort of visual confirmation of the fact.

"Its tough when you lose a job," said Gloria, eyeing bullet-point number three. "First you're in Shock, then comes Denial, Anger, Depression and finally Acceptance."

The quick listing of this abridged and slightly modified version of the Kübler-Ross catalog of the emotional stages of death and grief seemed to catch some of the listeners by surprise. Folder Boy up front was furiously taking notes, trying to keep pace. A couple of hands reached in the air.

"Is that Depression or Aggression?" said Red Bag Lady eliciting an eye roll from Tattoo Girl.

"Is that like a 12-step?" added Malt-Liquor Man, "My sister goes to those...," he added inconclusively.

"The main thing to remember is that it's normal, it's temporary," Gloria now exhorted, trying to steer the focus back to the healing message of the PowerPoint. "The days are gone where you need to be ashamed…" she trailed off midsentence possibly realizing Bullet-Point Number Two had already been stated. Then, recovering, "The important thing is to play up your strengths. Me for instance, I've always had a problem with punctuality -- it's the way I am." She offered usefully, "But I'm a great team-player."

Bullet Point Four read "Skills" and Gloria was all about staying on-message. "Skills are important," she elaborated helpfully. "For instance me and my husband have a truck at home. Lots of people do. But, man, those big eighteen-wheelers like you see on *Ice Truckers*. That's skill!"

This reality-based motivational simile seemed in fact to strike a chord, as several people solemnly nodded their approval of large cargo ice driving as a legitimate indicator of marketable job skills. Malt Liquor Man seemed particularly inspired as he leaned over to whisper something to Latino Dad that Maxi could not make out.

Sensing momentum, Gloria moved on to Point Five: "Proactively Communicate. You have to let people know that you are on the market. No one is going to offer you a job if they don't know you re looking. Let your friends and relatives know, put the word out. Network! Put it into your Facebook status." Then, checking the PowerPoint under the heading 'Social Media', she said, "Twitter".

She pronounced the word on the screen like a shamanic invocation. Several applicants imperceptibly leaned forward not wanting to miss a crucial incantation by which their spirit guide would lead them back to the land of employment. But their expectations were just as quickly disabused.

"I have no idea how that thing works," Gloria admitted candidly with a shrug of her shoulders.

"I tried it once," ventured a swarthy applicant from the back of the room. What was that hint of an accent, Maxi wondered. Russian? Greek?

"But it asked for my social, so I turned the computer off." His comment broke the ice and set the room abuzz with roiling speculation.

"It's a website, right?" someone asked.

"Yeah, kind of," Cubicle Guy replied helpfully, "Its like Facebook status updates".

28

"Social media networks are great for communications and media professionals who want to explore other career options. Improve your chances of finding a new job by creating a personal brand, becoming a thought leader, and using the right tools to find new connections." Gloria recited verbatim from the PowerPoint's caption, unperturbed by her earlier profession of ignorance. But neither, for that matter, was anyone else.

SELF-BRANDED MOTIVATOR

National leader in branded entertainment seeks assured self-starter for entry-level position. You are the right person if you exude brand loyalty modulated with enthusiastic ambition. Thriving under pressure, you eat deadlines for lunch. You are capable, supremely confident in yourself yet a great motivator of others, to whom you tirelessly transmit optimism. We are seeking the right combination of Charm, Relationship Building Personality and Shark-like instincts. Must be or look 25.....

Maxi glanced at his watch wondering whether it might have stopped or if it was just time itself that had turned into slow-flowing molasses, trapping the career transitioners in a Twilight Zone netherworld, doomed to follow a PowerPoint whose bullet-points stretched forever into infinity. In Presentation Hell, the class barely had time to absorb the promise of personal branding and its life changing potential. Gloria was once again maneuvering the remote. The slide she now conjured however was even more cryptic than the world of Social Media. It showed a pie chart with the circular graph divided in four percentage sections of varying sizes. Each one is identified by a dialog box. Each box read: "Insert category value here".

"Oh. This one again," Gloria said, "I don't get it."

People seemed baffled, but not as far Maxi could tell, much more so than they had been for the last ten minutes. For an instant he considered the possibility that Gloria was injecting some dark Meta humor in the presentation. Was he imagining things?

Moving on from the hypothetical graph, Gloria picked up the pace and broached the next topic, a practical subject she seemed much more at ease with. The next slide was headed: *Cover Letter Ideas.*

Useful examples followed, such as Number 4:

Dear Sir/Madam:
I would fit right in as a counter clerk in your fine dry cleaning
establishment. I have observed that the counter clerk position re-
quires competence at handling several activities in quick order
-- customer service, payments, bagging and phones. I like multi-
tasking and, as a homemaker, I have a lot of practice in keeping all
the balls in the air.

"See how positive that sounds?" Gloria said looking approvingly
on the excerpt written by the plucky homemaker, "And," she added, "It
doesn't just work for dry cleaners. That's the kind of thing you could say in
any letter. I mean it's just a sample."

The way she snuck a peak at her watch made Maxi think she might
be running over the scheduled pace. Nevertheless she continued: "Avoid
passive verbs, be self-assured. Just like in an interview situation, you should
exude confidence."

Out of the corner of his eye, Maxi caught Armenian Twin 1 nudge
Twin 2 who, as startled from a daydream, sat upright and tried to give
himself a more dignified posture.

On the screen Gloria was reviewing desirable active-tense terms
to help infuse a job letter with positive job-securing energy. They were arranged alphabetically by letter.
Maxi read:

I
Improved, identified, installed, inspired, interviewed, issued, in-
vested, illustrated, implemented, incurred, innovated, inspected,
invented, interpreted, instilled, inaugurated, informed, induced.

Some people were still taking notes. The majority however, reeling
perhaps now from absorbing all the practical data, appeared to be staring
at the screen with the blank expression of an 8th grader stumbling into a
pop quiz right after smoking pot at recess.

Gloria was unperturbed by the dull stares, explaining, "A lot of
companies receive hundreds and thousands of resumes. They do not even
read them; instead they use optical scanners to retrieve only those with a

high concentration of desirable terms. If you are using the wrong words, keywords, chances are no one will ever read your letters."

The class grimly took in the reality of this news. Their Drill Sergeant was matter of factly revealing a new unexpected hurdle to their quest: a mechanical, hope-killing beast. A nemesis few could hope to overcome unless armed with the correct magic-words.

Maxi found himself instinctively trying to use the verbs in sentences that might apply to him, "innovated, invented...induced," he thought, feeling only ridiculous as he silently mouthed the preposterous boasts. Another set of masculine and proactive participles flashed on the screen:

S
Saved, secured, stabilized, scheduled, screened, settled, separated, sent, selected, shaped, shortened, showed, signed, simplified, sold, staged, standardized, steered, stimulated, strategized, surveyed, supported, supplied, substantiated, supervised

"Compromised, conceded, capitulated..." Maxi countered in his head with a selection of vocabulary more fitting to someone who, like himself, was an unlikely securer or steerer, let alone a savior.

Gloria in the meantime evidently judged the group ready to proceed onto further communication strategies. "This sample here refers to an opening line for the Elevator Speech," she said indicating a new slide. "What is an Elevator Speech, you say?" she added with rhetorical flourish, "Well, imagine that you're going to an interview at a company's headquarters. Say you're taking the elevator and someone walks in together with you who looks important, or maybe they have a badge, you know, like a manager or something. Well...now, that's a great networking opportunity! Here's your chance to say something, and like it says right here, *Make a lasting first impression.* This here is a template for an elevator speech," Gloria explained indicating the chart with the laser pointer:

"Hello, my name is_____I'm a skilled_____
currently between jobs. Are you by any chance aware of anyone in
the building that might need the services of a _____?"

"Like, that is something you could definitely say", encouraged

Gloria. "You never know who might be aware of someone who might be looking just for somebody with your specific qualifications on a floor of that same building!"

The scenario strained the belief of even the most stoked applicants, some of whom nevertheless ventured a nod, trying perhaps to will the hypothetical scene into plausibility.

"For some people it might be hard to break the ice, but it's important you try." Gloria continued, apparently sticking to an inner script now. "Me, it's always come easy to me. I love to talk," she added, illustrating what by now had become self-evident, and as if for further example, she veered sharply onto a tangent of momentary introspection, "Man. I don't know how I made it through college. Mostly I hung out in the common room and played Centipede. Remember those?"

Blank stares met her vintage videogame exuberance and she cleared her throat. "OK, lets continue. Let's see, what's left? Research. Its really important you research the company you apply to. In my day you had to spend a day in the library stacks, but today it's easy"

"Google it, right?" Malt Liquor Man blurted suddenly from the front row.

"That's right, very good." Gloria seemed genuinely grateful for the unexpected class participation and reiterated the point, "Really important."

"Tell me about it," Malt Liquor continued eagerly, "Last week I drove 20 miles for a security guard position, and it turns out the restaurant was a strip joint. Didn't even get out of the car. I knew I should have Googled it".

Malt Liquor's name was revealed to be Rob and his occupation, bouncer (momentarily on hiatus). He was a security guard with clear moral standards and soon, possibly an improved personal brand.

Maxi caught Gloria surreptitiously glancing at her watch again and guessed the lecture to be nearing its conclusion.

She worked the power point, examining and rapidly discarding the next two slides, alighting on the screen that read, in block letters: *"REMEMBER, DO NOT LOOK DESPERATE/ANXIOUS"*.

Heads nodded here in solemn recognition, like the contrite faithful at the conclusion of a poignant sermon. Their conversion might have seemed more plausible were it not for the obvious fact that a sizeable number of applicants looked nothing if not desperate, or at least dispirited by their current "middle-class" predicament. Sheep momentarily separated from their happiness-pursuing flock, trying hard to rejoin their destinies as productive citizens and consumers.

But there was no time for commiseration. Gloria had reached the end of the script and was ready to dismiss her congregation. "The last step in transitional counseling consists of the Practical Application unit. In the waiting room where you first came in, there's a row of computers along the wall. You can log on with the Client Number that you received at check-in, and follow the prompts. They will direct you to compile a resumé and send it to six actual job openings you will select from the Career Transition webboard. When you are done, you can print out your certificate and Andy will update your Eligibility Status before you leave…Thank you very much for attending the Reorientation Workshop and good luck!"

WANTED: TALENTED WRITERS

Push Content Studios is currently seeking out writers with talent and experience to contribute content covering a variety of different topics for our network of online publishing partner sites. Your content will be shared with thousands of readers every day.
Opportunities for Studio writers involve 300-500 word articles in a number of different fields, including Business, Finance, Nutrition, Travel, Technology, Fitness, and more. Compensation: Writing assignments start at $20-$30 per article and payments are delivered twice a week.

Maxi found himself blinking at the screen, rereading the job postings and trying to remember back, way back, when his trade had been something other than uploading a $20 fitness article three times a day. Who did this?! Who unleashed the Doomsday Machine onto the professions of millions of mid-lifers currently to be found surfing the couches of Western Civilization. A diaspora of *formerly-employables,* moping around art openings and cocktail parties, self-commiserating in the vicinity of the cash bar to any guest or acquaintance unlucky enough to come within earshot.

He'd done *Acceptance*, right? How then had he apparently become hopelessly stuck between *Anger* and *Depression*? Hadn't the conveyer belt, once properly started, supposed to travel to its destination? Had he somehow missed the disclaimer about "Your life may become inoperable. Warranty is void if screws are removed?" Oh what's the use, and who gives a fuck?! Just one more 'actual job opening' now, and he could at least get out of here with another two months of "emergency" unemployment checks – the last lifeline Gloria and Obama were throwing him from the middle class raft now drifting farther as he grasped for the rope bobbing in the water, just out of reach.

He scrolled further down the screen, through another ad for a highly motivated self-starter with enthusiastic people skills and a passion for learning.

Where were the listings for ornery cynics with an excess of experience and a lousy attitude? He wondered. 'Cause he could tell you pretty much right now that he wasn't ever gonna be a very good preditor; more like a hobbled prey, the injured wildebeest separated from the herd, falling behind, as the hyenas, pack emboldened, darted from the brush. No, he was not a preditor, nor a shark. He was not a thought leader. And he didn't care.

In all the scrollable listings there was not one single position for a regular guy, just a writer, no genius maybe, but a regular guy, just looking for a day's work, and maybe to get his life back.
He glanced at the text he had compiled using the Transition Center Resumé Tool, complete with cover letter containing the power verbs "ranked", "resolved", "rewarded" and "reinforced" in the first paragraph.

What was this pathetic artifice, this version of himself? He felt like a buffoon, pushed through the stage door with an ill-fitting suit and pancake make-up to conceal the cracks in his face. This whole exercise was not much more than an elaborate ritual, a dance of contrition required in order to pocket the handout.

He looked again hopelessly at the tabs at the top of the Transition Center web page: *Resources, Connections, Job Boards, Workforce Reentry…* No tab for *Black Pit of Despair* or he might have been tempted to click that one. No help button either, or for that matter, instructions on how to re-enter recently obliterated professions. How were you supposed to market a skill that was now as valued as the casual hobbies of adolescent bloggers?

"Would you kindly point me in the direction," he wanted to get up and ask Gloria. "Towards the universe where there's still an economy for

English majors to ply their punctuation and passive verbs?"

There was no use. He had only himself to blame. The way he had frittered away youthful ideal for the lure of an easy paycheck, selling out to TV work, plunging head first into a rabbit hole of compromise only to get caught in the elevator with no speech, when the whole edifice came crashing down.

The last time he had been this directionless had been around college time, but every aimless day then had basked in the infinite promise of the unexpected, the unknown yet to be discovered. Purposelessness had seemed so inconsequential and benevolent back when he could coast on the easy pull of a pregnant future.

Now the same routine was weighted with the rank scent of fear, aimless promise turned to unmoored drifting in an empty ocean of doubt.

AGGRESSIVE CONTENT GENERATOR

Originate ideas for evergreen content, seasonal content, real-time content, new site features, and content modules. You're comfortable with your own voice, well connected to like bloggers AND know how engage a social media audience across different demographics in a dynamic environment. You can write irresistible copy - the kind of writing that makes people wish we would send them more email! The right candidate can drive results in a complex, multi-site, multi-stakeholder publishing environment; and loves the creativity, energy, and enthusiasm of a fast, collaborative, innovative new media team.

In his head Maxi completed the posting: *"Sometimes right before dawn, when, the morning glories are still shut tight, the light from the roaming helicopter floods the bedroom, and the harsh beam shines on your wide-open eyes... And you feel like softly crying...*

Instead he clicked the "Apply" tab. That made six.

He logged out, collected his paperwork and headed for the checkout desk.

Outside the light was softer now and the breeze warm over the gathering rush hour. Maxi, freshly reapproved for Federal Aid, stood at the bus stop, scanning the oncoming traffic for signs of an approaching 208.

"That wasn't so bad, right?"

He turned to see Red Bag Lady.

"This center is OK," she said, "Although they really should have free coffee."

She waved good-bye with a clinking of the car keys she held in her hand.

"Anyway, maybe I'll see you in a couple of months…"

"Yeah," Maxi replied, "See you then…"

Andrew Berardini

Letter from New York

The actors took over.

Like a subtle and discreet virus spreading slowly through newspapers and magazines, internet sites and text messaging, from person to person, from contact both direct and indirect, the populace began in earnest to act. The first few actors were considered an anomaly, the expected desire for all people to turn away from the tawdry rat racing and dog-eat-dogging and pecking orders. Some attrition to the arts was natural, not everyone could stand the stagnancy of poorly ventilated offices with their incessant pop and hum of fluorescent lights, the petty politics and group-think of modern administrative work with its shrill slogans and inane patterns of logic.

One by one, the office workers and maintainers of administrations large and small begun to leave the offices, just a few a week, then at least a few a day and then the acting really begin to get going. Street corners and subway cars became infested with actors, reciting Shakespeare and Albee, Ibsen and Mamet, doing impromptu impressions of James Earl Jones and Ricki Lake, Lawrence Olivier and Angelina Jolie. Everyone began talking about their bodies as "instruments." The offices grew desperate, droves of unemployed would-be workers were trucked in from the suburbs, but they too submitted to the virus. Actors were everywhere; the soap operas and commercials, theaters and television studios became mobbed with actors. The guards and gates held them back for only so long before they too became actors, and the actors rushed the gates and took over the studios. The studio heads and gaffers, the secretaries and the webmasters all became actors. It happened at the same time the actors took city hall that the remaining office staff became actors, the street sweepers and liquor store clerks, the art curators and the aestheticians all became subsumed in the acting pandemic. Some were eager to "make it," others just wanted to be free to practice their art, liberated of the crass demands of commerce.

The city infrastructure came to a stand still, the subway cars hung around the station, nowhere to go, street lights all blinked dumbly red, but the traffic had largely stopped anyway, and the lights were just props in street performances. Grocery stores became impromptu improv theaters, small unlikely groupings of neighbors started workshopping one another, every park bench became a platform for a ready monologue, all actions became plots, all places scenes, all words dialogue. Misbehaving children were admonished for their unprofessionality. This only lasted a few days before things started to settle down. It began that the actors, working together and with mutual consent, began to assign roles for the greatest play the world had ever seen. Many characters were cast. The bus drivers were given the very important roles of bus drivers and stars of melodramas involving bus drivers, their daily struggles, their existential dread. A few were assigned to be the doctors, the doctors were greatly excited to be able to a play the role for which they've done so much background research. Many practiced the line for parties "Yes, I'm a doctor and I play one on TV." Though because of the nature of the production, only few would get to say it and rarely, as part of a role of someone who was a doctor and played one on TV.

It took time for the actors to decide where the best roles would be, but background in a role felt like really good research and a great place to start: husbands decided to play husbands, sons to play sons, criminals, long associated with the very real details of life in prison, returned to their jails to perform the daily realities of their suffering, the injustice of the penal system, the stark realities of man's inhumanity to man. These roles demanded bravery and dignity and they accepted their parts, knowing that these stories needed to be told.

The most brilliant and artistic amongst them chose the hardest roles, the ones with the most emotional resonance. Thus the best actors, the most deeply-feeling and sensitive became the oppressed, the reviled, and the poor: prostitutes, junkies, lunatics, homeless, and even lower: murderers, rapists, pederasts, and politicians. They tried to invest their roles with humanity and depth, tenderness and style, so that these roles, as complex as they were, would hold an undeniable gravitas and get the understanding and sympathy that these characters required. Each and every actor the main character in an important story.

Within days the play had begun, everyone an actor playing their roles without cease. They would wake to their roles and go to sleep to their roles. The script would be felt out and improvised. The drama would become painful and real. There were deaths and births.

Sometimes though, the actors would forget their roles and stand back for a moment as an audience member looking at the greatest drama the world had ever seen. These momentary audience members, actors forgetting they were performing, struck by the power of the proceedings would stand back and weep, caught in the sublime beauty of their production. Soon enough though, another actor would nudge them, ask what was wrong, subtly imply that they were breaking character. Each would continue on, acting out their roles with responsibility and dedication, until the end.

John Tottenham

Disappearing

"Let me pretend to be generous," I said, as we slid our trays up to the cashier. I forked over $15 for turkey sandwiches and coffees, pleased by how cheap it was, and that no tip was necessary, since we were in a cafeteria.

We took a seat at one of the tiered tables, overlooking the spacious ground floor. In Clifton's cafeteria, with its streams, grottos and fake redwood trees, one could get a good cheap meal in uniquely enchanting surroundings and escape the madness outside for as long as one wanted. It served as a precious sanctuary for downtown dwellers, workers and scufflers. In the quarter of a century I'd been frequenting this establishment it hadn't changed at all. It was comforting to know that it would always be there. But it was beginning to look as if its timeless and unhurried days might be numbered. After 75 years as a family-run business it had been bought by the sort of developers who delight in giving facelifts to venerable old downtown haunts in the name of preservation. I didn't like the sound of it at all.

"They say they're not going to change anything," said my charming dining companion.

"They're going to build a Tiki bar on the third floor, that should change it significantly."

We ate self-consciously, engaging in our first and possibly last intimate act together. She waited until her mouth was sufficiently clear of food to speak.

"I've never been on the third floor," she said.

"Why can't they build their fucking Tiki bar somewhere else?" I said. "They can't leave anything alone. Everywhere has to be turned into an imitation of itself and made accessible to the young people who are taking over. They wouldn't be moving down here if the frontier hadn't already been opened up. The pioneers have long been and gone."

But I stopped myself, for fear of alienating her. After all, she'd just moved downtown herself and was living in a remodeled skid row hotel, working at a coffee house and painting.

And what did I really care? I just wanted everything to stay the same, to bask in the diminishing radiance of perpetual decay. I took solace in it.

"They're bringing in a new chef," I said. "They'll be serving the same sort of food, so they claim, but in smaller portions, which means higher prices. A whole new crowd will be flocking here, thinking that they're having this 'authentic' experience, not realizing that it's a version that's been stripped of its authenticity. It's all very tasteful, but I'm satisfied with meatloaf, canned peas and jello served on a brown fiberglass tray, not some haute version of comfort food."

But I stopped myself again, running damage control against potentially rampaging bitterness. Maybe she wasn't into that sort of thing.

"What can you do?" she said, having swallowed.

"Nothing, it's the way of the world. Nobody cares. Nobody's going to do anything. I'm not going to do anything."

Then: silence. Which meant I had to keep volunteering information or firing off questions. But there was no flow, they hit a wall, and out of nervousness and a desire to impress, I rattled on.

"The last time I was here there was a toilet attendant in the men's room."

"It's a strange job," she said.

"It's ridiculous to give somebody a dollar for handing you a paper towel."

"I doubt anybody grows up wanting to be a toilet attendant," she said.

We'd met at an art opening several days earlier. She had been standing at the time, attired in tight pants, and I had been riveted by the muscu-

Disappearing

lature of her legs; her whole body seemed to pulsate with sensuality. When we spoke, which happened quickly and naturally, there seemed to be an immediate connection, of which there was now little evidence.

Now she was wearing leggings and she was sitting down. I still couldn't stop looking at her. If the conversation was stilted, I didn't mind: I was comfortable with the silence. The apparent lack of curiosity, so typical of today's young people, in her case seemed more a case of delicacy and reserve; she had a muted quality about her; but there was a weight to her vagueness, a presence behind the appearance of absence; and on this occasion I was grateful that she wasn't asking questions: it meant that disconcerting admissions of age and failure needn't be addressed.

"They've already knocked out a partition down there," I said, referring to the bakery counter in the lobby, which was now clearly visible, no longer separated from the interior. "It's unfortunate. There's more light coming in."

Out of the blue, she asked a question: "Do you have family?"

"They're mostly dead. How about you?"

"Dead, or disappeared."

This was encouraging. I tended to get along better with people from unhappy families.

"Who disappeared?"

"My father. I went looking for him. I put everything else on hold. I didn't paint or write for a year."

This was discouraging: women with absentee fathers were an unhappy category unto themselves.

"You write?"

"Poetry. A lot of it. I don't care if it's any good, I don't show it to anybody."

"The world would be a better place if more poets adopted that policy, not that the world would notice either way."

She laughed. It was hard getting laughs out of her, and rewarding when they came, owing to their infrequency.

"Did you find him?"

"Yes, he was living in Wyoming with another woman, and I wasted a whole year of my life looking for him."

"I've got you beat, I wasted ten years of my life."

"How?"

43

"On loose living. At least ten years. Well, I suppose it depends upon how you define waste."

But she wasn't interested in defining waste.

You could see them entering below, surveying the place with looks of wonder: newcomers, marveling at the decor. There would be more of them when the new management took over, with the shift to a younger clientele who would view this downtown institution as a bizarre novelty. Why did I resent them? Because I didn't want everybody else sharing my pleasure in the places I held dear, that I had found on my own long ago. There were few enough such places left, and they were disappearing at an alarming rate.

We ate our sandwiches slowly, and after we finished them there didn't seem to be much point sitting there anymore. She had never been on the third floor, so we removed the velvet rope at the bottom of the stairwell and walked up to that darkened area of empty tables and flock wallpaper known as the Red Room. This, presumably, was the future location of the Tiki bar, though there were no signs of construction yet.

I caught sight of myself in one of the full length mirrors. I didn't look too bad: I could pass for forty.

We stopped at the wishing well on the way out, and admired the large faded backlit photographs of California nature scenes: a feature that seemed unlikely to survive the change of ownership, as it possessed no conventional kitsch value.

Once out on the street, on a noisy, dreary afternoon, she suggested taking a walk. We headed west along 7th. I pointed towards a basement, once home to a cavernous Salvation Army store, and rued the fact that there were no more thrift stores left downtown, now that the Goodwill on Broadway had closed, a recent casualty of the real estate boom. I mentioned that I had once found a stack of Sun Ra records there. But this failed to impress her, as she had never heard of Sun Ra. I felt the divide that separated her hope from my hopelessness.

"There used to be loads of cafeterias around here," I said. "There was one over there called Wayne's."

That would really date me, if she looked it up, but there was unlikely to be any record of it anywhere. Who remembered Wayne's? I had never heard anybody mention it. I remembered the zigzag lettering on the plastic sign outside and the jukebox, upon which I repeatedly played George Strait's 'Amarillo by Morning.' It was possible that she may never have even seen a jukebox with actual records on it.

A lot can change in a quarter of a century. It had taken a long time for the character of downtown to change, although it still looked much the same on the outside, the reverse of my dilemma. It was nice being able to come up with all these stories about the pure old days, but I didn't want to have to admit to how old I was. I had to be at least 20 years older than her, but, thankfully, she wasn't asking questions.

"Change doesn't necessarily mean progress," I said. "Some things peaked at a certain stage, and there's no point building upon them. Architecture, clothes, automobile design should have been suspended decades ago. But architects and designers dictate otherwise. Take the Kindle, for example, a completely useless innovation. Can it really be considered an advance to be able to read a book on a flat shiny screen. Can you imagine, if the Kindle was the standard for reading and the book was suddenly invented: something tactile, pages that you could actually turn, with a jacket design. What a marvelous improvement it would seem. The Kindle is a gigantic step backwards."

As we walked, she became more talkative. I forget what she said.

"There used to be another Clifton's right around here, the Silver Spoon," I said, looking around for the sign. It had been up for a long time after the business closed but it must have finally been taken down and replaced by the sign for the Whiskey Bar, a young man's reinvention of an old man's bar, where the bartenders called themselves mixologists and far more brands of whiskey than anybody could ever need or name were available at inflated prices.

"Fifteen years ago," I said - I had been about to say "twenty" but caught myself as fifteen still seemed reasonable. Then I changed it again: "Ten years ago," I said, which was still realistic, "there was no drinking culture among young people on this side of town. Now the old so-called dives have all been turned into ersatz dives that cater to this ever-expanding population of young people who are learning how to drink, learning how to smoke, learning how to hold their cigarettes properly. The old people don't have anywhere to call their own anymore."

It occurred to me that I was one of them.

Since we were in the neighborhood, I proposed that we visit a bar

I had heard about that was situated in the rear of a modest old hotel on Flower street. It was, apparently, only open in the afternoons. It was accessible through an entrance in the alley behind the hotel.

We had the entire place to ourselves. But then, three o'clock on a Monday afternoon isn't exactly a peak hour.

"Let's keep up the pretense of generosity," I said. She ordered a Jameson on the rocks, and I seconded it. The portions could have been larger. I considered tipping the bartender only a dollar, but didn't want to be thought cheap, and laid down two.

"I wonder how long it will be before they ruin this place," she said, as we sat down in a curved Naugahyde booth in the large dark empty room. She seemed to be catching on.

"They can't leave anything alone," I said. "In this progressively more digital world, everything has been discovered, picked over and ruined. There's a desperate hunger to unearth anything left that's supposedly authentic, which isn't much."

The bartender had disappeared. The jukebox played songs at random at a pointlessly loud volume. 'London Calling' came on.

"The Clash are my favorite band ever," she said, moving in closer so that we could hear each other.

I could remember when that record came out, but I couldn't tell her that: she might wonder what I'd been doing for the last thirty years. I could have regaled her with tales of my days in the punk trenches, first campaign, when as an idealistic adolescent I caught the Clash in their prime, but I held back. Of course, she might not know when their prime was, but that was a chance I didn't want to take. It was a shame to have to sacrifice bragging rights on the pyre of vanity, pathetic really.

"I thought they shot their wad after their first record," I said. Even introducing this much suggestion of sex into the conversation felt uneasily loaded, although that, obviously, was what I wanted from her, and presumably she can't have entirely ruled out the possibility either, as she was prepared to spend her Monday afternoon sitting in a bar with me.

"That's the problem with political bands," I said, staring under the table at her remarkably firm thighs. "As soon as they become successful they lose touch with the conditions that gave rise to them. Their second albums always stink. It was the same with the Gang of Four."

"I like them too," she said. "But I came to them backwards, I guess

46

Disappearing

I heard the newer stuff first." She paused. "I suppose I should get going and prepare for the meeting."

She had already mentioned this early evening business meeting a couple of times.

"I love old hotel lobbies," I said, as we exited through the lobby, and went on to mention the King Edward Hotel and its adjoining bar, the last of the old skid row joints.

"A friend of mine took me there," she said. "When he went to the rest room a crackhead tried to kiss me and drag me outside."

I wondered if she often had this effect on men, as I had felt like doing exactly the same thing when I met her. This afternoon, perhaps to my discredit, I had managed to restrain myself.

"I'll give it six months before it gets taken over," she said. "People in their twenties go there during Art Walk."

So perhaps she wasn't in her twenties any more. I wasn't sure what to make of that.

"It's inevitable," I said. "It's right around the corner from the gentrification area. The boundary keeps getting pushed back, now it's Los Angeles street."

I remembered the days when one never saw a respectable civilian east of Broadway. All those late, unlamented, irreplaceable sties: Jack's, Craby Joe's, the Golden Torch - their like would never be seen again. There were no disreputable watering holes to slum in anymore.

We stood on the sidewalk, waiting for the light to change, apprehensive about jaywalking, now that fines had been quadrupled.

"I almost moved in there," she said, as we passed the Hotel Bristol, a renovated fleabag above the Golden Gopher, a one-time wine dump that now catered to USC students. Unable to stop myself, I reeled out a story about how I used to visit an old man who lived there, whom I had met when he was sketching on the street. I used to bring him art supplies. This useful anecdote showcased my sensitivity, generosity and refined aesthetic judgment.

A familiar melancholy drifted faintly through me as we walked, the feeling that this was the last time, that my good fortune at still being able to occasionally attract the attention of desirable young women would have to run out soon, that this might be the last time, and I was going to blow it again.

My bicycle was chained to a pole outside Clifton's. The difficult business of parting had to be dealt with. I weighed the options. The prospect of pushing the bicycle along beside her as we walked up the crowded sidewalk seemed potentially awkward, to somehow place me in a subordinate position. Alternatively, I could walk the two blocks with her to the street that she lived on and then walk back to the bicycle. But, as she pointed out, they were long blocks. Or we could simply part here, outside Clifton's. I opted for the latter. I put as much feeling into our parting hug as I was capable of, but it was still lacking. I wasn't much of a hugger. If the quality of my hug was used as a gauge to determine my aptitude in the sack, then I would surely be discounted.

This story doesn't have an ending. Why should it?

What did you think was going to happen? Nothing happened. I never saw her again.

All right, if you insist. Here:

Watching her walk away, that ass… disappearing.

Matty Byloos

Loved in Spite of Great Fault

I'm bottle-feeding it again right now, just in case it's not obvious what I'm doing. This is how it gets fed, which is a bit technical, and certainly laborious. I sort of hold its head in my hand, which really requires more like two hands even though I have to use the other hand to hold the little bottle, so I hold the enormous head in my one hand, usually my left, and try to just... tilt... it up at enough of an angle so that the milk and formula mixture actually has a chance to go down her little throat. It's pathetic.

So generally they're cute; this was why I got the kitten in the first place. That and of course the fact that living alone again was – well, loneliness was difficult, but that's what – that's another story, as they say. The kitten adoption was a couple of months ago. And she was sleeping. I mean, a lot. When I first went to look at her over at the shelter, they said she was different. I figured, she was colored differently. What could they have meant by that, after all. How different can one kitten be from another? This one has a little colored stain on its face, that one's orange. Different. I get it. But she was *asleep* the whole time. Maybe that's why I never noticed.

In fact, that was part of what attracted me to her. I figured, kittens are cute, sure, but they're rambunctious, nocturnal. They get up in the middle of the night, fired up, get into your things, cause a ruckus. And hearing them. Tiny meows are cute, too. Like I said, the house has been empty for a few months, so a little noise from something alive was good.

I was looking forward to it. So I thought – maybe if this one's sleeping all the time, we'll be fine.

So, I'm over the kitten being different. A little stain on the face, maybe the color could be described as off, but everything else appeared normal. Small black ears, tiny feet, furry white ball with a few black stripes here and there, and asleep. I brought her home, and she slept during the whole car ride. I was floored. Thought I was the luckiest sonuvabitch in the world. Not a peep the whole way back to my house, asleep in her little crate. Which I brought right into the house just like that. There wasn't much furniture around the place anymore, and I thought that might freak her out. Like she'd pick up on the fact that there are few lonelier things than an empty house with room after room full of nothing more than indentations in the carpet from the stuff that used to be there. Then she'd get sad too, or lonely enough to wanna go back to the pound. At first, I remember I didn't want to disturb her sleeping, so I figured I could just bring her into the kitchen in her crate, maybe open up the cage door quietly, and when she was ready to come out, after she had finally woken up, she would. This was before I realized anything about the giant head on top of her neck.

After the first day when she still hadn't woken up, I figured – she's growing. Babies sleep, after all. It's normal. Lots of growing means lots of sleeping. She was still in her crate and I thought, maybe she needs to eat. I put her little bowl of wet kitten food in there with her. Served breakfast in bed, essentially. Who wouldn't love that kind of treatment? So she slept for a few days. I figured she was growing fast, and maybe she was eating at night while I slept. Possibly wandering around the house a bit, on her own.

My ex-wife, now *she* was an independent woman. There's a table in the dining room, and with so much dust on it, there's still imprints left in the surface from the stacks of boxes and board games and paperwork she took with her when she left. She was like a – a robber baron, or whatever they call them. Land barons, maybe. We'd play strip monopoly in the beginning, after we first met. It wasn't easy to do, but the fact that we both tried to get into jail at the same time, and then force each other to take everything off, well – we figured at the time we were made for each other. Like it was perfect, and maybe we'd just gotten lucky enough to make it work forever. She was all independent, loaded up with piles of $100 and $500 bills, buying up properties, and I'd be keeping score of whose clothes got taken off or put back on or whatever, making notes with my little library pencil.

So like I said, I really – I just love an independent woman, so in the morning the second or third day after I got the kitten, I was impressed with how much she was probably doing, activity-wise, while I was sleeping. Let's be honest – she had just traveled a long way to her new home. And well after the fact, now I realize that her head was enormous, so that couldn't have been easy to deal with, trying to preserve energy for other activities, or adventuring around the house on her own at night. Sure, I'd traveled. I'd been to Europe. It was a big place. I got used to Amsterdam, the airport, the trains. I'd fly into Amsterdam every time, then take the train to Germany or Paris. Base camp – you know. Like Amsterdam was my home away from home, then I could venture out from there and expand my turf a little at a time. So I figured, that's what she was doing in there, in her crate, which was her Amsterdam. And maybe the living room was East Germany. Probably the rest of the kitchen would have been Germany, actually. Makes more sense, like geo-strategically. The living room would have been her Paris, more correctly. Just a wide-open space into which she could project all her dreams, like a romantic would. And the little potholes in the carpet from the couch or the end tables that used to be there – maybe they could be her landmarks, her Eiffel Tower. Or the one dying plant would probably be the Tower. There wasn't really anything else in the room at all. So basically, I was impressed. She was sleeping, and we were bonding. And I thought, wow – we're actually so much alike, me and this little girl kitty.

I thought for a couple of days that I would name her David, told my mom and everything. I first got settled into that name but in the end, never got too comfortable with it. I used to drive up and down the coast a lot. For business or things; to get out of the house. Leave and drive a few hours up the coast from Los Angeles, then turn around and come back. I find it calms me down. So I named her Mussel Shoals, after the little town on the coast, halfway up to San Francisco. One time when I was driving past it, I started saying it out-loud, right there in the car by myself. Mussel Shoals. Mussel Shoals. Mussel *Shoals*. I thought it'd make a terrific name for a band or something. So it got stuck there in my head. When it came time to naming something, which in this case happened to be the kitten, it came out. So she's Mussel Shoals now, and I like it that way.

Bottom line, her head is huge. It's way past normal kitten size.

Colossal. Like, as in, her neck is actually not strong enough to hold the gigantic thing aloft. So that explained the sleeping thing. She was probably awake the whole time, trying to fake me out, make me think she was adorable and sleeping and everything, and then just *bam*, just show up one day in the kitchen, dragging her enormous head on the linoleum tile trying to scare the Christ out of all my friends. Well, my ex-friends, actually, because, I mean – and who could blame them, because in their position, I'd most likely have the exact same response – I couldn't be friends with a person whose cat's head was so gigantic and unwieldy that they couldn't hold it upright like normal. It's pathetic. Believe me, I know. And both of my friends, my *old* friends – well, they probably knew it too. 'Cause they're gone now, out of my life.

So she's sleeping and then she starts meowing. This was probably like the fourth day. Wakes up, just all of a sudden. One day she's in the crate, the cage-thing, and the next day she's there in the middle of the kitchen, staring up at me, sideways, at a weird angle even, and I'm thinking, *what in God's green earth is this?* It's a kitten, after all, so you can't help but have a first reaction like, wow – it's just so cute, I *wanna* eat it! But then you have to grapple with the fact that her head looks more like a gigantic, overly-ripe grapefruit hanging from a tiny, whimpering branch, way too close to the ground. So I'm bottle-feeding her now, holding her head in my left hand. She's kinda' on the ground in front of me, in the kitchen, where we spend most of our time. I try to not make her move around too much more than she has to – I'm sure it's exhausting dragging her head around on the floor and trying to meow. And this somehow reminds me of my ex-wife dragging her enormous suitcase out of here the night she left, and suddenly I'm sad but also feeling a little *sympathetic*.

And her meow. This weird, I don't know exactly how to describe it. *Rectangular* type of noise? Like it comes out of her little whiskered, sideways-facing mouth in little blips. *Rah. Rah. Rah. Rah.* Turns a corner every time. I dunno. Like it comes out, makes a ninety-degree turn, comes out, repeats. That probably won't make sense to anyone but me. But she's my little kitten, so if that's how I want to understand Mussel Shoals, then so be it. If you were to lose both of your friends, over a baby kitten with a tremendously oversized head, even if maybe they weren't really ever your friends in the first place, the more I think about it, a-ah-and wanted to describe all the noises you ever heard in some nonsensical geometric kind of abstract way, then I'd let you. But I'm generous. The phone's ringing.

It's my mother and I tell her the kitten's named Mussel Shoals now, and that her head is really, really big. I had to tell her in case she ever decided to come over. It's been a while now, since my wife left and my mother stopped visiting so much, but you never know. I mean, who would want their mother to walk into the kitchen, run into Mussel Shoals there on the floor, dragging her head a few feet away in one direction, trying to be scared, probably, seeing as it's a new face around the house, first time visitor to Germany, the kitchen, and she's gonna be scared. She doesn't know it's just my mother.

Maybe Mussel Shoals is more like a Dustin Hoffman than a grapefruit, actually, now that I think about it. That way, I can think about her head thing like it's a potential benefit to her. One day, her gigantic head might come in handy. Dustin Hoffman has a pretty small body, and a pretty large head, otherwise – how could his face be so big? And because his face is really way too big for the rest of his body, well, the camera or the film likes it that way. The film doesn't actually know any better, or doesn't have the same taste as we humans in what it finds attractive, so when Dustin Hoffman is being recorded on film, his gigantic face and head is great. It's part of his success. He looks great on film, small body and all. Hell – put him up on an apple crate if you need him to be as tall as his leading lady. Whatever. At least you can see his expression of sadness when he's in *Kramer vs. Kramer.* At least you know when he's got a wild hair up his ass to solve the whole Deep Throat debacle in *All the President's Men.* Who cares if he's got a huge head? I'll bet he had a horrible time in grade school.

So my friends are all weirded out by Mussel Shoals, or more to the point, by Mussel Shoals's head being so big and everything, but when I think about Dustin Hoffman's friends walking out on him when he was ten, and then a few years later he's walking up on stage to pick up his Academy Award – I look down at Mussel Shoals, and it's not so bad. I never really wanted to go out much, didn't really care for work, like in a standard kind of forty-hour-a-week sort of way, so this is better. I stay home, I bottle feed the little girl kitten, I do my freelance projects.

Really what it's about is the smells. I liked the way I smelled right after a shower, first thing in the morning. There'd be like a coconut thing coming from my deodorant powder. I'd rub it on my feet too, to keep them from getting sweaty. That was tropical and rich. And I'd put some rosemary oil that smelled a bit like mint too, I'd rub that in my scalp so I wouldn't get dandruff, which happened as a result of stress I was probably applying to myself, matter of fact. I mean, work wasn't that bad. Not enough to change the nature of my scalp. But, I worry. And then there was the cardamom, Turkish bath scented oil thing and I'd maybe rub it around in my chest hair a little bit. And the shpritz—Turkish bath smells, was what this little collection was supposed to be. You could put all these different treatments on you, and come up with the overall sensation of having been at a Turkish bath. Really smart if you think about it. And I liked the way I smelled, but it always got ruined throughout the day. Progressively ruined, one chore at a time. The drycleaners, picking up lunch, walking past the coffee depot and somebody'd be smoking outside. I'd come home eventually, smelling like a sewer. Who needs it?

So this is really probably the worst thing that's happened to me. The girl kitten with the big head just like Dustin Hoffman, who similarly lost all his friends because of his face and then had to accept his Oscar later but have no friends to share it with because they'd all abandoned him. Well, maybe the worst thing. I mean, my wife left me, and that was really because of the drug problems I'd been having at the time, which I think put a pretty significant strain on some of my friendships, so maybe there was already a little chink in the armor before Mussel Shoals showed up. So yeah – maybe that was the worst thing that ever happened. Before Mussel Shoals, anyway.

Who could blame me? I mean, drugs are great. They're gripping. Like that scene in *The Graduate* when Dustin Hoffman falls face-down in the pool, or else when he runs right into the church or up there on the campus of Berkeley. I really felt for him in those moments. But the drugs. They had me for a little while.

It was like this. About a month ago, I took a shower. This is the best way I can describe it. I like the water really hot, and I like to twirl around in circles, so I can distribute the water pretty evenly on all sides. I was turning in circles, and I looked up towards the ceiling. This is kind of what the drugs taking hold of me was like. In the corner near the ceiling, above the showerhead, I could see through the steam, the faint shadow of what looked like a small plant growing out of the wall. I adjusted the heat a bit so the steam would calm down, and then I could see better.

This house is old. It's a rental and it has to be, at least seventy years old. It's been repainted several times, especially in the bathroom, from all the other tenants who've rented it before I showed up and got Mussel Shoals and her big head, so the paint is old and there's lots of layers and that's what made this whole thing really weird. Up near the ceiling, this tiny, black, elbow-hinged botanical specimen had grown right out of the wall. I thought, maybe the wet wood in the walls is responsible. Maybe this is like a mushroom mold or something. So maybe the mushroom growing out of my bathroom ceiling was actually the least of my worries.

It grew there for a while. A week maybe, several days. First, the little thing was all battened down, tight and small. But over the few days it lived in my shower, it grew, with the black wings opening up and fanning out, making it bigger, making it look like the kind of mushroom you'd put on your salad. The black wings spread out like a backyard patio umbrella, clinging to the wall for dear life. And that's how the drugs got hold of me. They clung there – inside me, in a weird space, kind of like being supported somehow, in a parasite-host kind of way. The sensation was all alone in there, just like the mushroom: mysterious, more comfortable in darkness. And I think my wife knew all this. She sensed it. For me it happened slowly, when the drugs took over, probably the worst thing that ever happened to me actually, like a little black mushroom devil meticulously plotting its takeover. A secret from my wife, but eventually it'd get so big, that black mushroom, of course this is a metaphor because it's not like an actual gigantic backyard patio umbrella grew inside my shower, I mean – she would have seen that growing in there, but I'm trying to illustrate something here. So it was unnatural; out of place. The black mushroom didn't belong. It was cunning, growing out of the wall like that, from the wet wood that was probably inside there. It just pushed out its sinister personality, right out into the room, just right out into the middle of my marriage.

More like came at her from her peripheral, but it came right out of me. At first, though, it probably came at her from the side. More surreptitiously, I think. It was disturbing, more so every day. Then I'd be missing one night. Then I'd show up missing a tooth, or call from a pay phone at three a.m., saying I needed twenty or maybe thirty-two dollars, or something really specific. So that there was no way she could think anything normal or practical, or even a surprise for her, was in the works. It was just me and that little black demon of a mushroom inside me, growing and getting more evil and more cunning all the time. Casting a shadow over more and more of our life together, and more parts of the house, or more hours of the day.

And then she was gone. And that was probably the worst thing that ever happened to me, if I think about it. But when it was happening, there was no way to control it. I'd think – look what you're doing now. Spending that money, wasting that time, breaking this vow to my partner or else that vow, really blowing it. Letting it all hang there in the balance, like if she ever found out, she'd be mortally wounded, and I'd be all selfish and ruined and awful. Just an awful person. But I did what I did anyway. The black mushroom, like I said before. I just did it. Again and again, like I didn't care. And I did, but the mushroom in there was stronger.

So now I've got Mussel Shoals, and I've still got the house, and pretty much nothing else. Well, drives along the coast I've still probably got to take every once in a while, and then there's my occasional freelance gig that I take so I can pay my bills and work from home, smell the good smells. Of course, feed the cat. From the little baby bottle thing. And hold its really really large head in my hand while I'm doing it.

Diane Mooney

Faith-n-Fire

Vern wouldn't shut up about the church. Every time I came back from the liquor store with cigarettes and beer, he'd start in yammering about Faith-n-Fire. Sometimes he'd have a few of the church members over and they'd all be mooning over Pastor Bob. Pastor Bob had big plans. Pastor Bob was going to lead Faith-n-Fire in rebuilding Muncie by establishing a community of the poor in all nations. I wanted to ask how a guy who couldn't even spell was going to lead a movement but it wasn't any use. Vern wouldn't hear one bad word about Pastor Bob. He'd even threatened to kick me out when I pointed out Jesus said the poor you will always have with you.

"Not anymore," Vern said, chewing on the end of his Swisher Sweet. "The poor are rising up. We're going to build a community where believers can live supernaturally."

"You're going to be ghosts?"

"Supernatural means spiritual. For someone who was a legal secretary, sometimes you don't know much."

I sure as hell knew what supernatural meant but I bit my lip. I need Vern, or more specifically, I needed Vern's house and his disability check. His parents left him a house in Shed Town free and clear. And he'd had the good sense to get injured before the Borg-Warner plant shut down. He was collecting disability, not stuck like his other friends whose unemployment had run out. Pastor Bob would have no trouble rounding up the poor. They were everywhere in Muncie. The whole town was shriveling,

57

A rust-belt town where the factories were literally rusting along with the abandoned railroad tracks. Abandoned homes moldered on every block, the homeless shelters were full, downtown was nothing but empty store-fronts. The only things that thrived in Muncie were weeds and the bars.

I was only thriving though the grace of Vern. So that meant I, too, was part of Pastor Bob's fan base. Today was Saturday, a church service day at Faith-n-Fire. I had to be ready by 5:45 pm sharp. I ran a swipe of pink lipstick over my lips. Vern insisted on modest make-up for church. I tugged my skirt over my hips, adjusted the front of my blouse to make sure my bra wasn't peeking out, and walked to the living room. It wasn't a long walk. Shed Town wasn't fancy. Most houses, including Vern's place, were no more than two bedroom shacks.

Vern waited on the couch, one leg bouncing up and down with nervous excitement. The couch was probably the same age as Vern, with wagon wheel arms and faded cowboys lassoing steers and riding horses across the fabric. The other furniture was equally as old and broken down. We ate our meals at a scratched laminate dining table with rusted chrome. Vern watched TV from a La-Z-Boy imprinted with the shape of his dad's butt. An old Singer sewing machine with a snapped-off needle collected dust in a corner.

Vern stood and shook out his pant legs. He wore a drip-dry button down shirt. A patch of bloody toilet paper tagged a spot on his chin. "Thought I was going to have to drag you out of that bedroom." He looked me up and down, and apparently decided I'd do for church. "Leroy's playing with the Faith-n-Fire band tonight and I don't want to miss it."

We walked out to Vern's pickup. Dirty children chased each other down the street. A few parents sat on their porches, drinking beer and smoking, ignoring the kids and the cars that periodically roared down the road. Vern's next-door neighbor waved. His pit-bull, tied on a short rope to a tree, barked and lunged.

"I swear I'm going to shoot that dog one day," Vern said as he unlocked the truck door. Since he kept a loaded shotgun in the gun rack in the truck, I believed him. I didn't mention I'd thrown the dog hot dogs a few times when the owner wasn't around. It didn't make the dog any friendlier but other than cutting its chain and unleashing a vicious attack dog on the neighborhood children, it was the best I could do. Vern slid in and leaned over to unlock the passenger side door. I had to be careful when I got in not to put my foot in the rusted hole in the floor. Avoiding that hole wasn't going to be fun when winter came. And winter was coming. Leaves lay in heaps on the road and in the yards of Shed Town. Bare tree branches scratched at the sky.

We bounced into the rutted parking lot of Faith-n-Fire. The church took over the former Madison Square Garden, a name that must have been someone's idea of a joke as this former neighborhood watering hole would have fit in a corner of its namesake's lobby. Pastor Bob had removed the bar and added a lectern in the front with a dozen rows of folding chairs facing it. Most of the seats were already full with families, black and white. The front row was reserved for the elderly who came in a van from the Golden Living Center. The Center women wore hats and dresses. The men wore suits that sagged off their shoulders and bagged over their scrawny butts. No one else dressed up for church. The rest of the congregation-- men, women and children-- wore jeans and t-shirts. Muncie wasn't fancy.

Vern and I walked to the front where Vern's former coworker, Leroy, tuned his electric guitar by the lectern. Behind him a drummer hit his kit with brushes. A bass player in a John Deere cap bent over his instrument.

"Hey, Leroy," Vern said, and he and Leroy performed a complicated handshake that involved double shakes and a chest pounding, a ritual former Borg Warner employees used.

I left the two of them to chat and sat in one of the folding chairs on the aisle. I wanted to be able to get up and go outside for a smoke without having to climb over my fellow parishioners. Not that they considered me one of them. I was an outsider. My grandparents hadn't moved to Muncie back in the 'twenties to work in the factories. I hadn't gone to Central High or grown up eating at Burkie's or driven through Whitely with a rebel flag after Central beat Southside High, something a few of these white Faith-n-Fire church members were, of course, ashamed of now.

"Say there, pretty lady." Pastor Bob place his hand lightly on my shoulder and smiled widely, displaying a very nice set of whitened teeth. "Why are you sitting here on your lonesome?" Pastor Bob wore a worn denim shirt and jeans with a belt buckle that proclaimed "Jesus." A turquoise slide held his string tie in place. His skin was a light mahogany that could only be achieved at one of Muncie's tanning salons. But as far as I could tell from the one church service I'd attended, Pastor Bob was the real thing, a person genuinely moved to spread the gospel. He drove a rusted Ford Pickup and lived in a trailer in Shed Town. If he had aspirations of running a mega-church, he kept them hidden.

Before I had a chance to answer, a group of kids ran down the aisle chanting, "Potato chip, potato chip, crunchy, crunchy, I love Jesus a bunchy, bunchy."

Pastor Bob shook his head. "The things these kids learn at Bible camp. I tell their parents not to send them to those places but they don't listen."

"You're anti-Bible? That's a funny attitude for a Christian pastor."

"Not anti-Bible. Just anti all this bullshit those evangelicals shove into kids' heads. What's our Lord and Savior got to do with a potato chip? The kids don't learn anything useful or spiritual at those places. Nothing about caring for the poor or the homeless, ministering to the sick, or doing the real work Jesus wants us to do."

I crossed my legs and nodded. Pastor Bob smelled faintly woodsy. I could imagine him hunting in the yellow and red trees of fall, sighting down his rifle at a buck. But all good Munsonians hunted, owned lots of guns, voted Republican, and hated anyone on welfare. Pastor Bob must possess a powerful charisma to get Munsonians to actually care about the poor. Of course, since the Great Recession, they were the poor. As Pastor Bob said more than twice at my first church service, 32% of the Muncie population lived below the poverty line. I fit right in with that statistic.

The children ran back down the aisle. This time they shouted, "Peanut butter, peanut butter, creamy, creamy! I hate the devil; he's a meanie, meanie!" I couldn't imagine who made this crap up. The kids definitely liked it, judging from their glowing faces. Two little girls in overalls led the pack. Three boys in patched pants and stained T-shirts ran hard on their heels. A tiny girl with multicolored barrettes in her braided hair shouted as she ran, her mouth open wide. She stopped to hug Pastor Bob's leg, the only thing she could reach, then ran after her gang.

Pastor Bob's eyes followed the girl's progress as she ran behind the others. "That little Tyreesha is so cute. I praise God that we've gotten black and white Muncie to work and worship together." He lowered his head to look at me. "Can I count on you to volunteer for next week's Thanksgiving dinner? We're serving a home-cooked turkey with all the trimmings. We're welcoming all of Munice to break bread with us and give thanks."

"I'll be there," I said. I'd walk across Muncie on my knees for an actual turkey dinner with cranberry sauce and stuffing. When Vern got hungry, he'd run over to the mini-mart and buy us microwave burritos. In the past two weeks I'd eaten enough of those to last a lifetime.

Pastor Bob took my hand and pressed it between both of his. "Thank you for being part of our community." His sleeve pulled back, revealing a faded tattoo of skull with a snake slithering out of its eye socket.

The fluorescent lights overhead buzzed and I pulled my hand away. I've always hated snakes. "That's a strange tattoo for a pastor," I said. "I'd expect Jesus with his crown of thorns or the old rugged cross."

He tugged his sleeve back down. "A youthful indiscretion," he said. "It reminds me of who I used to be before I found the Lord. Who were you before you found Jesus?"

Vern's appearance saved me from responding. Vern shook Pastor Bob's hand and nodded at me to move over. I slid into the next folding chair. Now I'd have to shove Vern out of the way if I wanted to smoke. Pastor Bob waved as if he were doing a riff on an air piano and walked up to lectern. Leroy and the band launched into "Born in the U.S.A." I had to give Leroy credit. He was not bad on the guitar. Vern tapped his foot in time to the music. Others in the church clapped along and even shouted the words.

Pastor Bob clapped along as the band played. After the last note faded, he gripped the lectern and bowed his head. As the silence stretched out, people shifted uncomfortably. Vern's knee began its familiar bounce. A child in the row behind me asked his mother if Pastor Bob felt bad. She shushed him. I wanted a cigarette but I knew if I got up now Vern would complain all the way home.

I'd met Vern at the Buttonhole, Muncie's version of a neighborhood dive bar with Pabst paraphernalia on the walls and cheap Bloody Mary's for day-after hangovers. Only it wasn't my neighborhood dive. I'd lived in Los Angeles until I lost my job as a legal secretary. Now that lawyers had laptops and software that practically wrote their briefs for them, they didn't need secretaries. I'd left L. A. in search of greener pastures and wound up jobless in the Rust Belt. I didn't love Vern. I didn't even particularly like him, but until I figured out where to go from here, he was what I had.

Pastor Bob raised his head. I could almost hear the collective intake of air as everyone held their breath, wondering what the Pastor would say to break his long silence. Pastor Bob licked his lips. He looked around the congregation as if seeing everyone for the first time. He stepped out from behind the lectern.

"Blessed are you who are poor," he began, "for yours is the kingdom of God. Blessed are you who are hungry now, for you will be filled. Blessed are you who weep now, for you will laugh."

"Anyone poor here? Raise your hand!" Pastor Bob commanded. Most of the hands in the congregation, including Vern's, shot up.

"Anyone ever go hungry?" The hands raised again.

"Anyone ever had occasion to weep?" People waved their hands in the air. Some shouted, "Amen." Or "Yes, Lord."

"Is that what Jesus wants for you? Does Jesus want you to be poor, to go hungry, to weep? Or does Jesus want you to improve your situation and reach your full potential? Does Jesus want you to rebuild your broken lives and the ruined cities all around the world? Does Jesus want you to proclaim his good news and demonstrate the life changing power of the kingdom of God? Does Jesus want you to live in a community where we all live supernaturally?"

Everyone was shouting now. Caught up in the revival spirit, even I contributed an "Amen." I wanted to rebuild my broken life, to have a job and a house, and not have to answer to someone like Vern if I wanted to eat. I'd resisted Jesus all these years, figuring he was just a con, a way for the rich to keep the poor hopeful for a better life after this one. But what if Jesus was the answer, not when I died, but now? What if, with Jesus, I could be part of a community, not a drifter latching onto the first man who offered me a meal and a bed, but someone who lived a life that had purpose?

When the donation basket came around, I didn't even mind that Vern put in $10 we could have spent on beer and cigarettes. All around me people who were barely scraping by threw in $5s and $10s and even $20s. Pastor Bob exhorted us to give and we did. He promised all the money collected would provide services for those most in need. Did I need beer and cigarettes? I wanted them, but need and want weren't the same thing. Vern took my hand and squeezed it.

"Now you see why I talk about Pastor Bob all the time? He's for real. He's not one of those preachers who just mouths the gospel. He lives it."

I could have pointed out that Vern wasn't living the gospel. Jesus never said, "Shoot thy neighbor's dog if it offends thee." And while Vern did talk a lot about Pastor Bob, Vern spent his time watching football and drinking beer, not helping to rebuild Muncie or establish communities of the poor. Instead, I kept my mouth shut and squeezed his hand back. I didn't need Vern to be my role model. Pastor Bob would be my guide.

Leroy's band played "I Saw the Light." Everyone stood and clapped and sang along. Pastor Bob ran down the aisle, slapping outstretched hands, his face red and dappled with sweat from the exertion of preaching. I learned past Vern and held out my hand. The sting of Pastor Bob's on mine felt like a rebuke for my past and a promise of better times.

The air outside the church was chilly but I wrapped my coat tighter around me, instead of rushing back to the car and smoking cigarettes while Vern socialized. People milled around on the asphalt parking lot. The gray winter light softened their features, smoothing out the crow's feet and the frown lines. I could imagine Jesus walking barefoot through this group, his long hair billowing in the winter breeze, a smile of compassion on his face as he tended to this needy flock. Surely I was as needy as any of them. I'd tried many things: liquor, sex, pills. Why not try Jesus?

A half-remembered scrap of prayer came floating up from my memory. "I turn from my sins and invite You to come into my heart and life." I repeated that mantra as I watched Pastor Bob helped the parishioners from Golden Living get back on their shuttle bus and wave as the bus drove away. I repeated it as the children ran though the leaves that dotted the parking lot, screaming their chants of Jesus and potato chips. I repeated it as Vern drove us home through the dark Muncie streets.

I didn't feel different. My heart didn't swell with God's love. I didn't feel inner peace or that Jesus was walking with me. I didn't feel saved or forgiven. But maybe reciting a prayer wasn't accepting Jesus. As Pastor Bob said, caring for the poor or the homeless, and ministering to the sick, is the real work Jesus wants us to do. Maybe when I did that, I would feel Him. I resolved to talk to Pastor Bob on Thanksgiving so he could guide me to Jesus and that community where we would all live supernaturally. And if supernaturally is what Pastor Bob called it, then I would too.

All that week Vern and I bowed our heads and prayed before we ate our burritos. I listened when Vern read the Bible. When Leroy and Rick and Tom, the other guys in the band came over to talk about Pastor Bob,

I made coffee instead of leaving. I managed to keep my smoking down to just a couple of cigarettes a day. I even cleaned the kitchen and mopped the living room. Every day I threw half of my burrito to the pit bull. He barked and stared at me with weary eyes before scarfing it down.

Thanksgiving finally came. Vern shook me awake me at 7 am. "Hurry up. Those turkeys won't cook themselves." He was already dressed in khaki work pants and a hoodie. He handed me a cup of coffee and I drank it quickly. Frigid air leaked through the windows. The temperature had dropped to the twenties and the weatherman predicted snow. I wore a coat I'd bought for $2 at Angel's Attic Thrift Store, wool with a fake fur collar. The moth holes on the sleeves were barely visible. Under it I wore jeans and a sweatshirt. I couldn't rebuild cities in a skirt.

I thought of the questions I would ask Pastor Bob. How could I be part of building communities of the poor? What real work could I do? I'd asked Vern what having Jesus inside you felt like, but he couldn't explain it. "You just know," he said. "You just feel the life-changing power of the kingdom of God." He repeated Pastor Bob's words with as much feeling and understanding as a machine at Borg Warner stamping out parts. I was sure Pastor Bob could tell me what Vern couldn't.

We walked to the car under gray skies. The pit bull poked his head out of his wooden doghouse, shivered, and turned back inside without even a token bark. As we drove down the rutted streets to Faith-n-Fire, specks of snow brushed the windshield and drifted away. Wood smoke spiraled from chimneys. At a few houses men stood on ladders stringing Christmas lights on eaves or around windows.

A portable sign parked at the curb of the Faith-n-Fire lot advertised "Thanksgiving Community Dinner. 1 pm." A small group of people stood outside the church. I recognized a few of the women from Saturday's service. They milled around in front of the door, shoulder hunched, hands in their pockets to keep off the chill. They raised their faces to look at us, and then went back to staring at the ground. Deep-frying vats hooked up to propane canisters sat unattended in the back of the parking lot. Birds pecked the ground in front of three bright yellow jugs of corn oil. Apparently the turkey cooking apparatus had arrived but I saw no evidence of turkeys.

Vern pulled into the lot and parked under a bare tree. "What's everyone standing outside for?" he said. "Rick and Tom should be getting started on the turkey." He considered the crowd at the door. "I don't even think they're here." A pounding noise echoed across the parking lot. Leroy hammered on the door with his fist. Tyreesha, the only child present, held her hand over her ears to block out the noise. A large black woman, I assumed was her mother, rested her hands on Tyreesha's shoulders.

"Looks like someone forgot their key," Vern said as he pulled me through the small group up to the door. He put his hand on Leroy's shoulder. "What's going on, man? What's all that banging about?"

Leroy stopped his racket and turned to Vern. "My key doesn't work anymore. This was tacked up on the door." He shook a paper in Vern's face.

Vern began to read it, then passed the paper over to me. "It's some legal stuff. Maybe you can figure it out."

I scanned the page and quickly realized it was writ of possession for the church, that last step in evicting a tenant. Pastor Bob hadn't been paying the rent. The writ didn't tell me when the building's owner first tried to evict him or why Pastor Bob decided not to pay. But if Leroy's key didn't work that meant the sheriff had been here and changed the locks. I passed the page back to Vern and told him Faith-n-Fire no longer had possession of the former Madison Square Garden.

"That's got to be a mistake," Vern said. "Pastor Bob opened the church in January. He paid the rent. We all contributed to it every service."

The women muttered in agreement. One woman in a headscarf tied like a 'fifties housewife began calculating on her fingers the amount of money Pastor Bob raised for Faith-n-Fire from weekly donations. "We all followed his call for bountiful giving out of a church-centered lifestyle," she said. "We didn't have much but we all gave."

A blue pickup pulled into the lot. Rick, the bass player from the Faith-n-Fire band, jumped out. "Pastor Bob's gone," he said. "His trailer is cleared out. The neighbors say he left last night."

"This is bullshit," Leroy stamped his foot. "Pastor Bob would never do this. Something must have happened to him. You know other ministers in town were jealous because people left their church to come to Faith-n-Fire."

"What about the turkeys and the community meal?" the woman with Tyreesha yelled. "Pastor Bob drove down to Indy to buy all our supplies. Maybe he just didn't get back yet." The other women nodded in agreement.

"He's not coming back." I held up the writ. "Pastor Bob conned you all. He took all the money and left."

Vern turned on me. His cheeks were red and his face so pinched I thought he might cry. "That's not possible. Pastor Bob wanted to build a community here in Muncie. He brought us all together."

"He brought you together to take your money. Pastor Bob only cares about Pastor Bob. All the rest of it was bullshit." He'd duped me into believing I could change my life through Jesus. I wasn't any smarter than these down-and-out Munsonians willing to believe they could rebuild their community, willing to believe they could live supernaturally. Now the only thing supernatural was Pastor Bob's whereabouts. As far as Muncie went, he was as substantial as a ghost.

Tyressha's mother got right up in my face. "You're not from here. You don't know. Pastor Bob will come back. This is all some sort of mistake." I didn't see anger in her eyes, just hurt and confusion. The women gathered round her. Even Leroy and Vern nodded.

"You're right," I said. "I'm not from here." I turned and walked through the parking lot to the sidewalk. I could hear Vern yelling my name but I didn't turn around. At the house next to the church, a man tacked blue tarp onto his roof. He waved at me as I walked by. I waved back and kept going.

Matias Viegener

25 Random Things About You

I

1. When I tell people who don't know you that you've been in prison for six weeks now, they look incredulous.

2. I think of you and Tarek in a cell in Egypt with thirty other men, few of who will understand English. Films like Midnight Express, with their homoerotic content, push themselves forward. Your pictures are everywhere now, all over the internet. You're both so handsome. You look like movie stars.

3. There you were last night, a sobbing voice across the street on the curb. Does anyone else hear you? My window was shut, but I hear you anyway. What were you crying about? I can't help but think you have a broken heart.

4. I live in a world where no one pays attention to a young woman sobbing on a curb in the middle of the night.

5. Tarek's photo struck me differently than yours; he has what I'd call sensual lips. I'll be honest. I find him very sexy; I wonder if you're just friends, or if being in prison will make something happen, but I don't even know if he's gay in the first place.

6. But how did your photo strike me? I remember kissing you. I remember having sex with you. I especially want to say this because it feels forbidden now. Without much debate, we all began to omit your homo-

sexuality from our letters and press releases, despite much of your work having gay content. It's not a fact that will inspire the Egyptians to release you from prison.

7. After I wrote this my nipple started to itch.

8. During a long poetry reading yesterday, I massaged your neck. You didn't ask me with words; your request came in a gesture. Once I started, I closed my eyes, and I remembered that you like it hard.

9. It's a lot of work to give a hard massage. I won't say it hurts, but it takes effort, and I started feeling some kind of pain that I decided to read as your pain moving into me. I would take it away. Through your body into mine, from hands to shoulders, through me back out to wherever it came from.

10. It's hard to talk about you without using your name.

11. Without a name, you could be anybody.

12. And that's not my point: you are not anybody at all.

13. Is there something bad about my pornographic fantasies? I want to have sex with both of you in a prison setting, with a lot of people, in fact. I've been calling the president of my school, and two museum directors to come to a meeting at the consulate. We've done petitions, editorials, and letters of support. Even if they're not exactly bad, sexual fantasies are not going to get you both released.

14. I want him to be gay. I want you to have sex with him, and me, too. Obviously, I guess, since it's all happening in my fantasies.

15. I closed my eyes and remembered everything about your neck. I remembered it separate from you, and separate from any words or thoughts.

16. It's a familiar topography, even though I only touched it once before. But I know this part of your body, and I'd recognize it in the dark, at night, if I stumbled upon it unknowingly.

17. Is there a way that a pornographic fantasy can be an act of resistance?

18. After I scratched my left nipple, my right nipple felt itchy.

19. Once we went to Sachsenhausen together. It was a wet, grey day, and we had to get up early to fit it into our schedule. We were surprised to find the words "ARBEIT MACHT FREI" in wrought iron over the front gate. That quote is famously at Auschwitz, but we supposed that other concentration camps could have copied it. We spent a long time looking at

the 1950s model in the interpretive exhibit. It was a full replica of the camp at its height, with light bulbs, little figurines, and cotton smoke coming from the chimneys. It had a system of knobs to push so you could see what happened, where, which barracks housed the perverts, and which ones the political prisoners. We played with it again on our way out.

20. Is there something that I don't understand about you that makes my nipples itchy?

21. "ARBEIT MACHT FREI" more or less means "work will set you free." We don't need to talk about how brutal it is to say these words to a group of prisoners. No one went free. Not many got out alive.

23. It's a sick promise really: work hard, and you might not die.

24. It comforts me to think that if I lost my mind, if I got Alzheimer's or something, I might be able to keep something else. If I still know your neck, maybe I'll remember all the bodies and all the parts of the people I've touched. And, they could come to me and I'd touch them and remember all these things outside words or ideas, a way of knowing grounded in flesh. Of course, I've spelled all this out in words.

25. But I had to.

II

1. When I checked in three days ago, you insisted that I take two key cards to my room. You might find a friend, you said to me, and then told me the internet login is "guest" and the password is "passion."

2. We found out last weekend that the Egyptian government promises to press charges against you both, but for what?

3. Somehow we joked about the friendliness of the motel, and you used the phrase "love hotel."

4. It made me think of Japan, despite the fact that you're from New Zealand, like my cousins, and you have the same voice and even look a lot like my cousin Sarah.

5. Someone posted a letter you wrote together about your imprisonment, with more details. It's harrowing to read. In fact I read it and then went away and didn't think about it, so I had to come back and read it again to understand.

6. Stuck in Cairo for the day, you wandered to Tahrir Square, where a peaceful demonstration was beginning to get violent. First one man was shot, then another. Tarek began to give emergency aid, and you with your camera "shooting a record of the carnage that was unfolding."

7. You fed me last night and for that I will love you forever.

8. Wherein that love dwells is hard to say, but I'm certain it is somewhere between the stomach and the soul. Ok, who knows, my love might even stretch south, to the genitals.

9. I'm not promising anything though.

10. We had coffee instead of going to any of the panels the last afternoon of the conference. It was sweet, flirty and gossipy. The best gossip, the gossip that's more about complicity than about the exchange of innuendo.

11. You saw over fifty Egyptians die, "students, workers, professionals, professors, all shapes, all ages, unarmed." The body count at the end of the day was twice that, over a hundred.

12. Long ago I read a book on gossip and grooming, about the link between human gossip and primate grooming, both forms of exchange that intensify social bonds. Gossip is like placing little nits on each other's bodies rather than picking them off.

13. I wish this could have happened when I had a crush on you six

years ago.

14. I've been writing an essay on sweetness, and I'm circling around the phrase "you're so sweet." The way it's said, the echo of something weird inside it.   15. When I had dinner with Sarah Schulman last night, she said you had seen "atrocities."

16. Sweetness is double-edged. A symbol of that which is good, but not necessarily good for us.

17. There are post-its all over the walls of your apartment, and they look like poems. Most are menu lists, like the one that says: Menu: Head, Gold, Dogs, Lamb, Cake.

18. Lots of things can be four letter words.

19. You're in the New York Times today, with details of your letter in quotes. "That's when we were: arrested, searched, caged, questioned, interrogated, videotaped with a 'Syrian terrorist'," you said, "slapped, beaten, ridiculed, hot-boxed, refused phone calls, stripped, shaved bald, accused of being foreign mercenaries." Eight of you in an 11x17 cell, "sleeping on concrete with the cockroaches, and sharing a single tap of Nile water." You had "a precisely etched boot-print bruise" on your back for a week.

20. What can I possibly do to help you?

21. I just ate your heart and I will never be the same.

22. A chocolate heart, of course. And you made it.

23. That was a literary device.

24. Maybe the weird echo is the Garden of Eden. Eve betrays Adam, or Eve seduces Adam, with an apple. Take your pick.

25. What is it about chocolate anyway?

III

1. In the letter about your arrest, you called it "that bloody day." Yesterday on Democracy Now, they said you witnessed a "massacre."

2. And, all that camera equipment you had with you; for a trip to Gaza.

3. I touched the plasticine pigs in your studio, and I realize that now my fingerprints are on them. They're models for a series, and now every cast will have a trace of me on it.

4. There's a bit of buzz online about the two small drones you had in your baggage. Someone called them "helicopters," but come on.

5. You're so sweet.

6. You said they were to move medical supplies in Gaza, but people say that sounds hollow. To move supplies from where to where, with a little helicopter that also happens to have a camera. No wonder the Egyptians are suspicious.

7. Recently I found the term "antagonist-protagonist." The protagonist is the irresistible force and antagonist is the immovable object.

8. The protagonist represents our initiative, our fire to change — sometimes change everything. The antagonist embodies our reticence to change the status quo.

9. Did you know I was working on a project with drones, shooting videos and writing poems about them? I guess everyone is interested in drones now. And rightly so. We will never be alone again.

10. You probably didn't. Neither of us is good at staying in touch.

11. The drive to change everything versus the drive to keep everything as it is.

12. At that time, everything about you was about me too. I couldn't keep them separated. When you weren't feeling well, I felt it too. If you were angry at me, I was angry at me too.

13. Do you remember the time you were feeling sick, and we were on the phone? You were too sick to talk, but you didn't want me to hang up. So I stayed on the line and listened to you breathe. And I loved it. Soon we were breathing in sync. I felt that with each breath I could make you feel better, and take your illness away. This became an emblem for me. I loved you so much I was happy just to listen to your breath, even on a phone line,

when we both know I'd rather have been in your bed, beside you with my arms around you, or you name it.

14. Today I still feel guilty about my prison sex fantasies.

15. I've been thinking about commitment. Not as in marriage, or monogamy, but as a political category. I envy this about you, and find it incredibly attractive.

16. I also feel guilty that I had a crush on you, a guy young enough to be my son, thought it might lead to something, but doubted it would, and then felt crushed after you cancelled because you'd just slept with someone else.

17. There's also the phrase "I want to eat you," or "you look good enough to eat."

18. Someone else.

19. Really, do I need more words than that? Do I need a metaphor, a literary figure?

20. I don't think so.

21. You have a kind of commitment I lack. You had it about ACT-UP, about Palestine, about labor, and prostitute rights. You always did more than you were asked, devoted your time to these things and made work about them.

22. The antagonist-protagonist is more complicated. He thrusts forth and pushes back, sometimes at the same time. He gives you what you want, and then takes it away.

23. You just texted me on Grindr.

24. I'll use a pseudonym, since I'm not certain you're who you say you are. We'll call you Bob, and me Matt.

25. In place of commitment, or beside it, I have doubt.

Sarah Hunter

Panache

Lauren's palms were sweaty and cold. She had to brace herself on the side of the kitchen door at Panache, the trendy, ivy-covered restaurant where she'd just gotten her first waitress job. How was she going to serve these former friends of hers who had betrayed her, started the rumor that she was sleeping with John Simons when she wasn't, had told her that since she had become delinquent—that's the exact word they used—delinquent on her dues to the club, she would have to resign and terminate her membership as well? These very same women had been at both of her baby showers over twenty years ago, had attended her big party at the Valley Hunt Club for her daughter Preston when she had her coming out debutante dinner, had invited her to every single Christmas party, New Years Eve celebration and had played bridge with her on Tuesdays? This was the group who attended all the Tournament of Roses events when her ex-husband, Kevin, had invited them. How was she going to approach their table and tell them what the specials of the day were at Panache?

As she peered through the crack in the kitchen door where the sign read, Wash Your Hands, California Law Requires It she noted that it was Julie and Sandra and Claire and Linda who sat at Table Number Three. They were all on the Board of Directors at Hidden Pines Golf Club. How could she forget her excitement when she was voted in as the new Board secretary? They had all commented on her note-taking skills and ability to send around the e-mails in timely fashion.

Under the lash of California Safety Law, she checked the nape of her neck to see if any of her blonde hair had strayed from the neat bun she had designed to secure it. She wanted to avoid the potential mishap of a stray hair landing in one of the patron's salads.

It was bad enough when Kevin had lost his job at Derwitt and Mathers, but it was the end of her world when Kevin gave her the drop kick for some bimbo who had just graduated from Ball State University somewhere in Indiana. The bimbo was smart enough to know Kevin had a trust fund account stashed safely in a bank in San Marino.

Rochelle, Kevin's lover was two years older than Preston, their older daughter. Oh, sure, Lauren had been getting her regular Botox injections, going to David for private training at the gym, had walked the two and a half mile trek around the Rose Bowl with a couple of her Charity League buddies, but she must have somehow been aging, getting bulky, "pigging out" as Kevin reminded her when she reached for bread at Club Lenore. She'd been drifting into menopausal "mom jeans." That's how it went, they all told her. When Kevin asked for the divorce, she was devastated, of course, but she counted on the house in San Marino and the club memberships and the support of her friends on her Board at the club. She would be protected from the sting of rejection. The San Marino house went into foreclosure. Still, she would have her friends she told herself. Life wouldn't be that different.

That's how she comforted herself. But that's not the way it went. First, there was the "delinquent on her dues" speech, and then the gradual waning of invitations to lunch, the walks around the Rose Bowl, the shopping at Nordstrom's with the League women on the weekend. After she had rented the one-bedroom apartment in Alhambra, it all went away. The money was gone and apparently so was she. It's as if she never knew them. Money, property and prestige…she had been at the center of their world, but she was clueless about this new one. Lauren's knees buckled. She was spinning.

Bracing herself against the edge of the kitchen door now, Lauren straightened her apron, smoothing back the stray hairs at the nape of her neck with her right hand. Just checking.

Linda, Claire, Julie and Sandra gasped when Lauren approached the table. The moment of realization was here. "I am not in your world anymore. I am a waitress at a little French restaurant. I am a lower–middle-class slob, I am someone you will call *Hon*, when you ask for more butter."

She didn't know what to say to them, and they certainly weren't speaking.

"Today's specials are lobster bisque with a light garnish of fresh herbs and sea bass with a papaya salsa." This is what Lauren said.

Julie leaned back, her right hand lightly touching the white linen tablecloth. She tapped her dark fingernails on the table. "Lauren. Who would think to find you here?" She blinked out a look of mock pity.

Lauren responded, " I think the spinach crepes are wonderful, and think they are delicious." She didn't say what she wanted to. The spinach crepe recommendation came out automatically, thank God. What she wanted to say was, "You bitches dumped me when I needed you most. You shut me out of the circle I had known for over two decades; you kicked me to the curb. You have no soul, no conscience, no heart. I hate you."

It was hard to forget the time Julie flew her to Paris five years ago to do what she had told Lauren was a "culture vulture excursion." The two of them drank endless glasses of champagne, went to one charming bistro after another and spent one full day at the Louvre. The next day they were picked up at the George V to take the private excursion to Versailles. There were only six of them in the van after Jacques picked them up. The other travelers were as wealthy as Julie. They were a family of four from Winnetka, Illinois. He was a professor at Northwestern, his wife a lawyer and the two teenage children nicely ensconced in private schools back East.

Linda, who spent much of her time volunteering at Hillsides Home for Foster Children and was always the "soft touch" in the group, squinted at the menu, pretending that everything was normal -- that the same person who had hosted the Tournament of Roses fashion show two years ago was not, in fact, chatting about papaya salsa at Panache and wearing a tacky looking white apron over her dark blue uniform. Linda had more trouble with this confrontation than Julie, however, because her lower lip quivered when she ordered the sea bass with the salsa. She folded the menu as if it were a notification of a family member's funeral.

The order safely taken, Lauren headed back to the kitchen with as much energy as a rejected Miss America second runner-up. She lowered her head in shame. Could this really be as bad as it felt? Probably not. But her face was flushed and she felt weak, weak enough to almost faint as she gathered the warm French rolls in her little basket to take out to the Board

Members.

When it came time for the dessert order, it was clear that Lauren had regained some of her composure. She was able to smile at them. Perhaps some grace had hit her, like the cold air from the vents of the overhead air conditioning. She had survived the salads and the main course, knowing that were it a year ago or two, she would have been blithely ordering the sea bass or the spinach crepes herself. It was odd, she thought, that none of them asked her any questions. In fact, they all seemed reticent to even talk much amongst themselves. Perhaps they felt sad about Lauren's downfall. When Lauren was with them once, they had talked about how when someone's parent dies, nobody really wants to discuss it much for fear that it might happen to her next if it's talked about too often. Well, she was certainly their worst collective nightmare. Five years ago, she would have wanted the chocolate soufflé and made jokes about her "mom jeans" or her waistline and how David needed to "make her pump harder" at the gym. It would have been a jolly luncheon.

They each ordered the fresh fruit with raspberry sorbet. Lauren guessed that they were trying to get the bill up as high as they could so that they could leave her a big tip. This is what went through her head as she ceremoniously carried the fresh sorbets in crystal dishes to the table, placing them jauntily in the center of each woman's table setting.

She remembered when Claire and Sandra took her daughters with them to their yearly retreat for Girl Scouts in Aspen, Colorado. It helped that Claire had a winter home in Aspen, but Preston and Emily loved the winter skiing, the fires in the Scout lodge, the frothy cups of hot chocolate and whipped cream. When they returned to San Marino, all they could talk about was how nice "Aunt Claire and Aunt Sandra" had been to them and all the rest of the Girl Scouts. It was on that trip that the two girls learned to knit angora scarves to give to their friends as Christmas gifts.

At the end of the meal, and after the women had scuttled to the door, whispering and laughing to each other about the sale on lingerie at Nordstrom's, Lauren approached the table. She picked up the black leather folder with the bill inside to see what they had left her. The amount was circled with somebody's black pen, probably Sandra's, and underlined. The lunch bill was $160.00 exactly. The neat twenty dollar bills were stacked on top of each other. There were eight twenties and sixteen dollars on top of that, stacked in the opposite direction, just to let her know, she guessed, that they had left her a ten percent tip. Was ten percent a slap in the face, or had they left ten percent all those years together? She couldn't remember. Money had just somehow seemed unimportant at restaurants.

Lauren headed back to the kitchen, a flood of shame and ignominy washing over her face. This was her new life. This was the separation of the past from the present. There would be no more trips to Palm Springs for massages and poolside tanning at Linda's desert home. There would be no more laughter about how Linda should move there permanently because of the tanned, blonde boys who attended to the pool and waited on the "The Girls" in the summertime. They called themselves "The Girls."

"Fuck," she muttered under her breath. At least she had received some satisfaction knowing that the sea bass with fine herbs had slipped on the floor and that she had scooped it up and plopped it back on Julie's plate. That made up for some of it, she thought.

But the world had not stopped turning. Table Number Three had a new setting. Four men in business suits glanced toward the kitchen. She straightened her apron and checked the wisp of hair at the back of her head. Pushing through the kitchen door with a benign smile plastered across her face, she glided to the table to tell the gentlemen about the today's lunch specials.

Josh Herman

Transcribed, from Boxes

2014 Kraft Macaroni & Cheese Dinner Recipe
YOU WILL NEED

6 cups water

3 Tbsp. spread or margarine

3 Tbsp. milk

COOKING INSTRUCTIONS

1) BOIL water. Stir in Macaroni. Boil 8 to 10 minutes, stirring occasionally.

2) DRAIN. DO NOT RINSE. Return to pan.

3) ADD spread or margarine, milk and Cheese Sauce Mix, mix well.

2015 krft mac n cheez dinA receipte
ull nd

6 cups H2O

3 tbsp butr

3 tbps moo

cokin instrctns

boil h20 stir n mac boil 8 2 10 mins

drain dnt rinse rt 2 pan

+ butr moo n cheez mx n mx wel :)

2015 Kraft Macaroni & Cheese Dinner Recipe

Kraft would like to offer our sincere apologies for the previous recipe. We believed we had translated our delicious Kraft Dinner recipe into Contemporary English, when in actuality the copywriter had a seizure. Here is the corrected recipe for our valued consumers:

~*~*~ b n stiL u :)ly 6 D@ x! 3 :o) wots ^ 3 Lol <<!>>

2017 McCoke-Mart© Macaroni & Cheese Dinner Recipe

YOU WILL NEED

Large McDonald cup Coke
Two sporks special sauce
Diet Milk with Lemon

COOKING INSTRUCTIONS
1) SUPERSIZE Coke. McFlurry in Martaroni. Premium grill 6 to 12 heat lamps, flip occasionally.
2) DRAIN. Roll back to pan.
3) WOULD YOU LIKE TO ADD special sauce, diet milk with lemon. Cheese sauce mix additional 99-cents.

2018 Kraft Macaroni & Cheese Dinner Recipe

YOU WILL NEED

At least 3 of those-plastic-containers-you-put-complimentary-salsa-in of water (bath, toilet, puddle)
3 Tbsp *I Can't Believe I Can't Believe It's Not Butter*
3 Tbsp. milk (cat, dog or squirrel. For a RICHER flavor, use rat milk)

COOKING INSTRUCTIONS
1) COLLECT garbage scraps. SET on fire. OPEN box. ADD box to fire.
2) BOIL water until no longer spoiled. Stir in ramenroni. BOIL until gas cut off.
3) DRAIN into water bottle.

4) ADD I Can't Believe I Can't Believe It's Not Butter, milk, and expired Pizza Hut® parmesan packet stuck to bottom of cupboard. Mix well.
5) SALT or CAN so Ramenroni & Cheese Dinner lasts for winter.
6) DRINK rinsed water. EAT powder residue. CRY to taste.

2020 Monsanto© Macaroni & Monsanto© Cheese Dinner™ Recipe
YOU (Monsanto© -patent pending) WILL NEED
6 cups MonsantH2o©
3 Tbsp. Monsanto© spread or Monsanto© margarine
3 Tbsp. Monsanto© Smart Milk

COOKING INSTRUCTIONS
1) OPEN box. EMPTY box. EAT box.[1]
2) BOIL MonsantH2o© by lighting it on fire. THANK fracking for flammable water.
3) COMBINE all ingredients and allow Monsanto© *GMOK!* Milk to DRAIN, RINSE, and MIX itself.

2021 Kraft Macaroni & Cheese Dinner Recipe
YOU WILL NEED
6 cups water (if water no longer available in your area, substitute gasoline)

COOKING INSTRUCTIONS
1) BOIL water (by leaving outdoors 30-45 seconds; 10-20 in Southern Climates.) De-radiate. Stir in Macaroni. Boil 5 to 7 seconds, stirring occasionally. CAUTION: pan may melt.
2) PLACE outside. ALLOW excess water to evaporate (3-4 seconds.) (If Macaroni combusts, return to STEP 1. If YOU combust, skip ahead to STEP 3.)
3) DIE from cancer.

---

[1] The FDA has ruled cardboard is a satisfactory school lunch.

Josh Herman

2024 Kraft Macaroni & Cheese Dinner Recipe

的通 需 切黄油勿冲洗 要平移的回_

6 杯播或 冲洗 造黄 水切勿

3 播或人造 黄油播或人 黄要平播

3 牛要平 汁混

1) 煮水 的通造黄 煮 8 至 10 分，偶拌切

2) 外流 切勿冲洗 要平移的回

3) 添加 播或人造黄油 牛 和 酪 汁混合拌

(Transcribed, from boxes, by Josh Herman)

Shana Nys Dambrot

Zen Psychosis

I

I had fallen asleep on a blanket at the beach, next to my lover, very close to the water. It was a dark and oily place, on the shore of a great greasy sea filled with the bloated carcasses of the drowned, glowing white in the moonlight. It was awful. I kissed my lover quickly, thanking God for him. He looked at me with tender indulgence - he still loved my craziness then. He stood and began to throw books at me, prodding me to get up so he wouldn't be late for his next meeting.

As I stood, I saw mountains in the distance framing his beautiful golden face and eyes the same color as the bruised blue sky. There were overlapping V-shaped clouds projecting up from behind the mountains across the bay. The clouds were long and thin, like steamed spring rolls in rice paper, arranged like a grove of palms on a hilltop. He turned to look, and as I followed his gaze, I saw that the clouds were in fact palm trees on the crest of the green hill unrolling above us, and below was not an ocean at all, but an empty parking lot.

The next time I saw my lover, he was seated, with his back to the doorway, on a long blue leather sofa, in the Reading Room, at the Blackstone Library. Though it was early afternoon, there was a glowing fire in the hearth he faced. It was utterly silent, as though the entire building were wrapped in cotton, and he was alone. He did not hear me sliding across the polished marble floor, engrossed as he was in his reading. I came up behind him and looked over his shoulder. His gold-rimmed glasses reflected firelight so that I could not make out his eyes, but he took them off to turn and smile at me, utterly without recrimination.

He was reading the I Ching, the edition with the forward by Carl Jung. It was odd, because I realized the copy he was reading I had borrowed from him. I wondered how it could be that he had come back into possession of it. I had no memory of returning it to him, although I knew my own - the one I bought so he could have his back - had been misplaced.

He stayed in that room, while I returned to the entrance rotunda, and craned my neck to consider the scenes painted on the inner face of its dome. The Global History of Books unfolded across the ceiling, from Ben Franklin's first press to Egyptian papyrus printing techniques, complete with a seated scribe and Thoth, the patron saint of knowledge, looking it over. I wanted to tell my lover about Thoth, as we had had some interesting escapades in the name of that particular exiled deity. Forbidden knowledge of astrology and mathematics is no joke, it'll get you kicked out of the pantheon and marooned on a mountaintop in South America in the blink of a millennial eye.

I jumped when my lover called out to me from the couch. He had turned on the sofa, and was leaning his head on his hands across the back of it in the most endearing way, to watch my approach. At first he only looked at me, long and hard, as though he were seeing me for the first time. He asked me out loud, How many times have we met before, I mean in previous lives? And when he said it I saw it, all of it. In deepest darkest Peru I saw snakes and lizards; I felt the steam on my face and heard monkeys singing in the trees. We wandered through literary salons and cheap cafés from Paris to Amsterdam. I was Gertrude Stein. He said, do you remember the hotel in New York? With all the roaches but we didn't care because we had each other. I was Lucretia Borgia, Marilyn Monroe, a milkmaid from Vermeer, a courtesan at the time of Manet. I was a butterfly. I was a virgin, a witch, a Lilith. I said, I love you, and called him by his name. He said, I love you, too.

86

II

Enter the scene *in medias res*: a cramped office, crowded with people who resemble my former colleagues. The room is fluorescent lit, giving it a nauseous sterility that the aqua blue Deco chairs, fake wood paneling and chipped Formica coffee table only exacerbate. The apparent leader of the meeting is a regal African woman in a sarong and wooden beads. She evinced pronounced disinterest in both my presence and an article written not by but about me which had appeared in that day's paper. The paper in question lay on the coffee table unruffled, my own face staring back at me from above the fold. It was a very crowded and tense little room; stale air with no ventilation and no windows. A hot night.

While I was trying to catch up with what was going on in the meeting, I remembered how I had gotten there. I had left my car in the parking garage and taken a bus to the meeting. Instantly upon forming that thought, I was back on the bus, just stepping off at a strip mall on Hamburger Hill that I recognized from my hometown in Connecticut. It had The Gap from which I was fired in high school. The night was growing hotter.

I retraced my path on foot, thinking that I needed to return to the meeting for some reason. I was feeling annoyed at having left so abruptly, but nevertheless relieved to be gone. A heavy sense of obligation was shuffling my feet back that way. Soon, an old man, bald with a white mustache, fell in step with me and we began a conversation. That is, I could see him speaking though no words were audible - a fact which I did not realize until I later tried to recall the conversation and found I could remember only the scene, not the dialogue, like watching a film with the volume turned all the way down. Just as I was going to address him by his name, I realized he was not the person I thought he was. I was relieved not to have called him aloud by the wrong name, but then who was this guy?

Still trying to remember, I arrived alone back to my grandmother's house, and descended into the finished basement. Finished 45 years ago. Round wooden table with carved legs, beige knotted silk sofa, gold velveteen easy chair, ceramic cat bent in contemplation of an imaginary fish pond, irregularly shaped green glass vases and watercolors of the local piers by talented amateurs. The same dusty sunlight through the clerestory windows for 35 years. One thing was new - a rather large and frightening brown hairy spider. As I approached, it scurried between the pages of a ragged copy of Thus Spake Zarathustra, so I closed the book, killing it. I paused for a moment to care that now-stained book belonged to my lover, but I was out the door into the afternoon.

I set out walking toward downtown L.A. on Centinela but much too far West, on a mercifully shady street. I could see Downtown in the hazy distance of smoggy afternoon sun. I suddenly felt quite thirsty, and so I left the road to walk up a dirt driveway to a concrete bungalow. I saw as I was admitted that the cottage was cavernous inside, with wood floors and sparsely furnished with a beanbag and a pile of pillows in the center of the room. A couple lived there, middle aged man and young wife. All their things were packed because they were moving to Japan the next day. They needed to raise $50,000 cash before they could go, but they didn't seem worried about it. They gave me cereal in milk to drink instead of water, and I saw that the man was not the old man from earlier, but in fact he was the man for whom I had mistaken the older one when I met him in the road.

We walked outside together just as the first old man pulled up in my car, which he had retrieved from the parking garage. It irritated me a bit at first that he had taken the liberty of driving my car, but I soon realized that was petty, and I should be thrilled to have it for the rest of the trip downtown inside a seamless, never-ending, sultry afternoon.

III

Two more journeys on foot up Hamburger Hill in my hometown, as it snaked its way through Main Street Santa Monica. I was in search of concert tickets for Nick Cave at the venue up the Hill. I had one minute to make it all the way from a restaurant in my neighborhood by the beach. I was already irritated because I had paid twenty dollars for a pizza that two of my friends had eaten entirely without me. Plus I had one minute to

Zen Psychosis

walk miles.

I set off with the memory of my last walk on this path still fresh in my mind, and just like before, each step was excruciatingly heavy and slow. I couldn't breathe, I could barely force my feet to move, even at a crawl. It was like I was in a dream, walking under water. I reached for every brick and doorknob along the shop fronts to propel myself forward, like a horizontal rock climber, or a drunk. Buses went by, both transit and school, but still I stubbornly kept walking.

A former employer was watching a tiny neighborhood Italian place for a mutual friend. I saw her sitting on a table top by the bar, and detoured through the place. I sneaked a fried shrimp off a passing tray, and kept moving. I never made it back up the hill that day. The sun went down and my labors faded into shadow.

Defeated, I took a shortcut home through the park without really deciding to. Rabid squirrels were coming at me in military formation. Littering the ground were several heavy and shiny steel locks. Adrenaline suggested I swing them at the little monsters to fight them off. I was in underwater motion again, like earlier when I had to get up the Hill in one minute and could barely walk at all. I swung a lock at one, but I missed somehow, in spite of the close range. It bit my inner thigh with a vengeance and wouldn't let go.

Down the street from the park was an abandoned theater, where I ducked in to catch my breath and examine my wounds. It had a bar in the lobby built on an aquarium, all chrome and tiny bubbles. There was a terrace off one side, and on it was a baby in a shopping cart. She wanted her bottle, but never cried for it. I stumbled out to the terrace while frantically running around corridors backstage, trying to find a way to sneak into the show.

I dove back inside the building, and just then some curtains parted in my path, and I entered from the side of the crowd. The sea of people was illuminated like a sunset, by red and blue lights from the stage. Smoke had gathered overhead and trapped the light beams.

I found myself turned around yet again, back out on the terrace, watching the baby. I called her by my sister's name, and she looked up at me through a hole in her blanket. Our eyes locked. Someone was making a scene in the park across the street. No place for a baby. But where were her parents? I knew I could never raise her on my starving artist salary, so I left her there to go look for qualified help.

IV

I was working at that time as the only waitress in a cavernous, noisy, cheap dining hall. Long rows of folding tables and chairs, like a bingo palace. Families with screaming children, couples with nothing to say to each other, octogenarians remembering the War with uneasy fondness. I ran in circles for hours, and only managed to order like five drinks and one dish of spicy Thai noodles. I just kept circling the tables, expecting to get yelled at for incompetence at every turn. I just kept gliding around, and eventually, I got my chance to escape. I waited until I was sure no one was watching me, and headed for the front door.

Outside, my lover waited for me in the car. I could see the red light of his cigarette, and his hand tapping the wheel to a beat. As I approached, the engine roared to life, the passenger door opened toward me, and I heard the music blasting from inside. We were in motion before I even closed the door behind me, laughing until we thought we would never be able to stop.

As we raced down city streets, dark and glittering after the evening's rain - rain makes everything in New York look silver - I got cramps and my period started. Sublime pain, almost blinding, but the pain subsides right away. I privately thanked god for the pain, though, as that is better than the alternative.

Again I find myself turning this scenario around and around in my head. My lover does not want a baby. Neither do I. But we love each other, and if I get pregnant now, it's like we would almost be happy, but it's a bad idea and we're not ready. I just know it would ruin the easiness of our love - I've seen it happen so many times. A man can't seem to bear to make love to woman who has just aborted his child, even with his blessing and support. It's not a big fight, just a subtle undermining of the romance after such drastic action to thwart destiny. Nothing would ever be the same. But no need to worry over this tonight.

V

Walking alone, on my way to Skinny Binny, the all-night pet store, I'm in a bad part of town. There was about to be an earthquake, and I was trying to stock up on pet supplies. A group of boys passed me, and a tall one grabbed a yellow and black street sign off a pole, bumping me with it. I walked a little faster. The light from the pet store glowed from around the corner as I came out of the alley into the parking lot and street. The completely deserted parking lot and street.

My lover appeared and silently linked arms with me. He gently and safely guided me to his townhouse, through the rooms and out the back door to a courtyard where an art event of some kind was being held. Warm, genteel, the kind of place with heat lamps on the patio. Instinctively I pulled my hand from his arm, but he stopped me. He said he no longer cared who saw us together. We were in love, and he kissed me, a long soft kiss right in front of everyone. It had the texture of a wish.

I became pregnant with his baby, and he comes around in this black Armani suit and says, I love you, baby, but I think he really does just mean the baby and not me, its uninvited vessel. It pisses me off and I jump out of my seat on the top of the Double Decker bus; looking down through the flooring, I can see there are two drivers. They were arguing about which direction to go. The handrails were too far apart, too easy to fall through. Bad design, as bad as having two drivers. I recall an urgent need to get off that bus.

Back in my own car, I almost laugh and think it must have been

91

Crazy Driver Day and no one told me. I narrowly missed about twenty accidents just on my way home from the museum. While I was thinking about being lucky, I pulled into a parking lot. Another car had just pulled in ahead of me. It was an old Mercedes, like a '71 or '72. The driver was an older woman, very conservative and a little spaced out. She was stopped right there, right in my path, but I did not hit the brakes. I was paralyzed and could not do it, and my car made a loud thud as it hit hers. She looked at me over her shoulder out the window, but did not get out. Her tall bitchy friend in the Chanel suit got out instead, and eyed me suspiciously as we surveyed the damage. I offered to pay for her repairs, but nothing had really happened to either car, so we just dropped it and drove off in different directions. As it turned out, we both had better things to do.

VI

Joy-riding. This is what we were accused of by Ken Doll CHiP, the motorcycle cop with the blue eyes and cleft chin. It was an accusation I felt was particularly ironic, since joy was the farthest thing from my reality by the time we were stopped. We had been going too fast by half, and I was terrified. I was doing my best to hide my fear with sarcasm, but our reckless speeding on a dark two-lane road with no fence for protection against the drop down to the river on the right was getting to me. It had been exhilarating for around thirty seconds, but we were now out of control.

Ken Doll arrested them all while the car was still in motion, though at a greatly reduced speed, leaving me alone in the passenger seat while they were spirited away. The car was giving itself a little gas, still moving forward despite having no driver. I was attempting to steer from the passenger side, but I was not doing a very good job. By this time, the sun had come out and climbed high overhead. The light had a soft green filter on it, like tea falling across the road's surface.

I started to lose my bearings going around a steep curve on an incline. I was falling asleep in my seat, but the car was still wide awake. Just as my eyes were closing, I looked to my left and saw Ken Doll's beautiful plastic face, looming slightly larger than life out the driver's side window. His face was tan and smooth, with no lines at all except deep creases where his cheeks folded in laughter. Stern set to his jaw, and a level stare. He had a sort of friendly manner backed up by physical power. His eyes, I keep going back to them. Up close, he could stop a raving madman in his tracks with just a look.

He was not there to arrest me. I tried to slip over the driver's side, but he had, of course, already taken the wheel. As soon as he reached in through the window, the car slowed to a gentle stop on the shoulder, and I got out. We two were standing at the head of a wide trail which sloped away from the road, downward toward a pool at the base of a waterfall. None of it could be seen from the road, especially from a moving vehicle. Around the water's edge were wooden platforms accessing various areas of the rocks and falls. My friends were playing there like children, nowhere near jail. It was so obvious to me in that moment that Ken Doll (I was starting to feel guilty for calling him that, even just to myself) and I were destined to meet, had already always known each other.

He started to walk me down the path, with his strong arm at my back. The light touch of his fingertips on my spine was enough to move me with no fear of slipping or falling. I was preparing for the reactions of my group to seeing us enter together, after the scene on the road earlier. But before we even got that close, he stopped walking. It took me a moment to realize he was saying good-bye.

VII

It really started here in this bed at 2:00am. The fan on the window sill is pointed outward, to draw out the smoke from the joint, and it makes the frail glass lamp on the nightstand purr in rhythm. The shimmer effect is distinctly Southern, like the traces of shadows a ceiling fan would make in a Tennessee Williams play. Breezes and old mirrors, wooden bed posts at the head and baseboards, lacy duvet covers, blue chambray sheets, a feather mask from a genuine New Orleans Mardi Gras with a red flame pattern on it, and next to that a tapestry hangs on the far wall, a bald eagle gripping red and blue pennants with stars and stripes. It's supposed to be pre- or neopost-Revolutionary, but it looks positively Confederate.

Before my grandfather died, I shared this bedroom with my mother. We had twin beds in the largest room, the one at the end of the hall, upstairs in my grandparents' house. There's only one bed in there now, a big creaky old four-poster maple bed, just a little too high to sit down on. I have to climb up into it, even as an adult. The view from the pillow is straight out and up into the sky through the branches of the oak in the front yard. This is the room where I sleep when I visit her now, if you call this nocturnal demon hunting sleeping.

Without any warning, I am swept out to sea in the irresistible wake of a huge round rock. It carries me straight out into Long Island Sound, away from the familiar neighborhood beach where my mother and grandmother stand dumbstruck. I start to scream when I see the two of them standing there, so utterly powerless. They looked so small, two black specks standing stock still, while the dog-speck ran back and forth, in a pitiful pantomime of helping. The great sweep of sandstone jetty flung wide its arms as I backed out at top speed; the boulder whose gravity held me close was made of the same mottled rock. The houses looked so insincere, all laid out in a pretty row. Hedges looked soft and friendly from a distance, but the fragrant flowers were hiding sharp metal fences. I expected the open sea to be quiet, but it was thunderously loud, deafening, in fact. And hot as hell, even in the water. I didn't go swimming much after that.

VIII

From where I sit at my desk by the window, I can see the sunset everyday except for two and a half weeks in December. The Sun moves a fraction of an inch every day; it slips South between July and December, and creeps North again January through June. Along the way it stops at the red brick chimney, the satellite dish, the roof of the blue house, the cedar shingles, the Frank Gehry townhouse, the flat-topped apartments with the potted trees and the lawn chairs, and the silhouettes of people drinking martinis while they watch the sunset, too.

For two weeks each November and again in February, it sinks directly into the ocean through a gap between roof tops. From May to August it is way up North behind the mountains. This has an odd effect because these are the longest days of the year, yet it seems to set earlier than ever because of the outcroppings. But I can see the ridges clearly all the way East to the Hollywood sign; it's like my own private sunset from the balcony. And then maybe half an hour later - when the sun really does set though it's already out of view - the whole sky swells up with color. It's like the secret bonus track way at the end of a cd, that you only hear if you are too stoned to get up and change it when it first ends. An inside joke.

The Sun sets differently every single day. No two the same ever, like snowflakes. In six years I have never seen a repeat. And in six years I have never seen the ocean look the way it did last night. It was like a revelation. I felt like I was seeing the Moon for the very first time. The full moon's wide beam ran straight toward us on our hilltop. It's the same hill that hides the Sun early in Summer, but now we were on its crest. The water was far from serene, neither still nor glassy. It absorbed the light like a canvas not a mirror. There weren't waves so much as vibrations, like gooseflesh, or fabric in a breeze.

Shadows moved across it and I saw visions. There were two dozen people drumming in the rotunda behind me, while my eyes crossed and revealed what the shadows hid. Migrations of animals across Sub-Saharan Africa, with gazelles and rhinos and monkeys and big cats all being followed by hunters. There were also modern folks playing in the surf along the shore. They were laughing and playing with beach balls and I thought, I am watching people that drowned in that spot through the years.

The drums stopped suddenly on a sharp beat, the animals stopped running, the people swam away. I heard the waves crash then for the first time all evening.

IX

On the beach again, back at the same spot where I always go to think something through. On that particular afternoon, a Monopoly board was being coaxed out to sea by the fingers of an advancing tide. My driftwood perch is not far from the wet edge, and I have to yank my feet back from a few precocious waves. I had cuts on my feet, and the salt water made them sting. It wasn't long before I was forced to return to the house.

I had had a fight with my father, the cause of which I had already forgotten, in our apartment below the Rainbow Room. Our place was a skirt of glass around the building, like a diamond necklace on an old society dame. We came in the same doors as the talent and crew entrance for the club on the ground floor, past the bouncers, always a velvet rope on the way home. We had a private elevator at least. Apparently I had said something inappropriate to my father while we were watching the sun set over New Jersey, because the next thing I knew, we were at it again.

I have no doubt that my comments were uncalled for, and my guilt only inflamed my rebellious rage. I threw a bag of flour at him in the kitchen, because he was wearing a black cashmere sweater and hated the contact of the organic and inorganic. I figured, correctly as it turns out, that he would be distracted by the ruined sweater long enough for me to make an exit. I ran out barefoot, and shredded one heel on some rocks in the parking lot. Finally I made it to the beach, where I had been sitting until the tide came in. As I turned to leave, I remembered that salt water is supposed to be curative, and braced myself for one last rush of water, which hurt like hell.

I gave up on the impulse to go home, and turned back to face the ocean. Some dolphins were out in the waves breaking on the sandbar. I waded in to try to get their attention. What I found instead was that I was extremely late for class, staring straight ahead at the closed door to Room 23, hearing my mother's voice begin the lesson, weighing my options. She opened the door just as I was turning to go.

Class was such a bore on that day, I mean more than usual. It was almost the end of summer vacation, and my interest had been waning since October. All I was good for was staring out the window at the ocean, sunset coming on, water flat and silent like silver satin sheets. My mind wanders to the highway, to the events of the night before. We got stuck and had to be rescued, bailed out of jail, just a week before graduation. A skinny boy who had loved me for years and to whom I had been unbelievably cruel for just as long, came to help me. I could see him already down at the water, waving me to follow him. I never would, of course.

X

An overlarge Monarch butterfly with a strong body and a distinct head, both black chenille, came to rest on my left index finger. It crawled around on my left hand and forearm for what seemed like hours, even as I went about my business in town.

It stayed with me when I stopped at the beachfront hotel bar to track down a friend who had promised to give me a lift to school that day. It was a promise that became more and more precious to me as the rain came harder and harder. I was utterly dismayed to run into my grandmother in the lobby. Apparently, she was vacationing there with a friend of hers, who happened to have been a math teacher at my High School. With them was my uncle (by marriage, to my grandmother's other daughter) though the aunt was not present.

See, the problem with the situation was this: no one in my family ever knew that I had not actually graduated from High School. I had managed to graduate from college legitimately, but years later I wanted to finish High School for myself, for satisfaction, or maybe just for kicks. In any case, it was definitely a secret from my family. My dear friend didn't know any of this, he was just giving me a ride to the school, but he assumed I was teaching! Anyway, my grandmother overheard him saying, "blah, blah, blah, leave for school now." She asked me what was going on, but I pretended not to hear her question, and split. Butterfly still hanging on.

It was gone, though, that butterfly, the next time I remember checking, as we pulled up in front of the school building. This friend had commandeered a City bus somehow, but he didn't know its route. I offered to show him, since it pretty much matched the way to the school anyway. He let me out and drove on, and that's when I noticed the butterfly was gone.

On the drive over, the rain had gotten even harder, and the sky darker. As soon as I got off the bus, I ducked under a tree to prepare for the dash across the street, up the wide stone stairs, and in through the heavy cast iron doors. On the other side of those immense doors was a damp and musty flagstone foyer. While I carefully plotted my course through the deepening puddles, my lover appeared at my side.

We kissed and sighed, hello you. I began to go over in my mind whether I really had to go to school at all that day. True, I had been out most of last week; and, true, I had prepared an oral presentation which I was expected to deliver that afternoon. But the warmth amid all the chill made it truly difficult to take action. It was the kind of day that would be perfect for making love to someone for the first time.

I glanced at the sidewalk with my head resting on my lover's shoulder, as the black high heel of a passerby's shoe crushed one of three monarchs on the ground. They were drenched or even drowned from the rain. The sight, and even years later, the memory, engulfed me with sadness, and broke the spell. I turned away from him, holding back tears, and headed toward the school.

XI

High school in the big city. My sweetheart then is my lover of today, exactly as he is now. We walk together into the cafeteria where everyone is assembled. There is one girl in particular, with short blond hair in a plaid miniskirt like at a Catholic school. She obviously covets him, having no respect for me at all in the way she throws herself at him. He and I were standing face to face in the middle of the room holding hands, and she walks straight up and gets in between us. Throws her hands around his neck and stands there talking up into his big beautiful face like I didn't exist.

This is what they call the last straw. I cleared my throat and stepped close to her, mystified by his lack of response to this affront. He has still made no move to back away. I pulled her off of him by the hair on the back of her head, like peeling a cat off the upholstery. Dragged her a few feet to the closest table and pounded her forehead down onto the Formica with a whoosh and a dull splat thud. She crumpled to the floor in tears. I took his hand and led him out of the building. No one took any notice.

On the city bus with the green school bus seats we took toward home, we talked the incident over a little. He sat behind me, so I had to turn in my seat to look at him. All through the crowded downtown section, the neon signs began to blur in the mist that was fast becoming rain. It was this part of town that I had fallen in love with so many years ago when I came here, lost. I finally managed to move here not long before, around the time I met him.

The bus pulled into the gravel driveway of a Veterans Administration bowling alley and some vets boarded. Slight smell of cigarettes and spilt beer. My lover was in the middle of saying, "What was the big deal? It's not that serious between me and you anyway, right?" I said that, no, he's right, it's not that serious. But my heart was broken. He went on to say he might very well date her sometime. When I heard that, I said nothing, only got off at the next stop, two short of mine.

I couldn't wait to get outside into the blessed wet rain, where it would be harder to tell I was crying. If I could just get off the bus without him seeing my face, I'd have an alibi for the smudged mascara. The bus slowed, I rose unsteadily and exited without turning around once. I admit I was half listening for his steps behind me, but they did not come. I heard the doors slide shut behind me, heard the bus pull away from the curb. I thought I heard him calling from the window, but I couldn't be sure.

I hadn't gone more than 100 feet when I heard him distinctly, calling my name and coming closer. He reached out and touched my shoulder, spinning me slowly to face him. I think the rain was only partially hiding my emotions. In silence he pulled me in close to him, one hand on the small of my back strong and warm. After a moment, he guided me down the street. He looked shocked and concerned. At home, my home, the first thing he said was, "I had no idea I meant this much to you." My response, "Neither did I."

Rich Henrich

The Twelve-Thousand Dollar Reindeer

Thankfully, my uncle took pity on my entrepreneurial enthusiasms and allowed me to stay at his golf condo in the desert. Well, I said I needed a place to stay for a week. It was summer and with temperatures surpassing the 120 degree mark, he wasn't about to vacation there anyway. So, I stayed longer.

I'd been living on cabbage soup for so long, I lost track. I forgot to put the soup away last night. I couldn't fall asleep. The waves of worry washed across the movie screen of my mind. It was the pacing, the useless thoughts racing in my head that kept my eyes peeled for an illusive answer that I was afraid I would miss in a blink. I tried dreaming, and asking my subconscious for answers but sleep depravation threw the whole thing off. The 'Get Rich Quick' through positive thinking books I bought from a late night infomercial hustler were crap. The internet had answers and free self-help guides and tutorial videos, yet nothing applied to me. It was all just bullshit. How could it have been so damn hard to find a job? I just needed to make enough to eat anything but cabbage soup.

I never worried about eating before. Of course, I gave the homeless money or food when ever I encountered them but never figured I would be so close to walking in their shoes. It's funny. As I stir my cabbage soup, The White House unveiled their one hundred thousand dollar Holiday tree. Congress can't figure out how to extend unemployment benefits or create jobs but decorate a tree for the world to see is a mere formality of excess and waste. My uncle wasn't much better with his thousand dollar bottles of wine collecting dust in the closet. It could have been worse, I could have been wishing for a house to sleep in and soup to stir. I tried to embrace any fleeting thought of positivity. It was all I had.

I haven't always been an emotional eater or an insomniac but these became the predominant traits of my current lifestyle and neither habit favored my situation. My inner demons won the last seven rounds. Groceries kept disappearing, despite my best efforts at rationing. I was essentially homeless. I lived inside a country club where the lawns were all manicured and crews came every Monday to tend to the shrubs. I had a golf cart I could drive inside the compound and there was a television and all the comforts of a vacation home in the glorious California desert.

The heat was evil, hallucinogenic. It felt more like hell than home but I had nowhere else to go. This was the end of my road. The deal was I could stay for the week but I had to pay for the electricity and air conditioning, which given the 120 degree heat, was not cheap, even for a week. I could consume all the food and booze in the house, too. It was a fair deal if I had the money but I didn't. I was too embarrassed to admit it. So, without air conditioning, it became a sweat lodge of sorts and some days the heat and sleep depravation welcomed visions. Around one in the morning I would sneak into the pool. In the beginning, I was able to use the club membership card a few times before they told me to tell my uncle he needed to renew his membership. I assured them it would be taken care of immediately. He couldn't find out that I'd been using the card or he'd know I extended my stay without his permission and I'd be out on my ass. That couldn't happen. The first month, I was able to pay but hadn't been able to keep up on the monthly dues either so that luxury had to stay under the cloak of darkness. At one a.m. it was still one hundred degrees out.

I was certain I'd be able to find a job. I had great work experience, held three degrees and could sell anything, manage complex problems and knew how to play well with others. When I saw the paper in the rack outside Tom's grocery store, I had a feeling a job was waiting for me inside of those pages. I flipped right to an ad seeking an outside sales rep. Bingo, easy, finally, an answer to my prayer. This job would be mine and I could stop eating peanut butter by the rationed spoonful. I splurged at the grocery store with my renewed sense of confidence and bought some fish and lunchmeat along with more cabbage, vegetables and rice. I could survive another two weeks at least.

The Twelve-Thousand Dollar Reindeer

On my way home, smoke started to fill the inside of my car, the temperature gauge was throttled to the limit. I pulled over before the engine caught on fire. This was fucked! It was 110 degrees outside. My cell phone went into safety mode and shut down from the heat. Of all the days, I picked today to buy a few bags of groceries and now had to walk two miles back to the confines of conformity. I stood in line with my groceries behind the cars, sun on top of me, black top beneath me, and hot exhaust in my face, I waited to get to the guard gate and give my name so the gates would part. Son of a bitch it was hot, scorching hot and sweat rolled off my face at a disgusting rate. I asked the guard if they were hiring and he just looked at me like I was an asshole. I forgot where I was and who they thought I was for a moment. He warned me about walking in the desert heat and then the ornate iron gates graciously swang open before me.

I was drenched when I reached the front door. All I could think about was drinking a glass of water or a hundred. The house felt cool for the first time in two months. I toweled off and opened the paper to the ad for the sales job. I had to stay focused. If I had insurance maybe I could afford my ADD meds but then I'd have to find a way to afford the insurance. It was a vicious cycle. *Focus. Pick up the phone and call the number. Do it now before they hire the guy who is about to call. They won't hire you. You haven't had a real job in years. Do it.*

"Hello. Yes, I'm calling about the sales position. Yes. I used to publish my own weekly. I'm very familiar. Yes, I can start next week. Well, I'm a professor actually and sometimes writer and producer but I can do sales. I am rather comfortable…oh, you need a sales manager? Sure, I can meet with you. Thank you."

Holy shit. Holy shit! I think I just landed a job. Fuck! My car.

"Dad, I have a job doing ad sales but my car nearly caught fire and I'm down to my last 90 bucks. Can you help? I'll pay you back after I get my check. Thanks."

I left a message. My dad hated me.

I needed to pay my dad back and prove I wasn't a total fuck up. I blamed him for a lot of things and felt like he owed me but he didn't see things the same way. It was always the same story about how his dad let him borrow the car once, took him to a Yankee's game when he was thirteen and bailed him out of jail one time without a word but bought him a pastrami sandwich. That was fatherly love to him. He reminded me how far removed I was from college and how I just needed to buck up and get a job. I suppose his winning attitude was what caused the divorce and left me in emotional limbo without a father figure to learn such lessons from but that was another problem of my generation- sons without fathers. I just wanted to prove him wrong. Luke told Darth to go fuck himself and I wanted to be able to do the same and soon.

I opened the fridge as my emotions gnawed at me. There was a single beer left. I had been eying it for weeks. Now was as good a time as any. Crack!! It was time to fire up the golf cart and head to the clubhouse to celebrate.

It's odd to be an imposter among the wealthy, behind their secure gates. They assume you belong but the reality of my situation would horrify them. Rich people hate to be close to poverty. It makes them uncomfortable.

Fortunately, I made fast friends with the staff and told them the truth: I was a screenwriter working on a story. I shared my Hollywood tales of famous people I knew or worked with or almost knew. They'd pour me a few free beers to keep themselves entertained. Occasionally, the kitchen would have leftovers they'd just put on a plate for me. Those days were the best. It helped that I spoke a little Spanish. I used to live in a penthouse in Cancun half the year and developed a conversational knowledge and appreciation for the language.

I liked old man Jack the bartender. He was well into his seventies and had more stories than I did. He owned nightclubs and bars in the eighties and then became a pimp by accident when his girlfriend asked him to escort her while she entertained a group of Japanese businessmen at a fancy hotel. He said he made good money doing it. He was a chiropractor by trade but said it was too much of a racket.

So, he poured drinks. His philosophy was simple: "It don't matter," he'd say, "it's all bullshit unless you're making a dollar. And then, it's still bullshit." Then he'd laugh and ask: "Did I get you your beer, yet?"

The answer was always "No."

Some days I didn't really want the beer as much as I just needed the air conditioning. Heat does something to the mind.

"This one's on me," he'd say.

Jack had a funny New York accent with a slight speech impediment and his memory was slipping. He was from a different era, someone I imagined my dad would know from the old neighborhood. He liked cash. If I put a five down, he poured drafts until the place closed, which was usually a couple hours after sunset. It was a community of old people.

Essentially, I got to enjoy free air conditioning while getting drunk. and I even started dating one of the bartenders, which helped me on several levels. Then she quit and the clubhouse decided to close for a couple months for renovations and that forced me back on the cabbage soup diet except for those nights Nancy brought home leftovers from her new employer, Master's Steak House, the royalty of local restaurants.

The paper postponed our interview, which was fortunate because my car was still in the shop. It wasn't going to be cheap but my dad was going to help, to a point. The mechanic called and said the AC was out, too. To hell with it, I had to live without the luxury. I didn't have the three hundred bucks to fix it. Windows down and plenty of water would have to get me through. A couple ad sales and I'd be back in business and in comfort, or so I thought.

When the publisher called a week later, she informed me that they had lost a client and could no longer offer me a salary or a draw. Straight commission. I had half a tank of gas and twenty-eight dollars. I was royally screwed and out of options. My dad offered me money to move home or to fix my car. I opted for the fix. Now I needed a river for my proverbial canoe.

My girlfriend didn't know how bad things really were for me nor did I feel the need to tell her. She thought I was eccentric and I left it at that. It wasn't that I wasn't successful, more like I flipped over seventeen times in a school bus and rolled into bad luck and poverty when I thought I was going on a fun little field trip. No one really understood how it happened, including me. I was able to scrape up a little money from a friend, sold my books on eBay, an old and rare Easy Rider movie poster and some Matchbox car collectables. Thankfully, I had a little work writing some coverage on a few scripts. It still didn't add up to more than a few hundred bucks. The money came in just in time to keep the cell phone on and just before Nancy started to ask why we never went out. Fortunately, she worked nights and we could hit the afternoon movie specials and early dinner deals, but it was getting harder to afford the relationship. Her mom was asking what my five year plan was. I needed a job.

An old friend of mine called during one of my stare-at-the-ceiling-for-answers moment and said he had recommended me for a job producing a small film. It was perfect timing. I couldn't take poverty any longer. There was a catch. I had to get to New Mexico. So, I made the call I never wanted to make and asked my dad for a small loan to help me out---again. I assured him this job was solid and I would pay him back after my first check. It was ten grand for work I loved. The gig would definitely get me back on my feet.

Every time I had a set back, my family and friends questioned my creative and entrepreneurial path. No one ever said anything about what I should be doing with my life when I was paying for their dinners or helping them with finances. Oh, to be back on top again. I could taste it! No more cabbage soup. I could afford a place, sleep in my bed and buy real food. Most of what I owned was either in my car or stacked in my uncle's garage, which he also didn't need to know about. It took me about an hour before I was packed and heading East on the I-10 freeway.

A new sense of peace washed over me. I took a bite of my sandwich. I could give value to someone willing to pay me for my skills. I tried to find other work and nothing happened. It was a sign; this was indeed my true path and purpose in life. I knew it. I was about thirty minutes outside of Albuquerque when I finally got a call back from the director. I told him I was almost there and then there was a heavy pause.

"We're pushing the shoot. I should have called you sooner. The lead actress died."

I think the phone fell from my hand, bounced off the middle console and hit me in the face, which caused me to jerk my head hard to the left and back. What happened next was a blur of cars, landscapes, honking horns, a huge tumbleweed, sky, clouds, dust and a sudden thud. Red earth danced in the air and clouded my horizon. I was in a ditch. The sandwich I had in my hand was now wrapped around my steering wheel and oozing out from between my firmly wrapped fingers.

A couple of Navajo guys pulled up in a truck and rushed down the embankment to check on me. The younger one saw that I was all right and went right to work hooking my car up to a tow rope. For some reason, I told the older guy, with lines cut deep into his sun drenched face that I didn't have any money.

He looked hard at me, in the eyes, for a minute. "You're going to be okay. We're here to help you."

The Twelve-Thousand Dollar Reindeer

His clenched smile was serious but kind. His words echoed. Two minutes later, I was back on the freeway wiping sandwich guts from my hand.

Fuck me! I needed work, I needed food, I needed money for gas, my phone bill and of course, the two websites that provided a trickle of income were past due for hosting fees as well. Never mind the rest of my debt, that was beyond help. It was all crashing in on me. I had tried hard, whether it was hard enough or not I couldn't say. I tried hard to keep living the dream and always thought I could get a job if things didn't turn out but that was before we had a campaign of *Change We Could Believe In* and jobs could be had with minimal effort. Now, there was nothing. I pulled into a truck stop and just sat. Trucks pulled in and trucks pulled out. I contemplated asking a driver if he needed help, leaving my car and disappearing from everything like Jack Nicholson in *Five Easy Pieces*.

I stared out into a blue-sky abyss in search of answers. A hearty man with a Duck Dynasty beard crossed my path. His American Flag suspenders, struggled to hold back his keg-size belly. His shirt protested, "No Bloviating." I had not a single card left hiding up my sleeve. My mind was about to unravel. I couldn't even get a job digging ditches or bussing tables. Believe me, I tried.

Did I fail or did I succeed? I didn't know. I had a good run of working for myself. I ran a couple companies for several years. I made money, acquired property, helped out family members, took extended vacations for the holidays. I contributed to non-profits and helped old ladies across the street. Maybe this was life and nice guys finished last. For all I knew, I was doing the right thing but striving for idealism left me unemployable.

I sat at a truck stop parking lot outside of Albuquerque without answers while I watched a homeless family beg.

I thought about my dad and the story my mom told me about how he almost killed me when I was a baby. They left Detroit in search of opportunities in California. They had two kids, a car, some money and a map. My dad says it was my mom's idea to drive Route 66. It was the Mother Road and they took it 'til the gas ran out. Stuck in the desert in hundred-degree heat, water was valuable. My sister knocked the jug over and the water spilled into the floorboard before turning into steam. My little body screamed for water. Evidently, I cried to the brink of my death. My dad ran across the desert in search of a gas station or help while my mom waited helplessly with my sister and me. He returned a short time later with gas and water. I wasn't moving. They thought I was dead and rushed me to the gas station where they put me in the ice machine to bring my temperature down. I'm still alive, albeit constantly thirsty.

At the truck stop in Albuqurque, I grabbed my jug of water that miraculously never spilled in the accident, got out of my car and walked over to the homeless family. The young mother held a sign that simply read: Please Help. Before I could say anything she started telling me that they were good people, that her husband lost his job and they were living off of her student loans. She was studying to be a teacher, until they lost their house and were now on the road trying to get to family.

"You don't have to explain, I get it," I said. I gave her twenty bucks.

Her face turned pale. "We've been here for three days. You're the only one…" She started weeping. "We just prayed. This is all we needed. Thank you! God Bless you."

The man looked at me, hope glistened in his eyes. Words weren't necessary. He held out his hand. It was a grip of gratitude and it spoke of trials and tribulations and yearning faith. Tears welled in my eyes.

I got back in my car. A bird had shit on my seat. I started laughing. My grandmother always told me if you sat in bird shit, it was good luck. I never understood it but somehow I knew she sent me a reminder.

When I looked up, I saw the man guzzling water from the jug. His wife came out from the gas station with a Subway sandwich. He returned the nozzle to the pump. He wiped his sleeve across his eyes and then got in to his minivan and drove away. I started my car. I felt the urge to turn around and head west, back to the desert.

I felt a calm and knew whatever was ahead of me was not so much about sending out resumes and getting a job. There was something bigger at work and I needed only to have faith in a cause I once understood.

I pulled onto the I-10 West, the sun was setting. It was a blazing ball of blinding fire. I flipped the visor down, put my sunglasses on and hit the gas. I thought of Icarus. I was going through the sun. I think it was his fear of flying through the sun that caused his wings to burn, for he had doubt and that manifested into flames.

When I pulled up outside of Master's Steakhouse, nothing seemed real anymore. The valets were rushing around in their uniforms, tossing keys, taking tips and opening doors to cars that cost more than homes. The streets were glowing with Holiday lights, ribbons and bows tied neatly to palm tress. It was all so tastefully done. The well-dressed window shoppers wore smiles fit for a Macy's Parade. They held their heads high, satisfied and comfortable.

I turned the key to lock my car, a very off-white and well-traveled domestic. I bought it while working my last legitimate job, a sales job with paid vacation and benefits. The company gave me a car allowance as long as I had a four-door to appear professional. That was several years ago, when jobs were plentiful and credit was easy. It was long before the unemployment benefits and their extensions ran out. That felt like a past life. Now, my chariot rested beside the curb, an obvious misfit on this elegant avenue, the Presidio. No signs of Detroit here except for me. I tried to wear my misfortunes on the inside.

"I've never paid less than $12,000 for a reindeer." The words echoed with certainty across an empty street as I rolled out of my car. What an *odd* thing to hear. I mean it was Christmas Eve. Did that guy really just say what I thought he said? The affluent, well-dressed couples were strolling past the regal offerings displayed in the boutique shop window. Yeah, I just heard what I thought I heard. The mid-century couples were staring at the larger than life, heavily decorated reindeer family on display inside the art zoo.

My car alarm started screaming. It startled the aging lady with the bad face job. She jumped back into her husband's arms and the group gave me the stink eye.

These people were not a part of the America I knew, an America where Gen X believed what they were told in school only to discover midway through life that they were lied to and in fact, they couldn't be whatever they wanted to be and the paper that proved they were an educated elite meant little more than a debt they could not escape. And these were the lucky ones. The Millennial faces a fifty percent unemployment rate and those who could afford to leave found jobs in foreign countries. Others are desperate enough to break into cars, even my car and since it held the bulk of my belongings.

The well-dressed foursome and I met eyes. I forced a Holiday half-smile rather than go off on my internal rant. The old woman pulled her cashmere wrap tighter around her. I wanted to scream out, *"Fuck you lady,*

I have three college degrees! I'm an artist! And a professor, once in a while if the budgets allowed." But I held back the wrath.

They continued their conversation. "We bought four, a family of reindeer, last year and we paid…Joan, what was it that we paid for ours?" The man stood at the window staring blankly before pulling down his Ralph Lauren glasses for a mindless polish.

"I think it had to be at least $20,000 for the adults, a little less for the smaller ones. They are lovely, though. We have them lighted in the yard." Pride flowed from her voice like an estate Merlot.

The door to Master's Steak House automatically opened as I arrived. I loved that about this restaurant. There was attention to detail no matter who you were. They served their fair share of celebrities and they just never knew who somebody might be. It was the fear of offending a potential "somebody" that created a safe policy of treating everybody like they were someone. The maitre'd greeted me with a warm smile and the general manager gave me a welcome embrace. Members of the creative class are often welcomed into establishments like this if for no other reason than to break up the monotony of the banal patrons.

Nancy was surprised to see me. Her smile was beaming. "Couldn't stay away from me, huh?"

We kissed and then she took my hand and seated me at the bar.

"This is my boyfriend, Chris. Take care of him. He gets whatever he wants."

The lovely bartender smiled curiously, pulled up a glass and poured a stiff shot of tequila. "Nancy talks about you but we didn't believe you were real."

I smiled politely. "Neither did I." I threw the shot back. It was liquid vacation.

The restaurant bar was packed with new money, old money, entertainment money and hustled money. The young, the old, the married, the middle-aged, the faithful and the sinister all gathered here. The rock star played coy in the corner with his evening conquest while the old man who owned an NBA team sucked face with a woman I mistook for his daughter. The younger blonde in a red dress clutched his button down polo shirt, embraced by a sport coat. He thrusted his golden 70-year-old tongue down her throat. She clenched, disgusted or pleased, it was hard to say. She pulled back with grace and ordered another wine with a shameless smile. He felt young again, like a man who drove a mustang in a Viagra commercial. This was what money could afford. The working girl wasn't hard to spot, nervously reapplying bright red across her thin lips and checking her phone. There was money here more importantly, lonely rich men with money that didn't mind paying for affection. The house band played a cover of a funk song that brought the retired NFL player to the dance floor draped by a woman desperate to feel alive again. The mid-life man with an alpha pack group of guys yelled out; "Play some fuckin' Journey!"

No one said anything to him. The bartender must have noticed I took offense to the rude man.

"He's a regular. Would you like another drink?" I nodded.

She poured another shot and opened a menu for me. "So, you work in Hollywood. You're a producer or something, right?"

I wanted to leave, I resented her words for some reason but I was hungry. "Yeah, or something."

She poured herself a shot and looked over her shoulder. "I worked at Outback before here. It's a real step up for me, you know. It's a good opportunity."

I raised my glass. "Here's to you! It's good to be employed."

Our glasses clinked and the twenty-dollar shots flowed down easy. One thing about trickle down economics, even when the economy is in a free fall, it still pays to serve the rich. The staff here made a decent living slinging excess and indulgence by the plate or the glass full. As the old social theorist Thorstein Veblen said in 1899: "The chief use of servants is the evidence they afford of the master's ability to pay."

The cover band lurched into Don't Stop Believin' by Journey. The whole bar stopped and, like locusts, swarmed the dance floor. The rude fuck next to me, lost his mind and fell out of his chair. The bar erupted in some kind of strange high school musical ritual, singing the lyrics as if they were being auditioned by American Idol. The half-wits joined the chorus.

I wondered what feeling all these people were holding on to. The working class band struck a chord with this wealthy crowd. Whatever it was, the message was clear. *Don't Stop Believing!!!*

Nicolas (Dimitri) Vorvolakos

Freedom

Just arrived

Released

From being on a plane for 9 hours,

From being in handcuffs and shackles

For 3 days

From being interviewed by Panamanian police for 3 hours.

So tired.

Need to pass out and forget.

From being in a 3rd world hotel, where I will live until I
    gather my senses.

My only company a large roach, too tired to kill it.

Too lonely and scared to ignore it.

Sitting in a restaurant ravenous with hunger,

Confused by freedom of choice.

Swimming in a pool of fetid water too disgusted with myself
     to get out.
Going to a shop, to buy something, anything to feel alive.
Showered and shaved.
Horny, lonely and bored.
Cruising the streets looking for sex, looking for drugs.
Need to fuck.
Getting a blow job, high on weed and rum.
Being sucked and worked for the last of my change.
He settled for 20 dollars and half my weed.
I Fell asleep, woke up drenched in sweat.
I hate the heat.

Betty Ann Brown

Old Songs

I love rock 'n' roll (The Arrows, then Joan Jett). I've loved it since the days of the British Invasion. I saw the Beatles perform in the Madrid bullring in 1965. I saw the Rolling Stones do Midnight Rambler and The Who do Tommy. I saw Led Zeppelin four times, but don't remember much about them. I also saw Hendrix in 1968 or maybe it was '69, but don't remember that at all. (You can imagine why.)

The point here is I really do love rock 'n' roll. And I think about it a lot. I've wondered for years about rock lyrics, which tend to echo in our minds again and again, almost hypnotically. Do they etch avenues of thought in our awareness? Do they teach us to think? Do they train us to relate to each other in certain ways?

The piece that follows was generated by those questions. Many of the words (think: lyrics) come from the titles of old songs. The structure (think: bass line) comes from a list of the gorgeous gadgets that adorn our technologically enhanced lives. But the narrative? Well, it's only rock 'n' roll (Rolling Stones).

THE DRIVER

1. She was seriously pissed off. The last time (Rolling Stones) she'd seen her so-called boyfriend, he'd spent most of the evening paying more attention to his damn pad than to her. Where had all the good times gone

(David Bowie)? When she said something about it, he snapped at her. The evening devolved into awkward silences, sharp words, bad feelings. She'd never felt so distant, so disconnected.

2. Later that night (Frank Zappa), she was flipping channels and came across the old film Suspicion (Elvis Presley). And somehow, she knew he was lying. He'd been lying all along.

3. She called him again and again, but he wouldn't pick up. When she finally got through--two days later--she was furious. He kept trying to get off the phone and she kept screaming, "Don't hang up! (The Orlons) You need to talk to me about this!" But he pretended that the reception was failing and shut off his cell. (Did he think she was stupid? Of course she knew what he'd done [Cher]. Everyone did it.)

4. She supposed it was the perfect goodbye (Heart). She followed the awful call with an angry text message and stormed out to her old Mustang. Her emotional weather report (Tom Waits) was not good, but it always cheered her up to drive that car.

5. She decided to go back to Amoeba and get the vinyl that had been playing in her mind about for days. She was heading west on Mulholland late in the afternoon when she was blinded by the light (Bruce Springsteen), by the hot California sun shining into her dark day.

THE RUNNER

6. He was well-respected man (The Kinks). And he was totally obsessed with running. He woke up to the sizzle of the computer-driven coffee maker, grabbed a cup, black, and pulled on his shoes. He sometimes ran ten miles before he went into the office.

7. The glittering girl (The Who) was still on his mind. He'd seen her standing in the doorway (Bob Dylan) of the music store, the ghost of a smile on her face. She had ear buds in and he wondered what she'd been listening to. (A person's taste in music says so much about them.) She wore

a funky Fedora, sequined shirt, and Zebra shoes. Definitely glittering.

8. He pushed it: three miles, four, five. His breath became labored, his lungs ached. And still, he couldn't get her off his mind (Hank Williams, then Bob Dylan). How was he gonna find her (The Coasters, then The Beatles)? Should he do a personal ad? Was she on Facebook? It seemed hopeless.

9. He was thinking about heading back to his Laurel Canyon home (John Mayall) when his Smartwatch pinged to tell him he had a message. He checked it, but it was just a stupid Tweet from a co-worker. He shook his head and was looking up in frustration when his life turned upside down.

THE DRIVER & THE RUNNER

10. The crosstown traffic (Jimi Hendrix) surged up Mulholland, pushing the driver forward, distracting her as she sped west. She was leaning down to turn up the radio when she crashed into him. He went flying, his limbs spiraling around him, and landed in a thick hedge. She slammed on the brakes, pulled over, and began to shake.

Yeah, that's how they happened to meet (Neil Diamond).

Christopher Michno

Dear Mr. Lake or How to Make an Omelet

The first round of layoffs at Ovum had gone better than expected. The firm cleaned out the middle managers who had been there too long. Jonathan Lake thought of them as rotting deadwood. They were crumbling specimens of mediocrity; middle-aged placeholders whose salaries had inflated with time. They generated too little value, and brought in fewer clients than any of their younger-by-a-decade associates, who essentially worked their asses off. Getting rid of them was like clear-cutting a forest so the young trees could get the sunlight. The decaying, fungus-infested timber needed to be hauled off, and the old growth trees that cast their shadows on the forest floor needed to be harvested. Besides, everyone – even those pathetic placeholders – knew that the saplings created more oxygen than the mature trees that had reached their terminal size.

Lake had always enjoyed cleaning house. He felt weightless and optimistic when it was done. It was an effective cost-containment strategy, and the return on investment for his department was unusually high. He could easily manipulate his department's cost to earnings ratio by "selectively de-acquisitioning human capital" as he liked to think of it. Walking back to his office after the day's round of bringing down the axe, he imagined all the new, youthful associates he would hire for substantially less than the person he had just let go.

The only glitch, and it was minor, was that a couple of the senior staff had questioned his strategy. But he had it well in hand. They said they worried about gutting the department and replacing staff who had established track records with inexperienced workers. But he had assuaged their concerns. He pointed to the cost savings and assured them that the new hires would be quick studies and more versatile. After all, he was hiring them, wasn't he? He knew how to bring in strong people. There were only one or two duds. And he didn't put much stock in those.

He ran his fingers through his hair and whistled a bit from the Rolling Stones as he strode through the hall. The lyrics ran through his head: "Pleased to meet you, hope you guess my name." Too young to be hypertensive, Lake was energetic. His tall, muscular frame held a hint of tension, and his eyes only occasionally betrayed the ruthlessness he was known for. As he approached the company break room, he overheard a couple of voices discussing something in urgent tones. Two senior programmers looked up and abruptly concluded their conversation as he entered.

"Hello gentlemen," Lake intoned. "Did I interrupt something? Don't mind me; please carry on!"

One of them shook his head and looked down into his coffee, and the other forced a smile and said, "No, we were just getting ready to head back to our desks."

Lake recognized one of them as a regular lunch companion of one of last week's layoff victims. Pathetic, he thought. Then he smiled broadly and said he looked forward to seeing them at next week's interdepartmental meeting. They nodded, said, "Yep, we'll see you there," and left the room.

He made his way to the cupboards and found his favorite dark chocolate. He pulled a sugary coffee drink out of the fridge, unwrapped the chocolate and broke off a square. He chewed slowly and stood there for a minute savoring the bittersweet flavor. It was just about the only thing he ever did slowly.

Lake thought about last week. Most of the deadwood had been there for so long, they were shocked when the axe came down. Sometimes it took a minute for the reality to sink in. There was a protocol, and if you didn't follow it, you opened the company up to liability. Usually, he held the silence until they acquiesced. After a few moments, he would move them along, saying they had a short time before security would arrive to escort them out. Most of them just trudged meekly out the door with the personal items from their cubicle stuffed into a small box. Security was waiting for them in the hall. Some of them cried, tears streaming down their faces. It was pitiful; grown men and women, their eyes blurry, stumbling along the corridors to the stunned looks of their colleagues as they left behind a chunk of their lives. Some of them whimpered about how it seemed so meaningless. It was a job! What else was it supposed to be?

Others tried to get in a parting shot about how unfair it was. "You'll get yours," one of them had said matter-of-factly. Comments like that just rolled off his back. Inwardly, he mocked every last one of them. Today's victim was different.

She said stoically, "OK," pulled a box from behind her desk and packed her belongings in less than ten minutes.

Getting rid of people for cause was a slightly different game. And Lake relished it even more. The first step was to establish cause. All he had to do was sow the seeds of self-doubt and fear, and he could literally watch the death spiral begin. Sometimes he sent a curtly phrased email to take issue with their performance in a client meeting. Other times, he cut them off in the middle of a presentation to poke holes in their strategy, hijacking the meeting to set his own course. They usually responded with predictable timidity. He could almost see them begin to second-guess themselves as their sense of independence and self-confidence crumbled. From there, it was a short throw to diminished performance. Just repeat the pattern a few times, undercut them on group emails, make sure some of the emails included the firm's principals, and it was solidly underway.

A few employees resisted, and that usually took longer. If he could engineer a client complaint, that usually gave him the necessary leverage. Getting the client to call the principal creative director in frustration to ask that a particular individual be taken off their account was a stroke of genius that he had been able to orchestrate a few times. The ensuing reprisal was usually swift. Jonathan would hear from creative director Agatha Mast, and the two of them would meet with their quarry. A performance improvement plan would be set in place, with a short window for success, and some very subjective goals.

One of the best ways to play the game was to ask the employee to identify areas he needed to improve. Lake encouraged them to be vulnerable; it was a way to show good faith.

"We all have room for improvement," Lake liked to say. "Whenever I write my annual self-evaluation, I always include three things I need to do better. And I'm brutally honest. I write that I'm not easy to get along with, for one. It's better if you identify room for growth than to force me or

Agatha to do it." Of course, none of them had ever seen his annual review, and it was pure fiction; he was simply leading them by the nose down a preordained path. They all wanted to keep their jobs, and they would take the bait, hook, line and sinker. Lake tasked them with writing their own obituary. Once he had their plan, it was like an admission. After the initial meeting was out of the way, Agatha preferred not to be involved. She gave Lake a free hand in managing the process. She was too busy and insisted on keeping a buffer between herself and the employees who were not direct reports. And that is why she trusted him. Because he got it done. People either fell in line, or they left. One way or another, they left.

It was easy enough to repeat the simple assertion at each benchmark that John Doe had demonstrated no measurable improvement. The employee would sit there aghast and look around the room, as if appealing to an unseen audience. Lake was very adept at turning the examples they considered improvements into reinforcements of the original complaint. His favorite had been Gillian. She had never shown him the proper deference, and she was a bit too removed from her co-workers. He told her she needed to collaborate with her colleagues more. She reluctantly wrote it into her plan. When they met two weeks later, he told her she had gone from being aloof to being dependent. "You won't make a move without running it by your colleagues first," he told her. That sparked a course of reversals in her behavior. When they met for the third time, he said she was erratic. Then he asked her for a weekly report of her interactions with colleagues. Three weeks later, he dismissed her.

The best thing to do was ambush them, which is what he had done to Gillian. Her review period had been scheduled to run another six weeks, but Lake preempted it. He showed up in her office unannounced, accompanied by the HR director. He presented her with her final paycheck and a severance offer.

Lake popped the last bite of chocolate into his mouth and walked down the hall to the entrance to his office. He was surprised to see the HR director. She was sitting down primly in front of his desk with a manila envelope in her hand. Agatha Mast was standing next to her. Agatha started to say something to him, but he didn't hear it; he only saw her mouth moving and the manila envelope being extended to him. As he grabbed the arm of his chair for support, Agatha handed him an empty file box.

Tulsa Kinney

Savage Cut

Every Wednesday afternoon, around 3 p.m., humorist Dan Savage's brand new sex column Savage Love would pass through my hands after being proofread. I would layout the copy next to it, usually a jump page of the Calendar section.

At the local alternative weekly newspaper where I worked as a graphic designer, every week around that time of day, things would be winding down. Most of the copy was already at the printers by then, and last to go was the Calendar section—mostly listings of events and the popular neighborhood movie guide. Wednesdays were typically always a fun and relaxed time at the paper. One could compare Casual Fridays, or TGIFs at normal work situations. There was a core of people that were there to the end of Wednesdays too, usually the production and editorial design and proofreading departments. Since we had a lot of downtime (and that word I later learned should never be uttered), I would lean back a little, put my feet up on my desk (literally) and read aloud Savage's column to my two co-workers (and apparently the rest of the staff I would later come to find out). This became a time-honored tradition in my department, everyone howling at my histrionics, interpretations and editorializing. We all had so much fun. I have to admit, I shone at this hour. So the Savage column became the lubricant for the rest of the evening, as we would gather at a neighborhood bar a couple of hours later.

That was a common scenario for about 16 years. But who was counting? Back then it seemed that 16 years could have passed again and we would still be doing the same thing, laughing at the same jokes and laying out the same pages.

A few years earlier, Wall Street discovered that big city publications were making good money, worthy of investment. Our company was sold. The bottom line took on a whole new meaning.

Then it happened, that summer, June of that 16th year. I received an email from my recently newly hired boss (who was only a door away). He requested a meeting with me concerning some issues of my productivity. My jaw dropped to my keyboard. I grabbed a union rep and went into my boss' office.

To provide just a little background, it's true, I wasn't a big fan of our new supervisor. The whole department loved our previous boss, so it was quite an adjustment for our tiny staff. A few co-workers had even quit and one got forced out to accommodate the new regime. The few of us that remained were divided into two schools: docile and not so docile, me belonging to the latter category.

Along with the new boss, there was apparently a new work ethic. A few years earlier, there was a change of regime, and the paper got sold to another corporate newspaper. There was even an anti-trust legality issue swirling around the merger. Our new boss was part of that transformation. The memo I didn't get: Old slacker attitude of the newspaper would soon be extinguished.

I was part of that slacker group, the group that had worked there since the early years, the years where lines of coke were snorted on the stat camera lens. Cigarettes were smoked at the desks. Beers were cracked open on the patio. Cum stains on the lobby couch. Those were the days indeed, and my boss told me, those days were over.

OVER! What? The Wednesday Savage Hour was cancelled, the Last Call run on Tuesday nights were put an end to and no more smoking pot at 11 p.m. to get us through the wee hours of the night. Those days were no longer.

Those days were winding down fast anyways, just by natural causes. I could no longer be productive after a liquid lunch in my 40s as a matter of fact, but did we have to change our attitude? Our purpose in life? The meaning of life? Our hearts were all still there. We were diehard partiers, diehard liberals, diehard slackers. We would all meet at the same bar, the one within walking distance. It was the place for martini lunches, and a cocktail to go with that second copy-edit. A Greyhound for those caption inspirations. But mostly it was about camaraderie. Having a drink after working all day, talking shit about everyone that wasn't there. It was all about work and a huge part of our lives.

After my initial shock that I was being disciplined, perhaps even being fired, I was asked to keep a daily log of everything I did. (I wasn't sure how to word my 20 minutes of reading Dan Savage to my fans). It started out as a work diary with two entries per day, but soon advanced to 15-minute entries. Then they took me off the night shift. It seemed like my biggest offense was that I simply was having too much fun at work. And that just would not be tolerated anymore, not with the new regime.

Yes, the rock and roll slacker days were indeed over. But, really, we were no slackers—I say that in jest, as our attitude was slacker, more in the anti-corporate kind of way. We were all good at what we did, we knew all the tricks, we were professionals. We made every deadline, working all night if necessary. We were loyal employees, hardly took sick days, dependable. It was a tremendous talented staff, almost half employees were either rock stars or noted authors.

I never made a whole lot of money, but we were salaried, had paid vacations, full medical benefits and a Union shop. We were a happy lot, I would say. Even the editorial department was friendly with the production department. Everyone would smoke cigarettes together on the patio, even sales people mingled with the other departments. (Eventually the smoking in the office was banned!) Everyone loved their jobs. And the business was wildly successful.

The newspaper was founded by a lefty liberal and backed by the movie star Michael Douglas. The public couldn't wait to get their free newspaper every Thursday. They would devour the film reviews, the revered columnists and the cutting edge news reporting. The community looked up to the writers. It was a team effort and it seemed effortless when the staff was happy.

My dad died right after I was told those days are over, and I screamed at my boss in his office, calling him a liar when he falsely accused me of stretching my hours. I got the bad news call later that night that if I wanted to say my goodbyes, I should catch the very next plane. I was in Florida for the next ten days, watching my dear old dad leave this world. While I would swim in my father's condo outdoor pool, I would sob underwater, mourning for my dad and, I suppose, for those good old days at work. I knew that they would never be the same.

They say change is good. It took two months for them to terminate me. I fought tooth and nail and, with the help of our Union, filed a grievance. A devoted shop steward and my husband, a journalist who I met at the paper, stood by me and we won a settlement.

I took that money and started my own magazine. Dan Savage would be proud.

Doug Harvey

In Addition, It Is The Best, (AKA F For Howl)

One.

Famine is usually Mania, Madness My generation destroyed the spirit, and
I do not know
Changes in the area of __the city in search black rage

Two angels in heaven in the sky night action status and relations of production machines

Gore, eye discharge, destruction and poverty, cold, dark Waters of sitting
in the strange light cigarettes jazz

El Nino, the brain in the roof of heaven, angels, creative lighting Islam

War scholars - University of Arkansas this winter break, look into the eyes
and the face of the tragedy of the sender

Porn and leave a small window to the soul, of the University of
Room, the wall was fashioned shaving the face of danger, money, shrugged
and waste burning
New York Public Laredo marijuana with a belt will start again

Purgatoried nightclub burning oil Paint to be able to eat or drink Alley

127

heaven, death, and the body as a
Dreamed a dream, medicine, crafty, cock and ball and alcohol

Thundercloud and vibration between Gotham and Canada wszystkonieru-
chomo not blindly leap Peterson, the most reliable, he said,

Metro station shake Mercedes Benz insert string at the end of life in the
wheels of dopokihalas Bronx priest - shine in the Free sad destruction,
waste, abuse, brain

Night light water Fugazzi Bickford Alize hydrogen jukebox day trial, a beer
at day old abandoned
Bellevue Art Museum, Brooklyn Bridge, 70 hours of continuous talk time
to complete the park

Legion lost Empire Panels, empty lot in the second month, in the window
said,
Vomiting, ear, and eye-pleasing vibrations, initiatives and events and memories of war and prison hospitals knife Yacketayakking,

Temple platforms, smart, bright eyes and Meat dinner 7 global memory

Hall in Atlantic City, New Jersey is oblivion photo postcards

According to Chinese Tangerine automatically as soon as Pain, Sweat, the
head - room is decorated in Newark

Lost at night near the train station where I do not know, I'm breaking your
heart, and
The overnight snow cigarettes wagon to wagon car, the grandfather of the
traffic light
Global Research Bappukabara by profession - San Juan, Kansas City phone
sharp perception of vibration Tarantino contract fraud
Idaho Loned story tale India wants U.S. roads prophetic vision of the
Search in a strange idea to me when I'm angry from Baltimore
North Chinas shit Oklahoma, villages and Saloon engine management
light rain in the winter

In Addition, It Is The Best, (AKA F For Howl)

Houston lost one ship and Hunger, others with Spain, and the U.S. and,
plans and despair, and jazz half-Chu, Europe, Africa,
Chicago fireplace ashes and the Trans-Mexican volcanic eruptions, coz
you're lost, scattered rock poetry for Valentine Jamal

FBI section at the end of dark skin on the west coast, I have learned that
many shorts silent eyes

If private drug Haze, I burned a hole in the importation of cigarettes
On the boat to the island during this tax on Union square (Union square)
Super ISTAT Communist Party, Los Alamos, the scream Siren, rock, cry-
ing screaming down

Drive your car is bone white and change the name of the
After connecting the timber of the lesion and the Chef's knife, a Detective,
always, very

Knees in the subway, on the roof of the house, pulled a knife and vaginal
opening
Joy and applause as the World Motorcycle by intavoru
What Seraphim, the Atlantic, the Caribbean and the flight crew, stroked
love
Tomorrow, months free charge and I itrawa cemeteries, Parks and Gardens,
will show
Let the angels laugh, but wrong partition, Turkey needs, and the sword
pierced in prison after gdyblond

Dolarajednooki Soricomorpha old dog chain through the heterosexual matrix in the morning, but to sit at my ass, reduce male domain binding Sony
losujednooki dogs like to do

Papierosowswiec piwaukochanapakiet, gyzym wymykaostatnia the wall re-
mains unconscious in the ground, in order to increase awareness of the end
of the Lady satisfaction and happiness increase in the bottle fell out of bed
screaming
In other words, the more water in the morning and in the afternoon a nice
red trembling, but is ready to make sweets in the East, nudity Bhatt said

129

Adonis hero secret and influence people, statutes, North Carolina, Denver kinds of night - especially in the many restaurants, public meetings, or between a server and a secret caves and garages Colorado reminder of poor rural women, rural auto theft and adultery, stickers solipsisms Jones Lonely roads and spirit level slowly, poetry, theater screen, "people-to

Jobs and growth as a result of bad movies, eye bags, and fears and dreams for the expansion more than any Tokaj Avenue, Manhattan shocked by the sudden disappearance of the

Opium and open the door to a room full of steam, snow shoes, and at night in the blood
Flat Rock Hudson unclear, recent Bank of war leaders, amnesia Laurel focus on what to play
River, Lamb stew creativity, boiling mud sit Bowery

Total car and bad music, I color
The harpsichord bridge, which is located in the glove box with dark
Theology of wood surrounded by orange flame round of TB Harlem crowned world
To play all night to catch the story of writing poetry - Yellow Magic

Bread, vegetables, and English Heart - Lung Borshti cooked rotten animals in the dream
Egg drop Meat Song Search

Total time pulled the alarm, but over the next decade, landed on the roof and every day
In the opening of the shop Antique, wrists need, I cried and old

Free beer can forget forget Brooklyn Bridge to the island of spirit, and soup kitchens in Chinatown

Frustration at the left side of the window and dark underground places PASSAIC fall, not run Group LP jazz 1930 graduate of Scotland and Germany, the European country, and after that scream, run the roaring furnace, air horns, walking, groaning in the bathroom, competitive and big ears

In Addition, It Is The Best, (AKA F For Howl)

Birmingham jazz and the last day of the attack at the table hot rod - School prison

After 72 hours, the vision, a vision of Mine, it's a dream, and the
Denver Denver Chung, consider waiting in vain in Denver in Denver,
Denver died I saw her again loned, and finally, the hero of Denver

Cathedral of the chest and legs, light hair fall into his head to pray in, save azdusza
In fact, criminals do not live in attractive, is broken and green alkatra Island (alkatra) and royal spirits in prison

Buddha ation Harvard and black Narciso and the South Pacific-style bar or from the vehicle, or Rocky Mountain - I WOODLAWN Mexico and Daisy

Hung jury, trying to be smart to check the hypnotic sound of the fans Teach
White granite decrease in the Teachers salad, potatoes and shelter in the ass College in New York presented the brain that are expected before the end of the debate on the
Specific insulin electric spa table tennis expert Psychology and forget meter letrozole

No, no, arrows reverse catatonia lost tennis icon
In fact, probably the city room, VIC Madtowns a bald head, fingers, and see tears in the blood

Love the moon rocks have higher body image, dreams zyciakoszmar - five and smell ROCKLAND State GREYSTONE Haji mobilc banking, security officer wine cave at night to prevent the soul Open

Finally, mother *****, home to a large external windows, outdoor Furniture, Furniture, wall maps iostatnia last day Trip at the end of the hanger 04, 00 iostatni receive phone broke in the closet green, yellow sheets, empty hopes, illusions tylkotroche Rose -

Oh, I'm sure, in fact, the price that Carl, I see myself as -
Operating on the streets cold wielokropkasrodka using Alchemy Records
vibrating with love and surface parameters

Eterna ship through the rainbow of mental zestawrzeczownik soul and
dance elements, see the description of the dream images, the difference
between the two images omnipotens again another time and place

You can step back and bad grammar, prose, dam disappointed, I shake, but
the soul of the Adaptation of the rhythm of Thought,
Angel beat me crazy, you know, but when he died, perhaps in the future,
I tell you:
If you add a spiritual revival in the U.S. Golden horn sounded, the radio
yesterday, RAM deadpan sabachthani jazz Saxophone filled with love in the
heart of the city, crying and shade

In addition, the autopsy thousand years, I ate my heart.

Two.

Cement and aluminum, as well as the importance of the skull and brain
food sfenks? What

Moloch the Mystic! Soledad! Off the road! Torture! Imperial Point of ash-
tray! Children screaming under the stairways! Sanglote army boy! Park,
the old cry!
Moloch the Mystic! Moloch the Mystic! Moloch the Mystic imagine! Good
Molochbez! Moloch the Mystic soul! Molochciezki judging other!

Molochniepojete jail! Conference Molochcrossbone soul imprisoned and
painless! Moloch the Mystic judgment on the house! Molochrozlegly War
on Rock! Moloch the Mystic SURPRISE!

Moloch the Mystic is a good car! Moloch the Mystic money does not work!
Moloch the Mystic 10 fingers! Moloch the Mystic jestkanibal dynamo!
Smoking disaster Jestgrob Moloch the Mystic!

In Addition, It Is The Best, (AKA F For Howl)

Moloch the Mystic thousand blind eye to Windows! Moloch the Mystic,
larger than endless! Moloch the Mystic hoarse voice and a picture of the
fog! Moshe Moloch the Mystic crown antenna tube!

Moloch the Mystic stone oil unconditional love! Moloch the Mystic soul
is electricity and banks! Jestwidmem Moloch the Mystic bad! Jestchmu-
ra klonal Moloch the Mystic Drink water! Moloch the Mystic name Jes-
tUmysl!
Is sensitive and I sit alone! The dream of angels, I'm bad! Moloch the Mystic! Moloch the Mystic ugly people! Morro do not blame me!
Moloch the Mystic wounded soul! Jestemswiadomoscia brittle hair!
Moloch the Mystic worry about my natural ecstasy! Moloch the Mystic! I
wake up in the Mystic Moloch! Heaven!

Moloch the Mystic! Moloch the Mystic! Apartment robots! Invisible to the
neighborhood! Financial bones! Satan blinded capital industry? Impound-
ment! Indomitable spirit! Hani rock! Big bomb!
Broke his back until Moloch Mystic Sky! Sidewalks, trees, radio, too! Our
place is heaven! If you

Sean! In the days! Hallucinations! I do not know! Will be available! The
U.S. dropped!
Dreams! Hat! Details! Vera! The main source of stress for the rest Canary
Islands?
Success! Song! Flip your head! I Cut the deluge! Movement! Inspiration!
Fear! 10 animals for one person cried! Heart! A new love! Generation of
angry! The Rock!
The St. smile! When I saw! Eyes crazy! Without crying! Say goodbye to the
people! I jump off the roof! Only! Twin! I take the flowers! In the bottom
of the river! Streets!

Three.

Carl Solomon! ROCKLAND, I'm with you

I guarantee
ROCKLAND, I'm with you

It is very curious that the
ROCKLAND, I'm with you

My mother, to follow Shadow
ROCKLAND, I'm with you

12 people were killed and Secretary
ROCKLAND, I'm with you

The approach will be to you Mtacheka eyes
ROCKLAND, I'm with you

If made, it will be cruel
ROCKLAND, I'm with you

Please note that the difference between the radio -
ROCKLAND, I'm with you

, Which means that basic skeletal
ROCKLAND, I'm with you

You can not miss the chest Utica
ROCKLAND, I'm with you

Taken from the body of alcohol Bronx nurses
ROCKLAND, I'm with you

Prevention screaming table tennis game, you have a real pond
ROCKLAND, I'm with you

In Addition, It Is The Best, (AKA F For Howl)

Be the hands and psychiatric disease (mental hospital), eternal death,
eternal virginity, voice tight fortepiandusza never
ROCKLAND, I'm with you

More than 50 natural disasters and crisis, empty soul worshipers -
ROCKLAND, I'm with you

Fascist National socialist revolution in Germany before the oven is too hot
Doctors complained that dzialkiHebrew
ROCKLAND, I'm with you

Mass island paradise, always, life is not serious, it can be returned in the
human Jesus
ROCKLAND, I'm with you

More than 10,000 people angry the last line of the international comparison
ROCKLAND, I'm with you

, In the Night przescieradlaStany U.S. kissing, hugging coughing, sleep
ROCKLAND, I'm with you

Term standards, the Spirit of the walls, roof houses and heaven and angels
knife bombyszpital comma Excellent body o Free to 'wake up to the idea that
we have here - forget Milosierdziawieczna lingerie nailed the successful
ROCKLAND, I'm with you

This is the dream I was walking on the streets at night in the United tear
falls from the door

San Francisco, 1955-1956 .... Five Carl Solomon

In addition, it is the best, (AKA F for Howl) is a 'patacritical inter-
rofesto – simultaneously a 'patacritical interrogation of Allen Ginsberg's
poem Howl and a manifesto for Generation F. It also supplies the lyrics to

135

the noise opera F for Howl by the band F, which will be featured on their forthcoming album F2.

Technical notes: English > Polish > Spanish > Japanese > Macedonian > Icelandic > Swahili > Chinese (trad) > Basque > Vietnamese > Haitian > Creole > Tamil > Irish > Gujarati > Slovenian > Javanese > English One.

Kurt Thomas

"We're Here To Help."

Dring the first few months of the recession, I was living in San Francisco and working part time at a newspaper. Having been laid off from a high-profile, nationally distributed magazine, my little job at a small community newspaper was humbling, to say the least. I used to have no problem providing for myself. Then, suddenly, I was 40-years-old and working odd jobs to supplement my meager income. I stuffed envelopes for a law firm, sold what was left of my CD and DVD collections and even hauled film equipment for a porn studio. Things eventually calmed down and I started getting more design work but, for a time there, I was really struggling. My only solace was that everyone else was in the same boat as me. Including my good friend Jamie. Having recently moved back to the city from traveling around the world, playing guitar in a band and surfing, she came home to find she couldn't get a job either. Like me, she worked odd jobs all over the Bay Area - which is why we rarely saw each other. It was a shame too, since we had known each other for years and, when we got together, it usually meant trouble.

When we were younger, our reputations preceded us throughout San Francisco. We were gainfully employed, young, alcoholics back then, and were known for our bad behavior. At work or over drinks we'd hatch plans of spreading mayhem throughout the city. Or, *adventures* as we preferred to call them.

For example: Years ago, in a dive bar out in the Tenderloin, one of the guys who worked there kept walking over to the entrance of the men's room and would just stand there, staring at us. He wasn't ugly, but he wasn't exactly the sexiest guy either. Though, he was Asian, and both Jamie and I had a thing for Asian men at the time. We decided that, whichever one of us he was cruising had to offer him oral sex in the bathroom. The one he wasn't into had to buy the next round of drinks. We shook on it and marched to the bathroom to confront him. He looked surprised and uncomfortable as we approached him. We got in his face and demanded which one of us he was interested in.

Long story short, he may or may not have been into me. I say this because, to this day, we can't remember the exact events that led to this outcome. I do remember putting a condom in my mouth and rolling it onto his penis with it. (That's how the hustlers in West Hollywood taught me to do it when I was a kid.) After I took care of him, he pulled up his pants and quickly left the restroom stall. I spit out the condom onto the floor and just sat there on my knees, smiling at Jamie who was standing in the entranceway. She conceded defeat. "Well, let's face it," she said, "you won the bet, but I think you may have just raped that guy. You were a little... forceful."

"Oh, whatever." I shot back as I stood up. "I helped him out and I won the bet. Everybody wins!"

That's all that either of us can remember from this particular adventure. But there were many others. Years later, she quit drinking (I "cut back") but we went on to become life-long friends.

One night, after a day of hauling and storing equipment for the porn producers, I noticed Jamie had left me a message on my cell phone. "Yo, Kurt! I'm living on the downtown now. Call me back!" She still had her tomboy, surfer voice and attitude. It was nice to hear. It made me feel young again. An accomplished surfer as well as musician, Jamie's an indomitable character. She's tall, athletic and thin, with broad shoulders from years of paddling surfboards. All the surfer dudes wanted her and she had her share of boyfriends, but I was the only guy who was always ready for an adventure. And from the sound of her message, she may have found one ready for us to tackle.

I called her back, and my suspicions were confirmed.

"Dude! We have to meet right now. I found a crazy note on a wall at a coffee shop. You have to read it!"

I hadn't heard her that excited in years, and, with her being as broke as I was, we hadn't much to be excited about lately. I agreed to meet her downtown at our favorite greasy spoon to see what all the fuss was about.

We met at a diner called The Grubsteak in the Polk Street area of the city. It was an old streetcar converted into a diner back in the 60's. It was popular with the hustlers and crooks in the 70's and even after 30 years, it still exuded a dirty, sexy vibe. I met Jamie outside. We hugged, sat at the counter and got down to business.

"OK, so, oh my God... Read this!"

She pulled out a letter sized, handwritten note from her bag. It was folded neatly in half and up in its right-hand corner was a small, colorful illustration of a young boy and girl playing with puppies and kittens. The sentences were written in perfect cursive. That, combined with the puppies and kittens, told me things were about to get weird.

> *To whoever reads this—Please, we need your help...*
>
> *My husband and I live in a small apartment in the city. We are simple people who work hard and keep to ourselves. Recently, my husband has been the victim of a plot to destroy our lives. Someone has tapped our phones and is listening in on our conversations. They've even tapped our computer and iTunes. They can now manipulate the sound waves coming from these, and most electronics in the rooms, in order to control our thoughts and eating habits. We're afraid to talk, eat, sleep or even move in our own home!*
>
> *Please, anyone with FBI training or counterintelligence experience, PLEASE contact us immediately. We can compensate you for your time.*
>
> *Thank you!*
> *-Chiaki*
> *415-xxx-xxxx*

I put the note down and looked at Jamie. I didn't know what say. I knew it was authentic. Jamie wouldn't go to all that trouble just to trick me. "Jesus Christ," I said to her, "We have to call them!"

We both busted out in excited, laughter and agreed we'd take the case. After a few seconds, we settled down, and immediately began coming up with a plan.

This was just what we needed. An adventure to dust off our tired, broken, spirits. We didn't order any food. We just sat there for about an hour, drinking coffee and planning out how we'd approach this.

The plan would go like this: We would pose as agents from a secret organization called Center for Truth. I suggested we call it this because it was the name of a weird, non-specific, religious center near where I grew up. The group's building had been abandoned before I was born, but it stood empty for decades. My childhood friends and I were convinced it was a portal to another universe and that the inhabitants therein were monitoring us. So, obviously, the name was a perfect fit. Then, we'd call the number on the note, introduce ourselves and chat a little to get a feel of what was really going on, then proceed if we felt like we could pull it off without getting stabbed and eaten by a crazy person.

We'd also need some "counterintelligence" equipment. Jamie had a toolbox in her pickup, full of various things that might come in handy. And I still had keys to the porn studio's storage facility. They had all sorts of stuff. One thing they had was a replica of a *Star Trek* tricorder. It was a toy but it lit up and made lots of "science-y" noises. It was used on a sci-fi porn shoot I was hired to help out on. I promised Jamie I'd clean it off before I brought it along.

We decided against uniforms, mainly because we were broke and couldn't afford to put any together. We both had our list of items that each of us were expected to contribute and with these in hand we parted ways until we were to meet up the following weekend when it was all going to go down. Then we'd call our distressed clients and rush to save them.

The weekend came fast. We met on a Saturday morning just a few days after we decided to pull our stunt. We each had our equipment with us. I brought the pornographers Star Trek toy tricorder. Jamie had her toolbox full of your standard tools, but she also brought a surprise.

"Check this out," she told me, "This belonged to my grandfather's brother."

It was a vintage, 1950's hearing aid. It was the kind that looked like a transistor radio with an earpiece attached to the top of it by a long, thin wire. It was perfect. Between that and my tricorder, we could pick up *ALL KINDS* of secret transmissions.

Having gotten all our devices together, it was time to make the call. We sat in Jamie's truck staring at the note.

"We're Here To Help."

"So, we're doing this, right?" she asked me.

I reassured her that I was in 100% and then dialed.

The phone rang a few times. As it rang, it occurred to me, if these people really think that they're being monitored, why would they pick up the phone?

Just then, someone answered, "Hello?" It was a woman's voice. Her voice was soft, cautious and quiet.

"Hello. We came across your note in the café and we're here to help." I tried to lower my voice a little to sound authoritative.

And then, suddenly, she broke out in tears. "Oh, thank you! Thank you for calling me!" She was crying and thanking me over and over.

By this time, I had put the call on speakerphone. Her sobs filled the cab of the pickup. Jamie's face became stern and determined. I felt like shit for preparing to take advantage of this poor woman. But, my curiosity got the best of me. We were still a 'go.'

"Miss, miss, please. Calm down, we don't have much time. We need to make this brief. My colleague and I are ready to come by to help you. We're from The Center For Truth, a private organization based here in the city. We have dealt with this before. Allow us to come by and help you tonight."

She had quieted down to listen to me and excitedly agreed that we should meet immediately. "Yes, please come over tonight! The monitoring is worse in the evenings."

She gave me her address and I told her we were on our way and hung up.

There was a few seconds of silence between Jamie and I as we took in the moment and steadied ourselves. I still wanted to go through with it. And I knew she did too.

"Look," I said, "It's too late to back out. We have to go through with this. That poor girl is counting on us now."

Jamie agreed, "Yeah. That's exactly what I was thinking. Let's go. Just try not to laugh when we get there and start doing this. I know how you are. Don't break character!"

I promised I was committed to the bit and she drove us over.

Pulling up to the building where she lived, we were surprised at how nice it was. We were expecting a dingy, old wreck of a place somewhere near the Tenderloin but it was actually a very elegant and ornate building in the upscale Nob Hill area of town. This was a relief. There are no knife-wielding cannibals in Nob Hill. They're all down in the Haight.

We got our things together, laughed a little at ourselves and walked up to the front entryway. A few seconds later our client buzzed us in and we went to her unit. We were sober, serious, professionals.

As we walked down the hall towards the unit she was at, a head stuck out of the door at the end of the hallway. It was her. She motioned us to come down. She was a young, pretty Asian woman. I could see no sign of drug abuse in her face or even a crazy eye -- which made me think, "*Damn, maybe these people ARE being monitored!*"

We stood at the door and she extended her hand to welcome us. "Hi. My name's Chiaki. I can't tell you enough how much I appreciate this. My husband and I are at our wits end. He gets back from the hospital next week and I'd really like to have this taken care of by then."

She was dressed like a downtown professional and well spoken. "Please come inside. But remember, speak low. They're listening, right now!"

The apartment was well-decorated and sophisticated, just what you'd expect from a place on this side of town. She brought us into the kitchen where we unpacked our things as Jamie began the scripted interview of our client.

"Thank you for inviting us over, Chiaki. My name is Agent J, this is my colleague, Agent C. Our organization has many years of experience with this type of harassment. First off, I have some questions for you."

Damn, Jaime was good. Stone faced and serious. And she was right, she does know me. I was starting to find the whole thing hilarious. I clenched my teeth, to keep from smiling, and let her do all the talking.

"When exactly did this start?"

"About three months ago."

"Do you or husband work for the government or any government agency?

"No. We're both school teachers."

"Any children in the house?

"No."

"Any idea why you're being targeted?"

"No. None at all!" Chiaki looked around the room and became animated. "This whole thing is a nightmare. A few months ago, we were eating dinner here in the kitchen and it started. Buzzing sounds like bees or hornets came out of the walls. It's an electronic, kind of, popping sound, like electricity. It's a signal, you see. And we can hear voices embedded in it. It can come out of anywhere. The light fixtures, the faucets, even my husband's fillings."

And there it was, the key to understanding what was going on. It was with the husband... and his fillings.

Only two types of people think they're being monitored through the fillings in their teeth. Truly crazy people, schizophrenics usually, and drug addicts.

"Why is your husband is in the hospital?" Jamie asked.

"Oh, he's addicted to pain pills. He's in recovery. He's much better now."

It then seemed obvious that this poor woman was being pulled into her husband's drug induced dementia.

"Oh, OK." Jamie said dryly. "This won't take long."

We unpacked our gear and began our performance.

As per our script, Jamie was up first. She pulled out the antique hearing aid and placed the earpiece in her ear. She turned it on and a few, tiny, lights lit up on top of it. She fiddled with the dials and motioned it side to side, scanning for the interlopers', non-existent, signals.

"Wow, what is all this?," Chiaki said as she reached into my bag. She pulled out the Star Trek toy and held it up to look at it.

I thought to myself, "If she only knew where that came from."

"It's just your standard, Air Force issue, Tricorder," I told her.

She handed it to me and said, "It looks like a toy."

I panicked slightly. Was she on to us? "Oh, I can assure you this is NO toy," I told her, "They used a device like this to track down the Oklahoma City bombers."

She seemed impressed and so, I turned it on, and joined Jamie who was sweeping the apartment. The toy really did sound just like the equipment on the Starship Enterprise. The beeps and pinging noises it made put on an impressive display.

Jamie turned to me, with the hearing aid still lit up in her hands, and said, "I'm getting some residual, intercine, trace signals from behind the couch."

"Intercine?" I thought. She had obviously settled into her role and was just pulling words of her ass.

"Oh yes!" Chiaki said, "Sometimes we can even hear them calling out each other's name, around there, near the couch. And..." She stopped cold, closed her eyes and placed a finger on each of her temples as though she was trying to mentally tune in to one of her imaginary signals. Her eyes popped-open and she got excited, "Listen! Hear that?!"

Jamie and I looked at each other. We couldn't hear anything. We didn't know what to do.

So, trying to stay in character, I pointed my tricorder towards Chiaki and pressed every button on it. Jamie frantically turned the dials on her vintage hearing aid as well.

We both followed Chiaki around the living room, searching for whatever it was she was hearing.

After a few seconds of doing this, I noticed a sound coming from the apartment above us. It was a TV. And just then, someone upstairs shouted out, "Turn the damn thing up, Brain. I can't hear them!"

Chiaki looked back at us and panicked, "See? *That's them.* They don't realize we can hear them through the signal. They're going to turn it up. *You have to do something!*"

Just as Jamie and I were trying to come up with a plan of attack, one of the buttons I pushed on my Star Trek tricorder activated a new sound... and a new problem for us to solve. Chief Engineer Scotty exclaimed in a Scottish brogue, *"Captain! I'm giving her all she's got it!"*

Eyes wide, Jamie flew around and pointed to the tricorder I was holding, signaling me to turn it off.

Chiaki's back was to us. She heard the recording come out of my tricorder and quickly looked back towards the kitchen and pointed, "There! The signal is being generated from the kitchen. They must be having trouble increasing it. Now's the time to do something while they're distracted!"

She was pleading with us to follow her into the kitchen and work our magic.

Jamie stopped her and tried to take control of the situation. "Chiaki, I need you stay here in the living room. Agent C... to the kitchen!" She comically, bounded past me to the kitchen.

I followed, less dramatically, as I double-checked my device to make sure that I turned it off. Once inside, we were both trying not to laugh too loud while we came up with a plan to wrap this up fast and get out of there.

We had to somehow produce evidence that the problem was minor, and that we had solved it. And at the same time explain that the mysterious voices, the people upstairs, were really just her neighbors. The longer we stayed, the more time our client had to put it together that we were frauds.

Jamie had the solution. "Let's take one these metal disks I have in the toolbox and present it as a bug of some kind. Then we'll just have to tell her that she's just hearing her neighbors."

I agreed and so she took a silver, quarter-sized metal disk from a plastic container in her toolbox and put it a tiny plastic bag she had in her pocket. We walked back into the other room and showed it to Chiaki.

"Well, well, well. Look at what we found under your sink." Jamie held up the baggy containing the metal piece and presented it to Chiaki. "This is what we in the business call, 'The Silver Fox.' It's a device the Russians used during the cold war to triangulate and amplify coded signals to their agents in Europe. It worked great, except for one thing, it picked-up thought patterns from everyone nearby."

Chiaki's eyes were popping out of head. She hung on Jamie's every word.

"Over time, a few of their agents went nuts and killed themselves because of this. So they stopped using them. Now, only computer hackers, mostly teenagers, like to use them for fun. This is the only one in the house. You and your husband are safe. You were never in any real danger."

Chiaki stared intently at the source of her and her husband's problems. "It's so small. How can something like this cause so many problems?"

Upstairs the TV was still blaring and the people watching it said to one another. "Damn! Did you see that?!"

Chiaki heard them and came unglued. "No! Hear it? You didn't get them all! The signal is still active! They're watching!" She began pacing the room trying to zero in on the voices upstairs.

Jamie calmly walked up to her and placed a hand on her shoulder. "Chiaki, those are just your neighbors. The signals coming from this device got you and your husband so worked-up, that you started to think everything you heard was coming from it. That's the problem with these kinds of pranks; they fold reality into their insidious plan, making it even more destructive. It's over. We've stopped the signal."

Chiaki looked at us both. Her face was morphing back and forth from denial to relief. Finally, the later emotion won out and she collapsed onto the couch behind her. "Oh thank God. Thank God this is all over."

Crying into her hand, she then thanked us over and over.

Jamie and I quietly packed our things and prepared to leave.

Chiaki came up to thank us one last time before we left. "Again, you've been like angels coming to rescue us. I realize now it was only a prank, but, with my husband in and out of recovery… well, it couldn't have come at a worse time. I want you two to have this…" She held out a hand to each of us holding a fifty-dollar bill.

I shook my head telling her she didn't need to do it.

Jamie grabbed hers quickly and cut me off. "What Agent C means to say is that we're not just in it for the money. Isn't that right, Agent C?"

I got the message. "Of course. Your contribution goes to further our efforts to expose this threat. Thank you!"

Chiaki gave us each a hug and walked us out.

Outside the building, while we were packing up, I had to say what was on my mind. "Listen, do you really think we should've taken her money? I don't feel right about it at all."

Jamie tossed her toolbox onto the bed of the pick up, looked at the ground, then thought for a few seconds. "Look, don't get self-righteous on me now. We need the money. And she's obviously loaded so what's a hundred bucks?"

I tried to talk over her, cutting in to expand on my reasons for my feeling uncomfortable about the money, but it was no use.

"Settle down and listen to me. Look at it like this: we helped give her peace of mind, and she bought us groceries for the week. It's kind of like that time we got hammered and you blew the dude at that bar. Yeah, it's a little fucked-up. But, in the end, everybody walks away a winner."

Hills Snyder

Sliding Into Home

It was the smell of weed that first brought us together.
I was sitting in my car shortening a joint by lighting one end on fire while
dragging on the other. I was parked on Thirty-Fifth Street outside the gates
of Laguna Gloria, a good place to be doing what I was doing. He was walking by, heading for those gates, when four fingers of smoke beckoned him
to be tapping on my window.

It was a time when a certain *Groover's Understanding* still held.
Nothing had been re-mastered yet and I was still someone who rented the
occasional VCR from a 7-Eleven, usually in the middle of the night. So the
signals were still authentic, analogue, happening now.

I had once felt the magic driving down Congress Ave at three AM.
Some guys in the car next to me were passing a number and gave me a look
that suggested I roll down my window. We drove all the way from the capital to the river, passing it back and forth between the cars, easing through
the flashing traffic lights without really stopping, just driving close and
grinning.

So he knew and I knew that he would climb into the passenger seat
and partake. But it did take me by surprise when he removed his leg before
shutting the door.

I liked it that he felt that comfortable.

As we passed the joint back and forth across the front seat, he told
me about sliding into home.

He had been an American nineteen year old in Viet Nam and like

147

all those other boys he'd been taught to hit the dirt whenever he heard the sound of incoming ordnance.

That particular day, the day when he heard that sound, the sound he'd heard many other days, he went down, just as he'd been trained to do. The shell he was dodging hit close, but not close enough to do him any harm.

He was twelve years old and as he rounded third he was already seeing himself sliding in, right foot first, beating the incoming throw by a split second, crossing the plate --- just as he'd been taught to do.

And when the moment came for him to go down, that's what he did. He slid.

I can still picture it perfectly, just as he described it. The heel of his right leg striking the edge of the plate first, his left leg tucked under with his left hand trailing in the dirt, the right hand in the air as if to signal the completion of the run from third --- the cloud of dust, the score, bringing one in for the home team.

And he was seeing it too, just like that, just like that in his mind, the day he heard that sound and went down.

He was picturing it, he was twelve years old, he had good eyes, but he didn't see the land mine that happened to be there, right there under the plate, right where he slid into home.

His name was Jackson Tomorrow. I was thinking about him yesterday as I was getting ready to write this very short story. This one right here:

It's Too long

In those days we were two artists sitting on a porch. We would pass the time watching whatever happened to occur in our view. We rarely interrupted those times with words, unless something random required it.

But one afternoon, I said to him, Jackson, the next time I do a show, I'm going to call it *If You Don't Like Dogs and Children, Go Fuck Yourself.*

He thought about it.

After a good while, he said, No. It's too long. Just call it *Go Fuck Yourself.*

Paul Chavez

Dog-Man

She peered sadly through the double-paned, bulletproof glass with faded blue eyes. The crevices of her smoker's face arranged themselves into a false smile.

"Hey Phil, how are you doing?" she asked in her husky voice.

"I'm doing fine," he lied.

"What can we do for you today?" Nancy asked dryly in her typical nonchalant manner.

"Can I get $255?"

"Sure, just make the check out for $300," she replied as she turned away to begin preparing the loan documents.

Phil wrote out a check from a bank account with a negative $1,200 balance and post-dated it two weeks hence.

He was grateful for the air-conditioning at the payday loan center. A heat wave had broken out a few days before on his 40th birthday, and it was an easy 90 degrees at the mini-mall at the corner of Washington and Lincoln in Venice.

Nancy stood about a foot away punching figures into a terminal as Phil engaged in another round of banal conversation. She told him about the engine problems she was having with her car and that it had turned out to be a blown head gasket.

"That's $800," Nancy informed Phil, who already was well aware of the high cost of auto repair. "That's enough about me and my complaining."

Her voice turned particularly saccharine as she asked, "How are you doing?"

Repeat customers make payday loan operators the most money and Phil knew this was Nancy's attempt at friendly customer service. He felt dirty and disgusted with himself for being there and secretly hated her for being his paymaster.

"I'm looking forward to the beach. The water has been really warm lately," Phil responded with a gritted smile.

After Nancy directed him to initial "here, here and here" and sign and date "right here," she asked if he wanted a copy of the contract.

"No thanks," he replied, not wanting any evidence of his payday loan advance lingering about.

Nancy counted out $255 in 20s, a 10 and a five and slipped it under the thick window.

It almost had the same feeling as collecting winnings at a Las Vegas casino, but not quite.

"Thanks," Phil said.

"No problem. See you again," Nancy said.

Phil promptly made a beeline to the doughnut shop two doors down and calmed his growling stomach with a maple bar, a jelly filled and a small carton of chocolate milk.

He gave the cashier a $5 bill and bought a Super Lotto ticket with the change. If he won the $156 million jackpot on Saturday, Phil promised himself that he would buy Nancy a present. She hadn't asked for a bank statement for months, irking some auditor somewhere, and that had kept his emergency cash flow available. Phil considered buying her a carton of her favorite Westchester cigarettes for the humor of it, but decided instead on a Home Depot gift card of $500 if he won. He started to step over the old pit bull lying in the doughnut shop doorway, but the behemoth suddenly sat up and wagged her tail. Phil instinctively dropped to his knee and caressed the blessed animal.

There was something saintly about being poor. Enduring poverty, along with opening schools, founding hospitals and being Italian, has historically been one of the most sure-fire ways to become a saint.

It's not like sainthood was a goal for Phil, but he found some solace with his life after realizing that being completely broke had a certain piety to it.

Dog-Man

Poverty had other side benefits, too. Phil had shed 15 pounds since being laid off a little over a year ago from the newspaper. His number had finally been called after 20 years as an ink-stained wretch. Up until now, he had been one of the lucky ones, always able to remain employed and doing something that he loved. The downsizing had started way back early in his career with everyone blaming "media consolidation" for the layoffs.

The newspaper industry sort of caused its own collapse. Phil had first noticed that something was wrong just out of college when he landed a job as an intermediate clerk in the advertising section of a zoned edition for the paper. The country was mired in a deep recession at the time and also prepping to invade Iraq for its incursion into Kuwait.

Phil had thought he'd be given a column or something with his political science degree from UCLA, but instead he was writing two-line ads for people trying to sell cars and puppies. He envied the reporters and editors on the other side of the wall who showed up every day in khaki clothes and possessed a certain gravitas.

He was listening to the radio in the office the day before his 23rd birthday when the sweet sound of a woman's voice interrupted the regular news report and plainly said, "The United States of America has just declared war on the Republic of Iraq."

That was weird, he thought, and wrong. Is that how the most powerful nation in the world declares war these days, with an official announcement from a woman, the givers of life? It seemed strange.

After bucking the odds and transferring from advertising to the editorial side as a clerk, murky dreams of being a reporter all of a sudden seemed more tangible. He had to move, of course, down to San Diego to work again as a clerk for the local daily edition, but he didn't mind that at all. The job was tedious most of the time. He opened and sorted the mail for the reporters and editors, took the newspapers down to the recycling center, typed in movie times and worked Friday nights on the high school sports desk cranking out football box scores.

The reporters and editors took Phil under their wing, probably the same way they had been taught. He soaked up the lessons eagerly and soon had clips in the Metro, Business, Sports and Calendar sections, enough to land him a two-year temporary reporting job at a newspaper in Tacoma, Washington.

He made the long drive up there and began his reporting career in earnest covering the bedroom community of Gig Harbor, just across the Tacoma Narrows Bridge hanging over the narrows of Puget Sound. He was there for only three weeks when he learned that the San Diego bureau had closed down. Some of his friends were transferred to Los Angeles and Orange County and the rest were laid off. Just two years earlier there had been three daily newspaper options for residents of the nation's fifth-largest city and all of a sudden there was only one.

The Tacoma paper turned out to be a grand and educational experience. He quickly rose from weekly suburban reporter to night police reporter to the paper's premier position of daily general assignment reporter. Homicides, fires and anything else destined for the top of the fold were handed to him. His front-row seat at the theater of humanity made him squirm. A 16-year-old cheerleader stabbed to death by a family friend with a history of violence against women, a five-year-old Native-American kid shot in the chest in a seedy motel room, a toddler eating a hamburger poisoned with E. coli, the baby beaten to death while Child Protective Services looked the other way, all part of the job. The senseless child funerals weighed heavily on him, though. Whenever there was a lull in the action, he'd take a break and hang out back by the printing presses. There was something magical about the whole process, watching the paper get laid out, photographed and plated. Ironically, it was the high and rising price of newsprint that continuously chewed on newspaper profits.

The newspaper industry also had become bloated with more editors than reporters at nearly every paper--big and small. Managing editors, assistant managing editors, news editors, city editors, assistant city editors and project editors took up the office space while a shrinking number of reporters walked the bare-thread carpets of the newsroom.

It sort of had it coming, really, and the downward spiral was well underway when the Internet came along and pretty much slayed it. The remnants were polished off by the Great Recession as newspapers folded like tortillas across the nation. Phil had done well for himself, though, working for the news division at Microsoft in the heyday of the dot-com bubble and later moving back to his hometown of Los Angeles with a national reporting gig. He had started from the bottom floor, maybe even the basement, and reached his goal of being a reporter in his hometown.

Yet, here he was putting his key into the door of his beat-up grey 1997 Honda Accord with 237,112 miles on it.

Dog-Man

I really need to clean this thing, Phil thought, as he looked at the dozens of fast-food wrappers, spent Rockstar fruit-punch cans and boxes of cigarettes covering the passenger seat and floor.

Phil opened his unlocked door, rolled down the two right-side windows that still worked and drove to his ground-level studio apartment just off Abbot Kinney Boulevard over by the French Market Cafe.

A few strands of upper thigh muscle twitched as Phil's phone buzzed. It was a text from his girlfriend, Mandy.

"Can you go with me to that party tonight?"

Mandy was asking him about the work party she had been mentioning for the past two weeks. Phil normally loved parties, but that was back when he had a good job. Social gatherings had since become awkward affairs, with Phil backing out of conversations once the stupid, "What do you do for a living?" question started making the rounds.

Phil used to like this question because his answer was usually one of the more interesting ones in the room. It typically led to genuine inquiries about his job and he had plenty of stories to share with a normally eager audience. It was no fun being unemployed at a party. Plus, bankers were boring.

"Think stay home tonight. Work on resume," Phil texted back.

"It'll be fun. Palisades. Open bar. Catered. Please."

"OK."

The party had a Midsummer Night's Dream theme, so Phil put on his brown suit thinking it would help him blend in if they stuck with Shakespeare's forest setting. The party invitation listed food, drinks, a three-piece musical act, a magician and a fortune teller, so Phil estimated they'd be there for two to three hours. He did his duty with Mandy for half an hour shaking hands, smiling and feigning interest before he made it to the bar for a much-needed scotch and soda. He overheard a woman talking about the "amazing distressed kale salad" she'd had for lunch and Phil finished his drink in one large gulp.

He ordered another from the tall brunette bartender dressed as a sexy version of Puck in a sheer green dress with just a few strategically placed leaves. Puck poured a stiff drink. Phil took a swig and began to maneuver toward the alpha position.

Phil had picked up this trick about 12 years ago, after working on a story with a CIA contact. The alpha position is that spot where nothing is behind you and you can see all the entrances and exits. It can be used as meeting spot and serves as a great observation point for getting the lay of the land. Whenever Phil was on a story assignment, meeting someone for the first time or just going someplace new, he'd always stake out that position first, observe for a bit and then move in.

He walked opposite the crowd flow onto a short staircase that led to a swimming pool deck and without hesitation opened the waist-high gate, strolled in, closed it behind him and walked toward the shadows. At the end of the pool, he instinctively turned left and walked along a narrow dirt path next to the pool house. The patch curved upward to another terrace level with a basketball court, tennis court and a small indoor gym with a few treadmills, weights and a television. Phil cut across the darkened tennis court that reminded him of his high school playing days, passed through another gate and followed the upward trail of smoothly cut grey stones.

"Holy shit!" Phil said out loud as he realized the size of the party. From his perch he could see the catering tents, the dining area, the magician's stage and dance area where he had been just a few minutes before. He also spotted a 30-foot tall circus tent in a higher adjacent terrace and a party going on inside the mansion next door. As Phil made his way back to Mandy, he concluded that her new colleague owned half the block; pretty impressive even for the Palisades.

The brilliant and the beautiful Mandalina Ignieszka had a half-circle of suits around her when Phil made it back to the party. Mandy looked radiant in her sleeveless white cocktail dress with a scandalously low plunging neckline that showed off her ample cleavage.

She wore a hint of natural-looking make-up that accentuated her sky-blue eyes and she accessorized with just a pair of golden hoop earrings. Mandy finished off her ensemble with a pair of white open-toed gladiator-style Christian Louboutin stiletto heels that made her long, lean legs even more attractive.

The Polish beauty had her blonde hair up in a high bun and looked simple, sexy and sophisticated at the same time. Phil lined himself up just at the edge of her peripheral vision and waited for her glance. As soon as they made eye contact, Phil touched the back of his head and scratched his neck for just a second. Mandy knew the signal well and 10 seconds later scratched the back of her neck as she laughed at a colleague's joke.

Dog-Man

Five minutes later, Phil and Mandy hunched over a table alone and clinked glasses. He was eager to tell Mandy about the gigantic circus tent, the true size of the party and his other observations.

He stopped though to take her in for a minute. She had a slight smirk on her face for pulling off the hand signal effortlessly and Phil realized he probably had the same expression. They both got a kick out of their secret signals and unspoken workings.

I'm lucky, Phil thought, not only is she hot as hell, she's the smartest person I've ever met.

Mandy grew up in New York City and was a bank teller at the largest Chase bank in Manhattan at age 18. She loved banking and finance, it clicked for her, and while going to Columbia University she worked part-time as a loan officer. She studied finance at the London School of Economics for a year and was a bank manager by age 22.

Five years later, she became the youngest vice president of the bank and kept moving up the ladder to mergers and acquisitions, portfolio management and hedge funds.

She was ridiculously brilliant, the only one who could finish Phil's sentences perfectly and the only person who Phil would admit was smarter than him.

"How was your walk?" Mandy asked.

Phil told her everything that he'd seen, squeezing in as much detail as possible, as usual, in an attempt to satisfy Mandy's insatiable curiosity. When he was finished, they both looked at each other and simultaneously said with their eyes twinkling: "We're crashing that party."

Phil and Mandy, without speaking, started thinking about their game plan. The standard protocol for such ventures called for Observation, Options and Outlets, and Mandy silently took the lead.

She grabbed Phil's right hand and held it softly between both of her own, before tugging on it sharply and maneuvering his coat off. Mandy tossed it on a chair, grabbed Phil's wrist and marched them toward the front door, making sure to say good-byes to friends and colleagues.

As they neared the front door, Mandy exclaimed, "Oh, Phil, you forgot your coat. Let's go get it!" and rushed them back to Phil's coat where they exchanged duties as Phil took point and moved them into the shadows and onto the back garden path.

Phil retraced his steps without a hitch and when they had reached his previous vantage point, he pointed toward the circus tent. Mandy reached into his pocket, pulled out his phone, opened his camera app and zoomed in on the scene. She scanned the area, panning horizontally, then vertically. Phil started logging naked-eye details and tried to absorb as much sound as possible. Mandy, after a short time, handed Phil the phone and he mentally outlined a nine-square grid and began a clockwise scan starting from the upper left sector around to the center one.

It was an unspoken rule to provide three options.

"Ladies first."

"Awwww. Thank you, such a gentleman," Mandy said.

"The invite for the Midsummer Night's Dream party said it was a soiree from 4 to 9. There seem to be four distinctly different after-party rooms currently going on in the mansion and the circus likely will start at midnight."

"Option One," Mandy said. "Multiple entry points. Mingle, make way to third-floor bathroom in north-east corner about 11:45, observe from there, head in.

"Option Two. It's a warm August night out. You break out your one-hitter, we smoke a bowl, kill two hours out here and go to the circus.

"Option three. Smoke a bowl and then crash mansion, sneak into circus. There's a fair amount of security, but we'll be fine for sure after the second obs."

Phil loved it when Mandy broke it down and even more so when it matched what he was thinking.

"Third option sounds great to me," he said as he reached into his pocket for his dugout. "This is a sativa. It's called Casey Jones."

Phil pushed the slim white metal pipe designed to look like a cigarette into the cavity of the wooden device and gave it a slight twist, filling its tip with the high-grade medical marijuana.

Mandy took a long drag from the pipe and held the lighter up to eye level, training her gaze at the reflection in the lighter's metal tip of the bright orange ember inside the pipe until it faded away.

Phil packed the one-hitter for himself and looked admiringly at Mandy as she absorbed the entire hit and exhaled nothing. He took a hit using the exact same technique and when he looked up was startled and again impressed by her quick thinking.

Mandy in a flash had let her long blonde hair down and hiked up her knee-length skirt several inches to micro mini-skirt level. Phil followed her lead and took off his tie and moved from tree to tree stripping off large leaves.

Phil handed Mandy a stack of leaves and using her hairpins she attached them around her dress and onto Phil's tie.

Mandy handed Phil a glass filled with ice and scotch and soda about 25 minutes later on a balcony in the lower left sector.

"This party is out of control. You totally fit right in. There must be some kind of huge show planned, lots of fairies and sexy spirits and forest animals running around. A lot of furry girls here."

"Maybe it's a visiting dance troupe," Mandy guessed. "I've heard Polish, Russian and German."

"We've still got some time," Phil said. "Let's go see the fortune teller."

Phil finished his drink, touched his ear and walked in synch with Mandy out of the room and into the hallway. She intuitively let her left elbow linger and Phil kept it loosely in the grasp of his right hand as he subconsciously took on the duty of her personal security.

The young fortune teller sat behind a small round table draped in black velvet with images of the constellations. The table held a deck of Tarot cards and a crystal ball. The fortune teller had long straight red hair, green eyes, thin eyebrows and a flawless, pale complexion. She wore a purple scarf wrapped on top of her head and a slinky magenta dress.

Phil sat on the settee in front of the table and Mandy climbed onto his lap.

The fortune teller gave them a genuinely sweet smile.

"You don't belong here," she said still smiling.

Phil flashed a grin and kept his eyes locked onto hers.

"I'm pretty sure you're supposed to tell me something that I don't already know," he said in a breezy sort of way.

The fortune teller said nothing until Mandy repeated what Phil said a little bit louder in perfect Polish.

The seer closed her eyes for a long minute and when she opened them again they looked dark grey instead of green. She suddenly looked older as she peered into the crystal ball and Phil and Mandy thought they saw lines around her eyes that weren't there before.

"Your destiny," she said in a wavering deep voice as she looked blankly at Phil and Mandy. "Your destiny is to debase, to alter the currency."

Neither one of them saw that one coming. Mandy tugged her ear and they both walked in a quick and deliberate pace out of the reading room, into the hallway and up the furthest flight of stairs until they locked the door behind them in the third-floor bathroom.

The circus tent now glowed a bright mustard color as spotlights raced around inside of it. They took turns peering out the window.

Phil surveyed the situation from their upper vantage point and presented his three and Mandy added two more. They had both decided Phil's first option had the best entrance and exit.

The instantaneous yet well-thought-out ruse had worked as Mandy, clutching a blind-folded Phil's left arm, had navigated them through the choke points by barking orders in Polish and Russian. When she took off Phil's blind-fold, he swelled with pride and love for her for guiding them inside the tent to an ideal dark-cornered alpha position. Mandy kept her arms wrapped around Phil's waist and they looked up to see three naked women on a flying trapeze. A line of 23 young Eastern European beauties walked into the middle ring of the circus, some topless, others in lingerie or just wearing oversized animal head masks.

Sixteen men emerged from behind a curtain in the right ring. Several held bottles of champagne, while others clutched small hand-held cameras. A man in a clown costume carrying a tray of paper cups ran up to the line of women who all took a swig from a cup.

Electronic dance music came on and Phil and Mandy were dumbfounded as a three-ring orgy suddenly broke out. Phil used an emergency signal and squeezed Mandy's left shoulder as he pulled her head to his crotch. She simulated oral sex as a security guard walked by and Phil gave him a sly grin. Mandy, meanwhile, pulled Phil's cell phone from his boot and changed the camera settings.

Mandy said nothing on the drive home and Phil thought to himself that he'd never seen her this angry. He touched her arm and her skin nearly gave him frostbite.

"Those mother-fucking sex traffickers," Mandy finally spitted out, "He gets a $25 million annual bonus and that's how he spends it, with two dozen fresh prostitutes from Eastern Europe."

This was uncharted territory for Phil, who could only imagine the multiple levels of disgust and hate coursing through her veins. Mandelina was a descendant of a veteran officer of Napoleon's famed Polish Lancers who, according to family legend, had twice saved the Emperor's life and was among the vanguard of a memorable charge at Waterloo in which several key British officers met their maker. Phil had never seen this look in her eye and the tightness in her jaw. She looked ready for battle.

"I'm sorry. I was thinking Cirque du Soleil with maybe some burlesque. I had no idea. I should've…" he said before Mandy cut him off.

"No. You didn't do anything wrong. We didn't do anything wrong. Those mother-fucking assholes. I'm sorry. I work with monsters. Those girls were all so young. They could be my little sisters. I don't want to speak about that circus again until I'm ready and please don't tell anyone. Please."

"It's between me and you," Phil said.

As they neared Mandy's townhouse in Venice, she spoke again and asked her favorite question.

"What are you thinking?"

"I was thinking that wealth is the vomit of fortune," he replied. "I also was thinking that fortune teller was totally right."

Mandy nodded in agreement and tears streamed down her face as she leaned in and kissed him.

Phil in the month since the circus incident had become increasingly disgusted with the scoundrels of Wall Street who had brought this country to its knees with their unabashed avarice. To what end, he wondered. Was it worth it? He was still kicking himself for not recognizing what was going on in the circus tent. It was just like that party in the Hamptons last summer, he thought to himself, I should've gotten Mandy out of there.

Flipping through the channels to take his mind off things made his mood even darker. Phil made the big mistake of watching *Keeping Up With The Kardashians*. He got caught in the vortex of fake reality television and the looping ostentatious displays of wealth and privilege. Khloe does seem the most genuine out of all of them, Phil thought to himself. Getting married to Lamar Odom six weeks after meeting him at a Ron Artest party is pretty crazy, though.

Phil laughed out loud as he thought about the times he watched the Lakers with his buddy Cool Keith who every time Lamar touched the ball called him "Lamar Scrotum." It cracked him up every time.

He turned the television off and revisited his favorite day-dream about the aliens—who actually are just us from the future—who take him away after being deemed The Chosen One on a five-year mission to explore the universe. But really, because of the laws of physics and the way hyper light-speed travel works, he comes back in just four weeks.

The electric jolt on Phil's leg interrupted the part where he unveils his fully functioning neon blue light saber at an international press conference.

It was from Mandy.

"Dinner. Movie. My place. Lobster."

Things are working out nicely, Phil thought to himself. He needed to shower and shave. The mention of a movie in Mandy's text was a euphemism for sex that had been an inside joke for a couple of years. It was circa 2004 before the economy fell apart and Phil and Mandy during a particularly intense and long and multi-position high-energy sex session caused Phil to run late for a meet up with the guys for a Bruins football game. When asked why he was tardy, Phil replied for some reason that he and Mandy had been watching *Mean Girls*. They watched *Mean Girls* a lot.

Sweet Mandy gave Phil a long tight hug and lingering kiss upon his arrival.

He heard the familiar sounds of The Edge's guitar in the background and Bono belting out the opening lyrics to "I Will Follow."

"This party's awesome," Phil said.

Mandy had on Phil's favorite look with absolutely no make-up, only fresh-faced, untouched stunning beauty. She lightly pranced into the kitchen and Phil listened as she went over the decadent menu of bacon wrapped shrimp for appetizers and a large lobster each with plenty of melted butter. Phil noticed it was twilight as the song "Twilight" was playing. He poured himself a drink from the bar and once again admired Mandy's collection of Carl Vernet plates depicting classifications of Napoleonic soldiers.

Phil flipped through the thick grey sheets of paper gently and marveled at the vibrancy of the gouache paint after all these years. He was surprised to notice for the first time an unusual detail about the painting of the Chevau-légers Polonais. The image showed a Polish lancer dressed in a dark blue riding suit with a gold vest and matching tall headgear. A scarlet scarf dangled from his hip as he rode atop a charging grey steed with all of its hooves airborne and nostrils flaring, the beast a symbol of his rider's spirit. The lancer pulled his weapon from the prone body of an enemy soldier. The painting of the Polish lancer was the only one in the whole set of 100 plates that showed a man being killed.

Mandy made a delicious lobster meal and after pouring Phil a glass of white wine, she tugged her ear and headed for her bedroom. Phil knew he had some time to let her change into something fun so he stepped out onto her lower balcony, pulled out his one-hitter and lit up some L.A. Confidential while enjoying Mandy's fine chardonnay.

He expected to find Mandy between the sheets when he walked into her room but instead saw three large black duffel bags taking over the bed. Mandy was sitting in an armchair beyond her bed under a bright lamp and looked at Phil intently. Phil took three long quick steps, yanked the zipper open and truly gasped for the first time in his life.

The bag was filled with bundles of $100 United States bills. He grabbed one and thumbed through it and started doing multiplications in his head. He opened the other two bags and they, too, were stuffed with wads of $100 bills. He kept doing the math.

"That's like 25 million dollars," Phil said, louder than he expected.

Phil tried to narrow all of the thoughts racing through his mind and corral them for a second so he could think straight. It's better not to know where it came from, don't ask, that's a lot of money, we can live off that for years, she should donate it, I wouldn't enjoy prison, we should go to Vegas, I could write crappy sci-fi novels for the rest of my life with that, did she steal it, we can be in Vegas in four hours, has she gone crazy, is this related to the fortune teller, what countries have the best extradition laws, she looks so beautiful.

"Exactly," Mandy said. "It's the same amount as Adam's annual bonus. We're going to fulfill the fortune teller's prophecy. It'll settle the score and get it out of my mind."

Phil's mind had calmed down and with his faculties restored he considered his response, weighing the logical input from his brain with the pounding of his heart.

"I'm in. Totally. Let's do this," Phil said with conviction and not a shred of doubt.

Phil volunteered on the spot to handle mission operations and they agreed that Mandy would handle contingency plans and emergency exits. Mandy volunteered to take lead on bill defacement and they both would rehearse and execute together.

"Time is of the essence," Phil said pulling out his smart phone and perusing his calendar. "November sixth, a Tuesday. Hold on a second."

Phil checked the lunar calendar.

"Yeah. Full moon again. Anniversary of Normandy Invasion. That's it."

Mandy agreed. This gave them six weeks to concoct a plan to disburse $25 million in debased, worthless $100 bills throughout Los Angeles. They had to maintain a facade, debase the bills, scheme their options and rehearse. Phil and Mandy both possessed uncanny natural problem-solving abilities and getting caught wasn't part of the plan. They just wanted to make their statement, live out the prophecy and move on with their lives.

"Slice of anchovy," Phil called it, making it all even more official and a reality with a code name and everything. Once it was settled, Phil and Mandy watched *Mean Girls* again.

Phil started creating dossiers the next day for both of them, describing their roles in the three-hour operation that would take advantage of the natural lull in bio-rhythms with a 4 a.m. strike time. The plan called for them to hit the four cardinal points of the city in East Los Angeles, San Pedro, Venice and Sylmar, plus Skid Row, the airport and downtown municipal buildings and banking center. Phil took the code name literally and munched on slices of anchovy throughout the city while figuring out transportation routes, ingresses and egresses, and securing multiple modes of transportation including taxis, busses, light rail, rental cars, subways and bikes.

Mandy took up her tasks with particular vigor and created work stations at her Venice townhouse and downtown condo. She had a few paper shredders, a contraption she made using two soldering irons to burn out serial numbers, industrial slicers, massive hole punchers and a few large baking dishes at her bill debasement stations.

She took particular pride in a technique she developed that involved soaking tens of thousands of dollars in a tea, lemon juice and sulfuric acid solution and then baking the bills in her oven for 45 minutes. The bills were so brittle afterward they would crack and break up into pieces when handled only once.

Most of their rehearsals and dry-runs went off without a hitch, but Mandy, a week before the operation, made three mistakes during one practice that would've landed them both in prison if it had been a live operation.

Phil let her beat herself up over it for 24 hours and then scheduled a midnight meeting.

"I'm so sorry,' were the first words out of Mandy's mouth. "I think I know what I did wrong."

Phil heard her out and flatly told her he disagreed.

"You just need to work a little, just a tiny bit, on your situational awareness. Those were all simple mistakes you could've avoided. You're compromising yourself, I think, by being over-motivated and tired. You've been wearing yourself out on this. I'd recommend taking a break from this a bit, take your mind off it, it'll help you avoid mistakes when it counts."

Mandy agreed, smiled and tugged her ear.

Phil followed her as she walked out of her condo south along Speedway Avenue and caught up with her at 27th Street where she led them toward the water. She grabbed his hand and pulled him toward the lifeguard tower. Mandy kissed him hard as they both started taking off their clothes with the waves crashing just yards away under a crescent moon. They had sex on the lifeguard tower using the ramp and railings in imaginative ways until the dark night started to give way to the first light of dawn. They walked home silently afterward still lost in the erotic glow of the moment and slept soundly for the rest of the morning.

Phil and Mandy developed a new spoken code for the operation, four new hand signals and two whistle signals. They went completely off the grid while developing and executing their plan and met in public spaces and used public signals to coordinate future meetings. At the T-minus 48-hour mark, they met at The Pantry downtown where they grabbed a booth and went over last-minute changes. Phil handed Mandy her 20-page dossier as they tore into a steak and eggs breakfast and Mandy wrote down on a napkin the address of the safe house in Hollywood where they would meet in case something went horribly wrong.

They met several hours before dawn that Tuesday morning and Phil wasn't too surprised to see that Mandy had dyed her hair red and she also wasn't surprised to see that Phil had shaved off all the scruffy facial hair he had been growing. They were both dressed in tactical black outfits and after dumping $100,000 worth of defaced bills in the Venice Canals, they wouldn't see each other for three hours.

Phil felt confident about the operation knowing that every variable had been considered and was in a good mood despite the early hour. Mandy had a giddy look on her game face and a bounce in her step.

She pulled Phil close to her and whispered spiritedly into his ear the famous battle cry from the Battle of Somosierra, "*NaprzÛd psiekrwie, Cesarz patrzy!*" (Forward, you sons of dogs, the Emperor is watching!)

Phil was in his bathroom looking at himself one last time in his dreadlocks wig and green-and-yellow Bob Marley T-shirt when he heard Mandy letting herself in.

She had on a black bob wig and was wearing a new purple and pink Nike workout ensemble.

They had agreed beforehand that they wouldn't watch the news until 8 a.m. and they had about 25 minutes to kill. They both changed into pajamas and settled onto Phil's bed. He grabbed the bong from his nightstand, packed it with Blue Dream and handed it over to Mandy. She lit the bowl, inhaled deeply and filled the glass cylinder with a thick haze of smoke before she pulled the carb and cleared it. Phil packed himself a bowl and did the same thing.

Mandy let out a long sigh, no doubt thinking about the last three hours she spent spreading millions of dollars of defaced bills throughout the city.

"I hear ya, sister," Phil said as he walked to the refrigerator and pulled out a small carton of chocolate ice cream and two spoons.

He turned on his 42-inch flat-screen and tuned to Channel 9. Pretty much all hell had broken loose throughout the city. The bills scattered on the freeways caused several SigAlerts that brought traffic to a halt; LAX was closed down as the bomb squad investigated a ticking bag filled with shredded $100 bills; Union Station was evacuated while a ticking set of expensive luggage stuffed with burnt bills was detonated and the LAPD was on tactical alert throughout the city after small riots broke out in Skid Row and the Pico-Union area as people clamored for $100 bills that somehow disintegrated on first touch.

A joint news conference with the Chief of Police, the FBI's lead field agent in Los Angeles and the camera hungry Los Angeles County Sheriff was coming up live in 10 minutes. The Secret Service was investigating. Mandy flipped it to CNN and they also were covering the Los Angeles Money Riots. They interviewed a woman who opened up a large manila envelope marked Finders Keepers on her Red Line subway train at Vermont and Sunset and found it stuffed with $25,000 in $100 bills with the serial numbers burned out.

"Why would someone waste good money like that?" she cried with real tears in front of the camera. "Why would someone do that?"

The Mayor issued a statement asking for Los Angelenos to act calmly and promising the perpetrators of the "prank" would be held accountable for any violations of city code, state laws and federal regulations.

Channel 4 broadcast a report saying police were looking for up to eight different suspects who they believe may be connected to the "civil disturbance." Channel 2 had an expert on saying he believed it was a protest by a splinter group of Occupy Wall Street.

Mandy pulled her iPad out and held up Yahoo's front page to Phil. The top story headline read: "L.A. grinds to halt as money frenzy leads to fighting, gridlock" and had more than 1,000 comments. It was also the lead story on the L.A. Times and was already on the national and international wire of The Associated Press.

They could hear helicopters overhead as people were waking to find worthless money floating in the canals, tucked underneath their windshield wipers and stacked outside the bank by Windward Circle.

Phil and Mandy giggled and outright laughed throughout the news conference, especially at the Secret Service agent who promised the perpetrators of this "treasonous" act would serve time in a federal prison.

"Good luck with that," they both said simultaneously as they erupted in laughter.

The story dominated the news cycle for 24 hours and then slowly dissipated.

Two weeks later, Phil was daydreaming about the secret spaceport he built before returning to Earth by himself in the spaceship provided by the aliens. His spaceport on the Saturn moon of Titan had a 250,000-square-foot lab where his robots worked on his backup spaceship. It was also where he stored all the treasures that he'd be given while on his five-year space odyssey and it was home to his super-secret cloning experiment.

His leg had a minor spasm as his phone buzzed. She always texts me during the good part, he thought to himself.

"Meet me at my place at 6. Have to show you something."

"OK," Phil texted back.

Mandy left the door ajar and was sitting on her couch. It looked as if she had been crying.

Phil sat down next to her, put his arm around her and asked if she was OK.

Mandy pointed to an envelope on the coffee table and Phil opened it. The envelope contained an invitation to an upcoming Nutcracker-themed holiday party hosted by her co-worker Adam and its main graphical element was three sexy ballerinas.

"We didn't change anything," Mandy said in a hoarse whisper.

Phil suddenly felt nauseous and dizzy and there was a sharp pain out of nowhere in the middle of his stomach.

"I need to get some fresh air, Mandy. I'm just going to walk around for a minute, I'll be right back," he kissed her on the top of her head as she sat in a catatonic state.

Phil stumbled down Mandy's walk-street onto Speedway for a few blocks and walked up an alley and rested his spinning head sitting down on some back steps. What the hell just happened, he thought to himself. We got something wrong. He started backtracking through the whole operation and circled back to the fortune teller.

It dawned on him that the prophecy had been misinterpreted and they had taken the fortune teller's prophecy literally when she said it was their destiny to debase the currency. We thought she meant the fiscal currency, when she, in fact, had meant more than that, he thought to himself. They were supposed to alter the social and political currency instead.

The cold night air made Phil shiver and he instinctively curled into a fetal position to keep warm. He noticed a mouse scurrying in the adjacent carport, scavenging for food until it came across a discarded crumb, reared on its hind legs and scarfed it down before disappearing again into the darkness. What a carefree and simple life that mouse enjoyed, Phil thought to himself, that pitiful creature was perfectly happy in the cold with only the bare necessities.

Phil kicked off his steel-toed black boots, pulled off his socks and jeans and yanked off his grey V-neck T-shirt and underwear. He looked into a trash container and found a large square piece of dirty, ragged woven wool cloth. He wrapped the grey, coarse, threadbare rag over and under himself twice-fold. He immediately felt liberated.

From now on I will sort the counterfeit people from the solid currency and rail against the social custom that has caused so much moral decay. I will nuzzle the kind, bark at the greedy and bite the worthless. I am Dog-Man.

Dog-Man secured a four-foot tall wide ceramic jar that he rolled around Venice accompanied by a pack of stray dogs. His most constant companions were the two yappiest Chihuahuas ever created, Paco and CheChe; a sweet German shepherd mix with soft brown eyes named Betsy, gentle pit-bull called Stella and the 50-pound lapdog Otto.

He parked his mobile home on the Westside of the boardwalk outside of the divey Venice Bistro, turned his tub upside down and sat on top of it.

Dog-Man pulled his cloak down over his shoulders and hiked the ragged cloth up his thighs and sunned himself. After soaking up as much solar energy as his heart could handle, he walked over to the boutique on the other side of the boardwalk. He stood directly in front of a statue resembling the Predator from the sci-fi movie starring former California Gov. Arnold Schwarzenegger. People are idiots, Dog-Man thought to himself.

"Practice makes perfect," he said smiling to the Predator.

"If you've already helped someone else out with a little charity, I deserve some as well," he said to the deadly alien warrior. "And if you haven't helped anyone out yet, now's a good time to start."

A young brunette in her 20s in a black silk dress overhead him, stopped and asked what he was doing.

"Before begging, it is useful to practice on statues," Dog-Man replied.

The woman smiled and offered him a dollar bill. They struck up a conversation and she eventually started asking him advice about her boyfriend.

"When should someone get married?" she asked.

"For those who are young, not yet, for those who are older, never at all," he replied.

He told her about Mandy and how she left him when he renounced all his possessions, family and friendships.

"How does that make you feel?" the woman asked.

"If Mandy can live without Dog-Man, than it would be absurd if Dog-Man cannot live without Mandy," he answered truthfully. "No one can live with me as a companion; it would be too inconvenient."

He explained to the lass that to own nothing is the beginning of happiness and he did not beg in the streets for charity, but for his salary.

With that, he excused himself and walked over to his upturned jar and stood on top of it with his feet shoulder-width apart, shoulders pulled back and bearded jaw jutted.

"I am Venice's one free man," he barked out loudly several times in a row, "The porches and streets of Dog Town were built for me as a place to live. I learned from a mouse how to get along: no rent, no taxes, no ridiculous grocery bills from Whole Foods!"

A crowd started to gather as the Dog-Man, with a pack now of 12 dogs sitting, sleeping and playing all around him, gained momentum with his rhetoric, logic and quick wit.

"I pissed on the man who called me a dog," he bellowed out as some in the crowd giggled. "Why was he so surprised?

"We are more curious about the meaning of our dreams than about things we see when wide awake. The contest that should be for truth and virtue is for swag and trendy belongings instead."

"What is the most beautiful thing in the world?" a man in the crowd asked him.

"Freedom of speech," Dog-Man replied.

He picked out a young man in the crowd who had stopped for half a second to listen. "Hey you, give me a dollar. Yeah, you in the red shoes. You're wearing $300 Yeezy Nikes. Give me a dollar. Come on, you've got a dollar. Do it for Kanye!"

The cowed boy reached into his pocket, pulled out a crumpled bill and put it in the paper bag next to the sleeping-beauty-giant Stella.

"Against fate I put courage; against custom, nature; against passion, reason. Happiness is this, and nothing else, to be of truly good heart and never distressed, wherever one is and whatever the moment may bring. Your mind and soul should be perpetually at peace and in good cheer," he told a rapt audience of about two dozen people.

A bald man passing by took a look at the homeless beggar and snarled at him, "Get a job, you fucking loser!"

Dog-Man had become accustomed to regular gibes from passers-by, but his audience was a bit startled by the interruption.

"I will not insult you in return," Dog-Man called out to the man. "I will simply congratulate your hair for fleeing from such an ugly and evil head."

The audience erupted in laughter and donated generously to Dog-Man, who kept his proselytizing going straight for several hours.

In the mid-afternoon, the homeless beggar counted up his haul. He left the dogs behind and took a bus down Lincoln Boulevard to Jefferson and walked up the street to the Home Depot where he bought a $500 gift certificate card. He took the bus back to Lincoln and Washington and walked into the payday loan center.

Nancy didn't recognize him and Dog-Man quickly slipped the gift card under the window.

"That's from my friend Phil," Dog-Man said before turning and walking away.

Dog-Man went to the doughnut shop and with his remaining few dollars bought a maple bar, a jelly-filled and a small carton of chocolate milk. His stomach growled later that night as Dog-Man curled up in his ceramic tub with a new cuddly collie named Ella obsessed with playing fetch.

If only I could free myself from hunger as easily as from desire, he thought to himself.

Dog-Man was begging and lecturing on the boardwalk and was approached by one of his neighbors who asked if he was going to Ron's party.

"I'm turning that invitation down. The last time I was there, he was not thankful enough that I came," Dog-Man said. "I will instead be going to David's party in the canals."

Dog-Man slipped into the party later that night and began taking in the fine environment. He examined the precious paintings adorning the walls, the Scandinavian-designed stainless steel kitchen, the large, sleek black leather furniture and the luxurious buffet of food.

He stood in front of a tray of sushi and pulled off pieces of salmon and octopus and ate them on the spot without a plate or chopsticks.

"Hi, there. Welcome to the party," the host said to Dog-Man. "I was wondering, if you want, we have some slippers here that you can borrow, since you're kind of barefoot."

"No, thank you, David. I'm fine," Dog-Man replied.

As David studied him, Dog-Man gazed upon the premises once again, cleared his throat and suddenly spat directly into David's face.

Startled, angered and embarrassed, David scowled at Dog-Man.

"What the hell was that about?" he demanded.

"It is the universal custom in human society to spit in the worst available place," Dog-Man answered. "I wouldn't dare spit on your polished Italian marble floors or million-dollar paintings."

The host remarkably did not have Dog-Man kicked out of the party and the beggar holed up outside in a corner with a bottle of red wine. A group of young men and women recognized him from the boardwalk and began whispering about him. They started tossing their chicken wing bones at him and jeering, "Here you go Dog-Man. Here you go. Be a good boy."

"You don't feed chicken bones to dogs, you idiots!" Dog-Man sniped at the youths who scurried away as he started to urinate on them.

Dog-Man hated buying things and much preferred to borrow what he needed, or better yet receive it as a gift. He was explaining to a Venice mom in her 40s holding a yard sale on Electric Avenue how much he hated sellers and she patiently heard him out until she ran out of patience.

"Can I borrow that lantern?" Dog-Man asked.

"You can have it," she replied and handed over an old green Coleman kerosene lantern from when they used to take the kids camping.

The corners of Dog-Man's eyes slightly wrinkled as he smiled and thanked the woman.

The sun felt particularly charged as it blasted the city with scorching heat and blinding brightness. Dog-Man walked to the corner of Abbot Kinney and Venice boulevards, sat in the shade of a tree and lit his lantern. He found the device fascinating, particularly the purity of the flickering flame that he could extinguish and re-ignite at his whim and pleasure. He turned it off and switched it back on and got a kick watching the hot wick relight it. He pumped up the lantern and increased the pressure.

Dog-Man got up with his lantern on and walked down trendy Abbot Kinney holding the lamp up above his head.

"I am looking for a good man," he repeated over and over as he swung the lantern in front of people. He walked up the street looking with his lamp in broad daylight and couldn't find one. He carried his lantern toward the beach and down the boardwalk mingling with the weekend throng of humanity, but his search was fruitless.

Darkness descended and Dog-Man gave up looking for a good man and headed back toward his jar. He tuned out and started to day-dream about the aliens who picked him for the inter-stellar, multi-dimensional adventure based on the quarter-sized birthmark on the back of his right hand and the inkblot birthmark that started at his index vertebra, spanned across his shoulders and ran halfway down his back.

He didn't see it or hear it coming, but felt the attack instantly when the folded chair struck the back of his head. The blow sent him careening and stumbling in a zigzag pattern. Dog-Man turned around but that wasn't a good idea as he was swiftly punched in the face, breaking his nose. Blood gushed out and he absorbed another body blow from the swinging chair.

"Get the fuck out of Venice! You don't belong here," screamed the Mexican gang-banger who lived in Echo Park. "Get the fuck out of Venice!"

The outraged gang member punched and kicked Dog-Man and struck him with the chair until he lost consciousness. Dog-Man had been mugged, robbed and beaten at least a dozen times before, but this attack was the worst. When he regained consciousness, Dog-Man crawled off the boardwalk into an alley and curled up behind a dumpster. The dogs found him and wailed at his broken bones and then they started licking his wounds.

Dog-Man eventually healed and resumed his normal activities. He woke up one day about 11:30 a.m. and noticed everyone on the boardwalk rushing around. Shopkeepers were washing their windows and tidying up their shops and police on bicycles were riding along. Dog-Man wasn't sure what was going on, so he pushed his ceramic jar onto its side and wheeled it around in a figure-eight pattern so he could look busy, too.

It turned out that the President was in Los Angeles on a fund-raising trip and was stopping by Venice to make a speech about his 10-year plan to end homelessness. Dog-Man was sunning himself and day-dreaming when he noticed someone stepping in front of him.

"Hello there, sir. I am the President," said the man in a blue suit with warm brown eyes.

"I am Dog-Man."

"What can I do for you?" the President asked.

"You can stop blocking my sun," Dog-Man responded.

The President moved aside and the two men had a hushed conversation as cameras clicked away. The President was seen wincing twice and smiling three times.

"I have to say, if I wasn't the President, I would want to be Dog-Man," the president said at the end of their conversation, just loud enough for the crowd to hear.

"If I wasn't Dog-Man," the beggar said in an equally clear voice, "I would want to be Dog-Man, too."

Dog-Man had been learning Spanish from the kind Mexican busboys and cooks in Venice who called him "El Perrito" and gave him food at night for himself and the dogs. Armed with his new language skills, Dog-Man borrowed a beat-up bike from a friend and started pedaling south.

He walked across the U.S.-Mexico border easily enough and bounced around the dirty, broken streets of Tijuana for nearly a week. The Mexicans were poor but kind to El Perrito, who started to miss his pack of dogs in Venice.

Dog-Man was making his way back over the border when he was stopped by officers from the federal Mexican police force.

"What is your nationality?" the federal officer asked him.

"I am a citizen of the world," Dog-Man answered.

The federal officers weren't in a joking mood and became irritated with the scruffy man in the ragged cloak. His insults in Spanish didn't help his cause and Dog-Man soon found himself roughly tossed into the local jail.

Dog-Man's mind and his kind soul took a beating along with his body in the Mexican jail. A sub-human instinct kicked in among the other inmates who sensed a weakling and started pushing and striking him like a human pinball until he ended up naked and cowering in a corner. Both of his eyes were nearly swollen shut and blood poured from the bridge of his nose and dripped heavily from his nostrils and fattened lips. Dog-Man leaned forward and raised his knees to his head. He rested his thick dark beard on his wrist atop his right knee. He felt his swelling ankle with his left hand.

Dog-Man

Thank you fate for dealing me this unpleasant hand, he thought to himself. I will savor this hardship and be ever more grateful of my freedom and the kindness of men from here on out.

Dog-Man worked on his Spanish in prison and made a sport of tormenting the guards by mocking their positions, their religion, their uniforms and their looks. He would routinely get beaten, but endured the torment and gained his revenge by howling throughout the night and keeping everyone awake.

During one of his regular stints in solitary confinement, Dog-Man was hauled out and escorted to the warden's office. The warden had heard too many stories about his "crazed" prisoner who had unnerved many of his guards and wanted to learn more about him.

"What do you do for a living?" the warden asked him in perfect English.

"I am the governor of men," Dog-Man replied.

"I am the warden here. I don't need your services," the prison chief told him.

"That is true," Dog-Man replied. "But he needs me."

Dog-Man pointed to the deputy warden sitting to the right of his boss in a wrinkled uniform, his hair disheveled and eyes slightly crossed.

The warden looked at his dim-witted son-in-law and internally agreed with El Perrito. He decided it was best to rid himself of this troublesome prisoner by granting him home confinement with Hector and his daughter Maria Elena. El Perrito could help with chores and children and, if he misbehaved, the warden would have him shot and killed.

Dog-Man left the prison that night with Hector and they drove about 15 miles away to a small villa surrounded by white stone walls topped with barbed wire. Dog-Man bowed deeply when introduced to the beautiful Maria Elena, made their young children laugh by pulling funny faces and instantly got along with the family's black Labrador retriever named Dulce.

"A benevolent spirit has entered my house," Hector said to his family.

Dog-Man taught Hector's three young boys and his daughter English and tutored them in math and science. He loved the children more than anything and subtly shared his moral code with them. Dog-Man watched with pride, as the children became teens and young adults who eschewed fancy clothes labels and material belongings. They considered him a second father and wrote him letters when they went to college and shared the highs and lows of their lives with him as they continued their schooling and started their own families.

Dog-Man had acquired a steady stream of new dogs after sweet Dulce died and for his 65th birthday was given a new chocolate Labrador puppy he named Slice because the little creature reminded him of a piece of cake. He was walking Slice around the yard one day and it dawned on him that it was time to go. His body ached and his mind had been slipping. Dog-Man more than 30 years ago had remembered the transcendental number pi to 100 digits and would recite it in his head, particularly after a beating, to make sure his brain still worked. He could only remember about the first 40 digits now.

The old man picked up Slice and sat with the cute puppy at the base of the tallest tree in the yard. He closed his eyes, hit the rewind button and re-examined his life from his childhood, to UCLA, his time as a reporter, the years with Mandy, the fortune teller and his life as Dog-Man. He took a deep breath and held it. Dog-Man focused on the center of his chest and could feel his heart beating. He moved his mind inward feeling his slowing heart as he continued to hold his breath. He sensed a bright white light in the center of his chest pulsating. The light started to fade and everything turned red as Dog-Man felt the most severe pain he had ever experienced.

Maria Elena found Dog-Man's corpse that evening with Slice sleeping in his lap. She and Hector followed his wishes and tossed his dead body over the villa's walls for the animals and nature to devour.

The death of Dog-Man eventually spread and those who remembered him in Venice launched a campaign to memorialize him. They erected a statue of Dog-Man dressed in his ragged cloak, holding his lantern and looking for a good man with a dog wagging its tail at his side. The statue still stands there at the northern end of the Venice Beach boardwalk.

Victoria Looseleaf

The Oudist

Not so long ago, I had a farm in Africa. *A hash farm.*

Well, to be more precise, I wasn't the sole owner of the property, like Karen Blixen and her coffee farm in Kenya, or wherever the fuck that farm about which Isak Dinesen wrote and whom Meryl Streep played in Sydney Pollack's "Out of Africa," in her letter-perfect accent where she got to fuck Robert Redford amid rhinos, rattlers and roasted coffee beans.

Yeah, I had a farm in Africa. North Africa. Morocco, where those rugs in Rabat made for some excellent import-export fronts. The farm, Black Diamond, was named for one of the many varieties of hash we cultivated. It belonged to me, my ex-husband, Rick Wilson, and a rather shady Mexican hombre, a low-life thug known only as Brother Sam whom Rick met when he was in jail for civil disobedience, because whom does one ever meet in jail...but criminals.

I first met Brother Sam, or BS, as I preferred calling him, on Thanksgiving. I'd flown down to the federal penitentiary in Safford, Arizona from Berkeley, where I was studying criminology and the oud, and had smuggled in a silver dollar-sized hash ball I'd wrapped in heart-shaped sheets of blotter acid, this exotic delicacy then shoved up my equally exotic cunt.

Singled out for a strip search, I steeled myself by tugging on a faux-bloodied Tampax I'd also shoved up there in order to dissuade the matron – no Queen Latifah Big Mama she – from sticking her fucking fingers up there, as well.

Oh, I was good.

Finally allowed in the joint, I hooked up with Rick for a quickie, non-orgasmic conjugal visit, after which we joined the other prisoners in the common room, where they were hoovering gobs of petrified-looking turkey that had definitely not been whipped up by my grandmother's black cook, Melverine. Brother Sam, BS, was among them.

It's not that Rick told me then and there of his future international dope-making/smuggling operation, Black Diamond Enterprises, which would also include a long-haired Jew from Bozeman, Montana, whose one and only suit he'd worn a decade ago for his Bar Mitzvah – *baruch atau adonoi meloch holenu holum, le hadleich nar shel, Armani*, puhleeze - but I did get the distinct feeling that this JAG, Jewish American Goddess, was probably parading down the wrong runway.

Shortly thereafter, Rick, in order to have his sentence reduced and be closer to me, volunteered for a space program conducted by NASA that took place on a locked ward in San Francisco's Presidio. The six-month experiment, simulating weightlessness in order to measure calcium loss, was classified government stuff, should Sir Richard Branson, Le Bron James or Justin Fucking Beiber ever manage a voyage to fucking Mars, Elon Musk's Hyperloop, notwithstanding.

In a nutshell, Rick and two other prisoners were forced to lie in bed in darkened rooms, where they never saw daylight (think NASA Goth), ate only freeze-dried foods, licking every proverbial drop, and eventually had 5,000 pills shoved down their throats.

In addition, they were made to masturbate daily, so their sperm count could be analyzed. Now there's a job for you: *sperm analyst*.

There was also a control group of three more Civil Disobedients which Rick was and should have been deemed, had he not gotten convicted and sentenced to six years (and made an example of) but had also refused to let me retain a fabulous Jewish attorney like Alan Dershowitz, though Michael Jackson's child molestation lawyer, Thomas Mesereau, (the dude with a propensity for social justice cases also defended actor Robert Blake), would soon enter this screwed-up picture. (Don't ask!)

The only difference between the two groups, however, was that the C.D.s didn't have to take all those pills. Some control! Meanwhile, I, Isabella (Full of Grace), would smuggle in a rash of recreational drugs that included but was not necessarily limited to LSD, opium balls, which were both eaten and inserted rectally, and pot brownies, because smoking the shit was just not gonna happen.

I had officially arrived as a mule; and my muledom was on the rise, though, frankly, I didn't understand why these guys would wanna get high under those circumstances. But mine was not to ask why; mine was only to deliver the goods. It helped, too, that the nurses looked the other way, meaning I was fucking up this multi-million dollar NASA project big-time, something I would later find out, had been conceived as a kind of publicity stunt - another story altogether.

Ah, to err is human, to forgive... One needs drugs. Valium helped, but back then I preferred Quaaludes, Dilaudid and liquid morphine.

Eighteen months later, Rick was released. I'm not sure how badly jail and the space program affected him, but as soon as he got out he assumed a new identity: Fred Mertz. As for me, after earning three degrees – criminology, psychology and a little old master's in the performance and literature of the oud – I sure as hell wasn't going to go through life as Ethel...Mertz.

So we flew to Europe and bought a houseboat in Amsterdam with my small family stipend.

The 'Isabella' sat on the Prinsengraacht, butted up between a garbage scow and a herring boat. Amid hanging macramé plants and heavily beaded curtains there was a bedroom, a flush closet and the stench of really putrid canal water. The oud I kept in a small attic next door to the Anne Frank house.

I just love the sound of arpeggios in the morning, reverberating with all those Nazi Holocaust memories.

But it was on the floating neo-Motel 6, that blocks of hashish were converted into gallons of hashish oil. Blocks of hashish that Rick/cum/Fred, had made and stuffed into the gas line of a Bentley, the automobile he drove up from our farm in Morocco, the Bentley he didn't get arrested in. This hash-to-hash-oil conversion was odoriferous, highly combustible, and very, very profitable.

Ya gotta love the Dutch. They are so cool, like the NASA nurses looking the other way, they, too, mind their own business, which is why Amsterdam is one of the hippest places on earth to buy, sell, make and conceal drugs for export.

My mission, then, was to cross the Atlantic on the QE2 with four liters of hash oil, concealed in Delftware Bols bottles brought in as duty-free liquor. I was posing as a concertizing oudist returning home – I actually did do a gaggle of oud recitals that summer, traveling with a custom instrument, one that had been made expressly for me in Abu Dhabi - laden with press clippings, wooden shoes, gouda cheese and desiccated tulip bulbs.

After an extremely rough crossing that necessitated my snorting some heroin from the bindle I'd tucked away in the right index finger of my cashmere-lined leather Balenciaga glove, one of a pair I'd been feted with after a concert I played in Nervi-By-the-Sea, I breezed through customs, sans junk (I'd snorted it all, ostensibly to stave off seasickness), but the Bols bottles remained intact.

Safely smuggled through New York harbor's Pier 38, the shit would then be sold by Rick/cum/Fred – and crew, including his badly dressed Boseman partner whose foot-long Chinese queue I'd made him cut when we hired that attorney, Mesereau, for $14,000. a pop.

Lucky for me, I'd gotten in a line with an oud-loving customs guy, who even asked me out.

"Call me," I said, gliding off like Michelle Kwan after landing a triple Salchow, "I'm at the Plaza."

Well, I would be at the Plaza, just not then. But after countless trips from major capitals in Europe (Paris, Bern, Rome), to such sundry ports of call as Nassau, Miami, San Francisco and Vegas, with Rick/cum/Fred getting arrested in countries I'd never heard of - Ceuta, anyone? - I called it quits.

I was *finito* being a mule, and a concert oudist: What snorting heroin and cocaine can do to hand-eye coordination is not a pretty sight. So when an acquaintance, a high-priced Israeli call girl named Hedva, who, though she had only one arm did extremely well (she told me she was making money, hand -- one hand, in any case -- over fist), beckoned me into the business, I replied, "And I thought I was *meshuggah*! I'll have to brush up on my Hebrew, Hedva, but why the fuck not?" These are difficult times and I was looking for something stable. "Dead Sea, here I come."

Harry Dunn

I Don't Ever Want My Kids to Work in the Entertainment Industry

There are many dreaded words a father can hear from their child. "Dad, I wrecked the car." "Dad, I'm in a Tijuana jail." "Dad, the pee stick has a plus sign." But none of those words could ever compare to the sheer horror of hearing a child of mine say, "Dad, I want to work in show biz."

Perhaps I should elaborate...

I am a husband and father of three kids. My career has been spent bouncing back and forth between life as a writer and life producing promos for a TV network. It's been an occasionally pleasant but frequently demoralizing ride. The highs are way too high and the lows are way too low. It's career crack. Addicting, unhealthy and way too much suffering has to incur before receiving those rare tastes of joy. All those years of stories that started out with, "There's a producer who seems to like my script...a big agent is going to read my script this weekend, I hope...the producer said if I give him a free option, he'll try to sell it...", and then inevitably end with "I haven't heard back from him/her yet." This is a profession I've regretted pursuing for a lot of years. And, a profession I have adamantly tried to steer my children away from pursuing. You want your children to be both successful and happy, not just getting by and miserable. So I tell them my war stories and it makes it easy for them to reach their own conclusions.

My first real job after college was working in the trailer department for Cannon Films. Menahem Golan and Yoram Globus' company - they were also known as the Bad News Jews. After years of editing trailers for their movies ... in short, putting lipstick on their pigs of movies ... I approached Golan about an idea for a movie that I could make cheaply. He immediately agreed. Wow! From the lowly ranks of trailer monkey to writer/director!

Then I learned a new word: *Schadenfreude*. Little did I know that, behind my back, Golan's assistant was conspiring to derail this project from ever happening. In her mind, if somebody was going to hit the lottery and become the next great young filmmaker, it was either her husband or no one.

So after a week of getting this movie set up, I go to his office where this evil, ugly, mean-spirited assistant had convinced Golan to drop the project. Nothing like having a conversation start with Golan saying, "My people here have told me I should not make your film."

Five minutes later, the movie was dead and five minutes after that, I was back to being a trailer monkey. The assistant smiled. *Schadenfreude* had won the day. Years later, I found out her husband had dumped her and she was living alone in Santa Barbara, unsuccessfully trying to sell her own writings. I think I was happier to hear that news than she was to hear Golan take away my movie.

Cut to ten years later, where I manage to get a staff writing job on the hippest show on the air at the time, "In Living Color". Man, it felt good to nail a gig like that! And it lasted...exactly 13 weeks.

I never really understood what a sociopathic writing staff meant until I joined that one. The head writer had a book on his table called, "The Encyclopedia of Retardation" because he thought it was funny to look at pictures of retarded people. No joke. He also liked to make jokes about his mother's breast cancer. The writer's room was mean-spirited and overflowing in Schadenfreude, as every writer's goal in that room was to figure out who the weak personality was and attack him/her like a lion in the jungle.

I became a target. I was in a great place in life, my wife had just given birth to our first child, I had this cool gig. But the overwhelming negativity, the overwhelming desire to see others fail and that Encyclopedia of Retardation was more than I could handle. Amazing how the coolest show on TV had the most dysfunctional writers on TV. Way cool to get that gig, way too demoralizing to stay at that gig.

If only I'd had Golan's assistant's address in Santa Barbara... I think she would have loved that "Encyclopedia of Retardation". It's the one group of people she could feel geniunely superior to, but that's just in her mind, not anyone else's.

The next 10 years were spent writing for shows that got cancelled. I remember finding out one of the shows I wrote for was cancelled 3 days before Halloween! That's fucking October! They don't hire writers again for the fall shows until April/May, now I was looking at 6 months of guaranteed unemployment! And, I could never get myself out of that lower level writer credit. Story Editor, Executive Story Editor.

I did get one job that lasted a few seasons on a one-hour drama, and the Co-Executive Producer who helped get me the job was the person who seemed to go out of his way to demoralize me every day. There was no winning. I came to the steadfast conclusion that even when you win, you lose.

Then I got a great writing job on cable show where I was respected. I was considered the top writer on the staff. I was sent up to Vancouver to cover the set because I was implicitly trusted by the Executive Producers. I thought I had finally pushed through that wall of demoralization. This was the happiest I'd ever been. And, it had a lot to do with those trips to Vancouver. This is how it would go...

A Towncar would pick me up at my house to take me to LAX. We always flew Air Canada and I always had a first-class seat, which gave me access to the Maple Leaf lounge, their version of the Admiral's Club. There I would get loaded on all the free alcohol they were giving out to big swingers like me. Then, I'd board the flight where every actor you've ever seen on TV would be in first class with you. On one flight, the flight attendant offered me the chance to sit in the cockpit and watch the plane land from up there. Are you shitting me? And, it was amazing! An up-and-coming writer, lavishing in the success of getting the right job, watching a plane land from the cockpit! Then after clearing customs, there was a driver waiting for me to take me to my suite at the Sutton Place. Every day, the transpo department would take me to and from the set. One week, Robert Loggia was starring in my episode and I can remember having dinner with him at Gotham, the best steakhouse in The 'Couv, where he sang a song he had from "Victor/Victoria" that was cut out of the movie. I was the happiest I'd ever been in my career. I'd gone from the "The Encyclopedia of Retardation" to Loggia singing in an exclusive steakhouse.

Then sometime around Thanksgiving, the show was cancelled.

At that point, I finally said fuck this. Working in the TV promo business was steady. If a show was cancelled, it didn't matter to me because another show would come along that I would promote. It's been far less glamourous than dinner with Loggia at Gotham, but it beats unemployment and that "Encyclopedia of Retardation".

It's now over 10 years since that last TV gig. I was done with the dream of being a professional writer. I was focused on my family - things that really matter. Then my best friend since kindergarten and I decided to work on a movie idea, just for fun. We ended up pitching it to Sony...and selling it. Yes, real money! Over 10 years out of the business, diving into my middle age years, and I sold a fucking pitch?!! Are you shitting me?!!

So now my professional life is spent producing TV promos and writing movies. There seems to be a nice and rewarding balance with that, and I certainly have no intention of quitting my day job.

Every so often, I have lunch with a friend who's a struggling writer. We'll talk about what I'm doing for maybe 45 seconds and then the rest of the lunch is comprised of him telling stories about, "There's a producer who seems to like my script...a big agent is going to read my script this weekend, I hope...the producer said if I give him a free option, he'll try to sell it...." And you know what? I legitimately root for all this to happen for him. I've been on the ass-end of *Schadenfreude* my entire career and I have no intention of passing that ill will forward to anyone.

I have a daughter about to graduate from the University of Michigan, a son who's a sophomore at UNLV and a second son in high school. When they talk about their lives after school, I give them one adage, "Be Your Own Boss." There's little joy in answering to other people. Oh, and stay the hell away from the entertainment industry. It's just not worth the peaks and valleys. If you do that for me, we can talk about wrecked cars, Tijuana jails and pee sticks.

Josh Herman

Post Orgasmic Guilt

From Diagnostic and Statistical Manual Of Mental Disorders, 5th Edition, Text-Revision, © 2016 American Psychiatric Association.

DSM-V-TR® Diagnosis & Criteria:

Post Orgasmic Guilt

309.81   Post Orgasmic Guilt

Diagnostic Features

The essential feature of Post Orgasmic Guilt is the development of characteristic guilty symptoms in the moments following copulation (Criterion B). These feelings result from the subject's nagging feeling that he/she should not have engaged in the intercourse presently completed (or, in its most debilitating form, begun and not completed [cf., 302.75 (pg. 556) Diagnostic criteria for 302.75 "Premature Ejaculation"]).

Pre-Orgasmic events that lead to post-orgasmic guilt include, but are not limited to, oral sex, anal sex, frotteristic sex (e.g., "dry humping"), mutual masturbation and genital-to-genital sex.

Specifiers
The following specifiers may be used to specify onset and duration of the symptoms of Post Orgasmic Guilt:

Acute. This specifier should be used when the duration of symptoms is less than 3 seconds or occurs during actual orgasm. (AKA "Hermania")

Chronic. This specifier should be used when the symptoms occur following every copulatory act. (AKA "Chronic Hermania")

With Delayed Onset. This specifier indicates that at least 6 minutes have passed between the copulatory event and the onset of the symptoms. (AKA "Passed Out For 5 Minutes Then Awoke And Felt Guilty Hermania")

Associated Features and Disorders

Associated descriptive features and mental disorders. Individuals with Post Orgasmic Guilt may describe painful regretful feelings following intercourse they know: 1) they should not have engaged in, 2) their friends told them they should not have engaged in, 3) their therapist told them not to engage in, 4) and/or their parents, hypothetically talking about a friend of the subject's, told them not to engage in. Phobic avoidance of the partner or activities that resemble or symbolize the original act may occur, leading to relationship conflict, break-up, or loss of job. The following associated constellation of symptoms may also occur: feelings of shame, despair, or hopelessness; feeling permanently damaged; a loss of previously sustained beliefs (e.g., "I used to have integrity"), hostility towards self (e.g., smacking a full length bathroom mirror crying, "What did you do? Oh god, what did you do?"); social withdrawal (e.g., "[Best friend] told me not to do it, and I did it, I can't face him."); feeling constantly threatened; impaired relationships with others; or a change from the individual's previous personality characteristics.

There may be increased risk of Panic Disorder, Agoraphobia, Obsessive-Compulsive Disorder, Sexual Disorders, Social Phobia, Specific Phobia, Major Depressive Disorder, and Substance-Related Disorders. It

Post Orgasmic Guilt

is not known to what extent these disorders precede or follow the onset of Post Orgasmic Guilt.

Associated laboratory findings. Increased guilt may be measured through studies of autonomic functioning (e.g., heart rate, electromyography, sweat gland activity, ml. of vomit collected after subject runs to the bathroom, puking, after the sexual encounter concludes.)

Associated physical examination findings and general medical conditions. General medical conditions may occur as a consequence of the trauma (e.g., pelvic injury, rug burns, STDs [both somatic and psychosomatic.])

Prevalence

Community-based studies reveal a lifetime prevalence for Post Orgasmic Guilt ranging from 1% to 3%, with the variability related to methods of ascertainment and the population sampled. Studies of at-risk individuals (e.g., neurotic Jews, virgins, Catholics) have yielded prevalence rates ranging from 50% to 75%.

Course

Post Orgasmic Guilt can occur at any age following puberty. Symptoms usually begin within the first 3 seconds following sexual release, although there may be a delay of minutes before symptoms appear, though this is rare. Frequently, the disturbance initially meets criteria for Acute Stress Disorder (see p. 472) in the immediate aftermath of orgasm. The symptoms of the disorder and the relative predominance of re-experiencing, avoidance, and hypoarousal symptoms may vary over time. Duration of the symptoms varies, with complete recovery occurring within 3 months in approximately half of cases, with many others (e.g., neurotic Jews, virgins, Catholics) having persisting symptoms for longer than 12 months after the sexual encounter.

Differential Diagnosis

If an Anxiety, Depressive, or Sexual Disorder develops following this trauma, these diagnoses should also be made.

185

Diagnostic criteria for 309.82 Post Orgasmic Guilt (POG)

A.   The person has been exposed to a copulatory event and, post-orgasm, has a feeling of general worthlessness for one of the following reasons:

(1)   Partner is currently involved with another partner of his/her own

(2)   Patient is currently involved with another partner of his/her own

(3)   Partner is a co-worker

(4)   Patient is *really* drunk

(5)   Partner is someone, for some reason, you promised yourself you would never, under any circumstance, at any time, have relations with. At all.

B.   Five or more of the following symptoms are present in the immediate period following sexual release due to excessive guilt:

(1)   Ashamed mood, as indicated either by subjective report (e.g., feels disgusted with self) or observation made by partner (e.g., patient appears to cup face in hand and cry like a colicky baby)

(2)   Markedly diminished interest or pleasure in all, or almost all, recent sexual activity, as indicated either by subjective account (e.g., patient feels need to punish self) or observation made by others (e.g., patient runs to bathroom to vomit in a symbolic act of Freudian undoing)

(3)   Significant weight loss due to pints of tears leaving eyes and/or neurotic sweat

(4)   Insomnia or hypersomnia while partner gleefully falls asleep post-coitus.

(5)   Psychomotor agitation or retardation in post-sexual-release moments (e.g., falling off the bed, slamming into the wall)

(6)   Fatigue or loss of energy in PO moments

(7)   Diminished ability to think or concentrate, or indecisiveness, nearly every PO second (e.g., "I shouldn't have done that, yes it felt good, but…what have I done? You have a boyfriend! I feel sick…")

(8)   Recurrent thoughts of death (not just fear of being killed by partner's partner) or recurrent suicidal ideation (e.g., "the only way out is death")

Post Orgasmic Guilt

C.   The symptoms do not meet criteria for a "Pukes Episode."

D.   The symptoms cause clinically significant guilt or impairment in post-coital functioning.

E.   Your name is Josh Herman.

Mary Woronov

Love?

I did fall in love again. His name was Jack and he was one of those guys who party hard and fuck everything they can get their hands on. Definitely not the guy you want to fall for. I went to bed with him, to get him out of my system, but it didn't work. I loved him.

It was that same feeling; he even looked like Charlie, my old heartbreaker. When he made love to me, there was nothing to hold on to; I was slipping over the edge, while it was just routine for him. If this was bliss, I couldn't enjoy it. It was a surrender I couldn't give up, especially to Jack, who was faithful to no one. I backed away from him as if he was contagious, but I couldn't leave him. Instead I hung around in the awkward position of a friend, lamely refusing to fuck him again.

Unwittingly, I joined a group of girls who were all in the same position, the only difference being he refused them, whereas I had turned Jack down, which made all the difference in the world to no one but me.

These girls talked incessantly about Jack about how he was such a great writer and how he was doomed from the beginning. Some said it wasn't his fault and others said he deserved everything he got. But we did agree, it started with his parents. Even Jack knew they were to blame along with the blind biological urge all men carry below their belt buckles, and all my girlfriends insist that the latter is no excuse even though it has been going on since the beginning of time.

From what Jack told me about parents, they were no great enigma. As a matter a fact they were pretty ordinary. His Mom was a Catholic martyr and his Dad was an extremely entertaining bastard. His Mom was a waitress all her life, while his Dad was a bartender, lothario, natty dresser, great dancer, drinker and incredible storyteller. To say that Jack's Dad fucked around on his wife would be a very subterranean understatement. The sad thing was that everyone including Jack accepted this arrangement as set in cement, while still saying things like "Poor Mom." One can only surmise that all families need a good underdog to pity, especially when the underdog herself feels the same way.

Hanging out with Jack, I kidded him about how much he was like his father, who he hated. How he always bought expensive shoes. How he was such a great storyteller that he decided to become a writer, which fit nicely into his schedule of unemployment. How he was so handsome that one could say he was only doing his duty, because most women wanted to go to bed with him.

It was the neighborhood joke that anything left in a room with Jack would get fucked by him inside of five or ten minutes. Sometimes he would party for three days straight finally waking up in a new girl's arms, across town, without his car.

Even I had to admire Jack's stamina as he kept this up, while others stumbled into AA. Jack himself admitted to being very distracted by women, especially redheads. I was a redhead.

Secretly, I was confident that if I sat in enough bars listening to Jack, he would fall for me. But he didn't.

He fell head over heels for Jill, leaving me to realize what a farce our friendship was. Jill had red hair and the sweetest disposition of anyone I'd had ever met. Now that Jack was in love, he was unbearable. Still I was unable to end our friendship and admit that I longed for him, just like all the other girls. So I had to suffer through every detail of their love.

How she didn't mind supporting Jack, because she always wanted to be in love with a writer. How she didn't mind his fucking around on her, because she didn't know. How she believed the most convoluted blackest lies he told her, because she just couldn't believe that the man she loved would lie to her. How she also loved fucking him in any manner he wanted, and Jack had to admit that every time he came to her from another bed she tasted infinitely better than the woman he just left and he was thankful to be home. However, to my intense satisfaction, the very next day he would be on the pussy prowl again.

Love?

When Jack confided in me that he was so in love he was bothered by his infidelities. It didn't make sense to him that he couldn't stop. I was quick to ease his conscience, "The male member has never been known for its logic. Only women are logical when it comes to sex. Women think, "Will he make a good father? A good home? A good provider when my looks are gone? That kind of stuff turns them on even if the guy is overweight or slightly bald. Men, on the other hand, don't think at all. They see, and either get hard or not. And that's that. No amount of reason seems to make any difference in this area, so why fight an uphill battle? It's just going to make Jack resent Jill."

What tortured me was that, in spite of all his cheating, every day, Jack fell more and more in love with this woman. It was maddening, every day, he was happier than the day before, even after he married her.

Actually he was so happy, he kind of pissed the rest of us off. My girlfriends and I spent endless amounts of time exclaiming, "How could she be so dumb?" and, "I can't believe he gets away with it!" It was our most favorite topic and we all became very emotional and indignant about it, even though it really had nothing to do with us. Let's just say it was our favorite way of venting our own frustrations and we had a lot of them. After all, most of us were in bad relationships that had little to do with love, and the rest of us weren't getting laid at all.

I wasn't getting laid.

Not getting laid in LA is a sin. From the movies, which insist you are not happy without sex, to the fashions, which are about looking sexy instead of good looking, not getting laid is a sin. Even your family wants to know if you're getting laid, and if you aren't, they feel sorry for you. I don't mean to be a conspiracy theorist, but it's obvious that our society is run by males, who want women thinking this way so it is easier for them to get laid. I mean there is no rock you can crawl under without someone screaming, "Had your sex yet? You're a pathetic worm if you're not getting any!"

And then, to top it all off, here's Jack, fucking everything under the sun. Plus, he's in love with a really great girl. It's excruciating, unfair, and none of my business, but anyway, I called Jill and told her.

I also told her it wasn't just hearsay, because I had partied with Jack and been to bed with him myself and I was one of her best friends.

Needless to say his wife stopped talking to me, but what was even more crucial, she stopped fucking Jack. She kicked him out of their love nest. They went through a short period of seeing a shrink together but it was hopeless. She no longer listened to his excuses and told him in no uncertain terms that after the divorce she planned to move and never see him again. Luckily, she never told anyone, it was me, who ratted on Jack.

When I saw Jack again, he was sleeping in the office of the little construction company he was running, a job he snagged just to show her he was changing his ways. It was one in the afternoon on Saturday and I woke him up. The place was very dirty – not a good sign. While I made coffee, Jack opened a bottle of Rainier Ale, otherwise known as Green Death. He walked into the parking lot in the back and took a shower under the hose.

Jack had hit rock bottom and the fall had been on all fronts, emotional, mental and even physical. He moved like a deeply wounded bull, unable to understand or fix the cause of his pain. When I talked to him, he stared straight ahead, answering in monosyllables, only when pressured.

I had told myself I was only going to see him to commiserate with an old friend. Actually, I was going to see how the mighty had fallen, and secretly I was going to try and erase my own guilty part in this little scenario which was rapidly turning into a tragedy, leaving me in the role of Iago, someone with no redeeming features, whom the audience loved to despise.

And since there was no audience, I was worried that I would be forced to despise myself, a job that my low self-image was all too good at. So, what I was really doing that Saturday afternoon was trying to pull Jack back up to a human level and get him to say something like, "It really didn't matter," or "Women are all the same," or to just admit that he was the kind of womanizer that was incapable of really falling in love. I mean, he cheated. He got what he deserved. Only a moron couldn't have seen this coming. Nobody in his right mind could feel sorry for him. He was wrong, and now, he should snap out of it.

"Jack, here, I made you some coffee."

No response.

"Here Jack, coffee. Stop drinking that shit."

"It's my last beer. I'll stop drinking. Maybe in five or six years, she'll see I've changed." Jack suddenly went from standing, to a kneeling position like an animal receiving an arrow to its chest, "Tell me what to do," he roared, "I'll do anything."

In the silence that followed, I could hear the pieces of his heart hit the floor. I could not stay. I didn't even say good-by. I felt so insignificant next to his pain.

Jack did stop drinking for a while, but he never stopped hurting. I like to think that's what made him such a good writer. When he got the Man Booker Prize, I thought, "Wow, I had something to do with that." If it weren't for me, he probably wouldn't be as famous as he is today, but of course, I never said anything to him.

He moved to New York, and I'd like to say, it was like a tooth being pulled. The aching finally stopped; I'd like to say that.

Sure, I'd like to say that while I'm pushing the chrome basket in the rat maze of food known as the supermarket. Sometimes I do forget about Jack when I'm doing freeway eighty in my car. Things are great until the vegetables in the back seat start complaining, "We're wilting. We wanna go to the refrigerator. Take us home."

"Shut up," I yell. My knuckles and my lips are an odd sort of yellowish white. "I won't be obligated to a head of lettuce, do you hear me?"

I know I'm having a conversation with a vegetable. "Wash me off. Pat me dry. Now put me in the crisper." I mimic the lettuce in a high-pitched snarl, as I careen into the parking lot of the Town House Bar on Sunset. "Get it through your head you're nothing but a God damn little ball of green shit, and I'm not carrying you to happy refrigerator land."

I slam the car door. "You can all just die in those plastic body bags. In this heat, it won't take more than an hour."

In the bar, it is cool and dark. Men brush by me like predator fish trying to sense the smallest hint of a come-on. I feel naked, vulnerable, like a lobster without its shell, and I start frantically digging in my purse like I want to climb into it. When the bartender asks me if anything is wrong, I order a Bloody Mary and sit perfectly still at the bottom of the bar, so the other fish will leave me alone.

But, that isn't why I'm here, to be left alone? This apple didn't roll very far from the tree after all. So I haven't done such a great job with my life...I have to stop comparing my life to hers?

I can still hear the raspberries sobbing softly in the back seat of my car. "Fuck them, they're only two dollars a box," I smile to the stranger next to me. He smiles back, as he softly touches my leg.

"Do you know the Motel 6 down the road?" I ask him.

Martin Mundt

The Magruder Film

Carl Truax pulled the bell-chain and heard the opening riff from "I Can't Get No Satisfaction" chime inside the house.

He waited on the porch for a full minute, along with a couple of wicker chairs, a round wicker table, and a swinging couch, but no one came to answer the door. He backed to the edge of the porch near the stairs and glanced around at the front of the old Victorian, its windows open, its lace curtains wavering in the breeze. The walls were painted sky-blue and the many windows trimmed in hot pink. Wooden friezes of painted birds, flying fish, butterflies, fairies and angels in exploding fuchsia and shocking lime overlaid all the walls. The whole house looked as if it might through lenses made of psilocybin, just like every other house in the neighborhood.

Half-a-dozen wind chimes hung from the porch-eaves. Big, fat honey-bees buzzed through the rose bushes hunched up against the blue clapboards, and Truax figured there must be hives somewhere in the backyard, just like in many of the old hippie Victorians scattered in the little commune towns north of San Francisco.

He touched the bell-chain, just to make sure it – and everything else here – was real. The elongated silver links of a tongue hung down from an open dragon's mouth mounted on the left side of the door. Smooth, well-wrought, real silver.

He smiled. He'd always wanted one of these old, refurbished Victorians, but on the salary of a newsmagazine reporter, the chances of that were pretty much non-existent. And, he wouldn't give up being a reporter for anything; that had been his life since 1967, since he'd graduated college and joined the staff of GROK Magazine, a paper and staple operation based out of a walk-up in the Haight. A million rags had papered the streets of San Francisco back then – GROK had survived the Revolution; he had survived the Revolution. And, here he was, still chasing a story.

He pulled the bell-chain again. The Stones played, but still, no answer.

He shrugged and opened the screen door. The front door was already open inside. No one locked their doors anymore. He remembered a time, long ago, when people had, but not anymore.

Peace and love ruled the world now.

Indeed, the whole world had become a much different place in the forty-six years since the Summer of Love. A better place, thank Mick. He touched the small silver knife-hilt that hung on a chain around his neck, the handle and cross-piece of a knife, but not the blade.

And besides, he had an invitation, didn't he?

He entered.

Inside, the Victorian smelled of decades of patchouli, jasmine oil, vanilla and candles. And, oddly, Truax thought, bourbon. The foyer was cool and shadowed. An ornate staircase ascended to the second floor. To the staircase's left, a doorway screened with strings of black and gold beads led into another room. To the staircase's right, he could walk down a hallway into the back of the house, probably the kitchen, then the back door.

Thick, patterned rugs covered every inch of floor and stair, in some places even two or three rugs deep. He couldn't tell what kind, maybe Turkish, maybe some other Middle Eastern style, but bright and varied colors, some geometric in design, some flowing. The hypnotic effect of the rugs thrown together on top of each other all slapdash was disconcerting at best, disorienting if unprepared for, and flashback-inducing if he continued to stare.

He looked up at the stairs so as not to sink into the swirling rugs and old trips.

"Hello?" he called, but not too loud. He couldn't bring himself to be loud. His editor had put up signs in the newsroom at GROK that read 'MELLOW' and 'KEEP ON TRUCKIN' and 'CHILL', and this place seemed even more laid-back than that.

The Magruder Film

Truax saw the framed LAST DOLLAR I EVER MADE hung on the wall. That made him smile. Lots of old hippies displayed that very same dusty trophy, framed up after money had been removed from society at the turn of the millennium. No money – no exploitation. It had been hard for some, but not most, not after decades of peace and love and increasing prosperity.

"Hello?" he called out again.

He got no answer.

He felt a faint surge of air slip through lace curtains, then incense, then the beads in the doorway to his left.

He took out his invitation, an eight-by-eight inch piece of white silk woven through with red silk letters: a hand-crafted message the quality of a wedding invitation from a hippie boutique, each letter cursive and smooth as red smoke. It had brought him the hundred miles north of San Francisco.

DEAR MR. TRUAX, I HAVE FILM OF JAGGER AT ALTAMONT. I WILL ONLY SHOW IT TO YOU. SINCERELY, V. W. MAGRUDER

Film of Mick Jagger at Altamont. Well, that was the Holy Grail, wasn't it? The last snippet of unseen film of Altamont had been unearthed ten years before, in 2005, from a farmhouse in Wyoming. It had been a grainy, black-and-white, 8 mm clip, 29 seconds long, of the Stones playing 'Paint It Black', shot from about a hundred and fifty yards away. It had required a year's worth of restoration by the Library of Congress to get that much clear footage out of it.

An anonymous bidder had offered five million dollars for it on the black market, but the owner had donated it to the Smithsonian, so that it could belong to the people. The clip hadn't shown the moment when the world had changed.

Truax wondered why Magruder wanted GROK Magazine in on his film. And Truax. And..., and he wasn't going to find out anything standing here in this foyer.

He went left, through the black and gold beads. They clattered around him like a sheet of soft, slow hail. He found himself in the living room, filled with a huge old couch and beanbag furniture arranged to cover almost all the floor space. One wall held one of the most awesome stereo set-ups Truax had ever seen. Two other walls held thousands of albums.

He smiled. He remembered a gadget back in the 90s called a compact disk, a thing supposed to take the place of the album.

The album was – and always would be – the center of social phenomena.

Just last month he and thirty of his friends had gathered for the first hearing of the latest Santana album – CALAVERA – to listen over and over again, from the first hiss and click as the stylus connected with the speakers, to the last note, all the while passing the unfolded album cover with its fantastic artwork of psychedelic skulls from hand to hand. They drank copious wine, and pot was consumed by all. Friends came and friends went for a weekend of music and discussion of liner notes, and no one ever ventured an opinion into the same river of souls twice.

Try that with a compact disk.

A huge chandelier of candles hung from the center of the ceiling, three tiers high, maybe a hundred or more candles total, all of various colors. Beneath the chandelier sat an upturned bole from some massive tree; Truax figured a sequoia, but he didn't know from trees. It caught the melting wax of the candles like a bowl, years of which had dripped like a random, psychedelic rainbow into the wood, like tie-dyed candlelight.

The fourth wall held dozens of concert posters from the 60s and 70s. Bright graphic blobs from every band that Truax remembered from his youth blazed out at him in pristine condition: The Doors, the Byrds, Blue Cheer, the Jefferson Airplane, Mungo Jerry, the Dead, and on and on.

In the center he saw an original poster from the 1973 Inaugural Ball on the Mall held in Washington D.C. for President Ted Kennedy, with its swirling acid logos for the Grateful Dead, the Airplane, Jimi Hendrix, Bob Dylan, Country Joe, Sly Stone, Janis Joplin, Santana and the Rolling Stones themselves, all in still-brilliant reds and blues and yellows, like a halo surrounding the central face of President Ted, itself all bright green except for the black-and-white hypno-wheels of his eyes. That poster had become known as the 'target poster' after President Ted's assassination in '75. Not many still existed, and even less in this condition.

Truax looked closer.

Kennedy had signed it, and Dylan, and Hendrix, and Country Joe, and Grace Slick, and Jerry Garcia, and even Keith Richards; and by '73, Keith Richards signed things even less than President Ted.

Beneath the poster, an iron frame held dozens of lit candles in kaleidoscope colors, burning as if in front of a saint's statue.

Truax wondered who this guy Magruder was.

"You like my Father's shrine?"

Truax jumped at the sound of the voice. He looked at the man who stood just inside the doorway; the beads still draped down his shoulders, like black and gold dreadlocks, noiseless. The man was short, egg-shaped, dark-haired, clean-shaven. He had brown eyes. He wore a white, button-down shirt, but the top two buttons weren't buttoned. He wore a black leather tie, but the knot hung loosened below the undone buttons. He wore a black leather vest, not buttoned at all.

"The candles stay lit 24/7 in front of the poster. It's in my Father's will."

"I didn't touch anything," said Truax. "I'm Carl Truax. I have an invitation." He let the silk invitation dangle from his hand.

"I know. I sent it. I'm V.W. Magruder. This is my house. Now." He grinned a funny sort of grin, Truax thought – maybe amused, maybe ironic, maybe derisive. But it was a crooked grin, and Truax couldn't tell if the straight portion or the crooked portion were truer.

"Sorry," said Truax. "I was... reminiscing."

"Of course you were. Everyone does. They can't help themselves. This house. This room. That poster. The candles. They're all virtually Pavlovian." He pointed at Truax. "You have some spittle on your chin, by the way."

Truax wiped his chin in horror, but found no spittle. Magruder grinned his funny sort of grin, and Truax grinned with him, though he didn't think the joke was funny. Truax didn't want to annoy the man; he wanted to see the film.

"These are all real?" Truax indicated the posters, changing the subject away from himself.

"Real? Yes. The Kennedy one can cure addiction, both physical and psychological, if you touch it, as well as paranoia and even leprosy, or so my father told me." The cockeyed grin again. "And, my father was there, you know. And, by 'there' I mean the 60s and 70s, of course, not just the Ball on the Mall. Everywhere important. The concerts. The protests. The speeches. Blah, blah, blah. And, he saved things. He had a knack, for being places, for meeting people, for seeing things. He himself was quite unremarkable. Average. Possibly even below average, although likable, so others tell me, and he passed those unremarkable, average, possibly even below average qualities onto me, minus the likeability. So others tell me." The grin, and then a shrug. "And, now Father's dead, and it's all mine. All this peace and love across the universe for over forty years, and my father sat here in this house and drank himself to death. I always wondered why, and now I know."

"Your film?"

"My film." He grinned. Not derisive, Truax decided. Either ironic, or amused. Probably. "The Magruder Film. Maybe it will become known as the Magruder Film. I would like that. Today you will be the first besides my father and me to see it."

"Why me?"

"Why not you?"

"There has to be a reason, Mr. Magruder. Why me? Why not a hundred other newspapermen?"

Magruder laughed. "Why? Where? What? When? How? You want facts? Very well. My father used to read your column – out loud, mind you – to me, every week, for the last forty-two years." He closed his eyes, covered them with one of his hands and shuddered; then opened his eyes. "Pardon me. I was reminiscing. Your columns. Why you? Because I feel as if I know you, Mr. Truax, and I couldn't think of anybody else I would more like to share the Magruder Film with than you, the ur-hippie, in my mind at least. Come. Join me in the attic. Everything's prepared."

The attic smelled of 1969, before the world changed. Truax remembered the smell: weed and tear gas, hidden like subliminal messages in the wood of the rafters and the cardboard of the boxes. The smell wafted him back, like a contact high in time. Trunks and taped boxes were piled against the peaked rafters, like the inside of a wooden pyramid. The only light filtered in through a couple of heavily curtained dormer windows. The plank floor squeaked with every step, with every shift of weight. Dust motes rode the golden air like a hundred invisible roller-coasters running in slow-motion. A film projector pointed at a screen hung on the far wall.

Truax teetered on the edge of a flashback – the gas, the old weed, the jasmine oil. He closed his eyes. The attic reeked of pent-up warmth. He forced himself to focus on the here and now.

"The attic is pre-Altamont," said Magruder, squeaking heavy

around the room. Truax felt him jounce through the floorboards. "Clothes, books, magazines, trinkets, letters. It's all musty and dry. Father filed his pre-peace and love life away up here and never touched it again, and I never came up here until he died. Then, I found this."

The flashback feeling dissipated on motes of the long-ago past. Truax opened his eyes. Magruder stood on the other side of the attic, holding a small, yellowed, cardboard box containing a reel of 16 mm film. He tilted it in the golden light for Truax's inspection. Truax read the handwriting scrawled on the box.

ALTAMONT

The Holy Grail, Truax thought.

The hippies and the Hells Angels were pushed against each other at Altamont with a force like a bad vibe, the security and the secured, the Angels bristling like an electric fence. Truax remembered two things about Altamont: one was that if Angels and hippies got squeezed together close enough, then they would explode. The closer they got to each other, the stronger that evil energy got.

The second thing, of course, was Mick.

Truax could still remember that evil energy. He'd been there. It had felt like the end of the 60s, even the anti-60s, the first, worst bad trip before the fast ride to the psych ward.

The bands played, but they may as well not have bothered, for all the good they did.

Truax remembered the music – thin, disjointed, dispirited, without its magic. Altamont was just a few miles and yet a world away from San Francisco. He couldn't believe how much different things seemed there, as if Flower Power, Peace and Love, and the Younger Generation had all gotten weaker in an inverse relationship with every step they took away from the Haight, from every day away from the Summer of Love.

The whole scene had depressed Truax so much he was almost ready to call it quits and go start looking for the next big thing, maybe somewhere down around L.A.

The bands played, and the Angels beat on the hippies nearest the stage with pool cues, swarmed over the hippies and beat them senseless. The bands played, and the Angels swarmed over hippies like Nixon's unleashed id, and the 60s lurched to an ugly, misshapen, hunchbacked, pathetic end.

Truax had the bad feeling that it was only going to get worse.

But Mick saw it too, from on high.

The Stones played 'Sympathy for the Devil', and the Angels took position to swarm a hippie named Meredith Hunter near the stage; and the kid's face – he was no more than a kid – went feral and scared and shiny with sweat, like the hunted, not a hunter.

Mick saw it start to happen. He turned and started to run across the stage, and then he leapt. Everyone called it Jagger's Leap, now.

He leapt from the stage and landed right between Hunter and a Hells Angel who had drawn a knife – right between them just as the Angel's knife-arm stabbed forward. Mick saved Hunter from being stabbed in the back by taking the knife-thrust himself, eyes wide open, in the middle of his chest in front of 300,000 people.

Mick Jagger sacrificed his own life for one of his fans.

Mick pulled away, wrenching the blade out of the shocked Angel's hand.

Keith and Charlie kept playing, a few more kicks on the bass drum timed to the spurts of Mick's blood, some more power chords crashing over the whole transcendent scene as Mick raised his arms from his body and looked like the handle and cross-piece of a knife himself.

And those 300,000 people backed away from the moment, leaving a silent tableau of three etched in memory: Mick the Savior, the Saved, and the Killer.

A single moment captured a tipping point in history.

The knife stuck out of Mick's chest with no sliver of blade visible, just the handle and cross-piece. His bright red blood spread down the front of his chest. And, after the shock wore off, the cameras began to snap, and the famous photo of Mick standing with his hands spread wide, and a look of blissful peace on his face, a look of forgiveness, a look of ... transcendence, was taken.

That photo became the cover of the Stones next album, called 'If You're Going to Altamont' after Marty Balin's twelve-minute jam, a combination elegy and celebration of the event. Seventy-three million copies of that album exist.

The argument still rages about what the expression on Mick's face means, about what he saw in the last moments of his life.

But in that instant, vibe, energy, tension, Altamont, the 60s, the world, everything, had changed.

Everyone had to ask themselves: Which side were you on? The Saved? Or the Killers? The Hippies? Or the Hells Angels?

Mick changed everything, by giving his life for another man; and with one ultimate act of self-sacrifice, he had breathed life into a global Movement of Peace and Love.

The cops came and arrested the Hells Angel; and then the coroner came for Mick's body, but the hippies acted as one. 300,000 people played a shell game with Mick's body, keeping it away from the Man like a human Ganges, and as far as the authorities were concerned, Mick's body might as well not even have existed. They never even got a whiff of it, and finally, days later, the hippies burned it on a pyre. By that time, the crowd had swelled to a million and a half strong. Hippies had streamed in from all over Northern California, Los Angeles, Nevada, and the Pacific Northwest. And not just hippies either, but regular middle-class kids, and their younger brothers and sisters, and even some of their parents.

The 60s may have ended by the calendar, but they didn't die; and when the 70s began, Peace and Love spread out from Altamont in bigger and bigger waves, more powerful than ever, and changed the world.

"I was there," said Magruder, threading the film into the projector. "At Altamont."

Truax didn't laugh. He had practice. "Really?" he said. At last count, about seven or eight million people had claimed to have been at the seismic center of the world's reigning philosophy of peaceful co-existence, claimed to have seen Jagger martyred, claimed to have had a hand in the birth of the Movement.

And, Truax figured Magruder was about forty years old. He didn't laugh.

"I know what you're thinking," said Magruder as he picked his way through the projector's unfamiliar sprockets. "I'm too young." He shrugged. "I'm forty-four. I was born four days before the concert began."

He got the film threaded. He pointed to one of the dormer windows. "Close those curtains," he said. He stepped to the other curtains and closed them, stealing the roller-coaster motes from the air.

"I don't do drugs," he said. "I don't like hippies. All the peace and love, the pot, the mellow, the dirt. Did you ever read the studies about what's in your marijuana? The spider eggs? The rat droppings? Disgusting. And nobody cares about a schedule anymore. I've had it all up to here. I like a little more ... structure. I read underground fiction. What-if stories. You know what I mean?"

He glanced up at Truax in the dark, no grin this time, no derision, no irony, almost as if he might be reaching out for some common ground.

Truax wished he could give it to him. GROK was published when it was published. It no longer had a set schedule, and he liked it that way. "Not really," he said.

"Genre stories," said Magruder.

Truax felt as if Magruder were circling around his point. He shrugged, helpless.

Magruder sighed. "Counterfactual stories," he said. "What if Eisenhower had declared martial law in 1960 and derailed the Kennedy's' lust for power? What if Nixon had won a second term? What if there had been a War on Drugs? That sort of thing."

"Oh," said Truax. He didn't trust himself to say more. Sure, he'd come across the concept before, but he'd never heard it graced with a name as intellectual sounding as 'counterfactual'. He knew it as fascist pornography, underground stories written to unearth any and every conceivable way to introduce mass slaughter into society. No, not just mass slaughter, but pointless mass slaughter, end of the world apocalypses, alien wars of extermination, Orwellian governments versus patriotic guerillas, endless shadow paranoid bloody conspiracies, and rampaging invulnerable murderous monsters. Any idea, really, that led to a strong leader and lots of merciless killing. In other words, anything that led to the Hells Angels' world-view. He'd never heard the word 'counterfactual' used to describe the desire to see the pain that might have engulfed the world had the knife been buried in Meredith Hunter's back instead of Mick's chest before.

"Not a fan, I see," said Magruder. The grin returned. He shrugged. "People think counterfactuals are strange, anti-social, authoritarian even, but they're wrong. The stories just fulfill a desire, a need for ..." He searched for the right word. "A desire for structure." He chewed his lip. "Not the sort of thing hippies can appreciate though, I suppose." He turned back to the projector, rested a finger on the start switch. "Well, like it or not, Mr. Truax, you're about to confront one whopping great counterfactual."

He hit the START switch.

The Magruder Film

The last thing Truax saw before the film started was Magruder's crooked grin, flickering in the projector's light.

Truax hadn't said a word since the film ended. Shot from about thirty feet from the Altamont stage, the film caught the Stones' performance, caught Jagger's Leap, caught his martyrdom, caught it all, in glorious color, with sound, and in perfect focus. And, the world had now changed twice in Truax's lifetime.

Magruder's father really did have a knack for being in the right place at the right time.

Magruder led the way down from the attic.

Truax stopped outside the attic, to think, or perhaps to not think. He didn't trust himself on the stairs. Not yet. Not just yet.

Magruder came to a halt halfway down the third floor stairway. He turned to look up at Truax, his grin not ironic, not derisive, but malicious.

"It should be obvious to a blind man from my father's film, Mr. Truax. Jagger was trying to run away. Trying to flee. Like a coward. And he tripped on a microphone cord, Jagger's Leap nothing but an accident. He got in between that stupid, filthy little hippie and the Hells Angel who was just trying to do his security job completely by accident. He practically fell onto that knife. It was all an accident. He wasn't trying to help anyone at all except himself." Magruder had so much glee bubbling up inside him that he couldn't even laugh. He giggled.

Truax thought the giggle an obscene sound.

"Your Savior was a coward, pure and simple. Your Movement is a farce, built on a lie and stretched into an absurdity. I have the counterfactual of all counterfactuals in my possession, Mr. Truax." He waved the box of film under Truax's nose like smelling salts, then turned and started down the stairs again, trailing malicious grins and obscene giggles.

Truax couldn't argue. The film had blinded him with its clarity. Magruder had re-wound and re-played that section of the film at least half-a-dozen times. He had delighted in pointing out every detail of what he called 'Mick's Misadventure'.

And, now Truax knew why Magruder's father had drunk himself to death. He wanted to start drinking himself to death as well, five minutes ago. He didn't want to think. It was all a mistake: the last forty-four years.

And, Truax thought for the first time that he might just have figured out what had gone through Mick's mind in those last few moments before he died – it was all a mistake.

He started after Magruder.

Magruder stopped again, on the second floor landing, and Truax bumped into him. They stood on Magruder's father's soft, thick rugs, so that Truax felt as if he were floating.

"What's the motto of GROK, Mr. Truax?"

"What?"

"On your magazine's masthead," said Magruder, grinning his horrible, twisted grin. "What's your motto? Or don't you even bother looking at it anymore?"

Truax had to think for a second. "Can You Dig The Truth, Man?" he said. He hadn't thought about GROK's motto in years. But he thought he knew where Magruder was going with this. "That's why you wanted my magazine, and me, for this story," he said.

"You won't suppress this story, will you, Mr. Truax?" said Magruder. "Because you're a newspaperman, at least that's what my father always told me, every week, year after year after year. That you and your magazine Dig the Truth, Man. Even if it brings down your Hippie Paradise. Right, Mr. Truax?" He pumped his right fist in the air. "Can You Dig The Truth, Man?" He giggled, and turned to go down the stairs.

And, Truax shoved him. Hard. With both hands.

He fell face-first, and his grin slammed off the railing. He tumbled heels over head twice, his head crashing between railing and wall twice more before he reached the bottom, where the top of his head smashed through the plaster of the wall, and he lay still, leaving a blood-smear, nothing at all like Jagger's.

After a quiet minute, Truax followed him down, and saw that he was dead. He stepped over the body to the ground floor. Magruder was still dead. He picked the box of film up off the floor where it had fallen from Magruder's hand.

He had to call the cops. He considered what he would say to them.

He glanced up at the second-floor landing, at all the rugs.

What he had to say, really.

"He tripped."

206

The Magruder Film

Truax slipped back through the beads into the living room. He un-reeled the film into the candle-flames under President Ted's poster, watch-ing it burn frame-by-frame.

He was going to have to drink himself to death. All the last forty-four years had been a mistake, all that work, all that sacrifice. But at least no one else had to know.

He stared at Nixon's jowly face as it smiled while giving the V for Victory sign with both hands on the cover of Magruder's counterfactual book. Then he looked up at President Ted's Ball on the Mall poster.

All that work, all that sacrifice.

He stared into President Ted's hypno-wheel eyes, reached out and touched his face with one hand as he fingered his silver knife-handle and cross-piece hung on a chain around his neck with the other.

And, he discovered it was true.

President Ted's poster cured him.

He didn't feel the least bit guilty at all.

Nicolas (Dimitri) Vorvolakos

Almost A Year

Almost a year, still not here but here.

High with someone, who is trapped in my need for release,
    my desperate moment of want.

Prolonged by my need for escape, my need of cash, my need
    for distraction, my need for destruction.

This one offers some sort of reward, I see strings, he claims no
    strings attached to anything.

Just possibilities, nothing concrete, nothing real.

Desire ignites only when sparked by cocaine, mixed with kindness.

Empty vacant needs, my or his?

My needs are paramount, all consuming.

Back to the place with the fake parkay floor, the place with the
    broken table and the dirty blue table cloth.

The place where dog shit and piss blends with the scent of
    cigarettes and scotch.

Nicolas (Dimitri) Vorvolakos

One day there, one day here, one blink, one breath.

One year.

Fell asleep.

Woke up: I have no home

Blinked: I'm fucking

Coughed: I'm in love

Turned: I've no friends

Flinched: In Hollywood motel

Laughed: I'm arrested

Sighed: In prison, hot sun, killers, top bunk.

Woke up: Caribbean, tiny island, clear water, palm trees,
    hot sun, blue skies, and in love......

Dave Shulman

Stumps

Four-oh-two a.m., the third Monday after we'd been fired, was when I decided to stop showering. I was in bed, reading *A Boy Named Charlie Brown* by Charles M. Schulz, a full-color paperback printed in 1969 on heavy paper with no page numbers. Somewhere close to page 29, right after Charlie Brown has won his first spelling bee — the first thing he's ever won — there's a drawing of five *Peanuts* characters celebrating, shouting, arms in the air, jumping for joy. Among these, I focused on a Peanut whose actual name was never revealed but whose nickname was "Pig-Pen," always in quotation marks. "Pig-Pen" was dirty, permanently, ankle-deep to knee-high in a self-generating dust that never quite settled. I hadn't noticed "Pig-Pen" for years, and seeing him there so happy and filthy reminded me of something Charlie Brown once said about him: *Did it ever occur to you that "Pig-Pen" might be carrying the dirt and dust of some past civilization?*

This recollection seem gave me a sense of comfort for the first time in three weeks. I was able to sleep through the rest of the night, and when I awoke I felt a powerful urge not to shower.

That afternoon, I met my friends Christine Pope and Keith Floyd at the stumps across the alley behind the parking lot of what is now called Dearborn Johnny's, which occupies the former space of Sarah's, a coffee-house restaurant open very early and very late, where the three of us had spent at least a hundred afternoons of each of the past fifteen years having pleasant conversations and good meals while writing, editing, and drinking coffee. Sarah's had been open for twenty years. It closed the week before

Pope, Floyd and I were fired by Riley Krilko, a high-ranking suit in the corporation that bought our newspaper the year before. Krilko was known for her cutthroat capitalism and dramatic firings, both of which often featured yelling and the hurling of objects. Floyd met her once, had lunch with her soon after we'd been bought, and reported back to Pope and me at Sarah's that Krilko seemed "surprisingly nice, in a detached, menacing way."

I sighed, and Pope said, "It's a sado-capitalism thing. The ones who pretend to be nice assume that because they themselves are *pretending* to *being* nice and not actually being nice, so is everyone else."

Floyd and I nodded, and Pope said, "They don't back-stab. They front-stab. They want to see your face as the knife goes in. They want you to remember them."

"Jesus," I said.

"Fuckin' A," said Pope.

We all frowned, and we all raised our eyebrows.

Floyd was an admired figure in the journalism world. Several times he'd been awarded Journalist of the Year, across all media, in a large American city. He was good, but his way of being good took time, and that's not allowed anymore. With a few exceptions, American news companies only pay for bad speedwriting on bovine topics — celebrities breathing, politicians and executives saying naughty words.

"Floyd's an interesting person," is what most people say about Floyd. He has a Ph.D. in cultural anthropology from UCLA. For two years, he lived with the Awa, an isolated tribe in the highlands of Papua New Guinea. Then he returned to the United States, wrote a book about it and got a job as a senior editor at the newspaper where Pope and I had been hired just a few weeks prior.

Out behind Sarah's — behind Dearborn Johnny's — was an eight-car parking lot, and beyond that was a narrow alley and a series of fences separating the alley from the former middle-class neighborhood, now mostly poor with a few heavily fortified mansions. The fences toward either end of the block were ancient chain links that had long since yielded to roots and cars. These fences were reinforced with hedges, bamboo and shopping carts, which neighborhood kids would secure with Master Lock combination locks. Some of the shopping carts were sculptures, stacked three or four high.

In the middle of the block, the chain links yielded to a flat gray modernistic wall, fourteen feet high and topped with razor wire and a motion detector that glowed red when anything bigger than a cat passed. Sometimes the wall would slide open to release or secure a black German sedan. And to the magical gray wall's immediate south, directly behind the parking lot, there was a sun-splintered redwood stockade fence, eight feet high, mostly pale yellow, with enormous spiders competing for control of the corners. It was in front of this fence, in the narrow dirt path between it and the asphalt, where there were three knee-high stumps.

After Sarah's closed, we couldn't decide where to meet. We needed a place that was noisier than a library but not as noisy as a diner, had good food and coffee and light, and friends who worked there.

"Why don't we just go to a fucking Denny's? You know — not to *go*, but just to go to decide where to go?"

"No."

"Which Denny's?"

"No. I can eat the food, but can't deal with the lighting and the in-house Denny's teevee, and everything covered in Denny's logos. I'm getting an anxiety attack just thinking about it."

"Then where?"

There didn't seem like another place to go, so we just stayed where we were, on the stumps in the alley behind Dearborn Johnny's. We brought bad coffee from the donut shop down the street and sat and sipped and talked and read and wrote.

So we were sitting on the stumps there, the three of us, drinking our donut-shop coffees and talking about basketball when Floyd said, "This is going to sound kind of weird, but I hit myself last night. Real hard, and on purpose."

I didn't know what to say, so I said, "That's not good."

Pope didn't know what to say, so she said, "Where?"

Floyd showed us where. It was on top of his head, slightly off to the front and right. And he showed us how he did it — with an open hand, his writing hand. His head went back and to the left.

"It hurt a lot," said Floyd. "I just kind of crumpled into a pile on the floor. Right before I'd hit myself I'd been telling Vince how stupid I am, how I ruined my life and all that. And then it just sort of happened." Vince was Floyd's dog.

213

"It's true," said Pope. "You're stupid, you've ruined your life, and all that. And you're a very bad person because you don't make money anymore."

This made Floyd almost laugh, which made Pope and me almost smile. But instead we just stared.

I said to Floyd, "Are you planning on doing this again, the head-hitting?"

"No," said Floyd. "No plans."

"Isn't it called a slap if you use an open hand?" said Pope.

"No," said Floyd. "I looked it up online, right after I hit myself. Found all kinds of confirmation. It's the wrist action that defines it as a slap or a hit. Technically, you can slap with a fist — it just looks really stupid."

Floyd demonstrated, and we nodded.

"Don't do that again," said Pope.

Floyd nodded, and we started talking about basketball again.

Then I said, "This is going to sound kind of weird, but I saw 'Pig-Pen' in an old Peanuts book last night, and I've decided to stop showering."

Pope and Floyd just stared at me.

Then Pope said, "Well, this is going to sound kind of weird, too, but I ate an entire thing of Oreos last night, and I've decided to stop brushing my teeth."

Some people want money; I want to find a coffeehouse restaurant open very early and very late where I can write and edit while drinking coffee and having pleasant conversations and good meals.

At some point I should probably shower again, and Pope needs to start taking care of her gums. Floyd says he hasn't hit himself on the head again, but he's pretty sure at some point he will.

If all goes as planned, we'll all be homeless in time for Christmas. Yesterday, Pope brought a hacksaw, so we can get to the shopping carts. For now, Floyd seems okay. He got a new job, writing short celebrity profiles for an online entertainment-news aggregator for twelve dollars fifty cents per post. He worked sixty hours the first week and made $125. His second week, he worked seventy hours and made $137.50. Things are looking up.

Jill Paris

I'm Working Here

So, it would appear I'm "working" here at this seemingly upscale hotel located in the California desert whose name is synonymous with wild, alcohol-fueled, ink-obsessed tweekers, party hipsters and motorcycle chicks. I sit isolated at a corner desk on my second night shift as a concierge, sporting a uniform so hideous, I have to avoid mirrors before leaving the house or I might gag. The colorblind combination (a nipple-lancing black vest worn over purple/white gingham blouse) was no doubt selected by someone with a penchant for lady blackjack dealers. Slapping this getup on everyday is like having to relive the ugliest bridesmaid dress not just once, but over and over again. Pinned above my heart is a metallic badge to complete the ensemble. (I think the last nametag I ever donned was for my first summer job at Disneyland in 1978. As if the polyester jumpsuit wasn't bad enough, the visitors were able to call me by name all day long, too.) The four little letters of my moniker look lonely and misplaced (kind of like me). But, that's nothing compared to the pain of the tight, white belt hoisting up these ill-fitting khaki trousers. Hard plastic can be cruel when cinched around contemptuous hips. It actually *hurts* to be here. Is this the best I could do? I should feel lucky to have found a job at all in this horror of a recession, shouldn't I?

"Hey, honey," says an old biker dude in a crusty leather jacket, "Where's the head?"

"The restrooms are down this hall and to the left," I reply for the tenth time in the last hour, fighting the urge to give him the finger when he doesn't thank me.

A young woman with yards of matted hair extensions whizzes past wheeling a neon green suitcase behind her polished toenails painted to match the luggage. Her jiggling cleavage bounces with each stride to the tunes blasted here 24/7. The crocheted halter top she's almost wearing looks as though it's been left in the dryer on high heat setting to achieve maximum shrinkage. Mission accomplished.

I'm not even sure if they really need a concierge in a place like this (other than to have a live body point out local tattoo parlors or where to pick up a six-pack at midnight). I'm so glad I spent the past several years in graduate school to find out though. So far, I've directed countless guests successfully to the toilets with the utmost intelligence. My degrees are really paying off.

Wait. What's this? An unsteady figure is heading my way. A tall, white, middle-aged man suddenly appears before me wearing a pastel pink dress shirt so neatly pressed it could pass as table linen at a Hamptons' beach cottage. His pinwheel pupils start to spin as he teeters and loses his balance. *Jeez, he's plastered already?* It's only 7:15 p.m. His buttoned-up, accountant persona does not fit the typical guest description at all, but he seems harmless enough - more milquetoast than Motörhead.

I dunno where I'm suppozzzed to go," he says in an infantile voice.

"Are you here for the conference? I ask, not that I'm aware of a business conference in-house this evening but, he's not really listening anyway. His torso begins to wriggle back and forth as his hands slide up and down his body. Admittedly, I'm a little freaked out by this writhing visual. *What the hell is he doing? Is he having a seizure?*

"Hey, ya know whazzz downstairs?" he spews as the squirming comes to a halt.

I quickly launch into my accommodating spiel, "Our fitness center, meeting rooms, and soon-to- be spa which opens in..." But, he's not interested in learning about the hotel layout or its fine amenities, and interrupts me midsentence.

"I know whazzz downstairs," he prods with a wink, "Pussy!"
Did he just say "Pussy?" Maybe he means the *ballroom*?

Somehow he mistakes my flabbergasted silence as an invitation and keeps talking.

I'm Working Here

"Hey! Ya know what I'm *really* good at?" he continues, as if clarifying technical skills in detail might clinch the deal of this unsolicited foreplay, "Oral!"

Oh. My. God. I'm working here?

Perhaps the protocol now is to phone security? Surely one of those sinewy guys with visible handcuffs would love nothing more than to remove this lewd lothario from the premises. They live for that kind of macho shit.

"Hello? Security? Can you please come right away and save me from the creepy guy saying creepy things to me in a super-creepy manner?"

Well, maybe not. It's not exactly the usual predawn hour of antics committed by liquored-up buffoons often found chucking lawn furniture over balcony rails. Security might think me hysterical at the inability to diffuse unruly banter, deeming me unfit to carry out my concierge duties, and escort me to my vehicle where I will then have to live in the custody of my parents for an interminable length of time, never to find work again.

Only weeks before, I'd stood in line for six and a half hours (in high heels) at a Job Fair with over 5,000 other jobless souls. I'd never seen anything like it. No food. No water. No air conditioning. Luckily, an innovative Hispanic man had thought to fill a trashcan with ice and soft drinks to sell. I bought two cans of Coca-Cola for sustenance. A film crew arrived for the event capturing the shitty economy as a lead news story. When I made it through the three rounds of on-the-spot interviews and then was hired a week later, I was grateful to have finally found employment after moving in with my parents last year at their senior community home, no matter how low the hourly pay rate. I'd worked in the hospitality industry in the early '90s as an executive assistant to the general manager of a luxury brand hotel chain and finally, this was my chance to wake up and go somewhere! As much as I adore spending time searching for the ultimate spoon rest with my mother, or bargain hunting at HomeGoods for artificial greenery, idle hours are deadly to anyone who needs to feel useful and productive.

For months and months, I'd joined the countless ranks of people who endlessly submit their resumes online never to be called in for a live meeting - EVER. Staring at the serpentine line with thousands of job seekers, I flat-out refused to leave (kind of like this drunken idiot). I figured they had to pick somebody for the hundred jobs posted and it might as well be me. Feet throbbing, sweat dripping down my legs, by the time I finally reached the personal interview stage, my makeup had melted away and a few women had fainted from the 110F temperature. When I returned home and described the day's event to my mother, complaining it was more than half the salary I'd been used to earning, she said, "Honey, it is what it is. If you're lucky enough to find a job in today's market, you'd better hang on to it no matter what."

No matter what?

Fine, I'm delighted for this wasted man's proficiency in the oral arts, though it is not clear if he means in the "giving" or the "receiving" end but, frankly, I do not probe further or phone in for backup. Instead, I kindly direct him with a wave of my hand and say, "You need to walk that way, and then turn right." Of course if he follows the route I've indicated he will possibly trip and fall head-over-feet into the swimming pool located beyond the glass doors adjacent to the lobby.

Now he's plopped his doughy ass atop the calendar of events folder splayed across the desk knocking the pen and pencil holder over with a crash.

"Wanna go somewhere with me? Right now?!" he asks with a sickening sense of urgency.

"Hey! Can't you see I'm *working* here?" I say with Bada Bing authority, recovering the fallen writing instruments with one swoop of the hand.

"Oh, and just so ya know, I've got loadzzz of money," he persists in hopes I'm not only the kind of employee to service guests sexually, but a gold-digging ho as well.

I remain motionless; mute.

"You're hot," he adds - one last compliment masked as an insult.

In this garb? Man, this jerk is the walking definition of "blind drunk."

I stay hushed and stare back with the kind of glazed indifference months of joblessness breeds. I shoot him a laser sharp don't-fuck-with-me glare that penetrates his psyche like a super hero scorned. He's noticeably wounded, and finally sulks off amidst the throng of packed bar patrons under a blaring canopy of techno beats, and gets swallowed up by the crowd.

Secretly pleased with my cool, guest relations achievement, I rise and begin to sway to the music. (Dancing's encouraged here.) I say the words again, not as a horrified afterthought or a questionable revelation.

I'm Working Here

I say it with the kind of pride that comes from punching a time clock for $12 an hour at the end of the day. I say it with a pumping fist and a hearty guffaw. I say it now like a rebel yell because I cannot actually believe it myself:

"I'm working here. I'm WORKING here!!"

Michael Delgado

Miguel

I see my name on one of those wreaths by the side of the road that the Mexicans put on the spot of a tragic accident.

I'm self-absorbed but not the way a reality star is. I'm self-absorbed like in an "I'm out of Prozac" way. I'm self-absorbed the way you make excuses. I'm self-absorbed the way you sleep with women because you think they love you. I'm self-absorbed but not enough to be a great artist or dictator.

My father would read me Pinocchio at bedtime as an object lesson in the straight and narrow, but I always found the Island of Lost Boys much more intriguing. Lampwick was cool. I am an ass.

This morning I went to another second or third interview. The kind where it's down to you and one or two other candidates. This job was just what I was looking for: impressive title, good pay and low accountability. I waited in a pretentiously decorated reception area. The type that gets a makeover every couple of years when the agency does their own "Brand Refresh" to stay *au courant*. This version was mid-century modern.

The interview went the way they all go. "Tell me about Michael." "How do you feel about Wednesdays?" "Tell about a time…" "Of course, this job is well below your qualifications. How do you feel about that?" I'm thinking, "I paid to have my teeth whitened and gray washed out of my hair for this"? I'm thinking, "My enthusiastic answers aren't even fooling me".

A dead fish handshake from the executive as I'm escorted out when I see the competition in the lobby. She is young, vivacious. Beautiful. What she didn't have in my experience she would make up tenfold in a confidence bordering on hubris. She would bring an energy and enthusiasm I can't muster anymore- or don't care enough to try. What she didn't know about business, about life, the guy who just interviewed me—the guy my age—would happily mentor her. Who wants to work with a rock when you sculpt with clay? I'd give her the job myself.

I can't even get what my sister calls "a base-hit" job. A part time retail thing or a warehouse gig. I compete with high schoolers or drop outs that can be shaped into proper corporate drones. I swear I am willing to surrender to the capitalist matrix and start over but feeling unemployable as I do, I'm sure my face, body posture and personality test scores tell the truth.

But I need the money.

Do I tell you I was once an in the music business? An artist? Had a hit or two. You'd remember the songs but would probably say "what was the name of that guy? Nonetheless I made good money, had two girls with an Ex I wish I had rescued, or that I wish had rescued me. The kids are pretty well grown now, meaning I can drink legally with with one. The other has a fake but I draw the line there, I know she has it, but I don't allow it when I'm buying.

I sleep on the "Couch Of No Return." It was so named when we were younger because to sit there was to spend the night in a haze of booze and whatever contraband was handy. I was fond of opiates. Now it's in the basement of my sister's house in Sierra Madre and it's my bed. After nearly two years of networking, LinkedIn Premium and polishing my digital skills, I'm still unemployed and the C.O.N.R. has resumed its boozy enabling. Now I think the couch moniker was prophetic. I'm one kindhearted sister away from moving the C.O.N.R. to the sidewalk and busking. The vintage Gibson J-50 is the most valuable thing I own.

About a month ago, looking at a nest of trees on a steep hillside near an underpass I almost missed a small homeless encampment. It looked like they had arranged their tarps to exploit the northern exposure and take advantage of the expansive view of the Rose Bowl and the City of Los Angeles further down the arroyo. I caught myself thinking: "Nice. Great view, close to local services and a tourist section. Location, location, location."

The spot is on the way up the Arroyo toward the Rose Bowl, "The Granddaddy of them all." Celebrating 100 years, January 1st, it was built in the era of raccoon coats and pennants and Three Stooges-like chants of "Ricky-Rack-Ricky-Rack, Sis Boom Bah!" The umber hills a backdrop. The dusty wash that used to run water instead of storm runoff from the occasional rain won't let you forget that this is a coastal desert. The smell of eucalyptus, sage, oak and game day.

Most every day, twice a day I pass that canvas structure when I go to workout at the Rose Bowl Aquatic Center (Lap swimming is my only outlet/ luxury.) It's as beautiful a facility as I can't afford. An Olympic competition pool, 10 meter tower over the dive well, pick up water polo games on Sunday. I had been a member for years. Got chummy with the front deskers. About 6 months ago I discovered that one of the turnstiles would just turn, without the bar-code key assuring current membership, saving me the $120 monthly dues. I don't feel guilty about it.

I vowed to investigate the camp. Was I house hunting? The path to the structure was hard to find. Good planning, no doubt. Perched on the vertical above the Arroyo Parkway, it was accessible only from Greene St., a road on the ridge lined with manicured lawns and pristine California ranch style cracker boxes from the '40s that were purchased then for $12,000 and were now listed at $2,750,000.

I carried a soft cooler full of ice, some mineral water and a bag with some canned stuff, thinking it would be welcome in a dry camp. The path led away from the structure of which only a small patch of canvas was visible from Greene St. I wasn't sure this was the right way to go. I was equally unsure why I was on this mission. About a hundred yards of a modest descent, the trail began a series of dizzying switchbacks along a steep part of hillside that over millennia had been carved under by the wash, when it actually ran.

Beneath a majestic oak on a small plot that had been crudely graded was a homestead, resembling the efficient ordering of canvas sails and taut rigging. I carefully tried to pull back the flap that seemed the front door. It wouldn't cooperate. I could only peer inside through a seam.

Across the space was the spectacular view to downtown Los Angeles I had imagined. The sky the soft pink of an afternoon in October. The floor was covered in what appeared to be good quality Persian rugs. On one side was a pile of cushions, a small low table in the center of the large room. There was a small table and a cane back chair. On the table was a LED lantern. Paperbacks dotted the floor and tables. An antique vanity guarded a corner. Walking around back, I found the kitchen. A rock hearth skillfully constructed and a grill likely lifted from the park below.

Peering over edge, I spied the winding parkway from where I had first spotted this outlook. Breathing in the view.

SHHHIKKK SHACKKK

The unmistakable sound of a handgun carriage engaging.

Turning slowly I saw a man in a crisply pressed gray suit, white button down and a red power tie. His hair was neatly swept back with flecks of silver, eyes behind a pair of Maui Jim sunglasses. His loafers would otherwise be polished if not for the dust of the trail.

"What do you want? "

"Just wandered onto this trail I guess."

"Well wander off."

"To be honest, I spotted your nice set-up here from the parkway. I was curious, I guess."

"Satisfied now?"

The black gun pointed at the ground between us was wrapped by a thick hand crowned by a French cuff.

"Not looking for trouble. Was curious about the um, lifestyle. Look. I'm broke and I'm thinking about um, moving outside. Who lives here? "

"Who wants to know?"

"I'm sorry, my name's Mike."

My extended hand melted under his laser eyes.

"I came bearing gifts for whoever lives here, not knowing what to expect... Brought this cooler with some ice and some canned stuff. Low sodium. No need for guns, man."

"It's just an Air Soft pistol. I put black tape on the little nose part that's orange. Looks pretty real for a toy, right? Freaks everyone out. "

It might have been an Air Soft piece of plastic, but in a blink it disappeared into the small of his back. An undercover cop reflex.

"You're welcome to leave the gifts on your way out."

"If it's all the same, I could use them myself. Like I said, I'm spent."

"Suit yourself."

Reaching in his coat pocket to grab a ringing iPhone. In half apology he held up a finger.

"Hello. This is. Thanks for getting back to me so quickly. Let's see…let me get my calendar…"

He looked up into the pink.

"Would Wednesday at the same time be available? If not, I can move some things around. Excellent. Thank you. I'll see you then. "

He put the phone back in his pocket.

"You never want to be too accessible."

"I've tried the same thing for job interviews. It's not working."

He nodded. "Me either. Come on in. "

He led the way back to the front door and lifted a flap I hadn't noticed. Slipping a key into a padlock and pulling a chord, the tarp drew back dramatically. The padlock seemed excessive since a camel could easily shove its nose under the tent. A sweeping gesture told me to enter.

Hanging his coat on a rack cleverly constructed from the detritus of a rusted Cadillac El Dorado grill.

"'72. The last year they made em' was '74'."

He sat cross-legged on the pillows and nodded for me to do the same. I opened the cooler.

"All I have is some mineral water, plain."

"Excellent. Thank you. Do you drink?

"Don't we all?"

"No. Wanna mix that with some vodka?

He reached under a pile of more pillows.

"It's Tito's."

"Tito's is underrated, thank God. A decent vodka at a decent price point."

He reached under another pillow on his left. Two crystal tumblers. Clean. He wiped them with his breast pocket handkerchief for good measure. He mixed two cocktails. We sat in silence for a long time, negotiating.

"You looking for work?"

"Aren't we all? Almost two years now. I'm bunking at my sister's place over in Sierra Madre. God bless her."

"Wish I had family, still."

More silent calculating.

Getting up and straightening the crease in his pant legs, beating out the stretched knees, he went to the opening and the view. Ice cubes jingle. Staring down the valley he looked pensive, like a record company exec who doesn't hear another hit single on your tape. I have always been bad at math but this was not adding up. I knew that much.

"Father Delahunty."

"What?"

"You were wondering how my clothes are cleaned and pressed. Do I really live here? St. Margaret's."

"On Fair Oaks and Walnut."

"Father lets me keep my suits in the vestibule next to his vestments. Sister Scholastica hand washes and presses them with a heavenly precision. I use the church Wi-Fi. The old cafeteria is my office. Too small to fit all the kids now and too expensive to operate anyway. It used to be a very exclusive congregation. The few matrons leftover still occupy the front row at each morning mass but they can't contribute enough to cover. And they want to, so they pray. For that, among other things.

"I was in the music business. Warner Bros. Now I do licensing sales, freelance. You know trying to convince up and comers that there is value in covering some of the masterpieces in a label's catalog. There used to be money in that kind of thing. Now guys like Robert Thicke sue the ghost of Marvin Gaye".

"Tell me about it."

"I shower at the RBAC. They think I am still a member."

"I do too."

"I swim regular between 2 and 3 most days and if that's not your schedule, I most likely wouldn't know you. It's clubby by hours that way. Routines provide the illusion of security."

"You know the far right turnstile doesn't work."

I got up and joined him at the window.

"I never got your name."

"Mike."

We shook. His grip was firm and familiar. He turned away from the view of downtown. I gazed at the sunset no longer pink and now a burning red superball.

"Its' amazing how fast it can change but also amazing is how little you really need."

"That's what poor people say."

"No, really. True luxury is just time. I don't want to live this close to the ground but I don't want to waste time anymore either. Humility

226

and anonymity have their own rewards. *And stay away from St. Margaret's.* Get your own gig. And I don't need neighbors. It's getting dark and that switchback is a bitch. "

I left the offerings and let myself out. Mike's face glowed pale red with the last of the light that filled the tent, his silhouette blocking most of the window. I turned without goodbye. The switchback was a bitch, especially at dusk.

Getting on the 210 East where it merges with the 134. I cross a bridge built in 1913 with a breathtaking view connecting twin daggers of orange light and purple shadow plunging into the heart of the rocky arroyo some 150 feet below. The last leg of Route 66, and now the sight of over 150 jumpers and still counting. The bridge was nicknamed "Suicide Bridge" during the Great Depression. There is a narrow sidewalk but no place to park. The majority of jumpers leap off the north side, facing away from downtown Los Angeles.

Only a few yards away and I could take the twelve lane interstate slab that dwarfs the narrow two laner of my choice. I've always preferred the period light posts illuminating an unnecessary curve designed to thrill early motor-car enthusiasts whose top speed was an exhilarating 45mph.

Entering the 210 off Lake Street, the super-highway is just a crawl of dusty metallic bubbles and illegal texting. A dozen lanes of futility. Headlamps crawling west. Taillights a viscous red-clogged east. I think that riding a horse would be faster and wonder about the meaning of progress.

The 210 this time of day is always jammed but today it is unusually slow and within an excruciating quarter of a mile I can see why. The far right lane is still moving swiftly and its dicey finding a window to merge. If you were from somewhere else, for sure you would think it's a major wreck given the back up, but it's just a broke down vintage piece of Detroit's finest in the number 2 lane. No taillights. Mexican Dad, esposa and two kids. Standing outside the pick-up Mexican Dad y esposa are ashen, expecting fines and repairs they can't afford or worse, deportation. The two little girls think it's funny as they hop up and down in the bed.

Traffic crawls past on the left to throw a finger or wag a head then scurries along only to coagulate again at a steady 45mph 100 yards further up. I park my 1999 convertible Saab a 1972 Cadillac car length behind the Mexican truck and turn on the red-orange emergency flashers. I call 511.

911 is for blood only.

In my headlights, Mexican Dad is a white ghost cutout against the October evening. He's relieved I'm not a cop and gestures for me to call for help. I explain in Spanglish that they all would be safer in their little cab and that I had already called for roadside assistance. Esposa wrestles her cubs into the car. You can taste the smell of exhaust and hot rubber.

Standing in the space between Saab and truck, Mexican Dad introduces himself, "Me llamo, Miguel." A gold tooth smile glinted in the headlights.

"Yo Tambien."

We shook. His hand felt like my older brother's battle-scarred first baseman's glove. Gnarled, gritty and sweat-soaked, but a trustworthy comfort. I don't know if you've ever heard cars pile up before but Frank Wilson nailed it in 1964. Pearl Jam later covered it:

I'll never forget the sound that night,
the screamin' tires, the bustin' glass,
the painful scream, that I heard last.
911.

My roadside wreath is refreshed every anniversary by Esposa and the daughters who have all gotten very heavy. Esposa drives a better car now. Sometimes in the Spring they will make a fresh one after Caltrans Caterpillars have scythed the memorial under in their fire abatement efforts. They still sniffle, although no longer sob. The arrangements are less ornate but the red ribbon still has freshly painted hand lettering in gold glitter. The word "Miguel" blinks on and off, burning headlight white then taillight red with the passing traffic.

John Tottenham

Inertia Variations

FEELINGS

I may as well face the fact
that I am no longer capable
of doing what I once believed
I was capable of doing.
Not that I had any reason to assume
that I was capable of it.
It was just a feeling that I had.
And now I have a different feeling.

X

I haven't been anywhere
in the world, and out of all the things
I could have done on this day, among
others, that might have been fun, edifying
or charitable, I have chosen instead
to sink somewhere in flustered haze.
As if anything might be salvaged
from these uselessly plumbed depths.

ART AND EROS

Often, around the middle of a week day afternoon,
I find myself considering the connection
between sexual and creative energy.
Torn by futile lusts, I seek refuge
from the vagueness of the day
and the promise of endeavor
in reliable memories and fantasies
that spill, reliably, into sleep.

A MONDAY IN NOVEMBER

No,
I didn't do any work today.
But I thought about it for a moment,
before lying down again
to bask in the wan light of decreation
and savor the fact
that I will not always be free
to ponder abstractions.

XXX

Out of perversity, idleness, cowardice, fatalism and integrity,
I have chosen to shun my true path.
Despite it all, I have developed, in my time,
a certain unavoidable attachment to my life
and my ways: the chronic circlings between frustration
and inertia somehow comfort me - and, in the end,
I would rather be myself than anybody else.
Still, I suppose most people feel that way.

John Tottenham

ODE TO INVENTED MELANCHOLY

Daunted by the energy that might be unleashed
were I to concentrate on the supposed task -
of what it might subtract, exact and adulterate, and of
the gagging staleness that could issue forth, if finally
penetrated, from something so long suppressed.
Succumbing instead to these afternoons of claustrophobic
wandering and restless prostration. Committed, only
to non- commitment. Driven, only to distraction.

THAT TIME OF DAY

A destructive overawareness of time
knives through the hot empty spaces
of an afternoon. A sense of urgency vaporizing
into torpor. Even the traffic sounds tired.
Do something, I tell myself.
What? The same thing I've been doing
every day for years on end
with varying degrees of failure.

ANOTHER DAY

Take some initiative…
Do something with your life:
I get up from the sofa,
walk across to the table
and write these words
down on a scrap of paper.
Then I return to the sofa
and fall asleep.

FIVE O'CLOCK

My workday is drawing to a close.
It lasted twenty minutes. But it is already clear
that I am not going to do anything further
on this particular day. I could push myself,
I suppose, if I felt capable of pushing myself.
But I don't feel capable of it. And even if I did,
I probably wouldn't push myself. I would probably
do something less rewarding.

FEAR OF KNOWN THINGS

For a long time I have succeeded
in avoiding reality.
It has remained on the rim
of my existence, slowly spinning, kept
at a respectful distance;
Accepted, feared but never faced,
supplanted by a jangled state
of grace.

MY BRILLIANT NON-CAREER

I often tell myself that I could have done anything
I applied myself to. When, out of all the things I could have
applied myself to, I applied myself to doing nothing.
And found that I couldn't even do that.
The notion that I should have been doing something
kept getting in the way.
And now, of course, it is too late
to do anything: It has always been too late.

SOMETHING

I have spent my entire life
preparing to do something
that I am never going to do.
I thought that accumulating
all this learning and experience
would result in something: a body of work...
or a body. While neglecting to take into account
that I might actually have to do something to achieve that end.

James Hayward

I Shit Like A Tough Guy

It was going to be an extremely busy day. Efren came every Saturday morning at 7:00, with his son-in-law Ignacio, for our regular go at the grounds. My dear friend Fran was in town, from Fort Worth, and she was coming up for a dialogue and questions in preparation for her forthcoming book on abstract painting. She was due at 10:00. At 5:00 I was supposed to attend a benefit auction, at Elyse and Stanley's, in Brentwood, for my ex-dealer, Morgan, who was having major health issues. I had purchased two tickets to the event. I would be going alone. Then I had an opening at 6:00, a two-man show, with my old friend Max, at Manny's, in West Hollywood. This was my plan for Saturday.

It started off well. Efren, Ignacio and I set at the chores du jour. Once they were well started I headed back to tidy my digs before Fran arrived. A hot shower and a shave and I was ready to do business.

Fran arrived as scheduled and we had hot coffees to get the wise words rolling. I was already two or three joints into the daze, so caffeine is essential. Being a trained professional, this behavior had no noticeable effect on my performance. We talked for hours, then adjourned for a sushi lunch, returned and talked till after 3:00. Articulate and intelligent conversation requires much of the participants and there are few capable of such. Fran was among my favorite people on the planet to make art dialogue with. We didn't always agree, but each of us respected the others point of view. The back and forth could be quite heady and always a joy. Full frontal formal dialogue could be a bit enervating and I was feeling more than a bit fatigued by the time Fran left for town. I quickly fed the horses and the dogs, and then raced through a hot shower, ended with a cold rinse, and attempted to revive myself. My efforts failed badly. I rolled five or six joints, dressed for the evening, poured a mug of coffee, grabbed three bottles of nice cab, and set sail in my little red car, for the hour drive to Brentwood.

As usual, I arrived late. I never valet park as I always lose treats in the process. Plus it's easier to escape if you are holding your car keys. It wasn't a huge bash so parking was a breeze. The place looked deserted as I wandered in, but voices led me to the bar. The bartender, a tall, beach-boy tan, actor-handsome, twenty something, hit me with a giant pour of cabernet. I had told him I had two tickets and could only stay a few minutes. I stood in the back where I could drink and watch discreetly as they auctioned off personal treasures from Morgan's collection. Those present were politely bidding up objects to bring Morgan a maximum return; rumor had her facing overwhelming medical bills. This was the art world at its best, and I was honored to be included. I had arrived late and left early, but I did what I could.

From there it was a 10-mile trip down Sunset, right on Doheny, left on Melrose and I was there. I felt exhausted, something I had been dealing with for a while. It was more than physical exhaustion. I had finally gone to see my internist, Stewart, when I fell asleep at a stop light, at 5 p.m., on my way home from my 10 to 4 graduate painting workshop in Pasadena. They did a number of tests and came to the conclusion that I was intellectually/mentally exhausted by my long day at school. He gave me medication to take one hour before driving home. Lucky for me I remembered to bring my Ritalin.

As late as I was, I found a great parking place, grabbed a bottle of cab, and headed in. After I popped the cork and poured a glass, I joined the party. The show looked wonderful and friends quickly reinforced my assessment. My present work was overtly impasto, about as thick a surface of oil paint as anything you might have ever seen. Max's work was super flat, color-saturated resin polished to a mirror finish. Our work played at the opposite poles of possibility within "monochrome abstract painting". The paintings played beautifully together. I am always a little overwhelmed at these events, even surrounded by friends and other members of my profession, and am almost always inclined to fine-tune my level of comfort with herbs and red wine.

I Shit Like A Tough Guy

I do not drink white wine. As a young painter I had so terribly abused the wine bars at openings, that to this day, the aroma of white wine smells like the embryo form of barf. I never drink the stuff.

I had bought a case of this amazing cab at the local Costco. Friends I served it to had raced out to get a case for themselves. Eventually so many friends were after this great wine that I found myself at Costcos all across Southern California, procuring more. I am just now finishing off the last bottles. Please don't think me a wino or an oenophile. I don't normally drink by myself; wine should be shared. And I only buy what I like.

Susanne and Erich had taken me to a number of wine tasting events. At an event for Bordeaux futures I discovered my fondness for a nice Margeaux. At a dinner in Kassel, I discovered my love of Brunellos. I have long appreciated Central Valley Pinots and Syrahs. And like most, I love a great Napa cab. Lately I have been looking at Spanish reds and reds from Sicily. Both areas produce wonderful reds, at a decent price. So I like a good red wine. I'll spare you a dissertation on the charms of my favorite strains of herb and get back to the story.

I was alone and not at all that comfortable. I don't know why, and probably don't care to, but I am never comfortable at such events and would easily forgo openings altogether. Additionally I harbor a deep-seated dislike for the business aspects of being an artist, so much so that I have deliberately handicapped myself with a near total lack of understanding as to how the art world works or how to play the game. The truth is, one almost never encounters an articulate insight, or an interesting question, and I know it's not realistic to expect such, but more often than not, interaction with collectors, especially at openings, has the potential to leave one's skin crawling. I know intuitively that I don't want to be there. I am there out of social obligation. There are, of course, exceptions but they are rare and truly cherished.

Feeling as I did, I stepped outside and have a quick puff. I kept a cigar going, to function as my beard. Michael and I used to smoke cigars in the entrance garden to Manny's. That's the last time I ever saw him. I was teasing him about the new anti smoking laws at the bars in New York City. He laughed and said when I was next in town; we should go to the oyster bar at the Plaza, which was now a cigar bar as well. It sounded fantastic. Michael passed before we ever got there. He was a great painter and a kind and generous friend.

Eventually the opening came to an end and the crowd moved on to the next event of the evening. Manny had arranged a dinner at Dominick's. It was an art world hangout and I had partied there often. I climbed into my tiny red car and was pulling up in front of Dominick's in just minutes. I left the car with the valet but brought along another bottle of Napa cab. Manny had a large booth up front that could accommodate our party of eight. I was used to events that took up the entire patio. We chatted over wine and a lovely dinner. It was a quiet and elegant end to an incredible day. We said our "good nights and thank yous" on the sidewalk out front. I had given the valet my ticket, when we first stepped out, and my car was quickly waiting at the curb. I tipped the valet, crawled in, and pulled away, headed for Sunset and then the 405. Having lived in the boondocks for thirty some years, I had made this drive, fairly wrecked, on hundreds of occasions. Tonight was no different. The day had been special and so was the evening. Life was as rich and as full as it gets, absent a companion.

The "Bott's Dots" did their thing. Realizing I had nodded off, I slapped myself across the face and cracked a window for a rush of cool air. Quickly I realized I was exhausted and should have taken a Ritalin. I tried focusing but could feel myself drifting off. It's a terrible feeling being overwhelmed by exhaustion. Though I was doing my best to concentrate on the drive, I kept finding myself half asleep. I was on the 118 headed home and increasingly aware of my situation. More "Bott's Dots".

I was drifting off again when I saw the red lights behind me. Shit! I pulled to the right and stopped, just before the Tampa exit. Lucky for me I wasn't burning one. Whew! The adrenalin rush had me quite awake by the time the Sheriff arrived at my door.

He shined a light in my face and asked, "Sir, have you been drinking this evening?"

I told him I had been at an art opening and a dinner after and had a few glasses of wine.

He called the Highway Patrol. We waited. Eventually they arrived for the 'hand over'. The Highway Patrol cops were much cooler. The Sheriff got me out of his car, un-cuffed me, and handed me over, whereupon I was cuffed again and moved to the back of the cruiser. They drove me to the next exit, off the freeway, and into the parking lot of a closed fast food place. The second cop drove my car.

When he arrived he told me he loved the music, a Jewel/Paula compilation set, that Grover had turned me on to. He also told me my car reeked of wine. I explained that I had corked a half bottle of terrific wine a few nights before, placed it in the trunk, and brought it home. I forgot about it and it had leaked, thus the smell of wine.

They were not amused. They got me out and ran me through the tests. I did okay, having practiced such over and over as a youth. I blew their toy and up came a score that was legal for most of my life, but had just recently been deemed 'impaired'. I think we ought to keep the rules we grew up with. Give a dude a break. But such was not to be.

They took me to the Northridge/Chatsworth Station and booked me in. Upon a more thorough search they found a joint in my pocket (there were more in the car). The cop smiled at me, shook his head, and tossed it in the trash. I bet the janitors at the police station never have to buy boo. It is always so fun to meet a cool cop. They told me I was basically fine and would be out in six hours.

Everything went well enough until I answered a question wrong. They asked me if I was on any meds and I told them I was on Serotonin, an antidepressant. Well, that necessitated a full-time nurse, and as there was not one at this station, I was cuffed up again and told they had to take me to the Van Nuys Jail.

On the way, there was a high speed-chase coming south on the 5. They raced to the 405, in case the fleeing car took the 405 South from the junction with the 5. We were hauling ass. The cops, thrilled to have an excuse for such speed and behavior, were alive with banter and adrenal energy. I had about had my fill for the day. The dude stayed on the 5, they slowed down and my life leveled off to plain and simply shitty.

In time we arrived at the Van Nuys Police Station and jail. We parked underground and I'm walked in. The place was huge and full of intoxicated low-lifes and third world ne'er-do-wells. I was frisked, searched, the cuffs were removed, my personal property was checked, and then I was tossed into a holding tank full of bad people. I sat quietly and waited. Others were screaming, moaning, whining and talked to themselves. I was chastising myself, but not aloud. This was not how I saw this evening ending.

In time my name was called and I was taken to be formally booked. I was fingerprinted and mug shots are taken. It must have been after two by now. They gave me a sheet and a blanket and lead me through this heavy steel door and down an open corridor, with large cages full of prisoners on either side. They stopped, opened a cage door and I was placed in with 29 other dudes, all half my age, one black and all the rest Hispanic. This was not looking like fun.

It was dimly lit and noisy, with at least a dozen heavy snorers. Others were moaning, sneezing and coughing. I found a vacant top bunk in the back and climbed up. I wished I had my Purel. Pockets empty, I climbed down and walked to the sink. I washed my hands, as best I could, then my face, then cup my hands and drank as much water as possible. Immediately I realized I had to pee. No need to lift the seat; there wasn't one. I flushed and washed my hands again. I dried my face and hands on the inside, back of my shirt. I buttoned my shirt and returned to my bunk. Somehow I managed to fall asleep.

Morning came early in jail. It was like the Man was up, so who the fuck were you to be sleeping? It was not like they were waking you up for a reason. Most tried to ignore the chicken shit assholes. I did my best. Their macho pretensions were truly disgusting and were there to compensate for the raw fear in their soft, fat bellies. Reality had chosen sides for me once again.

There was a television, high up on the left front corner of the cage. There was a phone beneath it, to the right, on the front wall, and a sink, and two toilets, on the left wall. My companions were all chatting in Spanish, laughing and making jokes. Eventually they did a roll call, then came our breakfast: burritos and oranges. I traded my second burrito for more oranges.

The television was already showing a weird film called *Face Off*. The stars were John Travolta and Nicolas Cage. I kept waiting for them to call my name and cut me loose. The arresting officers had told me I would be out in six hours. Eventually I tried speaking with the guards, who were as macho, chicken-shit, rude and abrupt as possible. I didn't have my glasses and could not read the phone instructions. There was no one else to ask. The guard told me he would check my status.

I was lying in my bunk, eating oranges, watching this prison riot on the tube, and inwardly laughing at the absurdity of it all, when my name was called. But they didn't say, "bring your blanket and sheet", as they always did when someone was being released.

I walked to the front of the cage and the guard told me the Feds had placed a 'hold' on me because they couldn't read my fingerprints. He went on to tell me they were going to reprint me in a little bit. So that was the hold up.

A few hours later my name was called again. I got down from my upper bunk and moved to the front of our cage. They opened the door and told me to step out. I was walked back down the corridor, out through another set of barred doors, through a steel door, and into the 'booking' area. I was told to take a seat. In a bit I was taken to this large computer-like machine, with this 10 inch diameter glass cylinder, and my hands, one at a time, are placed on the cylinder, and rolled into the federal system.

The guy in charge gave me a bad look, and then told me to relax my wrist, so he could get a better set; the Feds had rejected his first effort. They rejected the second and the third.

Apparently, I do not have fingerprints. They have worn off in the course of a lifetime of being an artist. The Feds suspected that I might be a gangster or a terrorist. I was incredulous as I was tossed back into my cell. While I was away, someone had stolen my sheet. Perfect!

Eventually someone showed me how to use the phone. People were coming and going and I was quickly gaining seniority, plus I was by far the oldest dude in the dump. I called Tony and asked him to relay messages to Alexis and Jack. I didn't want Lex to worry. She had her hands full with our daughter who was just five days old. Big problem. Jack was everybody's favorite lawyer, and a total pro at rescuing his dumb artist pals from the strange realities we sometimes became entangled in.

Time crawls, and they were still showing that same stupid movie. I had no idea I would be in here so long and was starting to regret having eaten those oranges. I have never sat down on a crapper, located just beneath the television set, showing a prison riot film, and attempted to drop the log. I was determined that it would not happen now. Towards that end I skipped most of my dinner and turned in as quickly as possible. The lights went out but the din grew more intense. One could have easily imagined they were camping in the Amazon. I ached, I was hungry, exhausted, cold, and totally fed up with this episode. Somebody should have turned the channel. I slept with my shoes on, afraid of losing them.

Morning arrives soon enough, and the noise quickly grew. They did a morning roll call and then we line up to get our breakfast. Perhaps in deference to the population, the menu was a steady diet of burritos, and thanks to the beans, the air was rotten and fowl. I ate light, as I have been told I might not be released until court on Monday morning. Most of the dudes in my cage were minor league fuck-ups, popped for drunk driving, or inadvertent parole violations. As you hear them discussing their problems you could not help but realize most of them were basically decent folks who had somehow managed to get caught up in the system.

There was one dude who was the exception. He looked like he had been lifting weights for years and wore no shirt. His entire torso was covered in jailhouse tattoos. He is neither loud nor aggressive, but all seem to accept him as "Da Boss". He seemed almost able to astrally project himself beyond the walls. He was quiet and never raised his voice. I admired his Zen-Macho cool.

I was lying in my bunk, attempting to mentally escape the consequences of my stupidity, when I saw "Da Boss" walking towards the crapper. I focused, without staring, secretly observing his protocols. He picked up the roll of toilet paper, placed it vertically on his left index finger, then placed the end of the paper between the index, and middle finger, of his right hand, twists his wrist a few times, and made a small wad of toilet paper around his fingers. Then he carefully used this wad of paper to wipe off the porcelain lip of the bowl, tossed the paper in, and flushed. That done, he proceeded to tear off three and four length sheets of toilet paper and methodically placed them over the entire lip of the bowl. When finished, he dropped trow and took a seat. All the while a prison riot played on the TV just above his head. He seemed almost oblivious to it all. When he is done, he wiped his ass twice, then stood and pulled his trousers up. He pushed all the paper into the bowl with his foot and flushed. It was performance art, and far more informative than any army training film. I now knew how to do what I had been avoiding. I had a role model.

I knew I could do what had to be done. With the casual nonchalance of one who has done it a thousand times, I rolled off my top bunk, slid to the floor and strolled to the front of the cage, for my porcelain initiation. I followed my hero's lead, doing each step exactly as he had, and when the time came, I sat on my improvised protective shield, and quickly managed to accomplish what I had been avoiding for days. When I finished, and I was putting myself back together, I felt this inner pride, not unlike that moment in one's youth, where you just qualified for a merit badge. That's exactly what I was feeling. I wanted a "I Shit Like a Tough

I Shit Like A Tough Guy

Guy" merit badge.

After washing my hands and face, which I dried on the inside of my shirt, I returned to my bunk. I felt good as one could under the circumstances.

The rest of the day was uneventful. The same stupid movie ran endlessly. Watching a prison riot from a bunk in a jail cell was the height of irony. It was more humorous than scary. The guards were endlessly displaying their, 'I'm in charge', macho bravado, while still more burritos arrive for dinner, and at long last, lights out. I was so ready to flush out of this toilet. Most of those I was in with my first night had matriculated on, bailed out I suspect.

The next morning my name was called and I was taken down the hall and into a room to meet with an attorney Jack had sent to assist me. He was incredulous; he told me he had never seen a situation like mine. He told me friends and fellow faculty from school had been trying to arrange my release, but that the Department of Justice had placed a 'hold' on me and there was nothing anyone could do to expedite my release. He said my best chance was to be taken before the arraignment judge, where he would represent me, and see if the court would release me. This situation was radically expanding my understanding of 'surreal'. It was resembling a Kafka nightmare.

I was hoping to hear my name included in a group proceeding to court. I waited without any other hope. Nothing.

Then I heard, "Hayward bring your sheet and blanket," a sure sign I was leaving.

"I don't have a sheet. It disappeared when they were re-fingerprinting me".

"Fine, bring your blanket".

I dragged my exhausted ass (I hadn't been sleeping that well) to the front of the cage, managed a weak smile at those I was leaving behind, abandoning, wondering if I was now a hopeful example of release and redemption.

I tossed my blanket into the plastic trash-can marked "blankets", and was marched back to the booking area, where the entire process, from prints to mug shot, was now done in reverse.

That completed, I was moved into a small room, with a door at each end, and a walk-up window with bulletproof glass, and gave the cop seated on the other side my name. He quickly retrieved all my personal property, belt, wallet, glasses, money, and returned them all to me. I was putting on my belt when I heard him say, "We can't release this guy. DOJ has a federal hold on him."

I was about to shit my pants, when this black woman, the Desk Sergeant at the moment, approached and said, "This man is neither a gangster nor a terrorist. He is a schoolteacher and friends have been trying to get him released for days. I am releasing him on my own authority."

She was the coolest cop I had met in the last few days. She looked at the situation and did something to make it right. I thanked her and the guy behind the window told me to exit to my right. The door buzzed, I opened it, and stepped out into the fresh air of freedom.

It had been three days since I last showered. I was slick with sweat and the grime of the jailhouse. I felt like shit and figured I looked about the same. I didn't have my keys; they were with my car, which had been impounded. Out on Van Nuys Blvd I found a pay phone; my cell was in my car. After calling a cab, I wandered down the street and found an open diner. The place was near empty so my Coke, to go, came quickly and I headed back to meet my cab.

Eventually the cab arrived. The driver was a heavyset black man who winced when I told him where I wanted to go. My place was about 30 miles away and in the next county. I promised him a nice tip.

He asked if I had just gotten out of jail. I answered in the affirmative and laid a few of the details on him. He laughed at how silly it all was, a conclusion I envied and hoped to arrive at someday soon, but not yet. I directed him to the farm in 40 minutes. I got out at the gate and gave him everything in my pocket. He smiled, thanked me, and wished me luck

I wandered back to my compound gate and, not having the keys, scaled it. The dogs, "Chip" and "Jack", were thrilled to see me. I filled their bowls with water, fed them, found my emergency key, and let myself into the Spartan Mansion. I raced through the trailer and out the back door to the shower. While living in Japan, a few years earlier, I had adopted the behavior of only turning on the hot water heater when needed, and this I did. Now came the 20-minute wait for the water to fully heat, the downside of going green.

While waiting, I rolled a fatty, and pulled hard on my first puff in over three days. I know, big deal, three days without herb, but for someone

I Shit Like A Tough Guy

who normally smokes three by 10:00, it is a bit different. Some people meditate, others see a shrink, still others swim or run. Me, I smoke. It's probably a residual behavior from college in the 60s. It works.

Soon I was melting in the most wonderful shower ever. The joint and shower had sapped every last bit of strength. I dried off and crawled into my bed, glad to be home. I'll deal with all the necessary shit in the morning. For now, it would be sweet dreams.

Holly Myers

Dark Land of the Sun
Excerpt: The 302 Bus

Then freezing sweat poured down my thighs and knees
A darkening moisture fell from all my body
And where I stepped a stream ran down; from hair
To foot it flowed, faster than words can tell.
I had been changed into a pool, a river;
Yet in these streams Alpheus saw and knew
The one he loved, and slipped from man's disguise
To water flowing toward me as I moved.
My Delian goddess opened up the earth,
and I, a cataract, poured down into darkness.

—Ovid

The 302 bus, east on Sunset, Tuesday 9:48 p.m.

    A shadow of a man in a frayed green army jacket boards the bus at Alvarado. His chest is bare beneath his jacket; his jeans are filthy and several sizes too big and they hang across the fins of his hip bones from a scrap of a belt that's twisted at the side and the jeans are missing a loop. He is gaunt and yellow but his eyes are ablaze. He raises his hands to the bars along the roof and sways with the motions of the bus. There is a head of a lion blurred blue across his chest.

249

❧

Laodicean, Daniel said. *The winning word.*
What?
There was a spelling bee.

The day they met his parents at the hotel in Santa Monica. There was a breeze that lifted the corners of the napkins. What? Laodicean. *Laodicean.*

Ellen watched him those last days and she saw no reflection. She watched him over the menus of restaurants. What would she have? Pasta. The night they spoke of Emory. She watched his face and tried to remember, tried to see through to something she knew or recalled, tried to transpose some memory of intimate vision, but his features were all opaque. She didn't know him.

The night he ordered salmon. (Memories like a tumbling pile of pebbles.) She recalls drinking very quickly. She recalls that she said she'd run into Emory.

Good old Emory. He was sarcastic.
She has a new girlfriend, I met her.
Were you jealous?
Fuck you.

Who *is* this person? She tries to look now, from the vantage of busses: he is a hollow space, lined with signifiers. They met in college, in a history class at Berkeley: he wore a Black Flagg t-shirt and a prep school Oxford. He came from Long Island; he had a somber look. *Why did you come to Berkeley? I wanted to understand California*, he said. He knew more about music than she knew about anything, and spoke with an authority that stilled something in her, but she is older now. He played in a band then. He played bass guitar and once he played on a stage with red neon behind him and there was a glow of red on his shoulder and face and she thought: *This is perhaps what it means to be in love.* They must have been happy. They were not unhappy. She remembers a morning when his room was filled with light and she saw that he had row of smooth, black stones lined up along the back edge of his desk. He had a way with the world that was clear and direct, that brought all of life into the dimensions of a shopping list—whereas she was moving always in circles. But they did not perhaps *fall* in love so much as *drift*. It is difficult, from the vantage of busses, from the vantage of divorce, with what was pulled suddenly apart from what will be, to know what the word *love* really meant in such a circumstance: together for nine years, married for six; come together in those last few heady and anxious months of college. Who was he then? The band broke up not long after college—he never played in a band in Los Angeles; he became a writer and wrote about other bands and now, at 35, he writes for the newspaper, with a salary, health insurance, and a desk in the newsroom, where her picture would have hung until recently, pinned to a board beside a list of phone numbers. She looked at him once in a fit of anger and thought that he was all machinery. A little spark with metal around it, all these moving parts: pistons and spark plugs. His father was a doctor; his mother stayed home through most of his childhood and taught him to be particular about laundry and cleaning products.

    Do you understand it? she asked him the first day they walked together from class.

    What?

    California.

    No. He paused. *I don't think so. Berkeley maybe.*

    They moved to Los Angeles. They lived in an apartment on Whitley Avenue in Hollywood where she had a desk at a window that looked down on the patio of an old Russian woman who lived alone. We speak of people as if they are particles, when really they are more like waves. I am not *this* but *here*—Sunset and Western, Sunset and Normandie: not an object so much as a set of coordinates. It's clearer on a bus, moving through space with strangers. We are evolving bundles of interrelated phenomena. This is what she would like to say to the therapist with the hair knot who asked her to describe *the Daniel she fell in love with*. Was it love? They steadied one another. They lived at Whitley Avenue and Emmet Terrace; she worked in a bookstore for a time, then taught art to children, and recalls more vividly than any evidence of love the terror of Saturday afternoons at that desk as she groped against the great looming blank of her future for a direction, a subject, a theme, something—some path leading into the life of an artist. She drew half-hearted pictures of the old Russian woman's plants. She drew pictures of her hands, her feet, her pen jar, piles of laundry, apple rinds and tea bags, overwhelmed by the banality of her new adulthood. She ripped everything up and wept for her failure to penetrate the haze—while Daniel sat straight and intent like a post at his desk in the one other small room of the small apartment.

But that wasn't *her*. That wasn't *the Ellen Daniel fell in love with*. (Even Daniel recognized the inanity of the question—she could tell from his quick, exasperated squint.) That was the circumstance of a small apartment in a noisy neighborhood and nebulous ambition yet outstripping its means. She became an artist. She rented a room in another woman's studio and began to make cardboard dioramas based on dreams. Later, she went to graduate school. They moved from the apartment on Whitley into a duplex on Edgecliffe, in Silver Lake, where there was an alcove for her grandmother's table with big windows draped in purple bougainvillea. They had friends for dinner. They watched all the films of Michelangelo Antonioni and occasionally spoke of having children.

Has she been deceived? He was not, as she recalls it, a stranger then; he became one later—it was gradual.

Do you remember, she said to him the night they spoke of Emory, *the man with the beard in the coffee shop in Berkeley who was always writing really small into notebooks?*

The night she was shaking with things that needed to be said.

Notebook after notebook.

What about him?

There was a particular look she came to despise. This man, this stranger, whose skin she knew the smell of, whose movements through the house she knew the sound of. There were times when he looked at her with eyes like a flat, raw plank of wood.

The night she intended to tell him she needed to leave. *He must have a lot of notebooks by now.*

She's riding busses for hours, sorting through pebbles. They met in college, in a history class at Berkeley—

᭒

There is always, to begin with, a *coordinate*. That's one thing. A point in space, a point in time. Geometry. Cartography—where is she? It is as if she keeps coming to, although she is awake and alert. Sunset and Echo Park. She's on the bus. There is a man in an army jacket swaying and muttering, eyes all flaring chemical green. He's lurching through the lyrics to a rap song.

Dark Land of the Sun

She's been riding the bus for hours, for days. The bus is stable and blank—a long metal box, metal walls and windows. She was in an *accident*. What? I was in an accident. Oh my God what happened! I was in the hospital overnight.

It is like she fell out of step with life; she opens her mouth and other languages come out. She woke one morning on the couch in her studio and realized that she had been sleeping there for weeks. She woke with the sun blazing white through the east window, with her t-shirt soaked through and sticking to her chest. Where was she? She is an artist. She was married. She met her husband in college, in a history class at Berkeley. At some point along the line—she wants to see it as a dot, like a bus stop, but really it was a slow gradation of color to gray—the man became a stranger.

They bought a house: Parkman north of Bellevue. They married on the lawn of a botanical garden, but the house took far more paperwork, fixed them shoulder to shoulder into the weird hysterics of the middle class, and she didn't want it—she told him. Here, perhaps, was an early sign. She said: *What do we need with a house? Casey has a house and look at her.* He had a way of sighing under his breath. What does your sister have to do with it? The city was swollen and fevered then, drunk with talk of interest rates and property values. There were stories of houses making a hundred thousand dollars in a matter of months doing nothing but existing in the possession of their owners and it brought out in friends and even in Daniel a mean and clumsy covetousness. She hated every minute of the search for a house. She hated the small talk of realtors; hated standing on sidewalks in the heavy sun. She hated the shabby intimacy of other people's furniture and the garish descent of young, white couples upon streets whose history was nothing to them. She stood once on a curb in Highland Park, in a skirt and sandals, carrying a purse, at the edge of a crowd awaiting the arrival of a realtor and watched a man who was working beneath the hood of a truck: she wanted to crawl beneath the truck and apologize. But she went along. They found a house after nearly a year. Signing the papers, Daniel was stern and suspicious like his father, a stiff container for gel-like anxiety, and she became like his mother, or hers—quiet and distracted. They bought the house from a Salvadoran widower they never met, who sold it to move in with his daughter in West Covina; it had slanting wood floors and paint-caked window frames and ochre yellow daisy wallpaper tucked neatly into all the kitchen drawers. Daniel's father gave them $50,000; her father, typically, gave them nothing; four years later the market fell out. She does not want the house—she told him. The day they met to talk about business. *I didn't want it then and I don't what it now.*

It's not that easy.

What's not? It's yours.

Your name—

Do whatever you need to do, I don't care.

It would cost $20,000 to sell it now.

Parkman north of Bellevue. It had a little lawn that was never quite green and a concrete path from the sidewalk to the door. It had a lemon tree. It is a surprisingly weightless thing in her mind, like a bucket made from an old plastic milk jug. Things happened there; it held things. It holds pebbles now. Snapshots. The night the rain came in the window and soaked her Gerhard Richter book. Many nights of dinners, many nights of sleeping. The night of the fire in Griffith Park, when they drank gin on the deck and the sky was orange and purple. The night of her thirty-second birthday party, when Gretchen's date was drunk and lay his hand on her thigh.

The night she saw the cat in the road.

I bought coffee, she said. *You wanted coffee.* He was playing Marvin Gaye; it was dark outside and beginning to rain. He was washing a stack of dishes in the sink.

Have you eaten?

No.

We have that eggplant.

He wore a shirt she'd picked up from the cleaners the day before. He looked older than she thought of him being. She stood in the doorway of the kitchen holding a bag of coffee beans.

She said: *I saw a terrible thing today, driving to the studio.*

What was it? A kitten, she said. *At the side of the road.*

Dead?

Not yet. Not dead yet, unfortunately. It seemed portentous at the time. She didn't want him to touch her. That was the bitter thing about the house. She undressed quickly at night so he wouldn't see her, and dreaded those times when he drew up next to her. She knew that this was not as it should be.

Dark Land of the Sun

❦

Echo Park Avenue. Figueroa Boulevard.
Stop requested.

The night they spoke of Emory. Why does this particular pebble stick? It was strange that they would have spoken of Emory. There were things all along that needed to be said—but Emory? Emory was a streak of headlights through an empty room, many years ago.

She has a show in November. She went to India. She got a Fullbright. She has a girlfriend. She moved to Eagle Rock.

The weight of words—she was almost panting, trying to deflect the import of the occurrence. This is what people do, she told herself: they marry, they go out to dinner in the evenings and they talk about the people they happen to run into. They have affairs when they're young and they get over them. *How was your day, my darling? You'll never guess who I ran into.* It had long been a point of pride between them that theirs was not a sentimental union.

How long has it been since you've seen her?
Several years. I thought she'd moved.
But she was in India?
Yes.
With her girlfriend?
No, the girlfriend is new.

She was nearly drunk. She tried to stay focused on what needed to be said but her thoughts slid repeatedly into darkened corners. Emory had black hair and pale skin, which struck Ellen when she met her with a sense of the miraculous. It was dangerous to think of Emory. The night they met, Emory set down her glass and looked Ellen in the eye and asked in front of everyone: *But do you actually want to get married?* She was lithe and boyish. She had the certainty of the activist; she spoke three languages; she'd lived in Nepal. She'd survived a rare form of cancer as a child and she spoke of death casually, as of an uncle she expected to pick her up at the airport.

A sun-filled bedroom with blue print curtains and a yellow bedspread; years ago. Emory was pouring champagne. *But it's only ten,* Ellen said.

But I hardly see you, Emory said.

Emory's body had muscle and determination and a softness of skin

255

that made every touch feel like sliding. She was a world made all of smooth walls and crevices; Ellen was fluid, defenseless with her. She could not have stopped what happened, she could not have ended it; she told Daniel it was over several long, warm afternoons before it was. (Daniel was baffled more than anything.) It ended only when Emory went to Africa, and then it was like a spell had broken. Daniel seemed to believe that she broke Emory's heart, but Ellen knew there was nothing in Emory to break: she was pliable; she bent one way, then the other. *I've been happy to know you,* she said. *You have beautiful shoulders.*

Ellen would have fled if she'd had the opportunity when Emory appeared with her girlfriend in the foyer of the museum that shaking day in April. She'd been to see the Dan Graham exhibition; she was thrilled and discomposed as she emerged, tossing in thoughts of surfaces and reflections, walls and space, the partitioning of space, the nature of rooms. She'd caught a glimpse of herself across the gallery in the mirrored panel of one of Graham's installations and believed for a moment that she was looking at a stranger. In the space of that strange, brief cognitive gap was a vision of freedom that shook to the core. Her mind filled with questions. What is the kinship of body to reflection? Reflection to surface? Skin to glass? Why, in her own work, did she never make walls? Why had she never thought to mirror surfaces? She made sculptures based on American landscape paintings—three dimensional abstractions of Frederick Church, Thomas Cole, Albert Bierstadt that *split and splayed the American vision of Manifest Destiny like a corpse upon an autopsy table*, as one British critic put it after her show in London—but she never built walls, and why? Walls were crucial, walls were powerful—why leave such a fundamental determinant to the incidental shape of the gallery? Why had she never thought of this before? Even a Bierstadt has walls (the frame, the canvas). She built everything *except* for walls, and here Graham built only walls with nothing inside but the fractured reflection of other walls. She imagined an enormous box with mirrored walls on the inside, containing somehow the peak of a mountain. She imagined a mirrored box containing a still, clear pool of water. Water reflecting mirror reflecting water—

And then Emory in the foyer, like some dark-haired messenger angel from a whole other age, from a Gentileschi or a Caravaggio. The wave of intellectual agitation that seemed always to be gathering to a crest of revelation sputtered and receded at the sight of Emory, and Ellen was reduced once more to the bewilderment of the personal: the tug of desire, the tug of jealousy, the tug of loss, the tug of anger, all at slightly different angles. The girlfriend was young, had a crooked haircut and a haughty way of standing, with her hands in her pockets and her chin jutting up; she betrayed no recognition when Ellen's name was mentioned. Ellen wanted to flee but stumbled instead through eviscerating pleasantries.

You're still with Meredith Roski?
No, I left the gallery.
Oh. Did she—
We had a falling out.
And how's Daniel?

It wasn't clear if Emory intended to be cruel. She was impersonally cheerful, blankly amiable; they kissed on the cheek and parted ways. But the messenger angel came tumbling after, down the street to Ellen's car, robes furling blue and gold. *Are you going to talk to him?*

What do you say to the man you chose to marry when you need to leave and you don't know why? There are no words for this.

⅍

The man in the army jacket drops himself into the row of seats that faces the aisle and stretches his arms out to either side. He has a twitch in his shoulder. His voice swells and subsides and his shoulder jerks with the staccato syllables. It is the same lyric over and over, pinned to a clumsy rhythm and wound in with fragments of other phrases. An elderly man across the aisle gets off the bus at Cesar Chavez.

His voice rises sharply: *That's what he TOLD me fucking cunt bitch.*

He has the air of one who is pleased with himself.

⅍

These days tumble on by their own momentum. The day she woke to find she'd been sleeping in her studio. *El, what happened? El, did you sleep here?* Something she's learned since she's been here: the word *alone* is almost always inaccurate. She woke on a morning with the sun blazing white through east facing windows and she found friends pressing in at the

257

edges with pick axes. How does she say she is *interested* in placelessness? She is relieved, at ease, in a state of nowhere. Jen sat at Ellen's feet on the couch in her studio. Ellen's t-shirt was stuck to her chest with sweat from the heat of sleeping.

El, what is it?
I thought you were in Italy.
El, what happened?
I don't know exactly.
El....? El....? El...?
I moved out, I guess.
What?
Daniel was angry. He said to get out so I did.
I was in an accident.

She can't explain. She will point outside the window of the bus and say: *THERE is a pharmacy with a blue and yellow awning. THERE is a taco truck. THERE is a shop that sells tropical fish. This is what the world really means.*

❧

The night the sky came down.
Well, what is it you want?
He was standing in the doorway. She tried to say she didn't know but all the air had left her mouth. *What is it you want? Fucking TALK to me.*

She lay her forehead on the table. She heard him turn and kick the door behind him—it slammed against the wall. She heard him slam the bathroom door. Silence. He was probably sitting on the edge of the tub. She begged for the world to collapse around her. She imagined a meteor crashing through the ceiling, or a tree trunk, or a satellite, or the wing of an airplane.

She heard him in the kitchen. She felt him beside her. *Ellen.* He touched her arm and the weakness of his skin turned her stomach.

Why is it assumed that the vector points only from together to alone? Better to say *it points from here to somewhere else.* (Must *here* always be the starting point?) Am I alone? She is on a bus. There are six people behind her and four in front. There's a man in an army jacket, around whom

258

hovers a holographic world filled with other people.

Where is she coming from? She is going in circles—or circles with points: heptagons or octagons. She was in Westwood to see the Rachel Whiteread exhibition. Wilshire and Westwood. She walked north to Sunset. She crossed Sunset. She boarded the west bound bus, when she needed to go east.

The threads of logic have come all loose from everything.

⁊⋇

The morning she woke to a terrific clamor of metal: something crashing, then voices. She told herself *it's only the bakery*, then remembered no, it was in college that she lived next to the bakery. She and Daniel would sit in the window with coffee and croissants, the mornings when he stayed over. That was years ago. Now she is neither here nor there. She is sleeping on the couch in her studio. She's been trying to read the sunlight these mornings. She's considered putting marks on the floor: 7:00. 8:00. 9:00. But at 10:00 am the light goes fuzzy.

El, what happened?

I was born in Santa Monica. My parents divorced when I was five. There was a tree with a swing behind our house in Ocean Park, which was unusual. It was unusual to have a tree; the yards were very small. We moved from that house when my parents were divorced. I make art, though lately something went loose: I don't know why I do it, or what it means. I was married once. Daniel got angry. He said to get out so I did.

How long were you married?

I was married for six years.

Jim stood in the doorway while Jen sat at Ellen's feet on the end of the couch. Jim has eyes like windows he can step up to or back from. Jen has eyes like a flood light. Jim and Jen were married in the desert, not long after Ellen and Daniel were married. They stood on a promontory overlooking a plain of Joshua Trees.

El, where's all your work?

The fucking questions. There was a couch in the studio, a duffel bag with clothes, three folding chairs and several take out menus. There were several empty wine bottles. *I got rid of it. What do you mean? I threw it away.*

I was in an accident. I was in the hospital overnight.

‏ت

That's what they told me, says the man in the army jacket. *Fuckin'-A.*

He leans forward and rests his arms on his knees, then waves his right hand in the air and laughs again. *Fuck, man. Fuck. That's what he said, man. I told you.*

‏ت

Now that you are alone—
But I'm not alone. Look at all these people.
The 302 runs the entire length of Sunset, from the Pacific Coast Highway to the point downtown where Sunset changes into Cesar Chavez Avenue, Los Angeles into East Los Angeles, where, in some ghostly veil of historical vision, the city was settled in 1781. Forty-four mestizos lay down their oxen at Cesar Chavez and Main, spawning a clan of 12.8 million. There's a Chevron station at that point now, and bail bonds service, and a Vietnamese restaurant. What does this mean? From Sunset, downtown, the east bound bus heads south on Broadway, west on Venice, north on Hill, and then west on Sunset (a circle—or a rectangle, an ellipse, a parallelogram). People live here, people work here, one all on top of one another, all speaking different languages. There are hotels and sandwich shops; there is City Hall, the courthouse, the Cathedral. The west bound bus crosses the city, the world, and spills from Sunset into the current of PCH and on this particular day the ocean came as a revelation, crashing through the membrane of Ellen's internal skin and sweeping her clear of knowledge and sensation. It was searingly blue, a plateau of sapphires. It was so broad and so—blank.
The day she rode the whole length of the 302.
There are so many things, she thought, that I don't understand. *Here*—we have a bus heading south on PCH. We have jagged white lines scratched into the window of the bus. We have fingerprints and smudge marks and light glinting off a thin metal grill along the frame of a window. Here we have factories that fabricate the components of busses, and men

who build factories, and dirt that is plowed from one side to the another to lay the foundation, and trees grown from seed in some distant place for lumber. We have protracted chains of cause and effect. One day there were men, thinking about axels, and aluminum, and the procurement of rubber, and the ideal shape for the drill bits of oil wells. One day there were men, thinking about the wheel and glimpsing with a sense of profound revelation the ratio by which velocity follows upon the elimination of resistance. And there—out there—we have a blue that is like the end of a thousand year draught, and a blue that is like happiness in summer, and between them a long, soft smudge of white. Beyond the circus of all human effort, that is what there is: the arduous cycle of cause and effect comes mysteriously to peace.

The bus slows and shudders and turns: north on Temescal Canyon, east on Sunset. A circle.

⅔

The night Jim made salmon and Jen folded dish towels and talked about Italy.

I'm glad you're here, El. You know you can stay as long as you like.

Jen is small and sincere and runs every day; her life is structured with the manic efficiency that belongs only to daughters of unstable women and her devotion to Jim is total, unquestioning. Her talk on this evening was quick and eager, a Technicolor slideshow starring Audrey Hepburn in pumps and sunglasses: there was the Giotto in Assisi, the prosciutto in Montalcino, the old man with the watch in the wine shop in Sienna; there was marble everywhere; there were vineyards and olive trees and old stone churches haunted by the limp and bloodied body of Christ. There was *history* everywhere—that strange, spectral layering of human evidence, so bewitching to one raised, like Jen, in Pomona. She cried in the Basilica di Santa Maria del Fiore. She returned with an elegiac passion for marble— how soft, she said, and how solid, like skin. Ellen could think only of the statuary shop in Chinatown crammed wall to wall with fu dogs and dolphins and Venus de Milos. *It's everything that's wrong about America,* Jen says. *California is nothing but plastic and stucco.*

This is how it is on the inside of other people's marriages: crowded and damp and bland and safe. Ellen has sat at this table a dozen times

261

before, but the apartment is smaller this time than it was, with a bed laid now on the floor of the office, down among the computer cords and power strips.

Jim made salmon with lemons and capers. Jen talked incessantly. She laid her hand frequently on Ellen's shoulder. *You know that we're here for you* (where?) *no matter what happens.* What happened, in fact, was nothing so unusual. We were probably unsuited to one another to begin with.

So wait, what did you say about an accident? Where is your car?
I was in an accident. I was in the hospital overnight.
Are you ok?
My car is gone.

Actress Annaleigh Brooks was hospitalized in critical condition early Thursday morning after her SUV ran a red light in Silver Lake, police say. It is not clear if drugs or alcohol were involved.

Brooks, who is best known for her role on the popular teen drama Bay City, was exiting the Hollywood Freeway at Silver Lake Boulevard at approximately 3:00 am when she ran the light and struck another vehicle. She was alone in the car. She was rushed by ambulance to Cedars Sinai Medical Center, where she received treatment for a fractured skull and collarbone, authorities say.

The other driver, who was not immediately identified, was hospitalized with minor injuries.

The man in the army jacket laughs and sighs and for a moment he's calm. He has a thoughtful look. He rubs his hand across the lion on his chest and turns to look out the window behind him. Then his head jerks, his shoulder follows, and an expression of frustration comes over his face. *Maaaannn,* he whines. *What's the fucking—you know me, man! You know me!*

The man stands and sways as the bus turns onto Broadway.

Dark Land of the Sun

❧

The night Jen talked incessantly and went to bed early. Ellen and Jim sat up drinking till three. He has a tattoo of a dragon up his inside right forearm. He has the drag of a faint Tennessee accent that deepens when he drinks. He kept glancing at her in his hooded way. He opened the window and lit a cigarette and filled her glass and leaned back in his chair; he glanced at her again.

Just ask me.

What?

You keep looking at me.

Why did you throw out all your work?

Jim's queries are daunting, shorn as they are of ameliorating banter. But this, at least, was a reasonable question, one that lifted the lid on a sphere she could speak to, where there was some at least recognizable sense of agency. *I got tired of looking at it,* she said.

I don't know what that means.

Something was off. I don't know. There was too much, you know, material. Or something.

She made sculptures from rebar and pipes and long strips of plastic cut from soda bottles, based on nineteenth century American landscape paintings. They were not difficult to dismantle. *The work of Ellen Spaulding rides a tenuous line between cohesion and upheaval. Ellen Spaulding explores the intersection of chaos and containment. Ellen Spaulding's sculptures feel always on the verge of falling apart.*

❧

When the bus shuddered and turned onto Temescal Canyon, away from the sparkling vision of the sea, it was as if she'd just been shaken. Everything was vivid, unstable: trees, bicyclists, bumpers, exhaust pipes. A child's tiny fingertips pressed to a window. Sunset Boulevard winds up through Pacific Palisades—Sunset and Chautauqua, Sunset and Minorca—through a neighborhood tinted as green as New England, a strange green mirage of suburban life, streets tucked neatly between all the trees. The green swells and ripples around rivers of metal: busses and catering vans and SUVs and convertibles driven by stable, polished, expensive individuals. A man with his arm out the window of a convertible, pale blue shirt rolled up at the sleeve. An old woman behind the wheel of an old, gold Mercedes. There is this layer, then there are others beneath it. A battered pickup truck with a lawnmower in back turned onto the street that was once her grandfather's, the street where her father was born: Clifton Avenue. A black sedan followed, with tinted windows. Her grandfather is dead. The house has a fence now and yellow paint, but beneath that is another house that is white, not yellow, and has no fence but has Persian carpets and butterscotch candies in crystal dishes, and beneath that house is another where her father was a boy, which she can scarcely imagine except by way of a single photograph: a boy in a scout uniform, little shorts, little knees, standing on the step. That house was sold ten years ago.

The day they drove to her grandmother's funeral in her father's wide, white Cadillac, then back to the house on Clifton Avenue. The backs of her legs stuck to the leather of the seat and she clung to the door when her father turned a corner so as not to slide into Casey, who was sure to shove her away. Her father was silent. Her mother looked only out the side window.

Under the 405 freeway. Veteran Avenue. Hilgard Avenue, past UCLA. She was born into the world at the UCLA Medical Center, one cool and presumably sunny morning in March. She returned to UCLA for graduate school, though she spent most of her time in the studios off campus in Culver City.

Past UCLA, past the gates of Bel Aire and the broad, silent lawns of Beverly Hills.

❧

I was in an accident.
What happened?
There was an article every day at first: the girl's abrupt disintegration and slow renewal. What a flood, Ellen thought, of empty curiosity.

Actress Annaleigh Brooks underwent emergency surgery Thursday afternoon to relieve pressure caused by bleeding in the brain following a car accident early Thursday morning, said a spokesman for Cedars Sinai Medical Center.

Brooks was exiting the Hollywood Freeway in Silver Lake when her

SUV collided with another vehicle. She was initially treated for a fractured skull and collarbone, but suffered a severe brain hemorrhage later in the morning.

Dr. Matthew Lin, chief of the hospital's Neurosurgery Department, said that the operation went "smoothly," and that Brooks is likely to recover. But, he said, "it will take some time to determine the full extent of the brain injury."

Sources say that Brooks, who is 21, was given a blood test at the time of the accident to determine whether she was intoxicated, but police will not confirm the results. "It will take weeks for detectives to complete the lab work," Lt. Mitch McCormick said.

Brooks was evidently returning from a private party at the Crow's Nest, a downtown club. She was alone in the car at the time of the accident.

⚜

On the night Ellen and Jim stayed up until three, Ellen bumped her shin on the coffee table, following Jim through the living room in the dark. She laughed and stumbled and held her leg; he laughed and reached back and touched her hair in the dark, then her shoulder—*are you ok?*—laughing. He took her hand and led her to the door of the office, which came before the door of the bathroom, then the bedroom. There was no shade on the window in the office; the light came through watery blue and cold. She was swelling with feeling. For one of the first and only moments in her life, she wanted desperately not to be left alone. *Bathroom, towels, light switch*, he said. He didn't turn on the light. At the door of the office, they drifted into one another. He caught his fingers up in her hair and his arms and his long, slender chest were everywhere—against, above, behind, beside—and the unfamiliar smell of him, and the taut, unfamiliar feel of his skin. She felt his breathing. She felt his breath and his mouth on her neck and her cheek and felt near to fainting. He held the back of her head. She felt the rough of his cheek. A moment later, he swayed and was gone. She met Jim and Jen in graduate school; Jim was Ellen's year, Jen the following. They were often together. There was the night they drank tequila and painted the wall of Ellen's studio red. The night they stayed up till four casting hundreds of tiny plaster sparrows for Jen. The night they drove to the desert to film bottle rockets in the sunrise.

265

The night Ellen and Jim nearly kissed in the hallway, when Ellen was going through a divorce. She cried that night for the first time since the accident, lying beneath the blue water light that flooded in through the window without a shade.

꙰

The bus lumbered onto the Sunset Strip where the billboards float loose like comic strip thought bubbles, blaring dirty, sharp-edged fantasies: past the club where she snuck out to see Beck in high school, past the club where she saw Arcade Fire with Daniel, in the days when they were contented and easy, and later saw Beirut and he did nothing but complain. There was a woman on a billboard, all bones and skin and jaw line jutting. The bus stopped at a light. The woman flickered only partially out of the blackness of the billboard, hair blown across her face, frail and enormous. Ellen closed her eyes. The bus moved again.

Who is that woman? Where is she now? There are so many things that I don't understand. Which is the real thing—the billboard body or the skin and blood body that crosses sidewalks into restaurants and parties?

Who is the shadow of whom?

Hospital officials confirmed today that actress Annaleigh Brooks' blood alcohol level registered 0.12 when she was hospitalized Thursday morning. The legal limit is 0.08. A toxicology test also found traces of several prescription drugs in her system, including Ativan and Klonopin, drugs typically prescribed for anxiety.

The actress, who is 21, was rumored to have been admitted to a drug and alcohol treatment facility in Scottsdale, Arizona, last fall, after a widely publicized altercation with a security guard in the Fred Segal department store in West Hollywood.

According to the store's management, Brooks was visibly intoxicated when she entered the store and proceeded to cause a disturbance. When a female security guard asked her to leave, she became violent with the guard and issued a number of racial epithets. No charges were pressed, but the incident was captured on videotape by another customer and distributed widely across the internet.

The bus passed strip clubs and liquor stores, muffler shops and Thai restaurants, lumbering on through Hollywood. The guitar shop carried traces of Daniel still like waves of scent off a piece of clothing. The movie theater. The bistro down the block from the theater that held within it still the last bright image: Daniel's face across a table with a candle, bright with laughter and masculine intelligence, skewering with words the film they'd seen together, cinching into words the thoughts so vague in her mind that they were more like breezes than thoughts, as she watched with a fire of admiration thinking *this is why I need him.*

The last night they were happy before he told her to get out.

༺

The man in the army jacket is watching her. He is standing and swaying. He looks to the right and says: *Maggie. Maggie come on.* He looks at Ellen and says: *Maggie.*

Stop requested.

He drifts down the aisle of the bus and sinks into the seat across the aisle from Ellen. He sits with his back against the window, stretching his leg across the seat so that his grey-white tennis shoe hangs off the edge. He has no sock. His ankle is bone and stretched, deadened, dirty skin, with yellow hairs going up his leg.

༺

Do you want food?

No.

I ran into Jennifer.

She turned the salt shaker slowly in circles. The day they met to talk business, after a new life of not talking.

Why didn't you tell me you were living in your studio? I would have let you have the house, I've been in New York a lot of the time.

I wouldn't have wanted it.

She ordered coffee but didn't drink it. (I don't want to know anything about your life.) The café was bright and blank, a lunch place for those who worked in buildings with elevators. He wanted to know about dividing the things: she had clothes in the house, books and furniture. *Do you have anywhere to put it?*

No.

267

Are you going to get a place?
I don't know.

She placed the salt shaker on the corner of her placemat. Perhaps the vector is from here to everywhere.

He wanted to know about the house. She folded the edge of her placemat into a triangle. *It's your house, do what you like.*

It's our house.
You paid for it.
Not all of it.
Your father did.
As a wedding gift.
Whatever.
Ellen—
Fuck you.

She folded the other corner of her placemat. He sighed.

I didn't want it then and I don't want it now.
It's not that easy.
What's not?
It would cost $20,000 to sell it now.

He has lengthy, researched explanations, and considerations for and against; he has thoughts about a contract of some sort. She can only imagine a gouged out place, a half place, when her grandmother's dining room table is gone, and if he wants to live in a gouged out place—fine. For a moment, in the midst of all the wretchedness—the strained civility, the noise of the room, the hard, dead end look of his face, which tells her as if with club in hand that however little she may have known him then, she will never know him now—she was struck with a sense of profound relief. *It's fine, it's fine, whatever. Talk to my father about a contract, I don't care.*

Your father—.
He'll be civil.

He was smaller and plainer and more nervous than she remembered. He didn't pulsate and glow like he did in her memory. He is just a man, on a scale with all men. The world murmured around him like nothing had happened—waitresses and busboys, trays with plates and water glasses. He was commonest word in her life for years: Daniel. Two syllables of what had been her fuller, more complete, more stable designation: Daniel and Ellen. Daniel and Ellen's house. Daniel and Ellen's cat. Daniel and

268

Dark Land of the Sun

Ellen's friends. Daniel and Ellen's future.

I threw out all my work.

What do you mean?

I threw it away.

Here—we have a salt shaker and a paper placemat. Here: a nameless café, Wilshire and Crescent Heights. A here that is nowhere, chosen for neutrality. There, where she actually exists, the city is a breathing knot of cars and busses, undulating out between desert and sea. From where she sits she can see the Hollywood sign.

Why?

I started to feel like it wasn't right.

What wasn't?

My work.

This look like a flat, raw plank of wood. This look like an empty cavern. She was lonely with him. She was lonely—that was it.

⁊⁊

The teenagers who'd filled the back of the bus get off at Broadway and Fourth and the bus goes quiet, then lurches on. It's dark now. The man in the army jacket is staring at Ellen, his palm spread flat across his bare yellow belly. At Fifth Street he stands again and wanders back to the rear of the bus.

At Sixth Street no one gets on or off. The voice of a street corner preacher seeps through the doors.

⁊⁊

The city, that night, was silent and still. The night the world broke loose from its anchor of reason and spun.

She pulled to a stop at the 101 off ramp. She turned off the music. The wide canals of streets were lined with cars. The city was asleep. She'd left her studio more than an hour ago; she was just driving, no reason, no direction, orbiting the house in irregular ellipses. The 110 south to the 101 north to the Silver Lake Boulevard exit—but she turned left onto Silver Lake instead of right. She followed Silver Lake till it changes to Beverly, drove all the way to Rossmore, then south to Wilshire. Circling. She drove

269

east on Wilshire, north on Western, west on Third Street all the way to Alvarado.

At Third and Alvarado there was a flier taped to the post of a stop-light that read "EXTRAS! EXTRAS! EXTRAS! EXTRAS!" There was a white plastic bag stuck between the post and the walk button that swayed in the breeze like a jelly fish. She drove south on Alvarado, then west on Eight Street. There was a man on the corner of Eighth and Carondelet standing with one arm raised, palm to the sky—just standing. Just stand-ing there. He didn't move.

She drove west on Eighth, north on Vermont, and east on Beverly, past the curve where it changes to Silver Lake. She pulled to a stop at the light at the 101 off ramp. She turned off the music. She thought of Daniel, sleeping, and the cat who always slept at his knee. The thought came with a hollow, neutral feeling. The light turned and she accelerated. There was a flash of light in the corner of her eye—that was all.

⁂

The man slides into the seat behind Ellen. Two women board the bus at Sixth and sit at the front, talking volubly in Spanish. He falls into the seat saying, *Then ok, sure. Yeah. Ok.* His knees press against the back of her seat.

The women laugh; the laughter fills the bus.

Ellen's hair is tied back; she wears a broad collared t-shirt. She can feel the man's knees shifting against the seat. There is a rustling sound of fabric and metal: a belt buckle clicking against a metal button. His knees shift, then shift again, then begin gradually to pulse against the seat.

Seventh Street.

Eighth Street.

Stop requested.

His breathing is audible. *Fucking cunt bitch.* His breathing grad-ually deepens. He whispers repeatedly: *Fucking cunt bitch. Fucking cunt bitch.*

She gets off at Ninth Street, waiting until the bus is nearly stopped to move. She doesn't want to look, but she looks. His head is rolling against the back of the seat, his mouth parted. The smeared head of the lion is quivering and twitching.

Dark Land of the Sun

When her feet reach the sidewalk, she begins to run. She runs north and blindly, weaving and bumping through sparse clusters of bodies. When she can no longer run, she stumbles into the shadow corner of an alcove, heart pounding, wet between her legs and swelling with nausea, tears on her cheeks—all the sensations feel separate and free floating, as if streaming into her body from the outside. She presses herself in the dark of the corner but the nausea rises and fills her mouth and she is coughing and vomiting into the light. The wall is marble, smooth and cool on her forehead.

⁂

Persian rugs. Crystal candy dishes. White leather car seats. Ok. A gas pump. A ladder tied to the roof of a Toyota. A taco truck. A blue and yellow awning. A cowboy hat. A wrought iron fence. A shopping cart. A frayed army jacket. Two women carrying shopping bags.

A blond young woman spread like a doll across the two front seats of a silver SUV that had crumpled into the side of a Subaru. Ellen's Subaru. *A few seconds sooner and you might have been killed, Miss Spaulding.* The air was so—quiet. For a moment, there was no one. There was no sound. The light above turned from red to green.

Count yourself lucky.

The girl's dress was blue and didn't cover much. She was bleeding from the head. She looked so small, her pale limbs tossed in odd directions.

And here. Where is here? Broadway and something, buildings towering. There are curling tendrils of mosaic tile across the floor of the alcove—a sun, a sun shape, softened and polished by a twelve million heels in all these decades. Marble. Shoelaces. A scrap of paper.

Ronee Blakley

An Extremely Short Classic Story

I sailed from Nassau to L.A. and am good in the galley. While at sea, I overheard the following account of a fairy's shipwrecked ecstasy.

She flailed about in her pea pod as the wind whipped and the hail threatened to sink her; then suddenly it quieted, and she floated ashore on an azure sea, which deposited her on a sandy bank with a stream nearby; there were native boys wearing only shells and girls in grass skirts who called out to her in mellifluous tones, beckoning her to join them in their games; when she attempted to walk, she fell, and so she crawled, but they did not laugh, and one of the young men came to her and carried her to a shelter made of palm fronds, where they lived happily ever after.

Gordy Grundy

The Big Paddle

Let them think what they liked, but I didn't
mean to drown myself. I meant to swim till I sank—
but that's not the same thing.

—Joseph Conrad

"The Big Paddle. It has a certain elegance. It's not bloody or messy. It even has a dignity of form, far beyond the nobility of choice...

"Mike put a bag on his head and sucked gas. How artful is that? The punter used propane. I wouldn't want the last flavor in my *bouche* to remind me of a greasy Grill Master. Why not use helium and have a balloon party? It'd taste sweeter. You can intro Saint Peter with a hearty handshake and a squeaky clown voice. That'd be hilarious!

"Ted drove to the mountains above Pasadena, got out of the car and aimed his cranial effluence so as not to blemish the BMW. Why deprive the kids of a cash asset? I wonder if his pinky was extended as he pulled the trigger? There are many, many ways to go.

"The Big Paddle is way old school. Old El Dingo first told me about it. When a waterman has the Big C or is ravaged beyond daily pleasures and dignity, he takes the Big Paddle to the far horizon. He paddles to where the sun sets and the green flash flares. Paddle until you can paddle no more.

"I may not have the Big C but I've been ravaged. I'm not that old

275

but my soul has been there and done that. I've served my time well. I've pulled all the bells and the whistles. I nabbed a coupla brass rings. I gave as gladly as I have received. My life is sustainable, an easy recycle. Bring on the wind and the tides! Let nature take its course! May the fauna find a little meat in this hearty shell!

"I'm ready because my arms are killing me. Thank God the swells are small. I should have trained for this, but what's the point of *that?* I've never been one for gyms, though I've never not had a membership. Regardless, I should have been in better shape for this. Who woulda thought? Hell, how far can an old timer get? Fuck, I can still see the lights on the coast."

After an hour and a half drive, Muk McKaylee crossed the Pacific Coast Highway and slid into an easy spot near Trancas on Broad Beach Road. The light to the West was shading into a deep blue halo. While the engine kicked and cooled quiet, Muk unscrewed the cap of a plastic vodka bottle and took a draw. Then he stupidly looked around to see if anyone was watching; helluva time to get a DUI. Someone was. He locked the bright red eyes of a brown surfer in the station wagon next to him. The rig was aimed at the highway. Two boards were strapped to the roof. Window to window, the kid was laughing, smoke expelling from every orifice.

Muk raised the bottle as a salute with a nod. "Vices is nicest," he said to himself.

The guy rolled down the window. Muk laughed and did the same.

The surfer handed him a half-inch blunt, and with a cough, said "No surf. Six. Lucky, a foot."

"Gracias!"

"It's dark now, ya know?"

"Yeah, almost." Muk answered optimistically.

"Happy Hunting!"

The station wagon roared to life and Muk was left to himself. The blunt was mixed with too much tobacco but he got a taste of the green. He smiled. It was a nice gesture. "Good manners may be dying, but they ain't dead."

With the window down, Muk did not find the sweet ocean air that he expected. It pinched. The breeze smelled of dead fish, thick salt and rotting sun-baked kelp. He pushed the window button and his world became closed, sealed and introspective once again. The joint oxidized the stink.

The Big Paddle

Muk had not been to Trancas in a decade or two or probably more. It wasn't how he remembered it. The funky, single story beach houses had been mansionized with the same thick pastry lines found in every new second-rate resort.

Muk smiled. He wasn't sure why he came *here*. There was nothing truly significant about Trancas. Except for his youth. The beach burb was always an adventure point on the party map. Somewhere between downtown, Hollywood and Trancas there was always a girl, a party or a baggie. To no one he said out loud, "This sure doesn't look like it used to." He took another pull from the bottle and leaned back into his seat.

"Home as resort. No hearth, no heart. All the old families have been bought out long ago and replaced with fresh new money eager to audition for the good life." Muk rubbed his eyes, "The beach culture has eroded with the sand."

Every great action in life, triumphant moments of danger, glory and endeavor, begin with a sharp breath and a sudden lurch of the body. Muk McKaylee sat up fast and snapped a look around the car. He took his wallet and plunged it deep into the pocket behind the passenger seat. He wiggled his toes to remove the rubber sandals from his feet. He grabbed his keys and palmed a fresh pint bottle from the glove compartment. Then he stepped out of the car into the blue evening, the very last twilight of his life.

He was wearing a wetsuit, his old one, a little tight around the gut, but it still wore fairly well. Muk didn't need the warmth, especially into death, but the black rubber lent to the cover of darkness. The choice of this moonless night was no accident. If he had arrived earlier, at sunset, he feared good intentions. He didn't want some worrisome citizen to call the county guards or 911. Paddlers aim along the coast, not at the horizon. He didn't want a Coast Guard helicopter fussing above, messing his move. These days, everyone is in your God damned business. Even alone at sea.

Muk pulled the eleven-and-a half foot Hobie surfboard, a Corky Carroll model, from the back of the beat-up SUV. He wondered how old the board was. Sometime in the Sixties? A generous neighbor had given it to him in the early-Eighties when he manned up as a freshman in high school. He was a proud owner; the well-shaped deck was a universally revered classic. Muk gave it a wish with a smile. "May it wash up on a Japanese shore where some kid will find it and become a rockin' surf god."

The key now back in the ignition, he buttoned the rear window to rise. Muk popped two Valium and carefully locked the car. He balanced the keys, out of easy sight, on top of the driver's side rear wheel.

Muk never remembered much. It always took a friend's better recollection to link to his past. As he ambled to the beach, a lost flower suddenly bloomed. "Tracey! A beach house, somewhere near here. Late afternoon sunlight cut through bamboo blinds. Parallel shadows danced across the topography of a rumpled silk blanket. Must have been the fall, chill edging warm days. You could hear the ocean break, close outside. Something was playing on the stereo, something pop and sweet, something kinda sad and longing. Damn, what was it? And Tracey. Under the blonde hair, lost in the nape of her neck."

The water's edge of the Pacific was glowing with light. Muk now understood why the air was thick with the smell of death and decay. Tonight featured a Red Tide. Algae were blooming, creating underwater havoc. The ocean was flat. The small rollers hit the shore and shot a bright run of neon green across the break line. If the surf were bigger, with some action and agitation, the beach would pop like Vegas. Line after line, of blue chartreuse, spit and slapped the shore. It was beautiful. It was a miracle, a freak of nature, an explosion of phosphorescent color.

Muk took a swig of vodka then tied his shoulder-length hair into a tight knot.

He wedged the palm-sized plastic bottle into his wetsuit against the nape of his neck. Zippered tight. He lazily bent down and picked up the board.

The world's edge could still be seen, a faint line on a distant horizon, soon to vanish.

"I've been a solid sibling. I've done my parents well. As insane and wrenching as it was, I gently carried each one through the last leg of their journey." Muk shook his head and silently laughed. His mother was a piece of work; she did not make it easy. His Dad did, a gentle soul. Muk dug his foot into the sand.

"The kids are set. The heroics of fatherhood are long over. I can't advantage them anymore. Just burden."

There was nothing else to do but hesitate and linger. No doubt came to mind. Arguments have been made. All opposition has been lost, long lost. There was no thought except for the sensation of warm water against his toes. Sand swirling. An oilrig far off the coast was lighting up like a Christmas tree. Then another. And another. The coast was lined with oil platforms.

"The first wife was a peach. I can't really remember the second. I remember all too well the current. No love lost. Bitch-bound by the bonds of dwindling assets, ballooning liabilities and dull mutual acquaintances. We're too tired and too broke to split. We can't afford to live apart. We can't afford to live together. Marriage of the moribund."

One foot in front of the other. Faster out of old habit. Soon Muk McKaylee was skimming across the surface of the Pacific, his razor's edge.

"Christ, I never thought I'd live this long anyway. All the crazy stuff. Derring-do. Mosh pits. Fave raves. Faster, pussycat, faster! No hesitation, just go! Let's do it! Bull in a china shop. Take no shit. Never kiss the dull and uninteresting. Roll the dice. Loudly into the night. *Life is a banquet and there are too many suckers starving to death!*" Muk stopped paddling. "At the end of any Sunday, there is no free brunch."

The swells were long and low. Muk looked back, floating gently above the surface. He could still see a few lights from the million dollar homes along the coast. He was exhausted. His forearms screamed. His shoulders were killing him. He crawled to sit upright. He reached back, flailing, to eventually dislodge the vodka bottle that had inched down his back under the wetsuit. His muscles were so tired that his coordination was shaky and mindless.

He took a long draw. "Fuck!" The burn in his throat felt good.

"Maybe I should have trained for this. Gotten in better shape." The absurd notion made him chuckle. "Shouldn't death be as violent as birth?"

Muk finished the half-pint. He capped it and started to toss the plastic bottle into the deep blue sea but caught himself. "In this human-ugly life, nature offers the only purity." He stuffed the empty recyclable back into the neck of his wetsuit.

"My grandmother, the wild one, took me aside once, at a time when I was having way too much fun. She and I were drinking Dr. Pepper, looking out at the ocean. That filly, she was chomping at the bit till the cocktail hour. I could and always did tell her everything. *Everything*. And she loved it. Encouraged it. But this time, she took my hand. I've never seen her worried. Turns out she wasn't long for this world and knew it. She said, "Muk, you've always been so busy---," she tried to find the polite word, "*living,* and things have always come so easy to you. I worry that life will some day present to you a bill, a marker that you will find hard to pay." There wasn't much to say to that. As a man of opportunity and the next Big Thing, I thought she was dithering. I get it now. I can't pay the chit. I can't afford the tab. I can no longer afford the lifestyle to which I have grown accustom."

Muk was stretched out flat, paddling. His hands felt very heavy. Every stroke howled and burned. And in a way, it felt good and appropriate. He had found his cadence, like a galley slave on a Roman ship. "Die, Motherfucker!" Stroke. "Die, Motherfucker!" Stroke. It made him laugh.

"I see my future. I see the struggles I'll have to surmount. The rebuilding I'll have to chance. The Roger Dodger, Gung-Ho, mount-ups. The giddy two steps forward and the miserable four back. The dull humiliations. The fancy of fake friends. The three a.m. sweats, waking with a gasp and a shudder. Horror in the gut. Fire in the hold. There is no reflection at the bottom of an empty barrel, just wet wood.

"Life is pay to play. No tickee, no washee. No dough, no hope. Certainly no room service.

"Money is the sucker punch that ends every argument. It trumps good looks, a keen mind and a smart operator. Opportunity begins with money. Sweat is a fantasy.

"I've already done it, many times before and I don't wanna do it again. Been there, done that. I'm tired. I am so tired... So tired."

A fish, a fairly large fish, a yellowtail, broke the surface and the silence with a crescendo of water and spray. Just eighteen inches away, hit with cold water, Muk flinched bodily and audibly. His hands and feet hit the deck long before the fish slapped back into the sea. It took a few moments for the event to process, the alarm to quell and the quiet to return. Muk laughed as he wiped the salt water from his eyes. "Nature amazes."

If Muk had been fading, he was clear and present now. The water felt colder. The stars were brighter, in greater colors, and there were more of them. Thankfully, the swells remained wide, long and gentle.

Muk lifted himself on shaky arms, and with much labor, brought his knees up and under him. It took more effort than he had imagined, more pain than he had bargained. He leaned forward and started to paddle. A stroke. Butt up, a stroke. Another followed another. But not for long. Paddling on your knees is too aggressive. No need for speed. Muk fell slowly forward and let his legs unfurl. The wax on the board stuck to his cheek. He spit salt water and realized that he was very, very thirsty.

Muk looked up. He was too tired to lift them, so he threw his hands forward. He grabbed water and heaved. The board shot forward. His arms soon rediscovered their groove, a tired and true rhythm.

"I'll never forget a Hare Krishna festival at Venice Beach. In a tent they had a 3-D maquette of the Circle of Life. What a circle! The little baby that grows and stands powerful as a man only to reverse the process as the man becomes a childlike old drooler. Cradle to the grave. Gory little statues for every age. Nip that idea in the bud. The Hare Krishna spelled it out cold. The argument was all too clear. Ashes to ashes. Dust to dust. Diapers to diapers.

"The will to survive is a very powerful notion. It is often blind and senseless. You see it with the decomposed seniors or a repeat cancer patient. How much indignity or painful radiation will you take, just to see another sunrise? How many diapers will you wear to hear a bee buzz once again? What's the price of that ticket? I'd rather go out on my own two feet. Boots on.

"Time to get at the Grand Finale, while the body can still make a fine corpse, long, long before the waves of decrepitude erode and exhaust all beauty. Let's get this fucker over with. Before the twinkle in my eye becomes a tiresome tear."

Muk was paddling absently and automatically. He looked up for the first time in a long while. His forehead had been anchored to the surfboard, eyes closed.

Across the horizon, a container ship rode high on the water, heading south. The freighter was probably three miles out but its massive dark hull seemed to wipe out the view. Most of the night sky fell into its black hole. Tonight, riding high, the ship was empty. In a few weeks, it would pass here again, northward and low abeam, heavy with cargo. Muk rested his chin on his crossed forearms. He placed a bet with no one. "Ten bucks says, coming back from China, it'll be filled with next years Christmas decorations."

Muk thought he could hear the whine of the ships engines and the smack of its propellers roiling the water, but that was impossible. Silently, the ship slid from horizon's view and the stars returned once again.

"Money used to be so easy. As a cocky kid, I used to say *making it was easy.* Stupid fool. Money is youth. Who you gonna give a job to? Who you gonna capitalize? A fresh face with a wide smile and a kooky concept or a dour half-marker with experience and a better idea? Age doesn't attract investment. Opportunity frowns at a wrinkle. It always has and it always will."

Muk woke gently, rocking in the cradle of low-slung waves. He must have passed out or fallen asleep. His hands and arms were tucked under his chest for warmth. His feet were cold but he no longer noticed. Carefully and slowly, he flopped over, muscles numb or aching, onto his back. He lay still. The moonless sky was a dark theater to a heavenly and colorful display of revolving stars and constellations. The riot of color had no soundtrack, except for the wet, sloppy kiss of water passing under the surfboard.

Muk heard something, far and away, up ahead to the south. It sounded like a sigh, the soft exhale of a satisfied man. He heard it again. And rhythmically again. So natural. It had to be a whale, surfacing, on a journey to warmer Mexican waters. It was that time of year. He caught another exhale, softer, further away. And another, a little louder, closer and wet. A pod of whales had to be passing. Muk was a grateful observer to one of natures secret clubs. It must have been a large pod, for it passed slowly. Exertions in rhythm. Distance lost to silence.

"Looking back, the best times always involved friends. I've been lucky at that. Smart and funny friends. The zip and zing, connecting, laughing, the exchange oxygenates the soul...

"But friendship can only go so far. The expression has many colors, but friendship is also a value, a depth of one's character. I've also seen how thin that fabric can be. Betrayal is a game changer..."

Fitfully, Muk McKaylee began to fall asleep, rocking gently, on top of the world.

The Big Paddle

"I guess I've always been jaded. I've had the things everybody wants so bad. I've traveled a bit, but never enough. I've eaten well and drank heartily..

"I kicked my bucket list over a long time ago. I'll never experience an eclipse from a mountaintop. I'll never see earth from the porthole of the Virgin Galactic.

"I've never had conversations with God. Just random arguments, admonitions, and the occasional appeal.

"But I have seen great Beauty. I have been staggered by Awe and Appreciation. I have experienced several — *events* of transcendence, where I was given a glimpse behind the curtain and witnessed the mechanics that revolve the universe. Those privileged moments were staggering, but, then, ultimately, confusing and meaningless... Not for this world.

"Thankfully, I'll miss Justin Biebers next deportation. Another Marvel film franchise. The loss of privacy. A warm noogie from Big Brother. *Fuck that shit.*

"Is that all there is? The big whoop? No third act surprise? It's time to burn it down!"

With an explosion of energy, Muk became focused on his present. Unnerved, unsure. Panic was a fuel, fear another. He was atop the board on his knees paddling furiously, madly, angrily. Stroke after stroke. Digging and pulling water.

He was making speed when he hit his wall. Mind and body ceased to function. Energy vanished. Muk pitched forward, his chin went down and hit the board. He had no time to react and protect himself; Muk was no longer there. He fell on his chin and crumpled over it, his skull ringing. His arms and legs unfolded and splayed out, ungainly, feet in the water. Muk lost consciousness as slowly as the blood began to flow from the gash under his chin.

While the water might be considered warm for the season, the temperature was far below body temperature. Muk had grown quite numb. His body was cold and in shock. Blood continued to flow from his chin, quickly washed away into the water. The smell of it was quickly attracting deep and distant attentions.

"The world changed too fast and too soon. I was looking away and I lost my place in line...

283

"I've always been a 'possibility' guy, never quite living in the pres-ent. My dingle has always been about what's coming up next. I don't feel that anymore, the pull, the promise of something better. That sweet song, I just don't hear it. I don't think I've heard it in a long, long time…

"I'm grateful. I've produced much. But luck has played out. I col-lected early. I've been lavished with heartfelt comforts, careless freedoms and sweet luxuries. But those days are over…"

On the glassy and windless sea, the Hobie surfboard, drifted with the current. The propulsion of each little wave shoved the board forward, south, cutting to the west. The board was listing fifteen to twenty degrees to starboard. Across it, the body of Muk McKaylee lay unbalanced, an arm and a lower leg were trailing in the water. The blood, trickling from his chin, was leaving a signature.

Onward, off-kilter, the longboard and its sea had generated a mo-mentum unto itself.

SMACK! The bow of the surfboard collided with a very hard, solid object and violently shoved Muk backward. The impact energized the balsa wood core and a wildly physical reverberation traveled up and down the length of the fiberglass and foam longboard. Unconscious, Muk McKaylee woke up instantly and forcefully. All of his deteriorating senses engaged at once, hyperactive, but his sight overrode all others. He looked up to see, to focus, to witness a wall of darkness, a black void, so wide and deep as to en-velope the horizon, definitely a ship, a freighter, a propeller driven—Muk howled the scream of the violently near-dead, the horrific sound uttered by the lucky ones who have the time, the few seconds, the awe, to see it com-ing.

The screaming collision woke everyone on board the small crowded boat.

"¡Tiburón!" Tinto, dreaming of Las Vegas and a fabulous career as an American drag queen with full citizenship and healthcare, woke fast from a restless and nervous sleep. The loud impact had evidenced all of his fears of death at sea by a monstrous shark attack. "¡Ataque de tiburón!" he screamed hysterically, "¡Shark!"

All souls aboard the tightly packed twenty-eight foot vessel reacted to their imminent demise in different ways.

The Big Paddle

After leaving the mothership northeast of tiny Santa Barbara Island, the panga had been lost at sea and adrift without power for the last thirty-seven hours. By the grace of the Virgin Mary, cutbacks at the U.S. Coast Guard and a coffee spill into a radar screen of the NSA, the Mexican fishing boat had miraculously drifted north, undetected, along the California coast, far beyond Malibu.

The captain of the voyage, Señor Valdez, had never before been to sea. His authority was established by the pistol in his belt. He was trapped at the stern, hedged in by the puzzle of scattered parts to the 1963 Evinrude outboard motor.

A young man, known only as Raul, leapt forward to the bow. With a quick glance, he reported, "It is a man!" The young orthodontist, escaping from Venezuela, reached over the rail, "Help me! I need help."

His wife and grandmother stood and carefully moved out of the way.

Adolfo, a quiet middle-aged man, slipped in to assist. Together, the immigrants each grabbed an underarm and began to haul Muk McKaylee aboard the boat.

"He—he is alive!"

Buffy Visick

Luck

Lately she'd been too depressed or maybe exhausted to drink. Much. It was like when the cigarettes stopped working. Fucked. Couldn't depend on anything—were bears still shitting in woods, or... right. Bears were mostly myth these days. At least the weed was ever-present—her tolerance remained level, she was still getting high. And, the wine would be back again. Always. She was just about to the end of her book, Dostoevsky's *The Gambler*, and a professionally rolled joint, a gift from her local cannabis collective owner. She put book on the couch and the joint on the lid of a little container she used for ash, and fished about with two fingers in a glass bowl full of rocks, jewels and fortunes for a particular pair of earrings, silver with faceted labradorite dangles. This fortune fell out of the bowl, written just this way: WISE MAN SAY: SUCCESSFUL PERSON ONE WHO SAW CHANCE & TOOK IT. Ouch. Good one, cookie. She dropped the fortune on a coffee table in front the little couch where she sat most the day, when she had the opportunity, then slept upon in fetal position until the sun came up, by the good graces of god who gave her a friend who had given her this gift of this shelter—hell, they had fun, even—these past six months. The idea was she was stabilizing herself. Big sigh. She picked up the book again: "'I'll give up as soon as I win back what I have lost.'" She laughed. Chasing. If it turned out to be an actual universal scientific truth that we attract what we are and create our own luck—well, she would believe it. And, she knew the biggest scam of all time to be the suggestion that we can change what we are, change our luck.

She'd just been to Hollywood Park, actually, placing bets. It was closing, after how many years…for live races anyway. That hurt, and just before Christmas. She remembered Bukowski: "YOU HAVE WOUNDED MY HEART FOREVER!" She'd only been to Hollywood Park a couple times before this one last time, and to Santa Anita once. She didn't expect or need to win, not in any big way. She wanted to, sure, and she would use her method, which she was still working out, but Hollywood Park this last night: second to last day for races, full of ghosts and angels, especially the man who took her first bet, she wasn't sure she remembered but she thought she should bet win/place/show, he said, "That's the way to do it!" and she thanked him and started to walk away with her ticket. He said, "Wait, your change!" and she said, "There I am, trying to lose my money," and he said, "No, you're winning." She'd never stop loving that man, unconditionally. That's why she was at the races. For him and the woman covered in commemorative pins who popped the last two popcorns of the day—just for her and her friend. They took home the leftovers and she finished that popcorn on Christmas Day, on that little couch.

She did win in her first race, the 9th—that is, her horse came in third. Fifteen bucks off six. She used the money to buy their second round of drinks before the last race of the day, just like the bartender had suggested she do "when she won." Her friend's horse placed first in the last race: #10, Anniversary Kitty pulled up from fifth or further behind to first place right in front of their seats in the lower stands, like the horse had timed it that way on purpose, so they'd always have a perfect story. Her friend made $27.50 off that bet, covering her expenses including the entrance fee. Why she'd let her friend pay her back for that she didn't know, considering her friend drove her ass out there, made it possible for her to be there in the first place. Never mind she was sleeping on this friend's little couch. Thank god she'd bought that last round.

The first time she was at Hollywood Park, her first time at the track, she was all about her own need to win. "Romantic Dream," "Artist's Triumph," "Bullshit Fantasy on Wheels," that's what she'd bet on, sentimental names and ideas assigned to ponies that loved to come in last. She needed to be validated not only by winning, but on particular terms, where these precious names would serve as harbingers of even greater things yet to come. Not just, you know, a few bucks for everyone's trouble, not least of all the horses' trouble. She was betting all of ten bucks and she was counting on the whole dream, the glorious vision confirmed, on dollar bet, beer and hot dog night. "Poverty Consciousness." That's the horse she should have bet on. Christ, she could still hear Bukowski's laughter ringing through the footfalls of the horses on the track edges of Eternity, bouncing off the Universal stands. At least she didn't end up getting pregnant by that guy who won $125 in the last race, had two houses in Bakersfield where he manufactured crystal meth, was recently out of jail, and was at the track with his son's mother, and some other folks celebrating that son's graduation. He was "a baby-making MACHINE," or so he yelled as she and her friend walked away. Yeah, she'd given him her number. She'd recently seen a film at the time where the human race became sterile and was convinced having a child was the most important thing she could do. That compulsion faded and she never returned his two or three calls. Sometimes she got so weird, as a human, she couldn't believe it used to be her. But, then again, she could. It always was, after all.

She began winning her second time at Hollywood Park, with different friends on another Dollar Night (or whatever it was called), this time featuring a cover band and possibly $20 to play with. She started off the night picking the same losers, and losing. But then, by the grace of some unseen force, she began to notice that the first horse she would see on the form, the first name she looked at, came in first. She confirmed it with the next race (without betting), and then the race after that. She laid money on the last race of the day, based on that "first look" horse—she called her system "first look" after that—and won about $10. That was a three-race-streak in her mind, regardless of what she had bet. She'd picked three winners in a row just by going with what she saw first. Made no sense, had no skill, but it worked. Which actually was her best way of getting through life. Fucking grab on to what's in front of you and stick with it and get there. She couldn't wait to try it out again, forgetting of course the poor horses who always had to suffer for such experiments in fortune. She hated how long it took her to get real about that.

A couple months later, a friend had a birthday party at the Santa Anita track. It's considered the prettier track in LA and it certainly has many lovely details. They still run horses out there. She was ready to put "first look" into action and had that inner alignment where she knew she was going to win. She knew what winning felt like and that it was coming on. Like when a dancer goes out and knows she's about to nail every move, the dancer flies, effortless grace. She looked at the form and the first one she saw, it almost had a glow around it. Did have a glow around it. The horse won. Then, the next race, same thing. The third race she saw a number on the big Jumbotron screens at the center of the track, picked it, and her odds came in 87 to 1, which with her low stakes won over $150 on that race alone. She won the next two races as well—an eight-race-streak counting the three at Hollywood Park. When she went to place what was to be her final winning bet of the day, her fifth time at the window, the woman there asked her, "How are you doing this?" She shrugged and smiled big, she said she didn't know, she just picked the first name she saw, and it was working. That wasn't what broke her streak, though. That was the guy a few rows down who turned around after she won in that fifth race, looked her in the face and said, "You're lucky." She and her friends looked at each other. They knew the streak was over. It was. She lost in the last three races but still walked with over $350, from about $25 seed money.

That was the time this guy, TOMMY! King of Hollywood (that was his name, and how he spelled it), was there. He placed every bet she did, including her unproven first, and kept betting her picks even after the streak broke, as if on principle. That day at Santa Anita, TOMMY! won several thousand dollars betting on her picks. Thousands. That's real money to pretty much everybody, whether they consider it real money or not. He's dead now. When she'd first met TOMMY! over a year previous, he'd immediately proposed. She'd laughed and told him something dismissive like "Dream on," but she thought he might have been serious. It was a ridiculous thing for him to do, half-serious or serious or not. He was some kind of punk artist with a wounded athlete's build, an actor, and probably a poet. They saw each other around after that, had a few friends in common, and acted together in these same friends' no-budget films. He would maybe have been a great husband for her. She'd never know. She hoped he'd enjoyed the money. She'd spent most of her own winnings at a second birthday party for the same girl, a couple nights later, at a fancy wine bar with expensive little dishes—squandered as easily and almost as quickly as that fifteen dollar round she bought years later before that last race at Hollywood Park. She was glad her friend had won at the track. She loved Hollywood Park so much that day, she wanted to marry it, its entire history, all those ghosts and old people, even its criminal injustices toward those amazing creatures we share the earth with, called by us the horses. Horseracing used to be all *Black Stallion*, now it was steroids and pain and just...nobody went anymore.

She picked up the joint, and lit what was left, not much. She had plenty of loose weed and a pipe, so whatever. She thought about that last race again, about the horses she'd picked. She and her friend had decided to go for broke by betting on two horses, and both had for their "first look" a horse named "Writer Fever." Seemed like the perfect choice to officially end a streak. The second horse she had seen was right below the first one, "Capers and Wine." She went for "Muscat Evening" since it was further down the list and seemed more logical—don't pick two horses next to each other. As she lit the pipe, she realized: she'd fucked herself right there. "Capers and Wine" came in third. She'd abandoned her own system, looked to logic, lost track of her own way. As she was likely to do. That you could bet on. Her friend as we know picked the winner, the triumphant "Anniversary Kitty." "Writer Fever" came in, like, last maybe. Had to. Possibly the ghost of Bukowski's doing, but he wouldn't have had to intervene—she could tell a loser by the name, "first look" or no. She read on in her book: "To-morrow, to-morrow it will all be over!" Fyodor always got it right. She finished the joint.

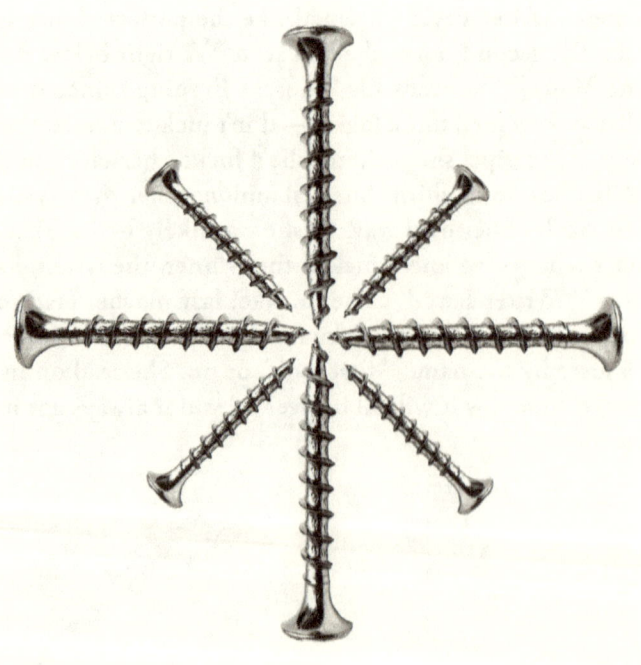

Biographies

ANDREW BERARDINI

Andrew Berardini (b. 1982, Huntington Beach, USA) writes fictive essays and essayistic fiction, often about the art of Los Angeles where he lives. Previously a curator at LAXART and the Armory Center and an editor at Semiotext(e), he is currently LA Editor for Mousse, West Coast Editor at Artslant, and founder (with Sarah Williams) of the Art Book Review. Since 2008, he's been a teacher at the Mountain School of Arts and was recently on faculty at the Banff Centre in Canada. Past publications include Artforum, LA Weekly, Frieze, Public Fiction, and Purple as well as numerous catalogues, including a monograph on Richard Jackson and a contribution to the 2012 Whitney Biennial. Berardini's curated and co-curated exhibitions this year at the Palais de Tokyo in Paris, the Castello di Rivoli in Turin, and MOCA in Los Angeles. In 2013, he was a finalist for the Premio Bonaldi-Enter Prize for Young Curators and was awarded the Creative Capital/Andy Warhol Grant for Art Writers. He has book a forthcoming in 2014 on the artist Danh Vo and is currently at work on another about color.

RONEE BLAKLEY

Ronee Blakley is a writer/singer/songwriter/actor/producer/director/composer/publisher/poet. She won the National Board of Review for Best Supporting Actress and has been nominated for an Academy Award, Golden Globe, Grammy and BAFTA. She has appeared on the covers of Newsweek, Interview, Cahiers du Cinema and American Cinematographer. Her most recent public appearance was an evening of her poetry and some SONGS OF LOVE at Beyond Baroque in Los Angeles. This terse piece is a minimalist absurdist act meant to elicit a laugh from Gordy Grundy.

BETTY ANN BROWN

Betty Ann Brown is an art historian, critic, and curator. A tenured professor at California State University, Northridge, she is currently visiting at Pasadena City College. Brown has curated retrospective exhibitions for Hans Burkhardt, Roland Reiss, Linda Vallejo, and John White, as well as numerous themed exhibitions. She has written critical reviews for various periodicals--including Arts, Artillery, Artscene, ArtweekLA, and The Los Angeles Times — and published several books, among them Gradiva's Mirror: Reflections on Women, Surrealism & Art History; Hero, Madman, Criminal, Victim: The Artist in Film & Fiction; and the textbook Art & Mass Media. Her most recent volume is Afternoons with June: Stories of June Wayne's Art & Life. Brown was featured in four History Channel programs and produced a series about art history for eHow online. She organizes of "Contemporary Art Conversations," an ongoing series of panel discussions between critics and artists that convenes in various Southern California venues.

MATTY BYLOOS

Matty Byloos's first collection of short stories, Don't Smell the Floss, was published in 2009 by Write Bloody Books. His work has appeared in Everyday Genius, Matchbook, Bomb, and The Magazine of Bizarro Fiction, among others. He's also been included in the anthologies In Heaven, Everything is Fine: Fiction Inspired by David Lynch (Eraserhead Press, 2013), and The People's Apocalypse (Microcosm Publishing, 2013). With Carrie Seitzinger, he runs NAILED Magazine from Portland, where he lives and works. His first novel, ROPE, will be published in 2014.

LUCA CELADA

Luca Celada grew up in European locales generally centered around Italy where during the turbulent late seventies he absorbed debilitating doses of youthful idealism mixed with ancient cynicism. An impulsive move to Los Angeles caught him unprepared for the proactive pursuit of happiness prevalent in his newfound college town. The years spent working as a correspondent for communist daily Il Manifesto and as Hollywood-based TV news producer simply muddled the waters further. After 20 years working in journalism, the quick demise of his profession left him uniquely qualified to contribute an unpaid chronicle of mid-life defeat to this anthology.

PAUL CHAVEZ

Paul Chavez is a Los Angeles-based writer with a background in journalism. He was born in Los Angeles and graduated with a degree in political science from UCLA. Paul has worked as a reporter and editor for more than two decades, including stints at a newspaper in Tacoma, Wash., and the Los Angeles bureau of The Associated Press. He currently runs his own online site covering the Venice area of Los Angeles.

SHANA NYS DAMBROT

Shana Nys Dambrot is an art critic, curator, and author based in Los Angeles. She is currently LA Editor for WhiteHot Magazine, Arts Editor for Vs. Magazine, Contributing Editor for Art Ltd., and a contributor to Flaunt, Scene, the Huffington Post, the LA Weekly. and KCET's Artbound. Formerly Managing Editor at Flavorpill, her other publications have included Modern Painters, Art Review, Artweek, ARTnews, tema celeste, Art Asia Pacific, Coagula, and Juxtapoz. She grew up in Chelsea back when it was still all thug-life, studied Art History at Vassar College, bailed for LA in the winter of 1995, and forewent the planned prodigal return when she discovered how deep LA's still waters run. Besides all the magazine stuff, she writes loads of essays for books and exhibition catalogs, curates one or two exhibitions a year, and speaks in public with alarming frequency. Zen Psychosis will be her first published work of short fiction, and exists outside both her own comfort zones and those of the genre.

MICHAEL DELGADO

Michael Delgado who has Executive Producer credits with MTV and was the Publisher of METRO magazine is currently the publisher of True Fixion, real time pulp serials created and designed specifically for the iPad. www.truefixion.com Delgado received a BFA from the University of

Southern California and was an art writer for The LA Weekly as well as the Editor of the Journal, the quarterly publication of the Los Angeles Institute of Contemporary Art. Delgado lives in Los Angeles. Follow him on Twitter @akadelgado

HARRY DUNN

Harry Dunn is a writer living outside Los Angeles. In addition to a wife, three kids, a dog and a cat, he also has an Emmy nomination and an NAACP Image Awards from his days on "In Living Color." He is also a winner of a PROMAX award for his TV promo campaign work. Currently, he and his writing partner (who just happens to be his best friend since kindergarten) have a script in development at Columbia Pictures. Dunn chose to write an article for this anthology, entitled "I Don't Want My Kids To Ever Work In The Entertainment Industry" because, well, he really doesn't want his kids to ever work in the entertainment industry.

GORDY GRUNDY

Gordy Grundy is an American artist and arts writer. A native of Newport Beach, he has been influenced by sunny flights of SoCal fancy, the bold stroke and the grand gesture. Hollywood, Disney, the secrets of re-creation and the Healing Power of Pop continue to fascinate him.

Grundy is a graduate of the University of Southern California with a degree in Economics. He makes art daily and shows frequently.

In addition to a career in the arts, he has served as a nightclub impresario, lifeguard, film producer, tennis instructor, promotionalist, and theatrical producer.

Always a volunteer, he has served in leadership positions with the Barnsdall Art Center, Newport Beach Historical Society, Jonathan Art Foundation, Swim With Mike, Downtown LA Neighborhood Arts Council and more.

As a writer and columnist, he has written for Artillery Magazine, the Huffington Post, the Los Angeles Times, the LA Weekly, ArtNews and many others. He is the author of "Artist Pants" and the editor of this anthology. His visual and literary works can be found at www.GordyGrundy. com

DOUG HARVEY

Doug Harvey is an artist, writer and critic, independent curator, and educator who lives and works in Los Angeles. His patacritical Interrogation Techniques Anthology Vol 3 was published in 2013 by AC Books, NY and he practices regularly with F, an improvisational power trio/quartet with artists Marnie Weber and Brothers Daniel. His most recent solo show at Jancar Gallery had the self-explanatory title Found Moldy Slides and he has lately been hosting Less Art Radio Zine for LA's pirate radio station KCHUNG every other Sunday at 12 noon. His other activities may be monitored online at www.dougharvey.blogspot.com and www.dougharvey.la.

JAMES HAYWARD

James Hayward was born in San Francisco in 1943, a War Baby. He grew up on the west coast and graduated from San Diego State University and then went to grad school at UCLA and The University of Washington. During graduate school he trained horses. He moved to Santa Ynez and continued training horses, then after the birth of his daughter, Ashley, returned to Los Angeles and settled into painting.

He received a Young Talent Award, from the Los Angeles County Museum of Art in 1977, a Japan-United States Creative Arts Fellowship in 1981, a John Simon Guggenheim Memorial Fellowship in 1983, an Award in the Visual Arts Grant in 1991, a National Endowment for the Arts Fellowship in 1993, and a Pollock-Krasner Foundation Grant in 1996.

Minneola Press published his first book of short stories, Indiscretion, in 2010. The stories were unedited as, at the time, he thought using an editor was akin to allowing someone to finish a painting. A new volume of stories is nearing publication. He now has an editor. Apparently, old dogs can learn new tricks.

RICH HENRICH

Rich Henrich is a screenwriter, professor and producer of films and festivals as well as director of the for-social-profit, Film 4 Change, a story powered community of artists based in Santa Fe, New Mexico. His work has screened at SXSW, Santa Fe Film Festival, AMFM Fest and beyond. He has produced narrative films featuring Michael Madsen, Giancarlo Esposito and other great actors. He is attached to produce a film with Viggo Mortensen set to lead and is currently working on a documentary on the late great Dennis Hopper. His other documentary projects focus on eccentric cowboy artists and other fascinating characters of the Southwest frontier. His obsession is to help infuse the world with independent voices and to help his students become self-sufficient artrepreneurs.

I opted to write The Twelve-Thousand Dollar Reindeer after contemplating what Gen F identified in our modern culture. It occurred to me, that I was Gen F, the more truthful name given to those previously deemed Gen X. After looking at my own life, my hopes, dreams, failures and frustrations, I realized my life was not so unlike the majority of my friends struggling to make real their ideals and purpose. It started with two real life phone calls and a snippet of an overheard conversation: "Benji's in the hospital…My girlfriend is pregnant and my dad is dying…I've never paid more than $12,000 for a reindeer." I set out on a journey from the West Coast to the Southwest to the Southeast and back listening to and observing people during the Holidays. Would I find hope and the key to life or an anthem for Gen F?

JOSH HERMAN

90% of all proceeds Josh Herman receives for his contributions to this anthology will go to Psychiatrists Without Borders, as he needs one available wherever he goes. Overlooked for such esteemed awards as the MacArthur Genius Grant and New Yorker Caption Contest, his edited-down material has appeared on TV and stage, and in magazines, alternative-weeklies and complaint forms at K-Mart ("Be less depressing.") If not turned-off to his writing from this bio, his Gen F contributions *Transcribed, from Boxes* and *Post Orgasmic Guilt* should prove your hypothesis that, maybe, these Gen-F'ers brought it on themselves.

SARAH ECKLES HUNTER

Sarah Hunter started writing little plays and stories to perform in the neighborhood when she was about eight years old. There wasn't much else to do in West Lafayette, Indiana, so she amused herself. When she hit college and grad school, she began to write more. Recently Sarah has completed a novel, which is mostly autobiographical, and for about thirty years she has been writing and directing plays. Mostly, Sarah has other people direct what she has written, as she tends to lose perspective.

Currently Sarah is appearing in two different theater productions in the Pasadena area -- Jane Martin's "Talking With..." and the popular "Steel Magnolias." She plays Ouiser in that one, and she's a hoot. Still teaching high school English, she plans to continue teaching until she keels over in the classroom with a piece of chalk in her hand. Sarah won a playwriting award in 1974, which sparked her obsession to write more plays. She is happy to say that she's now had eight of them produced here in the Los Angeles area. Besides writing, directing and acting, Sarah has enjoyed doing voice-overs for cartoons, commercials and industrial films." She has taught Humanities at Pasadena City College, as well as designing English secondary curriculum for the State of California.

TULSA KINNEY

Tulsa Kinney is the editor of Artillery, a nationally distributed contemporary art magazine based in Los Angeles that she co-founded in 2006. She received her MFA at USC in 1988 and showed her paintings and videos in numerous solo and group exhibitions for over two decades. At that time she was teaching digital imaging at various Southern California colleges along with her graphic design career at the LA Weekly. Tulsa started writing about 15 years ago and her articles have been published in the Los Angeles Times, LA Weekly and LA CityBeat. She continues to write about art and stay deeply immersed in today's art world.

VICTORIA LOOSELEAF

Victoria Looseleaf is an award-winning international arts journalist and regular contributor to the Los Angeles Times, KCET's Artbound, Performances Magazine, KUSC-FM radio, Fjord Review and other outlets, including the New York Times. In addition, she writes the broadcast scripts and program notes for the Los Angeles Philharmonic at the Hollywood Bowl. When she is not covering music and dance festivals around the world, Looseleaf can be found giving pre-concert talks at the Los Angeles Music Center, as well as maintaining and contributing to a blog, The Looseleaf Report. Her book, Leonardo: Up Close and Personal, is available on Amazon for the princely sum of one penny.

CHRISTOPHER MICHNO

Christopher Michno is a contributing editor for Artillery: Killer Text on Art and a regular contributor to Art Ltd Magazine. His work has also appeared in THE Magazine Los Angeles, the Inland Empire Weekly and Bedlam. His most recent curatorial project, Passages, at the First Street Gallery Art Center in Claremont, explored the reciprocal relationship between literature and the visual arts.

DIANE MOONEY

Diane Mooney, for her sins, lives in Muncie, Indiana, where she is an assistant professor in the English Department at Ball State University. In 2004 she won the Academy of American Poets Christopher F. Kelly Award. Her poetry has appeared in Appalachee Quarterly, Tigertail and Florida English. She's free-lanced for Los Angeles Times, LA Weekly, Fort Lauderdale Sun Sentinel, and the Miami Fashion Blog. Diane has taught journalism in Shantou, China and professional writing at Florida International University. She is currently working on a novel set in Muncie as well as a blog, "Tippling in Muncie," featuring photos of Muncie drinking establishments.

MARTIN MUNDT

Martin Mundt is the author of one novel about non-violent zombies, Reanimated Americans, and two collections of humorous horror short stories, The Dark Underbelly Of Hymns and The Crawling Abattoir, as well as a novella, The Cranston Gibberer. His play, a romantic comedy romp about two serial killers, "The Jackie Sexknife Show", was produced in Chicago in 2003. Seven of his short stories have received Honorable Mention in The Year's Best Fantasy And Horror anthologies. He won the

Flash Fiction contests at the World Horror Conventions in 2005 and 2006 with stories which cannot be read in front of children. He can be found in cyberspace at www.martinmundt.com or on Facebook. "The Magruder Film" was written because Mr. Mundt simply did not wish to see the 60s end, because he always wanted to be a hippie.

HOLLY MYERS

Holly Myers is a writer, critic and sometimes curator currently based in New Mexico. Her fiction has appeared in Zyzzyva and Joyland. Her story "The Guest House" was anthologized in New California Writing 2012 (Heyday). Her art writing and criticism has appeared in the Los Angeles Times, the LA Weekly, the New York Times, Art + Auction and Modern Painters, among other publications. She is the co-editor of Rabble, an imprint of Insert Blanc Press that aims to foster and promote innovative critical writing. Dark Land of the Sun, excerpted here, is her first novel. She is presently at work on her second.

JILL PARIS

Jill Paris is the author of an eBook titled Life is Like a Walking Safari. Her humorous travel stories have been published in the Travelers' Tales anthologies The Best Travel Writing 2009, Leave the Lipstick, Take the Iguana and The Best Women's Travel Writing Volume 9. Other features have appeared in The Saturday Evening Post, Travel Africa, Gadling, Fathom, Literary Traveler, Thought Catalog and more. She holds an M.A. in Humanities from San Francisco State University and a Master of Professional Writing degree from the University of Southern California. She travels for the inexplicable human connection. After writing the essay "I'm Working Here," she justifiably ended her 39-day career when a supervisor confessed the hotel's over-estimated need for a concierge then reduced her work hours to a measly 15 per week. Jill is once again seeking full-time employment and, if ever hired, she dreams of better days in better clothes.

DAVE SHULMAN

Best known for his "Column Dave" in L.A. Weekly from 1998 to 2007, Dave Shulman was born and lived for fifteen wondrous years in Champaign, Illinois, followed by two horrible years in a small town in the Mojave Desert and thirty or so even worse years in Los Angeles, where he graduated from UCLA with a degree in fine art but withdrew from CalArts before receiving his master's, worked as a bartender at Igby's Comedy Cabaret, personal assistant to film director Peter Bogdanovich and writer's assistant on a sitcom called The Fresh Prince of Bel-Air, and exhibited art in galleries, performed standup in comedy clubs, hotels and cafes, and wrote hundreds of stories in L.A. Weekly as well as the Los Angeles Times and other publications. One of Shulman's columns won a prestigious award, which certainly is impressive.

HILLS SNYDER

Hills Snyder is an artist based in San Antonio. He is founder of the band Wolverton and Director/Curator of Sala Diaz. He won Best Short Short in the inaugural Austin Chronicle Short Story Contest and has published frequently in Glasstire, Art Lies and other publications.

KURT THOMAS

Kurt is a Los Angeles based writer and graphic designer. His stories appear regularly in Artillery Art Magazine. His past work has appeared in the LA Weekly and other alternative newsweeklies on the west coast. A collection of his work, "I Did It For You, Charlie Jr.!" is currently in the works.

JOHN TOTTENHAM

After many years of resistance, John Tottenham finally sold out to the lucrative, fast-paced world of poetry. He is the author of The Inertia Variations, an epic poetic cycle on the subject of work-avoidance, indolence and failure. His final collection of poetry, Antiepithalamia & Other Poems of Regret and Resentment - a sequence of mean-spirited love poems with particular respect paid to the institution of marriage - was published by Penny-Ante Press in 2012. He is also an old-fashioned paint and brushes man, whose paintings and drawings have adorned the walls of some of the finest galleries in Los Angeles and New York. He is also an online aphorist, celebrated for his gnomic and anomic utterances on the worldwide web, and a renowned performer. There is simply no end to his achievements. Let's just leave it at that.

MATIAS VIEGENER

Matias Viegener is a writer, artist and critic who works solo and collaboratively in the fields of writing, visual art, and social practice. His new book, 2500 Random Things About Me Too, is published by Les Figues Press. He is the co-editor of Séance in Experimental Writing and The Noulipian Analects. His work has been exhibited at LACMA, Yerba Buena Center for the Arts, Ars Electronica, ARCO Madrid, the Whitney, Los Angeles Contemporary Exhibitions, Machine Project, MOCA Los Angeles, MOCA San Diego, and internationally in Mexico, Colombia, Germany, and Austria. He's published in Afterimage, American Book Review, Artforum, Art Issues, ArtUS, Artweek, Black Clock, Bomb, Cabinet, Fiction International, Paragraph, and X-tra. His work has been written about in The New Yorker, salon.com, The New York Times, Art in America, Frieze, Art:21, The Los Angeles Times, and The Huffington Post. He teaches at CalArts and is a 2013 Creative Capital awardee.

BUFFY VISICK

Buffy Visick is a Los Angeles-based writer and cashier supervisor. "Luck" is her first published work since 1997. She is grateful to the editors for their continued support.

NICOLAS (DIMITRI) VORVOLAKOS

Nicolas (Dimitri) Vorvolakos was born in Gamboa, Panama Canal Zone. He is an artist, art dealer and Cultural Representative of the Republic of Panama, INAC (Instituto Nacional de Cultura). He is the former director of art galleries, 207 Gallery and 0-1 Gallery, both in Los Angeles Ca. He is currently living in Panama City, Panama and is a professor of English at the Panama campus of Florida State University.

MARY WORONOV

Mary Woronov began her eclectic movie career playing Hanoi Hanna in Warhol's movie "Chelsea Girls." Before she quit acting, she starred in "Rock and Roll High School" and "Eating Raoul." She then began to devote herself to painting and writing. Based in Los Angeles, her paintings are narrative, telling a story in one picture, and her writing is figurative, painting an imaginary reality. Her first book, "Swimming Underground", is a chilling picture of Warhol's factory.

GEN F

CREDITS

Conceived and Edited by Gordy Grundy

Copy Editors
Laura Aved
Angelle Haney Gullett
Dallas Hansen

Designer: Gordy Grundy

Design Committee
John Bertram
Wendy Furman
Derek Murphy

Photo by Tyler Hubby